Vampire State of Mind

Vampire State of Mind

Jane Lovering

Published 2012 by Choc Lit Limited
Penrose House, Crawley Drive, Camberley, Surrey GU15 2AB, UK
www.choclitpublishing.com

A CIP catalogue record for this book is available
from the British Library

ISBN-978-1-906931-74-2

Printed and bound by CPI Group (UK) Ltd, Croydon, CR0 4YY

To the newest member of the family, Phoenix James.
Welcome to the world, little one.

Acknowledgements

Firstly, HobNobs, without which this book would never have existed – if biscuits are not one of the major food groups, then they should be. My fantastic partner, Steve, for endless chocolate, wine and other forms of encouragement, both edible and otherwise. My wonderful, wonderful beta reader, Sarah Callejo, for patiently e-mailing suggestions and not phoning up at two in the morning to shout them at me; also the whole of North Yorkshire for stopping me to ask how the writing is going and not mentioning that my pants are on my head and I seem to be wearing my slippers. My lovely friends at Choc Lit and the Romantic Novelists' Association who dragged me from my bed, removed the pillow from my head and kept me going when times were tough and Agent Kate for not letting me slide into despair or Lancashire.

Finally, for my wonderful, kind, considerate, gorgeous, clever and amazing children, Tom, Vienna, Fern, William and Addie and Tom's fantastic partner Becci, for being there. Right, children, please let me out of the cellar now, I've done as you asked …

Vampire history

From Wikipedia, the free encyclopedia

> *This article is about the recent vampire colonisation of the planet. For literary/film vampire history, see* Fictional vampires.

History

Scientists have discovered that, in 1910, the entire planet underwent a magnetic field shift causing, in the opinion of scientists, a fracture in the walls between this and other parallel universes [citation needed]. It is believed that this fracture enabled beings from other universes to cross into our world, where they became trapped by the reconfiguration of the magnetic flux.

At first the number of incomers, who became known as the Otherworlders, was very low and the incoming aliens remained mostly concealed, both purposefully and owing to their similarities to the resident human population.

However, by 1920 these numbers were growing due to infection of the resident population, reaching a high point of 1/30 by 1925. Humans began to fear both infection and uprising and sought to reclaim the planet for themselves, leading to the Troubles. After the signing of the Peace Treaty at Aberystwyth, Wales, the site of the original ingress, in 1988 a mostly equitable peace was formed and continues to be maintained.

See also: *Flux physics, Multiverse, werewolves, wights, zombies, Shadows, Otherworld, Troubles, Otherworld Treaty, Otherworld Pact.*

Troubles

This is the name given to the all-out war which arose between Otherworlders (led by the vampire contingent) and humans, officially declared by United States President Calvin Coolidge in 1927. The war was fought globally with each continent leading its own defence; problems occurred from the number of deaths by 'friendly fire' caused by the inability of the majority of the population to differentiate between Otherworlders and humans. After sixty years of conflict, during which the global economy was brought almost to its knees, a co-operative solution was sought by those on both sides and a workable peace was negotiated, enabling both Otherworlders and humans to live side by side.

See also: *the Five Per Cent, Peace Treaty, The Pact*.

Theories

Currently, studies in the field of social and political history have put forward the theories that the ingress of Otherworlders to this universe prevented mankind from waging war upon itself and that the Troubles may have defused a situation which could have led to a World War. The Alternate History Group of Great Britain have published papers on the subject and their studies are ongoing …

See also: *Germany, Iran/Iraq, Russia, AHGGB*.

Chapter One

Yorkshire Herald Tuesday 3rd February 1914
Increasing reports of 'monsters' appearing throughout the British Isles have been put down to the work of politicals, possibly Italian. The public are advised to disregard such anti-British sentiments ...

Jonathan Wilberforce smiled to himself, flipping the pages of his newspaper over to make walking and reading a little easier, then shook his head. The press seemed to have nothing better to report these days than rumour and supposition – although he almost hoped that these new Gothic tales of half-men, half-demons running amok through the streets of York were true. That beautiful new rifle that Christina had bought him this past December would be just the thing for hunting, whether lions, bears or those creatures that had been dubbed 'vampires'... he blamed that *Dracula* story. One man writes a slightly torrid novel featuring bloodsucking beasts with a human face and suddenly people are imagining themselves under attack from the creatures! He shook his head again at the gullibility of the lower classes. The whole event would probably turn out to be yet another escaped tiger from those circuses that constantly plied their tawdry acts around the open spaces, the brutes driven mad with hunger and confusion and forced to attack humans in order to feed.

'Sir! Sir, please, would you help me?'

Startled out of his pleasant dream of shooting an enormous tiger ravaging the streets of his own city and being heralded a hero, Jonathan stopped walking. 'Hello?'

'Oh, thank the Lord!' At the mouth of an alleyway stood a ragged but well-spoken woman, body hunched forward at the waist over a bundle which appeared child-shaped

3

and sized. 'Sir, please help me. My child, my daughter, she's taken suddenly ill and I am at a loss …'

Jonathan had a sudden image of his own daughter, an infant, held thus in her mother's arms, tiny arms and legs dangling, and his heart threw itself high in his chest. 'What is it? What happened?'

The woman moved a step backwards, the darkness of the alley preventing him from seeing her face in true detail. Not that he was really looking; his attention was captivated by the deathly stillness of the collection of ill-assorted rags that she held.

'It was here, sir, just here upon the ground, if you would care to look …'

'Where? In the alley?'

'She fell there, upon these cobbles, just slipped and lay so pale and still and now I fear she may have passed from us!'

He moved after her, two steps into the closed darkness, and the sounds and lights of the evening street he had walked down were blocked, as though by screens. Another step, following the huddled form, and he could hardly see his own feet moving over the slippery stones. One more step and he could just make out her figure bending down, dropping the bundle without care on to a pile of sacking and then straightening again to face him. 'I'm sorry, I really don't understand what it is that you would have me do,' he began, and then caught sight of her face. Even in this inadequate light he could see that she was beautiful, but her lips were drawn back to reveal teeth that had no right belonging in the mouth of anything human.

'You need do nothing, sir.' And her hand was upon his shoulder, her fingers like iron even through the fabric of his best evening coat. 'Nothing at all.'

His final thought was of Christina and the children; dear God, let them never know what happened here …

Chapter Two

York – 2012

Fangs dripping bloodstained saliva the vampire came at me from the far side of the graveyard, moving fast.

I saw him coming, dropped to one knee and came up hard underneath; felt the brief cold shock through me as our bodies made contact and then he was up, on his feet, coming back. I stayed hunched on the ground, breathing carefully. He broke over me, a hard, relentless block of power, but I wasn't about to let him get the drop on me and drew myself suddenly up from defeated bent-double to full-firing. As our combined weights sent us toppling slowly backwards I reached around and jabbed him in the neck.

'Oh, *bugger*.'

'Sorry, Daim. You know the rules.'

'But – ' It was all he had time to say before the tranq pounded into his bloodstream and he was out for the count, sprawled less-than-sexily on top of me, dribbling the remnants of cheap synthetic blood into my ear and with his tasteless death's head belt buckle snagging a hole in my tights. And I'd ruined yet another pair of heels.

Welcome to my life.

There was a splash of applause from the watching crowd, who'd all paused in their tour of 'York by Night' as though Daim and I were an alternative attraction, which was embarrassing because I was still flat on the flagstones pinned under the weight of the rubbish vampire from the far side of town, not exactly doing Buffy back flips. *And* he was snoring.

'Hey, cool fight!' One of the watchers exclaimed. Just my luck, a teenage American boy with join-the-dots acne and an expression which indicated that he was looking for trouble but hoping not to find it.

'Thank you.' It hadn't been cool, of course, more of a mad scramble for pole position, but I was prepared to take any appreciation I could get.

'You do much of this? Y'know, bringing down vamps n' stuff?'

'Only … sort of. I'm a liaison officer. It's my job to make sure they stay on the right side of the line.'

'And this guy didn't?' I thought for one horrible moment that the boy was going to kick Daim. 'What did he do?'

As I scrambled and pushed my way clear of the prone vampire, I thought how best to phrase the answer. Being crap wasn't a crime, although in vampire-land it was as reprehensible as being uncool. 'Wrong place, wrong time.' I limped a few, broken-heeled, steps and buzzed through to the office.

'Hi, Jessie!' Liam answered. Well, he would, he was the only other person in our under-funded department. He described himself as my sidekick, which, I suppose was true, if you took into account that there were no front or back kicks.

'Hey, Liam. I've bagged and tagged our man. It was young Daim, breaking territorial bounds. Could you send the wagon for him?'

'Sure. I'll let the Enforcement boys know.'

'Thanks. Who's on wagon-duty tonight?'

'Harry. Oh, and Eleanor. So, maybe you'd like to be somewhere else when they arrive?'

'Perceptive. Okay, I'll wait until they turn up and then I'll get on back.' I heard his grunt of agreement as I disconnected, and sighed. Eleanor and I had, as they say, history. Oh, not

6

in a romantic context, I couldn't imagine anyone feeling romantically inclined towards a woman whose fashion choices came in shades of khaki and, anyway, I'm one hundred per cent pure heterosexual. No, our history was more – well, shall we say that I wanted to kill her, and the feeling was mutual? But, because we were both employed by York City Council to help keep the human/Other peace, albeit in our case in an almost invisible capacity, we kept our animosity to ourselves.

Oh, and Liam. Liam knew all about it. You couldn't keep anything from Liam without a restraining order.

A mist was beginning to rise; greasy coils of white roping themselves around the already sinister outlines of St Michael-le-Belfry. I could smell a nearby chip-van doling out its wares to the clubbing crowd. It made my mouth water and I wondered whether I dared leave the downed vampire. I was *starving*. Lunch had been a Cup-a-Soup and, even with croutons, it frankly wasn't enough.

The mist thickened; tendrils of damp working their way through my light jacket as I returned to the downed Daim and straddled his body to look around. It was highly unlikely that any vampire worth his Armani would willingly wander about on this chilly damp spring evening, but there was always the chance that, unbeknown to all tracking systems, Hunters, Enforcement crew and all other mechanisms in place, someone had gone rogue and might think it was worth bringing down the entire Peace Treaty for the sake of a nibble at an official neck. Even though in terms of officialdom I was only marginally higher than the bloke who goes round checking the drains, the one with the wig and the bad breath. *And* I bet he got paid more than me. Probably had better shoes too, I thought sulkily, rubbing a sore patch on my elbow where I'd hit the ground. Still my job had its compensations – all the paperclips I could carry home and ... Okay, just the paperclips, but everyone needs paperclips, right?

The ladder in my tights shot suddenly from thigh to ankle and I wriggled around trying to straighten my gusset, lurching on my snapped heel like a horror-movie zombie. The watching crowd, bored by the lack of hordes of vampires piling upon me to wreak bloodstained revenge, had wandered off following their guide. Beyond me and the ratchet-snoring vampire, nothing moved and I was overwhelmed by a sudden wave of loneliness. Somewhere out there, I knew, the city was a hotbed of life; drunks and improperly dressed girls would be crowding the streets, but here in this graveyard it was like another world. I sighed again and thought of Liam tucked up in the warm office, probably getting his coat on ready to go home to his cosy girlfriend and their new baby, full of tales of what a hard shift it had been. Huh. A hard shift's filing was all he'd had to contend with, while I'd ruined another pair of Faith sandals. Honestly, it was bloody unfair. I sniffed miserably as the mist formed a drop on the end of my nose.

Suddenly something grabbed my ankle and pulled. Without thinking I twisted, but was already stumbling, as a cold hand clenched around my lower leg, the sting of acid biting through my skin. Down I went, over the body at my feet. Almost dislocating my leg I wrenched myself into a sitting position and was confronted by a reddish-yellow mass squatting on Daim's gently moving chest and gripping me round the top of my heel-less shoe. It looked like a partially microwaved cat covered in mucus.

It was Daim's demon, the thing that drove him, and not in a figurative sense.

'Tezrael? What – I thought I hit you with the tranq?'

'I fought it.' The voice was, in contrast to the body, quite pleasant. A little like a gust of wind caught in a chimney.

'Why? They're only going to take you back to the other side of river. We've got our quota of vampires over here; Daim's broken the terms of his agreement. And, I might add, put up a completely unnecessary fight.' I waggled my broken shoe, although why a demon would be interested in my footwear problems, I wasn't sure.

'This I know.' The demon wheezed for a moment. 'Cold night to be out, human woman.'

'Cut the pleasantries, Tez and tell me why you're bothering to talk to me.'

'You saved me once, Jessica Grant, and now I return the favour. There is great danger to you.'

'Danger?' I frowned at the demon. 'Are you sure? I mean, I'm not exactly at the pointy end of things, danger-wise. Unless the electric pencil-sharpener goes rogue. They don't let me do anything dangerous, because I'm the only one who knows how the petty-cash system works.'

'Yet you are here tonight.' Tezrael raised his scabby head and pale-green eyes met mine.

'Yeah, but I'm only doing a tagging. And it's only Daim.'

'And this is not dangerous?'

'They have to send someone who can tell a vampire from an estate agent, Tez. Well, a non-vampire estate agent, and I've not met one of those yet, there's something about estate agency that just seems to draw them in … You know as well as I do that it's only five per cent of the human population who can spot a vampire. I thought that was part of the attraction of this world, the general invisibility?'

Tezrael moved his body in what might have been, in another creature, a shrug. 'Listen. For this message I

9

brought my soul over the river, do not be hard on him when he wakes.' The demon was slipping now, becoming more mucus than solid form. 'Do not trust … family.'

'Tez!' But he'd gone, slithering back into Daim's possessed body in the form that I had once managed to prevent from sliding ignominiously down a drain when his previous host had been killed by an allergic reaction to the tranq.

Really, though … danger? I rocked back on my heel-and-a-half with the ridiculousness of the idea. I leave the big-gun work to the vampire-Hunters, the élite trained to deal with the beasts that go off the rails. The guys in the long coats, the bastards that get to sign all the autographs while the rest of us keep the files up-to-date and give them advance warning so that they can get their razor-sharp suits from the cleaners for the press calls. I'm Liaison, which means I deal in persuasion, in long, long telephone calls with leaders of various communities, with paperwork and, when all that fails, I tranq them. I'm in more danger from paper-cuts than from the street-level vamps. The higher-level ones, now *those* you have to watch. They can polite you to death.

But Tez had deliberately brought Daim over the river, to warn me. Me, Jessica Grant, queen of the safety-lock cabinet, whose main challenge in life was keeping the vampire-tracking programme up-to-date and the 'Mc' 'Mac' and 'McC' filing from going completely mental?

And what had he said? 'Do not trust family?' Whose family? My septuagenarian, retired teacher parents? They were hardly dangerous, although they could be quite sharp when grammar was wrongly used. My sister? But Abbie loved kittens and worked with sick children. Although she had inherited the parental severity if she detected any sibling favouritism, you'd be more likely to get an overdose

10

of saccharine from standing too close to her. But it wasn't really *danger*.

I poked Daim's recumbent form. It had to be a mistake, surely; if I *had* been in danger, how on earth would Tezrael know? He wasn't exactly a player in the demon community, otherwise he wouldn't be possessing a flat-out no-hoper like Daim Willis. He'd be driving one of the big boys; all designer clothes, scatter-gun stubble and high cheekbones. Like Sil.

No. I wouldn't think of Sil, not here. Not anywhere. All right, maybe in the private depths of my dreams, where I could pretend. But *definitely not now*.

A blue light strobed through the air and the vamp-wagon pulled into the area in front of the church, radio crackling. I could see Harry and Eleanor scanning the area with their portable detectors, checking for activity. I stayed where I was, standing over the body, until Harry left the vehicle and crossed the graveyard, still swinging his detector.

'Oh, hello, Jessie.' He gave a quick, nervous glance over his shoulder, but it wasn't vampires he was scared of. 'Didn't know this was your call.'

'Yeah, well. Take care of him, Harry, he's only here because – it was a mistake, all right?'

Harry looked down. 'Daim Willis? Didn't know he had the intellect to *make* mistakes. Sometimes you have to feel sorry for the demons, don't you? Okay, Jessie, I'll take it from here.' Another glance towards the van.

'It's all right, Harry. I shouldn't think she wants to talk to me any more than I want to pose naked for *Hunters' Weekly*. I'll head off back to the office now, take over from Liam.'

'Right.' Harry bent, slung Daim across his shoulder like an unlovely rucksack. 'Don't worry, Jessie. About Ellie, I mean. Things will work out.'

Yeah, I thought as I watched him cross the churchyard, things will work out. Right.

She's thinking of me.

Sil stood outside the club, sober, focused, eyes on the brick horizon fifty feet away. *She's thinking of me.* Somewhere out there, Jessica Grant – leggy, lovely, and probably totally unsuitably dressed – was letting her memory run away with her.

The connection pulled him again, briefly, like a thin silver wire attached to … well, he wanted to say his groin but it was more than that. He caught himself before a little sigh escaped; he was vampire, not a love-starved teenager. Supreme predator. Top of the food chain, master of all he surveyed and, although he shouldn't say it, *spectacularly* well dressed, and here he was mooning over lost opportunities and a woman who'd probably not even strain herself to raise two fingers at him.

He shook his head, quickly, dismissively, trying to lose the feeling that his immaculate suit was out of place, as though he should have been back in the old uniform of jeans and shirt, back in the office, back at her side. But – he allowed the sigh this time, knowing what it was for – that was never going to happen. *That was then and this is now and there is a woman watching me, I can smell the vodka and excitement coming from her. Well, that's tonight taken care of.*

You can stop thinking about me now, Jessica, you made your choice.

Chapter Three

I didn't go back to the office in the end, I went home.

Just because I work with Others – what the District Council in a superfluity of PCness keeps trying to call the Differently Vital – doesn't mean I have to live like Igor's second cousin, so I share a riverside flat with my best friend, Rachel. But then I bet even the best vampire-slayers have someone to record *Desperate Housewives* and load the washing machine when they're out. It can't all be moody silence and classical music, however much they'd like people to think that.

'You're late.' Rach spoke without looking up from the disinfectant bucket, where the Dettol-scented steam was making her hair curl into blonde ringlets. 'He's ill again, must be that old lady next door feeding him, I've *told* her and *told* her about his allergies, but she will keep doing it!'

The place smelled like a hospital ward. The patient was curled in a complacent cushion-shape on top of the fridge, purring slightly and looking anything but life-impaired.

'Okay, yeah. Is there anything to eat?'

'I left you some couscous. Oh, and somebody came over looking for you.' Rachel went back to scraping and sluicing. 'Some bloke.'

'What did he want?' I opened the fridge in search of something I felt like eating, closed it, opened a cupboard and then went back to the fridge.

'Didn't say.'

'What did he look like?' There was some cheese and salad, which would have to do. Rachel was into everything healthy, so even finding cheese was a bit of a triumph. Too much to hope that she'd weakened and bought some HobNobs.

Rach stopped scraping and sat back. 'Browny eyes, hair down to here,' she indicated her shoulders, 'tall, skinny. A bit ...'

I poked the cheese. Things had a tendency to live in our fridge until they evolved, and I wanted to know if the cheese would poke back. 'A bit what? Warty? Like Tom Cruise?'

She bridled. 'Tom Cruise is *not* warty!'

'There was a full stop in there. What, for the love of God, was he "a bit", Rach?'

She wrinkled her nose and her body twitched as though trying to shake off the memory. 'A bit ... he made me go all goose pimpled. Good looking, though.'

My stomach rolled. *Sil? Here? But why would he?* 'Did he look like a client?' By which I meant 'vampire', but Rachel is sensitive to mentions of my work. She prefers to keep the illusion that my job consists of acting as a kind of PR officer for the Otherworlders, rather than filling them with chemicals 'til they stop moving.

'You *know* I can't tell! He asked if you were in and I said no, and we chatted a bit, then he left. Friendly. Strange but friendly.'

Probably not Sil then. Friendship and he were mutually exclusive and he couldn't really be described as 'strange'. *And,* whispered that dark little memory, *his eyes aren't brown, are they, Jessie? They're the colour of skies in winter, of a cassowary egg, of a brewing storm ...* 'You didn't let him *in*, did you?'

'Of course I didn't let him in! Honestly, Jessie, you must think I'm stupid or something! We had a quick chat on the doorstep, then he went away. Didn't leave a message or anything, so I thought you'd know who he was.' She stood up and tipped the bowl of water down the sink. A cloud of steam puffed up, reminiscent of the mist in the graveyard.

'I'm only saying what happened, all right? I can't vet your visitors all the time you know. I do have a life.'

I manfully refrained from pointing out that her life consisted of working in a chemist's and looking after Jasper, the world's only Munchausen's-by-proxy cat. 'Sorry. I guess I'm just a bit weirded out. Daim Willis' demon popped by with some misguided warning. Even if it can't be true, it's still freaked me a bit.'

Rach stared. 'God, Jessie, that is sooo *coooool*!' She wrapped her arms across her significant chest, hugging herself in a silent delight. 'What was it like? Was it hideous – they're supposed to be hideous, aren't they? And how did it speak, is it, you know, actual *words* and stuff or was it that kind of mind-to-mind thing?' She gave an exaggerated shiver. 'I can't believe it, my friend, my really ordinary friend, gets to talk to demons!'

No wonder the vampire-slayers live alone with Beethoven's *Greatest Hits*.

'Imagine Jasper shaved, boiled and sneezed on. *That* is a demon. I'm going to bed, okay?'

'Are you taking that cheese?'

I stared at the block of Wensleydale in my hand. 'I seem to have lost my appetite,' I said, 'unless by some huge fluke and complete character switch you've got biscuits?'

Rachel pursed her mouth at me. 'They're bad for you.'

I tried *really hard* not to let my eyes flicker, but somehow they did. Rach gave me a mean look. 'Okay, all right, rub it in. I'm the mound of blubber and you look like a pencil in a wig, with boobs on, but even so! Think of the cholesterol.'

'I rarely think of anything else.' I shoved the cheese back on the fridge shelf, but my flouncy exit was spoiled by Rach's shouting after me.

'I read today that they think the five per cent of people

15

who can spot vampires are all a bit weird. Did you read that, Jessie?'

I shut my bedroom door, pacified my rumbling stomach with half a bar of Fruit and Nut and then sat on my bed feeling sorry for myself. Here I was, thirty-one, not bad looking (not exactly stunning, but no-one had screamed yet either), responsible job and ... nothing else. What I really wanted was a cuddle. Or at least – I stared at my ruined shoes and laddered tights – an expense account at Next. What I actually got was another night in with the telly and my best friend regurgitating *Daily Mail* headlines at me. Sometimes, just *sometimes*, I wished I'd handled my whole life differently.

'Bloke was here for you last night.' Liam hung his jacket over the back of his chair and sat down, pulling the filing pile across the desk towards him. His dark curls hung like an untidy tablecloth over his face. 'Said he wanted a word.'

'Ambidextrous,' I said, peering at the computer screen.

'Was he?'

'It's a word. Honestly, you do *have* a sense of humour, don't you? I'm sure it said on your job application.'

'Yes,' Liam said pointedly, '*I* do. Anyway, he left a card.'

'Journo?' I turned away from the computer, which was currently running the tracker programme, telling me that all our designated vampires were exactly where they were supposed to be, and that in the city of York the temperature was a cool 18 degrees. It was also, on a minimised screen, showing the Jeremy Kyle show, but Liam didn't know that.

'Didn't say. Don't think so; looked a bit clean to be from the local rag. Hold on, I put the card in the pile for filing.'

I stared across the desk at Liam. He was the most efficient man I'd ever met. He'd worked for me for five years, since he'd come at nineteen as a Work Experience placement and never left, and in all that time he'd never lost a single piece of paper. He wasn't bad looking either, as long as he never stood next to a vampire – but then, standing next to a vampire even Johnny Depp would come across as a bit *meh* – with dark hair and eyes and an onboard twinkle that made people warm to him. 'You were going to file a *card*? No, I'm sorry, that's just weird.'

An outflung arm indicated the knee-deep squalor that was the office. 'You ever want to see anything again round here, you file it. Well, I do. You drop it and wait for archaeologists. Cards go on the Rolodex ... ah, here it is. Might make sense to you.' He passed me the small square of card. 'Looks expensive. 'S funny that, don't you reckon, the more expensive those things are, the harder they are to read.'

'Mmm,' I said, without listening, tilting the white oblong back and forth to catch the light. 'Liam, are you pulling some kind of stunt?'

Liam rolled his eyes at me. 'Jessica, I am not pulling *anything*. Look, both hands, all right?'

'Ha. But this card is blank.'

'Nah. That would be stupid, dropping in a blank card.' He took it from me and squinted at it. 'What would be the point?'

'And *how* long have you been around the Otherworlders? Come on, Liam, if there's an opportunity to be posey and mysterious, have you ever known one pass it up?'

Liam frowned. 'I'm not actually sure he *was* an Otherworlder.'

I took the card back again and dropped it on the edge of the imminent landslide that was my desk. 'You couldn't tell? And here's me thinking you were one of the five per cent ... So what did he look like?'

He shrugged. 'He was a bloke – contrary to what you might like to believe in your dirtiest dreams, I don't really notice blokes.'

Same man as called at the flat? Could be. Definitely not Sil then. Liam and he were … *had been* friends; even after a night on the Pernod and black Liam would have recognised Sil … 'Did you tell him where I was?'

'Course not. I said you were out, that was all. If he *was* a journo didn't think you'd thank me for having him turn up all over a tagging, and if he's not, well, he'll find you.'

'You didn't mention where I live, or anything?'

'Yes, of course. I also told him that you like reading, you're a Gemini and you want a man who's sensitive and smart – of course I didn't bloody tell him where you live!'

'Sorry. And what makes you think I want a man who's sensitive and smart?'

Liam rolled his eyes.

I pointed in the general direction of the card. It had already been subsumed by paperwork and vanished somewhere under a pile of reports. 'So. He wants me to know he's been here, but the ball remains in his court.'

'Being mysterious on purpose. Get your curiosity going.'

I curled my lip. 'Come on, Liam, did he look like he might want me for something urgent or just as a matter of interest? Or was he competition?'

'You mean, did he look like a Hunter? Not really. Not enough of the Hugh Jackman thing going on, too skinny.' Right, yeah, Liam, Mister 'I don't notice blokes'. 'And if he was a vamp, he's not one of ours – didn't look right for a vamp anyway, didn't *feel* right, if you know what I mean. Oh, and you're due in that school in twenty minutes, to give your talk.'

Great. Not only do I have to tag the bastards if they get out of line, but I have to do their PR, which is how

I regularly find myself standing up on a stage in front of a bunch of kids, giving them the 'Otherworlders are quite safe, that's why we have a Treaty,' spiel, tempered with a little 'but it's not cool to be a vampire. Honest. Don't let the being gorgeous, rich and successful fool you.'

We don't know how it happened, even after a hundred years we're still not quite sure *where* they came from, but we do know this – when it all kicked off, the vampires were at the heart of it. Oh, they weren't the only species to come through, or pass over or whatever you might call it, the werewolves came too, and wights and Shadows and ghouls and zombies – we got the full set, but the vampires were the ones that fronted it. The acceptable faces of an alternative dimension, at least that's what the *NME* call them, but they've always been good at the sound bytes. I just call them bastards and have done with it.

The thing that most people don't understand about vampires is that, basically, when you get right down to it, they're transport. That's all. Transport for a nasty little demon, its eyes and ears and food supplier. In their home dimension, apparently, all the demons live without hosts, and even here they can get by on their own but … well, there's a limit to the amount of fun you can have when you look like an irradiated rodent with an ooze problem and no form of protection. So in this dimension one of the enhancements that having a top-of-the-range demon on board tends to give you, is physical attractiveness. Vampires can be abso-bloody-lutely drop-dead-and-swivel-on-the-ground gorgeous. Demons need that kind of thing, something to do with all the hormones sloshing around, they get off on adrenaline, dopamine, oestrogen, testosterone, the whole alphabet of human regulators gives them a huge high, so they make sure that they are first in line for the thrills.

Here's how it works – you get bitten by a vamp and you have one of three options. If you're lucky it just feeds – leaving you weak, lightheaded and looking favourably upon nearly raw steak for a month or two, also wearing a mark that you're *never* going to get away with explaining as a love bite. Or, they just kill you, because to a vampire another vampire is competition, but sometimes, you know, if they're feeling procreative, you get really unlucky, and they inject demon-seed into your blood. Then you've got, probably, an hour – ninety minutes tops – to get to a hospital which has a blood-wash system, otherwise, in the words of Liam who tends to panic about these things, you're screwed. It's happened to me twice and, believe me, blood-washing *hurts*, so you try not to get bitten, right?

If the worst happens and you end up with demon-seed in your bloodstream, then you hatch a demon. Inside you. And like any other parasite it forms links within you so that if it dies, you die. And, because if *you* die, and they separate from you in time, it leaves them unprotected and vulnerable, they like to keep their hosts in tip-top condition, so being demon-infected means that you get a kind of super-human strength, great vision, hearing, speed, all that kind of crap. Oh, and you tend to live a long, long time – not quite immortal, but the Queen's going to get writer's cramp doing your telegrams.

Most vampires these days tend to live on synthetic blood and the successful ones spend their time running corporations, becoming hugely rich and powerful and sleeping with supermodels, so you can see the attraction for the kids. But for every top vamp there's a whole pyramid of lower vampires, the ones that, even with super-human enhancements, are never going to make it. Like Daim. Like the hundreds of other spotty youths who thought that being a vampire was the end of their problems and not the beginning of a whole new load of even more complicated problems. And if you're even the *slightest* bit tempted, then go and read your history books, study the Troubles that broke out when the numbers of Otherworlders reached pandemic status, when the humans decided it was time to fight back …

And that, give or take the occasional use of bad language, is what I tell the kids. Takes twenty minutes, half-an-hour, then we do the Q&A, and I'm back in the office by lunchtime.

'I bought you egg-and-cress.' Liam dropped the sandwiches in front of me. 'Any amusing questions today?'

'Not really.' I tore into the packet. I was *starving*, my own fault for getting sniffy and not eating the Wensleydale last night. 'A Year Nine boy asked if you could catch vampirism from drinking out of the same glass as a vampire, that's about it.'

'And you said?'

'I said you're in far more danger of getting vamped if you spill his pint.' I chewed. 'Anything happen while I was out?'

Liam flipped his computer screen. 'A lot of movement,' he said. 'And I mean a *lot*. They all seem to have permits though; they've been scanned through from their city of origin, no probs.'

Every city has a vampire quota. Stops anywhere getting overloaded, and keeps the Hunters in work. God knows what *they'd* do if all the vamps stayed put and behaved; form a rock band probably. Our quota for this area of York is seventeen, and most of them worked for Sil.

'How many do we have?' Liam tilted the screen towards me. 'Two *hundred*? What the hell is going on? And it's not just vampires, we've got zombies, ghouls, were-creatures. When did we become undead central?'

'There's some kind of thing on, apparently, a gathering.'

'Right. So the vamps are having a social? That is weird. No, it's more than weird, it's *nasty*.'

Liam gave me an old-fashioned look. 'I'm only telling you what I know and, given that there are dust-mites in this office that rank higher than me, that's not a lot. The Enforcement team might have some info, it'll be an "all leave cancelled" occasion.'

'Harry didn't say anything last night. I'm not sure they've even *heard* about it.'

'You'll have to call Sil, then.' Liam solemnly pulled an overlong piece of cress from his mouth.

'Is that meant to be a joke?'

'I'm only saying.'

'Well, don't.'

There was a slightly stiff pause. I concentrated far harder on my food than an M&S sandwich really merited, and it was Liam who cracked first. 'Why not ring Zan?'

'Could, I suppose. But is it really his brief? Sil is meant to be in charge of York.'

'Yeah, but Zan is the nearest thing to an assistant he has. He might know *something*, and that's more than we know now.' Liam averted his eyes. 'If you're serious about not speaking to Sil.'

'I'm not merely serious about it, I'm stony-faced.'

'Yeah,' Liam said slowly. 'I can see that.'

Sil had come to the office and offered to work with us ... how long ago now? Three years, four? Said he wanted to get some experience in how things were done from the human perspective and he'd sounded so keen, so eager to make things work, to make the city a better place ... And, of course, he'd looked so amazing, with that switch of dark hair and those eyes ... not that that had influenced me at all, of course. No. He'd purely come to assist and he and I had worked together so well ... *so* well until ... We'd been talking about that day's tagging – Sil had been investigating a Hunter we suspected of taking bribes – and then he'd curled his fingers into my hair, cupped my chin with his other hand, and kissed me. Nothing more, nothing less. But I'd responded. For that one moment I'd given Sil the benefit of years of pent-up emotions, stresses and lustings. The desires I'd kept locked away for so long – he'd got it all.

Because I wanted him.

And then I'd felt the fangs and I'd pulled away. Shouted something, I can't remember what, slapped my open palm against his face and watched him grow even paler, felt his demon react to the sudden withdrawal of desire – and known that I'd blown it. And it was anger with myself more than with him that had caused the huge argument with accusations on both sides, mine of his taking advantage of his position, of trying to indoctrinate me, cultivate me until he could infect me, his of my prejudices, my unfounded fears.

You don't love a vampire. You *can't*.

'I'll give Zan a call. When I've finished eating. I can't talk to him with my mouth full of egg, you know what he's like.'

'You could get in touch with Head Office. They might know something.'

I snorted. 'Yeah, right! They think that you are a five-year-old child prodigy and that my name is Maximillian Snowbottle.'

Head Office set up the Liaison department to run as back-up to Enforcement, but they seemed to get a bit embarrassed about our role as communicators. In a lot of people's eyes (particularly that ninety-five per cent of the population who couldn't tell a vampire from any other slightly deranged person) vampires shouldn't be acknowledged, as long as they stuck to their side of the Pact and we stuck to ours. *Talking* to them, in the eyes of the tabloid fraternity, only made them worse. The only good vampire was one who blended so totally with the human population that it was invisible; and it ought to be hard working and clean living, too. Therefore Head Office thought it more politic to forget all about us, so although we're technically part of the York District Council, in practice we look after ourselves. They pay the wages and throw occasional lumps of money our way, for 'equipment', but apart from that we're on our own. Certainly as far as the media is concerned, anyway. We work stupid hours, three weekends in four, and supposedly have days off 'in lieu'. We haven't worked out what they're in lieu of yet – a living wage is our best guess.

I finished my sandwich and put an Internet call through to Zan. He's sort of my equivalent in the vampire world; while it's Sil that keeps the Otherworlders in line, Zan is the one who has to file the complaints. He's very together, stupendously attractive, and makes me feel clumsy and stupid. Which, I think, is intentional. And, probably, not hard.

'Ah, Jessica. How lovely to see you again.' Just my luck, he was web-camming. 'You appear to have egg on your chin.' His eyes moved off me and took in the office background. 'Also, you seem to have been burgled.'

'Sorry,' I muttered, and wiped the egg off with my wrist. The jibe about the untidiness of the office I ignored. I could see behind him a team at work, and the Otherworlders believed in keeping everything electronic. They had a budget; we had Liam and me. 'What's this big do that's happening, Zan? And how come I didn't know anything about it?'

'You probably need to talk to Sil. I'm not sure I can say anything.'

'Zan ...' I let the inflection do the work for me. His general distaste for personal interaction meant that he hated any display of emotion, and putting a tiny 'I might just cry' wobble into my voice worked more often than you'd think.

'A get-together, a gathering of the clans.' Zan's voice, even when he was trying to avoid 'distressed female' syndrome, sounded like old silk being rubbed with cat-fur. 'Vampires like to have a knees-up as much as the next man.'

'There's zombies and werewolves as well,' Liam helpfully pointed out over my shoulder.

'Yes, well. We are very sociable.' He moved so that the camera focused fully on his face. He'd been in charge of the Otherworld's administration in the city of York for sixty years, and had held the city apart from the worst of the Troubles, and he still looked like Colin Firth's younger brother, perfect pale skin and come-to-bed eyes, the bastard.

'Come on Zan, what's happening? I know as well as you do that vampires only like a knees-up if the knee in question is connecting with someone else's soft bits.'

'It's the Dead Run,' he said at last, sulkily. 'Thursday night. At the Hagg Baba restaurant.'

Liam widened his eyes. 'Hang on. I read about that ...'

'Oh God!' I slumped back in my chair, an unheeded piece of sandwich falling into my lap. 'I can't believe they've let this happen here!'

Liam was searching for the e-update sheets that periodically got sent to us. He actually prints them out and archives them when they arrive, in case of computer failure. I roll them up and use them to kill wasps. 'Where is it?' he muttered. 'I'm sure I put these in date order. Jessie, have you been using them to stand on again?'

'Well, you will keep putting the Kit Kats in the top cupboard.'

'That's because *someone* has to keep you from overdosing. Ah, here it is.' He pulled a two-year-old issue free and it slid from the pile with a shower of dust.

'It was supposed to be Manchester!'

'I know.' Zan sounded aggrieved. 'I know, and honestly, Jessica, I would not have had it happen here. Can you *begin* to *comprehend* the amount of paperwork this is involving? But somewhere along the line something happened and the powers-that-be moved it to York. Believe me, I am not happy about it either, do you have any idea of the complexities – '

I leaned forward and turned my computer off at the mains switch. Liam gave a tiny moan of protest, but I think my expression stopped him complaining out loud. 'So why have they switched it to York? '

Liam gave me a pained look. 'If you hadn't just shorted out our entire system I think Zan might have been about to tell you.'

'I only turned it off.'

'Without backing up.'

'But ...'

'It was felt that York was more conducive to atmosphere for an interspecies competition.' Liam and I swivelled away from the computer and towards the interrupter's voice. 'After all, the whole point is to allow Otherworld races to compete against one another and it was decided that Manchester was insufficiently, how shall I put it ... impressive.'

'For the Goth Olympics,' Liam said, helpfully.

'And who on earth are you?' I stared at the man sitting perched on the edge of Liam's desk. 'And, more to the point, why are you here?'

'This is the guy who came asking for you yesterday.' Liam was taking the opportunity of my gawping at the stranger to re-boot my computer. He thought I couldn't see the reassuring way he stroked its casing.

'Malfaire.' The visitor straightened himself away from the desk; didn't offer to shake hands. But then, that was human behaviour, and this man … My usually reliable senses were letting me down. I didn't recognise him from Rachel's description; she'd said he had shoulder-length hair and this guy had his tied up in a pony-tail, she'd also called him 'strange', and, as far as I was concerned, this guy had long ago passed through strange and out the other side into 'read far too many horror novels late at night and practised the look way more than was healthy'. Eyes, seville-orange-dark, swept over me and I felt a cat's paw of fear stroke down my spine. 'And you must be Jessica Grant.'

I drew myself up to full height and tried to project cool, capable business-woman, decently proportioned and not harassed, scruffy council-employee, wishing that she'd worn a suit rather than these elephant-arse jeans. 'Why were you looking for me?'

He *couldn't* be a vamp; there was something Otherworld about him – he certainly wasn't human – but I couldn't get a fix on him. And it felt as though he was trying to work something on me; some obscure kind of magic I didn't recognise was washing up and down the surface of my skin like an oily psychic skincare product.

'I came to tell you about the relocation of the Dead Run, actually. Seems that I'm a bit late on that score. Still, never mind.' He gave a smile, but it was an unsettling one. 'Please excuse me for letting myself in, but you were concentrating on some vampire or other.' The way he said vampire made me think he wished it rhymed with 'turd'. 'And I also came to invite you to attend. Well, it's not so much of an invitation as an order, but you know what the vampires are like. They've heard of Free Will but to them it's an interesting concept.'

'Sil sent you?' There was something 'off' about the proportions of his face; that was what was so strange about his appearance. It was symmetrical, should have been good looking but ... I inwardly berated myself for judging him for not being as stupendous as the top-notch vampires; he wasn't exactly a gargoyle, just ... odd.

'Not exactly. Anyway. Here's your invite, I'd better not outstay my welcome.' A thick envelope was pressed into my hands and I felt the soft motion of a velvet sleeve as it brushed against my skin. 'Please do come.' His head inclined my way and he was gone, leaving only the trademark magical exhaust fumes which smelled like rubber.

'Jessie?' Liam had to shake my shoulder to attract my attention. 'You all right?'

'That,' I said, carefully, 'should be on screen, putting sinister character actors out of a job.'

'But you fancy Christopher Walken,' Liam said, mischievously. 'You wouldn't want *him* starving on the streets.'

'He was just ...' I rubbed my hands up and down my arms as though trying to remove any molecules that Malfaire might have touched. 'Weird.' The envelope contained a classy, gold-printed invitation to attend 'The Dead Run, Thursday at 8, Hagg Baba restaurant. Jessica Grant plus One.' 'I wonder why Zan didn't just post the invite. Or mention it when we were talking ... oh, no, silly me, it might mean he had to sound like he was inviting me himself and that would be dangerously close to sociability for Zan.'

'Zan's got social phobia.' Liam brought up the tracker programme on my screen again.

'It's a good job the Troubles are over. Can you imagine a

vampire hunting on the streets who hates actually having to have contact with people? He *would* starve to death.'

'And who on earth am I going to get to come with me as my Plus One? That sort of thing always has press attending and I don't want to be photographed standing on my own, they might give me some "comical" caption like "Liaison once again without a liaison".'

'That really upset you, didn't it?'

'It was a Charity Ball! I had a lovely dress on and all I got was that stupid subtitle.'

'I'll go with you.' He lowered his head so that his hair hid his blush and coughed a bit, then said, 'I mean, like, as a works outing kind of thing. Not as, like, a partner, thing. It would save money – we could call it our works Christmas party. Eight months early. To beat the rush.'

I patted his arm. 'Nice thought. But Sarah would *kill* you, and quite rightly so – why should she get babysitting duties by default while you go off and have a night out? It's okay, I'll think of someone to ask.'

'There's always Sil.' Liam kept his face averted.

'I'd rather take my chances with the humorous tagline.'

'Yeah, okay.' He stared at the screen for a few moments. 'Exactly what goes on at this Run thing?'

'I thought you read the handout?'

'Yep. I'm just checking that *you* did.'

'They pick names of volunteers out of a hat, the runners have to make their way down a course and the winner gets the honours. Do I get extra points for mentioning that it's taken place every year since the Pact was signed?' I looked at the back of Liam's head as he read through the list appearing on the screen of all the incomers' names. 'Liam.'

'Mmm?' He clicked the mouse over a name, nodding when 'permitted' flagged up.

'That guy, that Malfaire, were you getting anything from him?'

Liam swivelled the chair. 'You, too? Thank God. I didn't want to say anything, thought I must be losing my touch. I've been sitting here worried to death that you'd chuck me out if you found out.'

'I'd never chuck you out, you're the only person who can get the computers to work. And, you're right, I wasn't getting anything either.'

We shared a round-eyed look. 'And – tell me if I'm talking out-of-turn here, Jessie, but you're the best I've ever seen at scanning the Otherworlders. You even knew about that Ian, and he'd fooled a whole television crew. You never get it wrong, you never even mistake one form for another. I'm an amateur in comparison.'

'Are you after a rise or something? 'Cos if you are, a mention of my ravishing beauty never offends.'

He grinned. 'It's true though, isn't it?'

I shrugged. 'It's a knack.' I began to pace the floor of the office; it didn't take long, there's barely room for Liam, me, two desks and our computers. 'So, any thoughts?'

Liam steepled his fingers and rested his chin on his hands. 'Not vamp, we'd be able to tell. Didn't seem to think much of them, either. A were?'

I shook my head. 'Nah. Too slick. They at least *feel* half-human, this was way beyond. Could you do a computer search for me?'

'I can try, but I think this might be a bit outside Google's parameters. Might have to hack in to Zan's system.' Pause. 'Again. I'll have a poke around, see what I can turn up. You off out?'

I grabbed my coat and hunted round the office for my mobile. 'Thought I'd go and ask Rach if she fancies coming out on Thursday night. Then I might just take a turn around the streets, see who's out and about – someone might know something about our mystery man.'

'Like his phone number, perhaps?'

I threw my mobile at his head. 'I take it all back, you've suddenly become dispensable. Anyway, someone should be out there checking up on all this movement. There's a lot of kudos goes attached to getting chosen and I don't think the organisers care overmuch about whether or not the runner has all his paperwork properly signed and his movement permit in order.' And besides, I wanted to get some fresh air. Our 'mystery man' had left me feeling as though I'd been in the vicinity of some kind of chemical accident, all clammy-skinned, and even my teeth felt dirty. Plus the little shop around the corner sold HobNobs, and Liam *still* hadn't got the message that real meals should be at least 50% biscuit.

Chapter Four

The streets were oddly quiet, given that we'd more than ten times our quota of Otherworlders flittering about. Admittedly most of them wouldn't rear their heads until after dark. The zombies would all be at work, ghouls *couldn't* go out in the light and the vampires would be waiting for twilight. Not because of any aversion to the sun – it turned out that Bram Stoker had met the world's only vampire with a photosensitive skin condition – but because the buggers were so concerned with being cool that they spent the daylight hours getting their look *just right*. I idly speculated on whether Sil had ever got his Gucci back from the cleaners; he had looked *fabulous* in that suit. Particularly when he'd let his hair grow long. The beginnings of a smile tried to part my lips at the memory, but I fought back as I felt my heart squeeze and the familiar sensation that my lungs were full of pins. I was *so* over him. Course I was.

I wandered around the narrow maze of streets in front of the Minster. The usual crowds of tourists were clotting around the sights of interest, and a party on the Vampire Walk were being entertained by a tour guide dressed as Dracula. A casual scan of the area turned up nothing unusual; a pair of werewolves prowling along together in human form greeted me with a smile and an indication towards their bag of butchers' offal – it being easier to shop for your predilections rather than risk going hunting and catching the inevitable silver bullet.

Talking of which – a figure in a long brown coat straightened up from where he'd been leaning against the wall of Betty's Tearooms, lighting a cigarette. 'Good afternoon.'

Great. A Hunter. Not a local, they all slouched about in designer suits and Converse trainers, this guy was working the full Van Helsing, down to the open-necked shirt and uncombed hair. He even had a monogrammed cigarette lighter, which put him beyond the merely poser and right out into 'look at me!!!' territory. I'd give him about twenty minutes against one of the real hard boys. Still, nothing to be gained by being rude, so I slowed down.

'You're Jessica Grant, aren't you? Liaison? Thought I recognised you from the ident list we got handed … I'm just on my way down to Enforcement – should have gone in and introduced myself this morning but things kind of took off on me. Ken Symes. I'm from Dorset, came yesterday accompanying a bunch of monsters up for the Run.'

I didn't know vampire Hunters could be called Ken. I thought they only recruited blokes with butch names like Grant or Jez. And he called the Otherworlders monsters, which earned him minus several million points with me. And, yes, he should have gone and introduced himself at Enforcement HQ. They were almost as cagey about incoming Hunters as we were about Otherworlders: the Hunters 'pose' level was nearly as high as the vamps' and there's only so much admiration to go round.

'Yes, that's me.' We shook hands while he smoked at me. Minus another few points.

Ken swirled his coat and let the wind ruffle his naff rock-video hair. 'Ah well. Nice to have met you, heard you're well in with the city vamp, might score me a few brownie points with the bad guys.' He dropped the stub of cigarette on the cobbles and ground it out with his heel (good job Ken wasn't going for my Man Of the Year award), turned and headed off down one of the narrow alleyways. He wore built-up shoes, the big wuss.

I watched him. He walked enough steps to think the half-light that filtered between the buildings would conceal him then, with a quick glance over a shoulder, headed through the door into the local branch of Specsavers.

I tried not to giggle. Hunters had their work cut out maintaining an image; it must be hard never being seen to do those things that ordinary mortals did without thinking. And then I bridled at his words 'well in with the city vamp'. What *exactly* did he mean by that, considering that I would quite cheerfully have offered to tranq Sil right this second had I heard that he'd so much as mentioned being slightly peckish within four miles of a human?

Then I cast around in another mental sweep of the area. Everyone seemed to be behaving unnaturally well, probably didn't want to risk anything upsetting the status quo and getting the Run cancelled. It was a big thing in the Otherworld calendar, according to ... well, I had my sources. Or used to have. Maybe that's what Ken had meant – maybe he hadn't heard about our ... falling out.

And this time I couldn't stop myself from conjuring an image of Sil's face. Steel-grey eyes, determined unsmiling mouth and hair so dark it made crows look as though they could have tried harder. My insides gave a little shiver of pain. So, here I was, living a miserably chaste life and he was out there screwing harder than a carpenter with a lot of shelves to put up. Sometimes – and I would have punched something if I hadn't been standing in the middle of York's main shopping street – life was just plain *wrong*.

There. Again. Sil raised his head from the pillow and stared blearily at unfamiliar curtains, letting the twisting in his gut subside. His mouth was clagged with the dry residue of bottled blood, powdery instead of the rich aftertaste you got with the real thing, and he wrinkled his nose. *Should have gone for it last night, Sil.* He turned to meet the blue, but less-than-innocent, eyes of the girl from the club, feeling his fangs sliding down, locking into place before the sensation caught up with him again. That odd jerking awareness deep inside, as though his demon was writhing and flipping through his chest on a hormone-burn. *Jessie?*

He let his mind run the connection, feeling the white heat of it dragging inside his head like a parachute, slowing his reactions. *Could she feel it? No, too human. And there's the problem, isn't it? Jessica Grant, with her human outlook, her human preconceptions …*

'Hey, big boy, are you going to bite me, or what?' The question brought him back, back to this rather sordid little hotel room, back to the blonde girl with the whisky-breath.

'Are you sure you want it?' He made his voice light, ran his tongue over his fangs, playing her.

'Well, it's what you do, isn't it? Drink blood?'

And that uncertainty was enough. His fangs retracted. 'Can we just have sex?'

The relief in her sigh told him all he needed to know. 'Like last night? Oh *yeah* …'

And as he turned to her the regret burned a hole in his gut. *Wrong woman. But when the right one doesn't want me, and my demon wants the lust … what am I supposed to do? Head for a carpentry shop and hope to catch a renegade splinter through the heart? No. Make a life, a half-life, as best I can. Just as after the bite, when the demon took hold of my body and mind. Adapt. Cope. Survive.*

'Your mum rang.' Rachel was at work, stacking boxes of hair-dye on the shelves in the little chemist's shop. That's the shop that was little, not the chemist: he was six foot ten and looked like he'd got some werewolf in his ancestry. 'Said something about popping round this evening. They're going to the pictures, apparently.'

Great. That would mean more questions, and I'd better remember to wear long sleeves, as I'd acquired some spectacular bruises falling over Daim last night. 'Lovely. Is that her and Dad?'

'And your sister, I think.' Rach slotted the last 'Shock Pink' into place and turned to the toothpaste. 'It'll be nice. You haven't seen them for ages.'

Because they always ask after my job, that's why, and I don't know what to tell them. Although they're good, broadminded people they seem to have a bit of a problem over me working with demons and suchlike. I'm not sure if it's prejudice or fear – are they the same thing? – or the protective parental instinct, but they're all really sensitive to mentions of the Otherworld. Maybe that's why they've chosen to live so far out in the countryside. They pretend that it's for the rural quiet, and Dad loves his smallholding so much that maybe it's true, but it doesn't stop me suspecting that the very low density of Otherworlders outside the cities has a huge appeal.

They've got a barghest living in a lane not far from their house. I haven't dared to tell them yet.

'Fancy coming out on Thursday night?' I leaned casually back against toothbrushes and floss. 'There's a bit of a do on.'

'What sort?' Rach had assumed an air of uninterest, but had frozen in the fluoride section.

'Work. It's at the Hagg Baba, thought you might like to come, but, if you're not bothered, Liam said – '

'I'll come!' She stood up so suddenly that a little rain of dental-care products resulted. 'Will there be, you know, *vampires* and things?'

Rach lost both her parents and her older brother in 1986, the year when the Troubles reached their height, two years before the Treaty was signed. She was four. Always maintained that she didn't remember her family, didn't remember those years of fear, of ordinary citizens armed and never chancing nightfall. But sometimes I wondered … was there something buried deep that accounted for her fascination with the Otherworlders? She persisted in seeing vampires as romantic double-edged creatures, haunters of the margins of life and misunderstood heroes.

'There will, almost certainly, be vampires and things,' I said, assuredly. 'It's sort of the point.'

'Wow. No, honestly Jessie, wow. You don't usually invite me to your work do's, why now? And what shall I *wear*?'

'That's because the nearest thing we've ever had to a works do so far is when Liam and I had to go to the Guildhall to get our wrists slapped over breaking the old tracker programme. We don't even get a Christmas party. Well, I make mince pies and Liam does his Widow Twankey impressions, but that's as close as we get.'

I ducked, suddenly, under cover of the shelf. Over Rach's shoulder I'd seen Harry and Eleanor come in to the shop, uniformed and armed. From the way they were leaning over the pharmacist's counter and talking urgently I didn't think they'd come in for Tampax and aspirin. Harry was scanning the place with his detector while Eleanor had slipped behind the counter, showing the pharmacist the readings on her hand-held, trying to do so inconspicuously whilst they pretended to be consulting about a prescription. It wasn't fooling me, not with the weaponry they were carrying.

'Jessie?' Rach bent down beside me. 'It's all right, if you don't want her to see you I can smuggle you out the back way. It goes into the alley, and you can get down to the river from there.'

'It's not that.' I crawled on hands and knees around the end of the shelf and hunkered down behind the toilet rolls heaped near the window.

Rach followed, carrying the large cardboard box she'd taken the hair-dye out of and placing it to conceal me from view. 'What is it, then?'

'Look at their *eyes*!' I glanced once, quickly, then ducked back down.

Rach obediently stared at Harry. 'He's quite cute, isn't he?' she whispered. 'Are you sure they're not dating?'

'*What?*' I pushed my head over the bog-roll parapet. 'No, their *eyes*. They're … wrong.'

As Harry swept his detector once more around the inside of the shop, I looked again. His eyes, normally a sunny sky blue, were clouded. Almost as though something else was looking out from behind them. Eleanor's were the same; a kind of hard, unfocused darkness instead of human pupils.

'This is so not right.' I fumbled for my mobile. 'Need to get a message to Liam …'

But it was too late. Eleanor nodded Harry's way; he pulled out his weapon, standard Enforcement issue – energy ray, silver bullets, the lot – swung round to face a corner and yelled, 'Enforcement! Get visible, get down on the floor!'

The entire shop went silent, then exploded into action as customers panicked together, packing towards the door. Eleanor and the pharmacist, plus another assistant, shepherded them outside on to the pavement. They stayed outside but Eleanor came back in. Her eyes were stony.

'Anything?' She called over to Harry, who was still facing the corner, weapon drawn.

'Not yet.'

'She's here. I know it.'

At that point I stood up. 'What are you doing?'

Harry swung around to face me, but didn't lower his weapon. 'Jessica.'

Behind my back I was making little 'down' motions, indicating to Rach to crouch behind the box which, from the anxious bobbing at my shoulder, she was ignoring. 'Harry, there's nothing in here.'

Then Eleanor waded in, her gun half-raised at hip level. 'The readings say there is a Shadow. Our informant says it's a Shadow. It is our duty to apprehend it.'

'Ellie.' I tried to keep my voice level. 'The only things in this shop right now that aren't cosmetic or health related, are you and me. There is no Shadow. Your instruments are wrong.'

'We have information that a Shadow is hiding in this shop.' Harry's answer was automatic, like he'd been programmed. 'Shadows are negative energy. They will sap the life out of living creatures. It's our duty to remove dangers to the public.'

'Harry, listen to me. You were looking for someone, I heard you say "she's here." Was it me? Did you come in here looking for me? And if you did, then there's no Shadow. Which was it?'

There was a beat, during which I really thought the logical approach had worked, and then their guns moved. Both came up to shoulders and rested there, trained on me. 'Are you assisting an Otherworlder to resist arrest?'

Shock made me giggle. 'It's such a good job you don't lisp.' I couldn't seriously believe that Harry, or even Eleanor, would use a gun against me for doing nothing more than telling them they were wrong. But then I looked in their eyes

39

again and it wasn't Harry or Eleanor looking back. Their pupils were distended and flickering.

'But Jessica, everything is on our side. There is a Shadow in here, refusing to concede. You are aiding it.' Ellie shrugged, and it was an alien shrug. 'I think we can kill you.'

'Oh, my God,' I whispered. 'You've been glamoured.'

Another shrug, and behind me, Rach squeaked. 'They're under a spell? And they're going to kill us?'

At the sound of her voice, Harry's gun jerked away to point at the floor. 'She must be alone.' His voice wasn't right, either. Emotionless. 'No witness.'

Eleanor wasn't so easily distracted. 'Then we kill that one, too.' She was sighting me down the barrel of the Enforcement rifle. I wondered what ammunition was loaded. Not that it mattered; anything that would kill an Otherworlder would leave me deader than dead.

My knuckles rapped against something cold and hard. I looked down to find my hand resting against a large bottle of hair conditioner, and reflex action cut in. My fingers closed around its reassuring weight and I curved my arm up and over, flinging the bottle in a delivery that a world-class cricketer would have been proud of. Unfortunately, I hadn't trained with the British team and my shot went wide, but the two Enforcement officers broke their concentration for a second, their misted eyes following the bottle like two cats seeing a fast-moving furry object. There was a fumbling behind me and something plastic was pushed into my hand as Rach armed me for another strike and I followed up with a more successfully aimed family-sized bottle of Nit Control shampoo which hit Harry on the side of the face. He staggered, and, re-armed by Rachel, I flung another bottle, which connected with Ellie's wrist as she squeezed down on the trigger. Her shot went wide, piercing through the nappies and into the shelving, whilst the lid came off the bottle and splattered her in blue gloop, smelling of chemicals and detergent.

Then Rach and I began flinging everything to hand. A box of old-fashioned curlers caught Harry on the temple and he went down. Eleanor, trying to wipe splattered shampoo from her eyes, was felled by a joint attack of Storm Red and Honey Highlights, her feet slipping from under her in the pool of glutinous liquid. For safety's sake Rach and I continued the barrage for a few seconds then, when neither Harry nor Eleanor got up again, we cautiously crept towards the door.

The two Enforcement officers lay unconscious. Rachel stared at the Rigid Wave box by Harry's head. 'Eat shampoo, bitches!' she said triumphantly, and then, 'I didn't think I hit him *that* hard.'

'It's the glamour. It must have cut out.'

She started to giggle as the shock caught up with her. 'They wouldn't really have shot us, would they? Harry's your friend.'

I stared at the spreadeagled forms. 'That wasn't Harry. When you're glamoured, it's like being hypnotised, you'll do anything you've been told to.' I crouched down, trying not to get Head & Shoulders on my shoes; I was still a pair down from last night. 'They won't remember anything about it when they wake up.'

'You're trying to stop yourself from writing "I'm a cow" on Eleanor in lipstick, aren't you?'

'Quietly happy that she's going to smell of anti-dandruff chemicals for ages, actually.' I stood up. 'And "eat shampoo, bitches"? That is *not* a line from any of the Rambo films I've seen. Why didn't you shout "dye, bitches, dye!"? That would at least have had the comic element.' I'd started to giggle too, but tears were pricking behind my eyes. In my back pocket my mobile beeped its ring tone and I seized it with out-of-proportion gratitude.

'Jessie, are you coming back today?' Liam sounded petulant. 'Because I've got Zan nagging about this Dead Run thing, Head Office want you to chase up some paperwork, and it's bloody boring stuck in here on my own.'

I had to clear my throat to answer. 'Yes, sorry, I'll be back soon.'

'Anything happening out on the streets?'

I stared down at the gunk-covered Enforcement officers. 'Actually, things just got a bit weird.'

Chapter Five

Abbie stared around the flat. 'It's even smaller than I remembered.'

My sister thought I should have bought my own place by now, somewhere to put the collection of art originals and antique furniture that I also should have but didn't. She regarded my sharing a flat as some kind of attempt to hold on to my youth – as though Rachel and I held wild, drug-fuelled orgies every weekend and spent weeknights piercing one another's bodies or tattooing outlandish symbols on our thighs. On quiet evenings, i.e., all of them, I laughed quite a lot about this. 'It's nice,' I said, defensively. 'It's handy for work.'

'But it's not *yours* though, is it? Doesn't it belong to Rachel? Don't you ever want to have your own place, properly yours? There's a nice cottage in Farndale. Reasonably cheap. Needs work, but it could be lovely.'

Abbie is fourteen years older than me and sometimes she behaves more like my mother than my mother does.

'We were thinking of moving up north,' my dad, balancing a cup and saucer on his knee and with Jasper comfortably occupying the central portion of his lap, waved a hand, 'maybe getting a croft on the islands. You could come with us, Jessie. Try a change of career.'

'And what if Rachel gets married? You'll have to move out then, and Mum and Dad won't have room for you, and you can't come to me – I suppose you could always rent somewhere in the suburbs.'

'The Orkneys are very beautiful, I've always thought.' Dad carried on his parallel, and not quite continuous, conversation. 'Bit chilly, but the grazing's good, apparently.'

Nice. Abbie, much as I love her, have *always* loved her, tends to plan her life out in ten-year segments, which drives me mad. And, I noticed, she'd got Rach married off but never contemplated that it might be *me* settling down. And Dad was always trying to get me to do something other than Liaison work, but even by his standards, moving to the Orkneys was a bit extreme. I ignored both of them and pretended to dust a shelf, a move they would both have seen through at once, since dust and I had a complicated, and slightly symbiotic, relationship.

My mother came in from the kitchen, carrying a plate of Battenberg. I noticed, with a sudden shock, that she was looking old. Her face was more lined than it had been last time I'd seen her, her hair more wispy and she was stooping. I'd been a 'last-chance' baby, born when my mother was forty-three and my Dad forty-eight, so I'd been used to her being the oldest mum in the playground, but she'd always worn her years lightly. Although her hair had started going grey before I was born she'd kept it pinned up so the white hairs didn't show, then later she'd started dyeing it strange colours, meeting me from school with purple hair or electric blue – just to see my face. Now, however, it was completely white. My heart squeezed.

'Mum.' I shuffled up on the sofa to make room for her. 'Are you all right? You look a bit tired.'

'We've lambed forty ewes this spring, it takes it out of an old body. You ask your dad about it. It was his bright idea to buy in some Jacobs, and they're stroppy old buggers at the best of times.' She settled back against the cushions and fiddled in the sleeve of her cardigan for a handkerchief. 'But I'm all right really.'

I looked up, and met Abbie's eyes. She has our parents' eyes, bright blue like cornflowers, although Mum and Dad's have faded a little over the years to a bleached version of their former glories; I'm the odd one out with my orange-brown pair. 'Different milkman,' Mum always used to say when people remarked; apparently I was the spitting image of her grandfather. Only without the pipe-and-whisky habit and the inexplicable fixation with Bakelite that I'd heard about from Dad.

Abbs was giving me a 'tight-mouthed' look, as if something was my fault. When the parents had left to go and watch their film, I cornered her. 'So? What's been going on?'

'Nothing.' Abbie coaxed her large frame into a particularly unflattering tweed coat. 'I'd better go, I promised to drop in on some friends while I'm in town and then give the parents a lift home after the film. I'm on duty in the morning.'

'You're not going until you tell me what's up with Mum and Dad! They both look worn out, and you've been doing bum face at me over their heads all evening.'

'They're *worried* about you! Can't you see that? At the moment all they seem to talk about is you; getting you away from York, wondering if they can persuade you to leave your job. All this wrestling with vampires stuff, they are absolutely terrified that something is going to happen to you!' She sounded bitter, with reason. Our parents had never worried that much about her. But then, they'd never had to. She spent her spare time helping around the smallholding and working at the local Cats' Protection League; was large, unfashionable and, if it hadn't been for her twelve-year marriage to the deceased Andrew, a born spinster.

I was always described as the young, flighty one, but I think my parents' definitions could use some work. Thirty-one is barely young and working for the council is kind of the antithesis of flightiness. 'I'm perfectly safe! Honestly, Abbs, you can tell them, I know my job looks weird but it's about as dangerous as giving out parking tickets, and about as interesting.' Carefully not even *thinking* about Harry and Eleanor and this afternoon's high strangeness, I patted the tweedy arm. 'Abbs, I like what I do. I'm *good* at what I do. It's not a patch on what *you* do, of course, but it's me.'

In my back pocket my mobile rang.

'Well, as long as you're careful.'

'I don't really *need* to be careful, Abbs, honestly, my job is bagging and tagging and watching a computer screen. The newspapers like to blow everything out of proportion and make the Otherworlders sound exotic and dangerous but really they're as interested in keeping everything running smoothly as we are. No-one wants …' I stopped. Abbie remembered the Troubles. I didn't need to remind her of how it had been. 'Honestly,' I repeated. Then I flipped open my phone and Liam's breathless voice spoke, louder than necessary.

'You'd better get down here, Jessie. We've got a live one, and they reckon they need you.'

I gave a kind of apologetic grin at my sister. 'Where are the Hunters, Liam? This is their call, surely?'

'They're there, but they reckon the detectors are going insane, what with all the Otherworld activity, so they need a reliable person and, guess what, your name came up.'

'What do they expect me to do, alphabetise something to death?' I muttered.

'They can't see what's coming at them, that was the message I got. Well, the actual message was 'Ahhhhh, fuck, what the fuck … can't tell … get help,' but you see what I mean.'

'And?'

'And you're the nearest person that can tell a vampire from one of the Hunters up for the Run. Someone gets downed, it had better be an Otherworlder otherwise things are going to get messy, so … guess it's you, Jessie.'

Sweat broke out on the palms of my hands. 'That sounds like a posh name for bait.'

'Jessie, the place is swarming with Hunters. Plus, you know how to handle yourself. You went on the self-defence courses, didn't you?'

I had, but only because I thought they would be full of blokes. All fourteen of us girls who'd signed up had thought the same. 'Yes, but administering a groin-kick to a padded-up ex-rugby player isn't the same as fighting something that wants to fight back.'

'It's double time, evening rates.'

'Wow. And suddenly I'm interested.' I still owed Rach last month's rent. Liaison came way down the list of priorities when it came to pay rises and I swear we were still being paid at 1988 levels. 'What is it, a vamp gone rogue?' That wasn't too scary; all I'd have to do was point the Hunters at the right body. I could be home in time for *Shameless*. 'Where and when?'

'It's in the Museum Gardens, you know? Near the river?'

As I struggled into my jacket, Abbie gave me a surprising hug. 'Take care, sis,' she said, squeezing rather tightly. 'I don't want anything to happen to you.'

'Not as much as *I* don't,' I said, squeezing back. 'Tell Mum and Dad everything is OK. Tell them, oh, I'm fine, work is fine, you can even tell them that I've met a nice man if you like. I haven't, obvs, but it should keep them quiet for a bit.'

We smiled at each other, a sisterly smile of complicity, then she left to go visiting and I left to go detecting.

Chapter Six

It felt odd to be passing through, under the Enforcement-green chequered Incident Scene tape, past the stationary ambulances with their ominously still sirens into the unusually quiet park beyond. Normally this part of York was crowded out with picnickers and visitors to the Museum, but now it was only occupied by little clusters of Hunters, edgily smoking in tight groups and keeping half-an-eye open for *Hello* magazine telephoto lenses.

'Where's it all happening then?' I said, approaching the nearest group. They were locals, Paul Smithed to the eyeballs, discreet little tie-pins proclaiming their identities.

'You tell us.'

'That's what you're here for.'

I sighed, and looked towards the only woman in the group, who'd dressed like something out of *The Matrix*, all black leather and dark glasses. Hoping for some kind of female-affinity, I spoke to her. 'Is it true all the detectors are on the blink?'

'Are *you* getting anything?' Her voice was as tight as her hold on her gun, nervous, wound-up. No solidarity here.

'I'd hardly be standing here talking to you if I could tell a vampire was about, would I? Or is this what it's all about, use me as a human canary – when I run, you all run?'

The group followed me as I inched forward over open ground. If there *was* a vampire about – and I couldn't feel anything at the moment – then it would attack from cover. As long as we stayed away from the bushes and trees, we'd see it in plenty of time and the vamp would be coming at us half-blind.

Creeping along, I wondered. *Something* had glamoured Harry and Eleanor. Something powerful enough to get past the usual Enforcement screens. Something that knew malfunctioning detectors and mistaken identity could have got the blame for my death. Was that 'something' here, now, hiding in the increasing darkness and the ridiculously Gothic ruins that littered the park as though a vampire Capability Brown had designed the place?

As we moved across the park, other small knots of Hunters joined us, circling slowly on the periphery of our group. From above we must have looked like a very well-dressed puff of smoke, coiling our way inevitably towards the ruins of St Mary's, which hung against the skyline. A few of the less agile of the Hunters stumbled over the scattered stones, too busy scanning the horizon to watch their feet – which is a nice kind of metaphor for the Hunters themselves.

'Oh!' I stopped suddenly, half-under one of the arches and three Hunters cannoned into me from behind. I noticed that the stress of the situation didn't stop one of them from feeling my bottom. 'It's here.'

The whole group dropped into an instant crouch, guns bristling in every direction. 'Where?' someone hissed.

'It's not a vampire.'

And as soon as I'd realised that, and all my assumptions about attack from cover were wrong, it attacked.

It came from above, took the first Hunter in the shoulder, wrenching him backwards and dropping him to the ground while the others waved their guns around, desperately searching for the right ammo to load against what suddenly wasn't what they'd been expecting.

'It's a demon!'

I caught a sudden view of it, full face, raising its head to sniff at the air, while the wounded Hunter shuffled backwards, heeling himself out of range to crouch behind some decorative stonework; huge pointed ears above a dog-like muzzle, viscous body like mist formed from treacle. 'It's a hell-hound!' I shouted back, not knowing if anyone could hear me above the yelling and the demonic screaming, flattening myself back against the stonework of the Abbey and hoping that those red eyes wouldn't notice me as fifteen separate guns emptied fifteen separate magazines into the creature.

They were good and they were efficient. Within seconds the creature was gone, two Hunters were bending over their fallen colleague, several were forming a protective circle around me, and the one Hunter who hadn't been hiding behind the door when the sociability gene was handed out, was patting my shoulder.

'It's okay,' he said, 'it's dealt with.'

I found I was shaking a bit. This wasn't what I was here for. I'd come to identify a vampire, something that could be taken down by a good shot; sod it, distract the vampire with a 50 per cent sale leaflet from the Designer Outlet and you wouldn't even need to aim. This was something else, something serious. 'No, it –'

There was an abrupt 'uggh' from beyond us, a dragging sound, all over in about two seconds, then everyone was on their feet again.

'It took Daz!' someone called. 'Came from nowhere, and took him!'

It had left his hat, though. Hell-hounds have a comic-book sense of style.

'No, he's here!' Another voice shouted a reply. 'We need a medical team, stat, he's wounded.'

'You can't kill it.' I tried to measure my voice carefully, knowing that they'd only listen if I sounded as though I had authority. 'You'll have to trap it, tie it to the earth.'

A suddenly much-tighter bunch of Hunters grouped around me. 'How do we do that?'

My stomach lurched. People could *die*. I could feel the adrenaline-sting in my blood as shock shouldered all my emotions out of the way to make room for action.

And then, there it was, sliding up from the earth to form on our side of the wall, hanging for a second between reality and nightmare. Truncated muzzle, tiny red eyes like glass beads in a plague-pit and a mouth which swept open, loops of stained saliva roping from it and smelling of everything sour.

Watching me.

'What do we *do*?' The whisper was urgent, as a matter of reflex the guns were all raised and aimed but we all knew how much good they were. 'You'll have to tell us, Jess.'

I kept my eyes on the creature in front of me. 'Look. There's an ice-cream van abandoned down the path there; we came past it on the way up. Empty out the freezers.'

I don't know how it was communicated, but two Hunters from the back of the group moved slowly away, peeling off towards the path. The hell-hound didn't seem to notice. It was watching me. Still.

And now it was getting dark, too. The stone arches of the ruins stood stark against the dying light. The vampires were gathering down by the river. I could feel them and their interest; they'd be able to smell the blood by now.

So quickly that I didn't see it coming, the hell-hound struck. Snaked forward as though growing through its own skin, bulging towards me and I turned and fled through the limestone eyebrows of St Mary's with the Hunters at my back, three of them helping the injured Hunters to run. There was another burst of gunfire – you had to hand it to them, they kept trying – and a muffled yell and then we were all running, flat out across the open parkland, heading downhill towards the path where the ice-cream van was innocently parked.

The demon wasn't fast, it wasn't particularly agile, but it could dematerialise and reappear anywhere. It could also keep this up all night – forever, if it had to. It was hunting us, herding and chivvying, safe in the knowledge that we were vulnerable, squashy and tasty and I was *damned* if I'd let some overgrown demonic Labrador finish me off before I'd ever had the chance to own a pair of Jimmy Choos.

'Here!' I led the running band into the shelter afforded by the flimsy side of the ice-cream van, where we all collapsed against each other. 'I thought you lot worked out!'

'What for?' A be-suited Hunter wiped his forehead with the back of his hand. 'We kill. There's not a lot of working-out you can do to prepare for killing.'

'Don't you ever have to chase anything?'

He patted his gun. 'Ammo does the chasing, not us.'

'It's gone.' One of the more observant Hunters, the Matrix-Trinity-lookalike, I think, was watching round the side of the van. 'Just, kind of, sank into the earth.'

'Then it's moving in the Underworld, coming round in front of us,' I said.

'How do you *know* this stuff?' Ken Symes, our Visitor from Dorset, was slumped on the other side of me, still wheezing.

'I watched *Buffy*,' I said, shortly. They stared at me. 'You know, *Buffy the Vampire Slayer*? TV programme? Teenage girl who fights demons?'

'Yeeeesss,' said one of the York Hunters, impeccably dressed but with mud marks on both knees, 'but we never thought of using it as an instruction video.'

I rolled my eyes. 'Right. We need to be ready. Everyone grab as much ice-cream as they can carry. The big plastic buckets for preference, but lollies will do.'

'This is a wind-up.'

'No, this is extemporisation,' and then I had to add, 'it means, thinking on your feet. As soon as you see it start to come back up, we need to tip all the ice-cream over the top of it.'

'*What?*'

'Just *do it*!'

'There it is!'

The bubbling pool of smoky-black was beginning to rise, trickling up through the earth on our side of the van, and I jumped for it. The others, thankfully, followed, copying me when I emptied the sludgy, half-melted contents of my plastic container over the ground, sloshy yellow foam and chunks of vanilla cascading in a waterfall of rancid lumping.

The earth shrugged aside and the beast burst free, but the running pool of artificial additives, flavouring and colours flowed smoothly over the top. Where it encountered the smoke-like semi-formed lines of the hell-hound it solidified into a sticky entangling web. The creature shook its head, trying to break the bounds, but the stickiness was tying it, binding it, making its insubstantiality into something concrete and solid.

'Do you carry tranqs?' A small pistol was passed over someone's shoulder and I fired the unfamiliar weapon into the neck of the hell-hound, once, twice, until I felt the creature stop struggling and go limp. 'Mr Whippy, one, hell-hounds, nil.' Someone at the back applauded. 'We tied it to the earth.' I was surprised at how strong my voice sounded. 'They can't fight that. You'll need to call Enforcement to deal with it now, but make it quick because once the ice-cream has dried it will go all stiff and they'll never get it in the van.'

Hands heavy with dignity, I passed the tranq gun back to its owner and managed to walk all the way back to my parked car before shock caught up with me.

Chapter Seven

Next morning, as soon as I arrived at work, I was greeted with, 'Well, if it's not the hero of the hour!'

'Don't. Just don't. It was horrible, Liam. Really. Never let me get volunteered for anything like that again.'

Liam shoved the daily paper under my nose. There, spread across the front page, was a truly dreadful picture of me leaving the Museum Gardens, ice-cream stains across the front of my shirt and an inexplicable, but heroic, smear of blood across my cheek, which I suspected someone had Photoshopped in. 'You "helped save lives", apparently. You should be proud of yourself, Jessie.' His voice was gentle. 'And, for the record, I wouldn't have let you go if I'd known how bad it was.'

I stared at my picture. 'Does my nose *really* look like that?'

'Only sometimes.'

'Great! Well, they can keep it. I couldn't be a Hunter, going through that all the time. There's plenty of people like me out there, let them recruit from that five per cent and leave me alone.'

'No, Jessie,' Liam laid the paper down, folded so that the 'nose shot' was less visible, which unfortunately meant that my chest was on the crease-line, 'five per cent of the population is like *me*. I don't think there's *anyone* out there who works like you do. By the way,' he swivelled his chair so that he faced his computer and couldn't see my expression, 'talking of that, Sil came by earlier.'

All the reactions that I *should* have felt facing down the hell-hound – the nausea, increased heart rate – hit me like delayed shock. 'What?' I asked faintly. 'When?'

''bout ten minutes ago. Came to find out how you were.'

'Yeah, right.'

'Honestly. He looked shitty, if that makes you feel better.'

'What, not brushed his hair?' I pretended to be immersed in sorting through some of the papers on my desk, not even seeing them, just keeping my hands busy.

'Come on, Jessie, we both miss him. I'm sure he'd come back if you asked him. With Zan doing the admin I bet running the city doesn't take up *all* his time.'

It was far, far too late to tell Liam the truth now, so I muttered, 'Budget cuts. It's him or you,' which shut him up, and an unusually sullen silence descended on the office.

I stared at my e-mails, all documents, giving various Otherworlders permission to enter the city on a temporary basis, until the print ran into a formless blur. Remembering, whilst trying not to, that evening when the place had been full of swirling paper, falling like moths around us as Sil and I had screamed at each other with a passion which could only ever find its outlet in fighting and vehemence.

And then I'd thrown him out. The best associate I'd ever had, Liam's friend, my nemesis, my downfall. Sil. Because he was getting too close, *because I was afraid*.

'Penny for them?'

I jumped, and dropped the sheaf of papers. 'Bloody *hell*! Where did you come from?' Malfaire, cross-legged and elegant on Liam's desk, raised an eyebrow. 'I didn't hear you come in!'

'No. You didn't.' He stood up and stretched, gracefully and oddly familiarly. 'Too busy navel-gazing?' He was wearing a navy-blue suit with a collarless shirt which laced up down the front, dark glasses hid his eyes. He couldn't have looked any cooler if he'd slithered in coated in ice.

'I was thinking. Where's Liam?'

A flash of eyebrows: was that meant to be suggestive? 'Making coffee. I think he might be leaving us alone together.'

'I'll kill him, I'll bloody *kill* him,' I muttered, still trying to switch my head from thinking about Sil to talking intelligent English. 'So, what can we do for you today?'

'Apart from make me coffee and give me the opportunity to chat with a, quite frankly, delightful young woman?'

'I'm not *that* young!'

'She's not that delightful, either.' Liam came in, carefully balancing three mugs and a plate of our best shortbread. Weird though our visitor may be, he clearly merited top-class treatment – Liam usually just brushed off the custard creams when someone new came in. 'Trust me.'

'I came to get your RSVP for the Run tomorrow night. The organisers need exact numbers, you see, and they were slightly concerned that after all your excitement yesterday, you might not want to attend.' Malfaire removed his glasses, and marmalade-coloured eyes met mine. 'Are you still planning to attend, Jessica?' Although his words were business-like, he was scanning me up and down in a way that made me feel slightly uncomfortable; a tinge of magic ran along with his gaze and tickled my skin like a snake's tongue.

'I'm not sure.' I took my mug from Liam and tried to conceal the 'a woman needs a man like a fish needs a bicycle' logo by cupping it in my hands. 'Last night I ...'

'I read the papers. Quite a triumph, by all accounts.' There was a note of amusement in his voice again.

'Yeah. But Jessie is still a bit shaken.' Liam wasn't looking at Malfaire, he was watching me with concerned eyes. 'There was a bit of a misunderstanding with a couple of Enforcement officers too, and we still haven't got to the bottom of that. So maybe mixing with Otherworlders isn't such a great idea right now.'

He was completely ignored. 'It is something of a triumph to be invited. Certainly for a human. In fact, I cannot recall *any* human being requested to attend the Dead Run. A great coup for your department, in fact.' Hot damn. He certainly knew the buttons to press. York Council would be absolutely wetting its collective padded underwear at the prospect of scoring one over all the other districts that had hosted the Run to date. There would be so much triumphant crowing that the Town Hall would sound like a free-range chicken farm at dawn. 'And I can promise there won't be a single hell-hound.'

I pretended to think, propping my chin in my hands and wrinkling my nose, whilst in reality giving our guest a once-over. He should have been good looking. Heart-shaped face, small mouth, just enough stubble and dark-blond floppy hair randomly scattered with lighter streaks, like he'd been on a surfing holiday. There was just this ... oddness that stopped me from puddling at his feet, this slight sense of wrongness ... *What the hell was he? Vampire, demon, or a lucky human?* His eyes gave nothing away, neither human nor Other, and trying to scan him was like running my mind over sheets of glass.

If I went to the Dead Run, at least I'd have a chance to find out. 'I suppose, if it's safe ...' Plus, think of the kudos. We might even get a rise ... hell, we might even start getting paid at post-decimal rates.

Liam groaned. 'Jessie, are you sure?'

But Malfaire cut his words off again. 'You will enjoy it. A spectacle, I think they say, something worth seeing. And the Run is being done a little differently this year, had you heard?' Malfaire carried on conversationally, ignoring Liam's narked expression. 'In a simulcrum of the City of York. I think they felt it might add a little more drama to the proceedings.' He sighed. 'It's all about "visual experience" these days, not a pure exhibition any more.'

I almost asked if there would be an attendance fee; after all, I still needed to replace those sandals, and I was already on first-name terms with the girls in the shop where I bought my tights, but when he cocked his head inquisitively towards me, I realised I was supposed to come up with something slightly more intelligent.

'I … err … I don't really know very much about it.'

'No? And yet you knew how to bind a hell-hound?' His lips twitched when I shrugged. 'But I suppose you would.'

'This is the first time the Run's been held on our patch,' Liam chipped in. 'And, from what I gather, no-one else gets told much. The organisers are very "need to know".'

Malfaire looked at Liam with his head slightly tilted. 'You are very protective of Jessica, aren't you? You care a great deal.'

Liam flared red. He opened and closed his mouth a couple of times, making a spluttering noise, and finally managed to breathe. 'She's my *boss*. I just want to make sure I get paid!'

'Of course.' Giving off stylish yeah, pull-the-other-one vibes, Malfaire set to flicking imaginary fluff from an immaculate trouser leg. This drew my attention to the slender length of his thighs and his perfect, form-fitting, tailoring. My mouth should be watering, but wasn't. Dear God, don't tell me Sil had ruined me for other men; I'd be doomed to a life filled with cats. *I'd turn into Rachel …*

The telephone rang and my brain pinged back to reality with an out-of-proportion gratitude. While Liam dealt with the call, my visitor smiled his honeyed smile. 'So. Can I tell them that your answer is yes?'

'I …'

'Is something worrying you? You seem very hesitant, Jessica. Surely you wouldn't want the vampires to think you are afraid of them and their kin?'

This made me bridle. How dare he imply that I'd ever be *scared* of a bunch of overly image-conscious, dentally challenged creeps? But he was right. If the word got out that I'd turned down an invite, then someone somewhere would draw that conclusion, and the next step might be an *en masse* attempt to give me something to be scared of. 'Malfaire – I – look, it's just that … I had a warning. About some kind of danger? At the time I thought it was stupid, but with what happened with Enforcement, this invitation, and the Run and everything … are you *sure* it's safe?'

The lazy smile died from his face, his eyes hardened. 'Danger? To you? Where did you hear this?'

'Vamp called Daim Willis. His demon is Tezrael of the Asgarths. I once did Tezrael a favour and the other day he returned it.'

Malfaire put his coffee mug down very carefully and leaned towards me. I noticed that he smelled of lemon-water and something smoky, and that his skin was very cold when he touched me, cupping my chin in his hand and brushing his eyes over my face to take in all my features. 'If anyone wished you danger, Jessica, then they would have to go through me first.'

'That's,' I had to stop and clear my throat, 'very kind of you.'

He released my chin, but his fingers trailed over my skin slowly before he pulled back. 'I must leave now, so much to do. Take care, and I hope we shall see each other tomorrow.'

And he was gone. Disappeared out of the office as though he'd never been; apart from the half-drunk coffee and the biscuit crumbs, he could have been an illusion.

Liam hung up the phone. 'Enforcement. No-one there has a clue what happened or how anything got past the shielding. They're "investigating", for which read "ignoring the whole thing"'. He stared at me. 'God, Jessie. You look like you're going to pass out.'

I touched my face, feeling the cold ridges Malfaire's fingers had left. 'Is he, or is he not, totally freaky?'

'Dunno about freaky, but he's a bit too smooth for my liking. No-one can be *that* smooth without having a whole load of weirdo under the surface. He looks like one of those guys you start talking to at a party only to find that they're a secret train spotter and you have to listen to the lists of "engines that got away".' He sighed. 'Shame they won't let us shoot train spotters on sight; the Treaty wasn't all good news.'

'And still nothing?'

He shook his head. 'Nope. I was trying like crazy, but, it's like he's metal or something. Impervious.'

'Did you Google him?'

Liam tapped a finger on his keyboard. 'Couldn't get anything. Maybe using a false name?'

I chewed my lip. 'Could be, I suppose. Not like an Otherworlder not to want us to know *exactly* who they are, though. Do you reckon Zan would have anything on him?'

'Hard to tell, if he's using a false name. We could try getting a furtive picture of him, but that's your job not mine. Last time I did the "concealed camera" thing all we got was four shots of the inside of my pocket and an inexplicable photograph of a pigeon.'

'Oh no, I am *not* creeping around taking secret photographs. Can't you just describe him to Zan?'

'I'm not sure Mr Social Phobia has a baseline to go from, we'd have to start with defining "walks upright" and I haven't got that many years left to me. Picture would be better. You could pretend it's for your "album". The special, secret one you keep under your bed ...'

I threw my phone at him. This was getting to be a pattern; if I wasn't careful I'd need a new one.

Chapter Eight

The Hagg Baba restaurant was located in one of York's better streets, one where the cobbles still stood proud. Its simple, understated exterior bore only the carefully symbolic sign, and mirror-effect windows of any other York eaterie, only the folded-back shutters and faint slaughterhouse-whiff of the fresh blood cocktails gave it away as an Otherworld favourite.

'What're these for?' Rach fingered the black shutters as we went past.

'Blocking out the light. It's as good as midnight inside for the creatures that can't take daylight. Ghouls, that kind of thing.'

'Oh.' She glanced around to see if anyone was looking, and then adjusted her underwear with a swiftly subtle hoik. 'These tights are murder.'

'It's worth it, you look very nice.' Rach was clad from head to foot in borrowed dark-blue satin, while I wore a more serviceable knee-length dress in a kind of black-and-red embossed velvet material which looked as though it had been copied from the walls of a Chinese takeaway. My dark hair was piled up on top of my head and pinned loosely in place, a style that was meant to look carefree and relaxed but actually made me look more as though I'd been in the vicinity of a small detonation. I caught my reflection in a window and cursed under my breath. I'd made a real effort tonight, but I was still one windy day and a mixed-wash accident away from presentable.

A uniformed man took our coats, and Rach hissed at me, wide-eyed, 'Is *he* a vampire?'

'No. Human.'

'Oh.' Disappointed, she stared out of the windows into the street outside. 'How about him? Over there? The foxy looking guy with his arm around the blonde?'

'Human.'

'Oh, *blast.*'

'Can you really not tell? Doesn't looking at a vampire make you feel all …' I waved an arm in lieu of words, '*odd*?'

Rach gave me a look. 'You mean horny? I've heard about what they do, how they mess with your head to get you to – do whatever they want.' She gave a half-scared, half-hopeful shiver.

'They can. But for some reason it doesn't work on me.' I shrugged. 'Don't know why.'

She turned away to stare around the restaurant foyer. 'But then you've always been a bit strange yourself, Jessie, haven't you? Maybe that's why.'

Gosh, thanks Rachel.

We were shown to our table (not a good one, right at the back, but at least handy for the toilets) and sat down. I adjusted my dress carefully, so as not to let the three tranq syringes I had in my pocket show, which would be the equivalent of pumping a shotgun in a crowded bar.

'What's that lump in your skirt?'

'Ssssh, Rach! Just a precaution.' I pushed the narrow tubes with their sleeved, wide-aperture needles further down so that they lay flat along the pocket seam. I'd decided that the gun would be overkill and I could work the little hypodermics by hand if it was essential.

'Why? Do you think it might be dangerous?' She shifted in pleasurable fear. Like most of the generation too young to remember the Troubles, vampire attack for Rach was a sexy, moodily lit scene from a late-night film, rather than the subtle back-alley assault that it tended to be in real life.

'No, but it is my job to be prepared. I'd hate to see the headlines if I let something kick off that I could have prevented.' Yeah, I needed another sarcastic caption like I needed two holes in my throat.

'Oh.' Rachel lost interest in my sartorial peculiarities, and stared at the waiters coming in with laden trays. 'We don't have to eat anything *funny*, do we?'

'No, it's all right, there's a human option for us.' I turned my attention away from her again, scoping the room but coming up with nothing more menacing than the blackness caused by a Shadow squatting near the bar, invisible in this non-light, drinking gin. The place was crowded out because the Hagg Baba was one of the few places in the city where real blood, brought in from the States where they paid a premium to donors, was served. Apparently, human blood is as different from synthetic as low-alcohol lager is from Stella. I'd investigated the Hagg Baba a couple of times during boring moments, but the paperwork all checked out, so I had to assume it was legit.

The human menu turned out to be more than adequate, with roasted quail served alongside exquisite terrines of vegetables, and lovingly embellished Beef Wellington sitting amid a vat of onion gravy. 'So, now what happens?' Rach asked, refilling her glass with the, seemingly, limitless free wine.

'Dunno. From what I'm told, they read out a list of the runners and then everyone ... well, it's a bit hard to explain but ... the race doesn't actually happen *here*.'

'So there's, what, like a bus or something?'

'No, it's here, but it's not *here*, if you see what I mean. The actual race takes place in another dimension. Y'see, what it is, this world is where a lot of dimensions touch,' I used the cruet to build a demonstration model, 'and some clever dick has found out how to open the door to certain places. A hundred years ago, no-one knows why, it opened by accident to the demon dimension, hence the vampires and the werewolves and everything, but today it might be ...' Earth was destroyed as the pepper pot fell over. 'Are you listening?'

'Yeah. Weird.' She was busy adjusting her tights again. I took advantage to look around once more, fingering the tranqs. 'Don't look now,' Rachel whispered at me from a semi upside-down position behind the table, 'but there is a *very* gorgeous man over there, and he's looking right at you!'

Gosh. Now *that* was something else that didn't happen every day. 'Where?' I whispered back, hunching forward across the table to try to see behind me.

'Over near the stage area. Oh, God, Jessie, he is really, absolutely, pant-wettingly, amazingly *stunning*; quick, look, I can't bear it!'

I glanced across the heads of the crowd between us and the area set up with microphone and notepad for the announcement of the race.

'*Shit!* What's he doing here?' I flicked back around and fixed my eyes firmly on the cutlery.

'Jessie? You've gone all pale. What's up? Do you know him?'

Standing in a clear space, with his gunmetal-grey eyes turned our way, was Sil. Tall, with the effortless elegance inherent in the vampire added to by his own titanium-sharp cheekbones, a surprisingly gentle mouth and dedicated stubble in the planes and angles of his face that drew attention to their sharp definition. Totally gorgeous. Totally devoid of human emotion. A total heartbreaker.

With obvious interest Rach stared across the restaurant. 'He's very pretty, isn't he?' she carried on. 'Who – oh, I see, he's with that dark girl.'

'What? Which one?' My neck cracked as I swivelled, in time to see Sil sliding his dinner-jacketed arm around a coffee-skinned young beauty, her long hair tied in a high ponytail, but still long enough to cascade down her bare back to where her dress, and bottom, started. He was no longer looking our way, but speaking animatedly to his companion, so I covertly studied him. He was thinner but as casually glamorous as ever with his night-dark hair messy over the collar of the dress shirt and his bow tie askew. So attractive that he didn't need to try, and he knew it. Unfortunately, so did I.

'Jessie? What's the matter?'

'Nothing!'

'Well, stop banging that wine bottle with the spoon, it's really irritating.' Rach stared around her again. 'You never see vampires going round with their teeth out, do you? I mean, out fangy out, not, like, gummy. I suppose they get fed up with biting their own tongues. They sort of slide them back in when they don't need them, don't they?'

I laid down the spoon very carefully and set my jaw. After all, Sil was nothing to me, had *never been* anything to me, apart from my assistant. Okay, so he was good looking and all that jazz, and we'd had a great time working together but, well, really, that temper. 'Yes. Like cats' claws.'

A whine of feedback indicated the opening of proceedings and Rach and I pulled our chairs to the same side of the table to watch. To my astonishment, Sil left the girlfriend at a table and came up to the microphone.

'Now, we all know why we're here,' he began – there were a couple of catcalls but he ignored them – 'so I'll cut the crap and get down to it. Tonight's race will be –' a dramatic pause gave me long enough to wonder why Sil was acting as MC; it was hardly the sort of thing I'd expect to find him doing – 'through the carefully hand-crafted vision of York. And the runners, chosen by random draw from those who have applied, are,' Sil opened the envelope handed to him by one of the uniformed human flunkies, 'for the vampires, Caro.' A very pretty female vamp stood up and acknowledged the cheers, looking stunned. 'Tangent D, running for the Zombie nation.' There was a small, muted cheer from a party seated so far over to the left that we couldn't see them. 'The Hog, running for the Wild Folk,' a more raucous cheer. The whole audience looked over. The Hog turned out to be something I had taken to be someone's guide dog. 'Tasster, for the Night,' a ghoul, I presumed, but couldn't see, 'and, running for the Humans,' Sil's eyes were fixed on the piece of paper he held. Watching his face I saw his mouth move and his eyes darken. 'Jessica Grant.'

I imagined it. I must have done. '*What!*'

'Jessie?' Rachel was on her feet, knees banging against the table, forks jostling out of the way. 'You didn't tell me you'd entered anything!'

'That's because I *didn't*!' I stormed out of my seat and began to zigzag between the crowded tables towards the Master of Ceremonies with sheer indignation overriding my desire to never speak to him again. 'Look. You know as well as I do that humans don't do the Dead Run.'

Sil seemed to be struggling with himself for control, a muscle twitched in his nicely stubbled cheek. 'Jessie.' Eyes narrowed in an artificial smile. 'It's been an age.'

'Just drop it, Sil, I'm not impressed,' I snapped.

'Don't tell me, you can't keep away.' Sil's grimace-grin became more real. 'I ought to have known that even *you* couldn't keep up the defiance forever.'

'Don't start changing the subject, you bastard!' I hissed. I must have looked serious, because Sil started back, hands held defensively in front of him.

67

'Hey, hey, calm yourself! I'm only saying.' He lowered his arms and bent down to look into my face and the sudden familiarity of the smell of him took me back so fast that the breath puffed out of my lungs. He always smelled good, Sil, a mixture of dark chocolate and earthy scents, like a wooden box of cocoa overlaid with the subtle alluring vampire fragrance. The bastard. 'Jessie, there is danger brewing, a whisper that something big is going on. I came here to try to find out what it is and now I am beginning to think someone has fixed this draw.' He was almost whispering now. His dark hair had fallen across his face and was curtaining us from the room. 'Someone wants you in the Run for some reason.'

I lowered my voice to match his. 'But the Run ... well, it's just a race, isn't it? And I'd stand no chance against a vampire or a zombie ... I know how fast you lot can move. Or shuffle, in their case. Does someone want me there just to prove how useless humans are?'

'Perhaps.' Sil's mouth was so close to my ear that I could feel his lips moving against my skin. I toyed with the idea of shoving him in the chest to force him to back up a little, but stopped myself. Physical contact with Sil – not a good idea. 'But, as you said, humans don't participate. There must be a way to get you out of it.'

I stepped away and his head came up. His eyes followed my movements, as vampires tended to do, like cats watching very clever mice of whom they are slightly suspicious. 'What, you think it's beyond me? You think I can't even stagger a couple of miles to prove a point?' All my earlier indignation had gone, subsumed under the desire to demonstrate that I was just as good as a vampire. Well, maybe not *as* good, but certainly partially adequate. 'Don't you dare dismiss me like that, Sil!' Being angry with him was the only thing that kept the feelings at bay. It's hard to want someone when you want them to shut up and leave you alone.

He raised a hand and long, pale fingers flickered as though he was about to touch me. 'Jess...'

'Back off, Sil.' I turned so that my whole body indicated the end of the conversation. 'My name got chosen. I'll run.'

'In that dress?' There was a momentary heat in his words, whether desire, anger or sartorial comment I couldn't tell. 'I thought you always said you needed considerable undergarments simply to walk briskly?'

'Excuse me.' An intentional elbow caught me in the ribs, as purposeful as a pickaxe in a pavement. 'Do you know this person?' It was the long-haired girl, returning from the bar with jealousy raging in what passed for her heart. Thin as a knitting needle, she looked like someone who wore three wisps of lace under her frock, and had never needed the full-on support of a cantilevered bra in her life.

'This is Jessica. I used to work with her.' His eyes were calm now, misleadingly gentle.

'Really? You never said. Was that how you learned so much about the human way of doing things?'

Sil's eyes met mine as we both remembered that night, the spectacular fight that had led up to him storming out. 'Yes,' he said smoothly, but there was a flicker of yellow across the grey, 'that was how I learned.'

'How lovely. Well, if you'll excuse us,' and she grabbed his elbow and steered him away, deep into the crowd, not wanting a proper introduction, not wanting history. If only it was that easy.

Sil edged himself gently away from his date and rubbed the centre of his chest. *Jessica. You can't feel it, can you, that impenetrable net that encases us both, that unknowable, indefinable essence that binds us. You look at me and you see – what? An enemy of the kind that only a friend could become?* He turned to watch her as she stood sulkily, both hands bunched down by her sides, talking to the chunky girl she'd arrived with. Despite everything, he had to force himself not to grin at the sight. She'd still got that aggressive out-thrust jaw, still kept her head up so that all that wonderful, curly hair sprang from its restraint, coiled around her face and made her look ... innocent. Was that what attracted him, her innocence? Or just the body? Was he really that shallow?

He breathed carefully and fixed his eyes on the dull carpet until the incipient erection subsided. Yep. He *was* that shallow.

So. She was still Jessica. And someone had entered her into the draw. She'd never have come over so aggressively if she'd put herself in; besides, as she said, humans didn't run – it wasn't the point. Vampire versus zombie versus ghoul ... that was how it went; putting a human in the mix was like entering a chicken in the Derby.

He ran his tongue over the tips of his fangs, descending now as the anger burned its way through his bloodstream. His demon shifted, feeding on the rising adrenaline, pushing its way towards the surface and making him ride the situation in a way no human could understand. She couldn't run, of course she couldn't. She'd be a laughing stock. Or, more to the point, she'd annoy the other entrants until everyone started fighting everyone else and in that other dimension he wouldn't be able to wade in and stop it. Hell, there must be some way that he could pull her out or rearrange the Run, something. *Because if anything happened to her – what would happen to me?*

Rach came up, panting. 'Wow, quick work there, Jessie! He is *gorgeous*, did you get his number?'

'I've had *his* number for years,' I said, sarcastically, watching covertly as Sil stood surveying the crowd. 'A difficult man, our Sil. I hope that hag knows what she's doing.'

'Oh, so *that's* Sil? The guy you used to work with?' Rach stopped wrestling with her gusset for a second. 'Wow. I thought you said he was a complete bastard?'

'He is.'

'He doesn't *look* like a bastard.'

And there's everything you ever need to know about Rachel in a nutshell. 'Don't let the looks fool you,' I said, my upper lip curling as though I'd bitten into something delicious only to spot the mould when it was too late.

Rach fiddled with her underwear again. 'And you're being very hard on his date. I thought she looked quite sweet.'

'I meant it literally. She's a hag. Like, you know, a kind of witch.'

Rach's mouth fell open. 'What, really? Wow!'

Yeah, wow. And she'd better not cross *me* one dark night, quota or no quota. 'Look, I'm going to have to run, Rach.'

'But I thought you said humans didn't run? And anyway, you're not dressed for it. Remember that time at school when they made you do the hurdles and you hadn't got your kit and you tucked your uniform into your pants and one of the boys said ...'

'Yes, I remember.' I thought about Sil's offensive dismissal of my chances. 'But I reckon I know more about the streets of York than anyone else who's running out there. I just might be able to sneak ahead – and what will it say about humans if I can actually *beat* even just one Otherworlder?'

'So you will run?' A familiar, soft voice beside my ear made me jump.

'Malfaire!'

'The very one. Hello.' He'd carefully subverted the whole

71

evening dress thing and was wearing a ruffled shirt with no tie, a tail coat and a pair of exquisitely cut trousers. I couldn't see his feet, but I'd take bets he wasn't wearing Jesus sandals and grey socks. I introduced Rach but Malfaire's eyes kept swinging back to me, almost as though he couldn't believe I was actually here. They were the clear gold of syrup tonight.

'I will, yes.'

'Good.' I felt the brief pressure of his hand on my shoulder. 'Someone needs to show these vampires that they are not as supreme as they think.'

'I'm not sure that they do, actually.' And besides, my chances of beating a vampire were less than remote, more like non-existent. My only real hope was that I could cut off some corners unknown to the others and maybe get home before the zombie. They weren't fast but they didn't let a little thing like a leg half-off slow them down.

'We'll have to see, won't we? I am sure that you have hidden depths, Jessica.' And, with a scalding smile, Malfaire let the ebb and flow of the crowd take him across the room, leaving me wondering where on earth he'd got his opinion of me from, because it certainly wasn't the local press, with their sarcastic taglines and peculiarly angled shots of my nose.

'So, he's going to try to get you out of it?' Rach had stopped yanking at her tights and was staring after Malfaire.

'No, I'm running,' I said, still wondering about Malfaire's faith in me.

'Ooh, Jessie, your *face*! Are you in "luuuuurrrve" with the luscious Malfaire? Or is it something a bit more – primitive?' And Rach did a lewd dance, with much recourse to her rapidly lowering gusset.

'No!'

'Mmm. Think I'd rather have the other one, Sil. Malfaire's

a bit smooth for my liking; give me a bit of the scragged-up rough stuff any day.'

I let her words flow over me as I performed the metaphorical equivalent of tucking my skirt into my knickers. Malfaire seemed very keen on my performing well and I wondered why – there had never been a human runner in the history of the Dead Run. The whole *point* of the Run was supposed to be for the Otherworlders to show each other their individual prowess, not for some poor outclassed human to get stomped into the mud. They can stomp on us any time.

The restaurant was so crowded that at first I didn't notice what was happening. There was a general current of people moving towards the corridor which led, via the toilets, to the kitchens, funnelling out so that they passed through the doorway in single file.

'Where's everyone going?' Rach popped up at my elbow.

'Dunno. Maybe they've all got cocaine habits.' I tried to smile at her, but my mouth wasn't cooperating.

'The doorway has opened.' I twisted my head to the other side and found myself gazing at Zan, dinner-jacketed and with his hair slicked back, looking establishment for all he was worth. He was very tall, at least six foot three, and quite slender, so he should have looked like a well-dressed broom handle, but there was something eerily imposing about him. 'They are heading down to the viewing point. Jessica, are you all right?'

'What's going on, Zan? Sil said he thinks something is happening ...'

Zan looked at me directly. 'I don't know,' he said, and normally Zan knew everything; like I said, he's run the paperwork for this area for sixty years. 'But Sil thinks you are at the centre of it.'

'Where is he?'

'Trying to stop the Run.'

'So, do we go now, or what?' Rach stepped forward and Zan put out a hand to stop her.

'I'm afraid you cannot join us, Miss Marwood. Humans are forbidden from entering the portal. Even Otherworlders will not be actually *present* for the race but will watch through a special scope device. I'll see that you are escorted home safely, however.' Then, catching my glance, 'Honestly.'

'Not even a tiny nip, Zan.'

'You truly believe that *I* would break the Treaty? That it would be *I* who would bring back the warfare and the times of fear?' His smooth, impeccably handsome face creased into lines of horror at the thought.

'Joke, Zan.'

Rach looked from me to Zan. 'You mean, he's a – ' Her eyes widened. 'Gosh. Really? You look perfectly normal to me.'

'She doesn't mean to be rude.' I soothed the vampire, who was looking rather taken aback. 'She's a bit over-excited.'

There was a smooth movement at my elbow. 'Obviously.' Sil appraised Rach, who, with her shining eyes and blue satin dress, looked a bit like a hyped-up nine-year old at her first sleep-over and was gazing at him as though waiting for something to happen.

'Is he another one?' Rach whispered but, since she was amplified by the loud hailer of overexcitement I think the bus queue outside Tesco's heard her. 'You never told me he was a vampire, too!'

'Oh yes.' I heard the tone in my voice and even though I was using it, I didn't really understand why it was there. 'He's a vampire, too.'

'Would you like me to prove it?' Sil addressed Rach

directly, drawing back his top lip to let his fangs descend. It changed his whole face; rather than the slightly untidy, casually sexy young man he had appeared, he was now a predator: marble-hard eyes and a sense of coiled elasticity.

Rach squeaked. 'Don't tease her!' I said, rather more sharply than I would have done if I hadn't been facing an ordeal that sounded less fun than painful surgery, and Sil moved away from Rach to stare directly into my face.

'You would give *me* an order?' His fangs were still down and now locked into striking-position, his expression and voice cold enough to blister skin. 'Jessica? *Really?* You think you still have the right to tell me what to do?'

Sil's demon was moving inside him. I could sense it scratching and scrabbling its way to the surface, eager for confrontation, resolution – anything which would provide it with more of the hormones it was currently getting off on. Anger, stress, sex, it's all the same to demons. They're like little chest-dwelling junkies. And Sil's was driving him to the edge. I'd seen him let loose, I'd even seen him close to killing before, but I'd never seen him in danger of losing control like this.

'Sil, steady.' I put a hand out, but he flinched into the new silence as if I'd been about to hit him. Flinched, then shuddered, as though somewhere deep inside himself he'd forced his demon back. I was quietly impressed. Sil had obviously learned a new level of self-control. 'Of course I'm not trying to tell you what to do, I'm just saying ...' I nodded towards Rach, who had a look of horrified fascination on her face, 'ease up a little.' Then I added, '*Pas devant les humains*,' because I knew it would break his mood, make him smile.

He gulped a sharp breath of air and swallowed hard, clenching his teeth, then shook his hair away from his face and grinned. Fangs were gone, I was pleased to see. He made a little bow in Rach's direction. 'Miss Marwood, I apologise.'

'Aren't you going to apologise to me?'

I saw Zan give a tiny smile which he tried to hide.

'No. You I am going to yell at.' Sil took my elbow and steered me into a corner. 'Jessie, you have to pull out of this. I can't stop it, the Committee won't allow it, but you can't run.'

I could feel his grasp as though he held more than my arm. I'm immune to the whole vamp glamour thing, although I've seen it at work on several people and can testify to its efficiency – they'd burble around the streets like people who'd gone shopping and forgotten what they came out for, bearing at least one double-pinprick and a look of blissed-out stupidity. But here something else seemed to be at work. Something harder, something deeper. 'Sil?'

'What?' He pushed his hair away again as though it irritated him.

'I'm not that pathetic, you know. I've got a bit of a game plan. All right, I know I'm never going to win but I can at least keep my end up; not disgrace my entire species.'

'Like that time you ran the London Marathon?'

'Er, yeah, I suppose. Only with less breaks for cappuccinos and Kit Kats.'

Sil gave me a look. His eyes were flipping between two colours, the metallic grey and a softer, bluer shade. Apart from that he looked almost human. 'Well. If you're sure.'

'I'm sure. Besides,' I lowered my voice so that the general hubbub around us covered my words, 'if something is going on, the best way to find out what it is, is to go along with it. Don't you think?'

'Jessie ...' But he didn't follow this up with anything, just shrugged.

'Zan, will you take Rachel home, please?' I turned to the tall, skinny vampire. 'There's a lot of things here for the Run and I'm not sure I trust Enforcement at the moment.'

Zan hesitated, then looked to Sil. 'Hey, go ahead,' Sil said. 'I only run the city. Jessica is clearly pulling rank on me tonight.'

I glared at him, but he turned away.

'Miss Marwood?' Zan held out his arm, still hesitantly. I half-expected him to request a HazMat suit. 'I shall escort you to your door.'

'Oh!' Rach looked at him and at the proffered arm. 'Gosh. I mean … so polite!'

'Yes, well we don't all behave like something out of an Anne Rice novel,' Zan said, dryly.

I stood, buffeted by the crowd for a moment. Zan and Rachel left, joining the humans outside in the street, enjoying their evening, wandering around between the pubs and clubs of central York. Sil smiled at me and there was a complicity in it that left my heart thumping uncomfortably. Being so close to him again was raising ghosts I thought I'd laid a long time ago.

'Ah, there you are.' The crowd seemed to part, everyone else fell into black-and-white as Malfaire moved smoothly across the floor towards me.

'Oh, there's … have you met Sil, Malfaire?' To annoy the vampire I leaned a little closer in to Malfaire until our hips jostled, and the grey eyes went nearly black.

'We were introduced,' Malfaire said shortly.

'Yeah.' Sil was nearly as dismissive. 'You're about to go through, Jessie.' To my shock, he came over and put his arms around me. 'Good luck,' he said, over the top of my head as he forced Malfaire to either step away or risk being involved in a group hug situation.

'What are you doing?' God he smelled fabulous, and even the touch of his hair as it brushed my cheek made me shake. Too close, he was too close ... but, *damn*, it felt good ...

'Checking that you are armed.' Sil lowered his head to speak directly into my ear. As he did so, his hands ran along the sides of my body with a familiarity that I'd only ever before encountered in dreams. 'Ah, I see you are still breaking the rules.' His voice was even lower now as his hands brushed the giveaway hardness of the tranq tubes in my pocket. 'Good.' Then, with a grin, 'Are you enjoying this?'

'If you don't get off me,' I matched his low voice, 'then demon or no demon, I shall punch you so hard that when you land you'd be advised to ask what year it is.'

'Don't worry.' A hand, taking advantage, brushed my buttocks. 'I haven't forgotten your prejudices.'

'Prejudices!' I snapped my head up. 'Get *off* me!' I pushed him back two steps, and regained some measure of control over myself.

He moved away without another word, melting back into the crowd now heading for the large space in the middle of the restaurant.

Malfaire gave a smile that looked like the kind of grin that a cat might give, if the cat had been fed amphetamine-kippers. 'I'll take care of you from here,' he said, as though he'd scored some points. Then he held his arm out to me. 'Shall we?'

I hesitated. I didn't like to admit to it, but I was in the throes of a kind of panic. 'It will be all right, won't it?' I said. 'I mean, it's not, like, dangerous; they wouldn't let a human run if it was dangerous, would they? Don't the Committee have some kind of rules, or something?' I was babbling, aware of it but unable to stop myself.

Malfaire stopped and turned to face me and I hated my

shallow, appearance-led brain for the way it dwelled on the strangeness of his looks. 'I am sure your hidden inner strength will rise,' he half-whispered. 'There is so much more to you than meets the eye, Jessica Grant. So much more than even you know.'

Okay, so maybe he knew about the tranqs. They were the only hidden strengths I had.

Sil dragged himself into the kitchen, crouched in the dark space between two freezers, and snarled when the maître de asked him if he was all right. *I thought she understood …* He banged his head gently on the tiled wall, then harder, stopping as he felt the stretched-string sensation which was her passing through the portal into the far dimension, and slumped down on to the carefully swabbed floor. *How could I be so stupid? Why? Why am I doing this to myself, to her? Why can't I let it go?* Fangs slid down as the anger took the place of the softer emotions, slicing at his lip and drawing blood; the pain making him snap back to himself.

Zan called him sad and a disgrace to the species – well, not *sad* because Zan had been one of the first vamps and his behavioural tics meant he found adapting to the increasing pace of modern life exquisitely painful. He'd never say 'sad' in that context. Or 'cool' or 'sick' or 'bro'… any of the contemporary vocabulary peculiarities that made Sil quietly despair – but it was what he meant. Still stuck in his ways, whereas Sil had *adapted*. It was what made him dangerous, what gave him the sheer balls to be the acceptable face of the Vampires of York.

Yeah. He was Sil, and he was in charge. He didn't just rule, he *rocked*. Any woman, any man. Anything. He could have anything. March in there and take it, with his demon feeding him the power as long as he returned the favour and fed it with the razor-blade edge of emotions in a way that the humans would never understand. And the blood, oh, yes the blood ...the feeding and the frenzy and the huge, whole, sexual high of it. Which, he remembered as he shifted from foot to cramped foot, had caused the whole problem in the first place.

Where was she now? It was okay for her, she was human, she didn't have this constant *thing*, this harpoon-in-the-gut sensation all the time, like she was a whaling ship and he was ... Moby Dick or something. *Unflattering comparison there, man. Forget that one.* Okay, more like a spider-and-web scenario.

He hoped she knew what she was doing.

Chapter Nine

The huge room beyond the corridor couldn't exist in human space and time; there simply wasn't enough vocabulary in our world to do justice to it. The nearest I could come was 'the space inside a skull when the brain's gone'. Chambers off to either side ranked back in the gloom in infinite number and a central passage divided the room; I couldn't make out any more detail than that. I was going to be running through something that looked like the Library of Hell.

'Is this it?' I whispered. Everyone was whispering, the whole crowd. 'Is this where we're racing?'

'No.' Malfaire looked around. 'This is the reception area.'

'Oh,' I gave a little, half-hysterical giggle.

'We're waiting for the gates to open so that the race may begin. Do you have a plan?'

'*Plan?* I didn't even get *pudding*. I only came to give Rach a good night out and suddenly I'm …' Hysteria. Not a good look. But the part of me which contained my pride didn't want to reveal how scared I was. 'This place is really intimidating, I wonder if they know that.'

'Of course.' Malfaire was gazing up into where the ceiling would have been if there'd been one. 'It's rather the point.'

Suddenly there was a communal gasp from the crowd. The floor rippled as reality shifted once more, to reveal a huge pair of bone gates. There was a noise like a pain in the soul, a deep sonic groan which came in through my feet and my ears simultaneously, and the crowd began to fall back. If I'd been less panicked, I might have admired the artistry that had created those gates – the designs picked out in fine detail, the intricate way in which the bone had been carved to allow the arch to follow the vaulting of the room, so that the gates formed a kind of cartilaginous echo of the vastness.

'Right. The rules.' I found myself pushed right to the margin of the group of runners, who were assembled in front of a vampire I didn't recognise, while the rest of the crowd moved back, clustering around a device I couldn't see. 'You pass through the gates, and from then on you are in strict competition, understand? No holds barred. The first runner to reach the matching gates at the end of the course will be the winner. Remember, the honour of your people is in your hands.'

I think I'd already given up my human honour, together with hope. And faith in my deodorant.

The officious vampire giving us the pep talk glanced over his clipboard. 'And any death, or fatal injury, is the responsibility of the runner themselves. There is a disclaimer on the paperwork, if you wish to examine it and this will be made available on the noticeboard at the end of the race.'

Death? Fatal injury? I don't remember the London Marathon having that kind of disclaimer ... The zombie and I made eye contact and gave one another an apologetic grin. I knew him vaguely; he ran a greengrocer's shop in Acomb and had, if I recalled correctly, once had a run-in with a bunch of bully-boys trying to burn him out. I couldn't see the ghoul runner, but The Hog, whatever it was, was snuffling around the legs of the female vampire, who looked slightly disgusted at the liberty. The sight of them gave me confidence; neither one looked as though they intended anything more dangerous than a slightly scraped knuckle. One at a time, each of them stepped forwards and vanished from sight, until only I was left, with rapidly moistening palms and an increasing awareness that I really wasn't dressed for this.

And then Malfaire was back. His suit was soft against my skin, raising the hairs along my arms. 'It's your turn.' He gave me a little push forward. The vampire with the clipboard was standing in an alcove with an expectant look on his face.

'Miss Grant? Step over here, would you?'

I moved towards him hesitantly. As I stepped into the alcove the surroundings melted away like a bad dream. Not-quite instantly the vampire, the alcove and the crowd were gone, replaced instead by a familiar scene. The change was so total that it made me giddy for a second.

I was standing in the middle of York, outside the Minster, facing Stonegate. Everywhere was quiet and there was nobody on the streets. I staggered, unbalanced by the speed of the transition and the odd familiarity of the location – like the city, and yet not, more like a film set built by someone who had seen photographs but never the real place. No birds sang, no pigeons stalked the pavements, the medieval buildings stood like watchers. It was three-dimensional yet nothing cast any shadows. There was no trace of the room I had left, nor of Sil or Malfaire.

I felt sick, needed to sit down, and I groped my way through the oddly painted-on sunlight to the bottom of the Minster steps. Sod the bloody race, I didn't care if I won, lost or got carried home in disgrace, there was no way I could run when I felt like heaving my dinner up on to the road.

As I sat I felt the skirt of my dress pull across my thighs. I put my hand into the small, satin-lined pocket for the reassuring touch of the metal syringes – a contact with the world that contained Jeremy Kyle and *Shameless*, my world.

The body-warmed smoothness of the containers stood as a little link with reality.

Which was how I came to be holding a tranq tube when the creature struck.

It came at me out of nowhere, silent and rank, and the first I knew of its arrival was the blow to the back of my head which sent me toppling forward off the step to lie sprawled on the pavement. Whether or not the flagstones were real, landing still hurt and pain always makes me angry. It also makes me act instinctively and my instinct was to tranq the bastard.

I brought my hand up and round behind me and dug the needle-end of the tube into the flank of the creature just as it flung its weight on top of me. The head of the beast crashed down on to my skull, enormous paws slid to either side and stinking fur carpeted my entire back. It was like being pinned under the world's largest bearskin rug. I wriggled my way free, coughing at the smell, and tried to identify my attacker. Superficially it looked like a huge dog, but the wide shoulders looked wrong and the feet were much too big. Some kind of demon, then.

I shook my head, backing away, and looked up at the south face of the Minster. Funny, I'd never noticed the statues before. Set between arched rebuttments in the stone, their features largely rotted away and their garments now rendered indistinguishable drapes and mouldings. It seemed an odd place to have statues, surely their accessibility would mean that they got climbed on or graffiti'd or bits were broken off by souvenir-seeking tourists. And as soon as I realised this, the statues' eyes opened –pop, pop, pop – with a noise like a stammering grindstone.

'Run,' said the nearest, a nose-less crowned figure, in a voice which made me think of heavy smokers, 'run, now.

We *like* to chase,' and they began levering themselves down from their podia, scraping and grunting as their legless forms met the pavement, eyeless and browless, in some cases even headless, with truncated, acid-eaten limbs held out towards me.

I'm never one to pass up a suggestion, so I ran. Along Stonegate, head down, powering through the narrow street, until I stuttered to a halt on the corner, where it widened out into a square. The noise of my stone pursuers had faded, but I could still hear, above the thumping of my heart, the sound of pavements being macerated; they were coming and they were coming fast.

Well, this was fun, wasn't it?

I leaned forward and panted for a moment until I managed to catch my breath, then off I went again heading towards the bridge, where I had to stop because it curved into nothingness. I peered between the railings, down towards the water, but the river wasn't there either, and here they came again, the stone figures. I wheeled away. Tranqs wouldn't work, not on rock, and I had no other weapon apart from my desire not to be caught. Turned back to run down a parallel street, and nearly tripped over the body in the road.

'Hog?' It was the black beast, the one running for the Wild Folk. He was dead, or at least he was flatter and more spread out than live creatures usually are. I bent down and touched his head with the tip of a finger. He was still warm. But dead. Still warm. *But dead.*

I looked around for someone official, and had to remind myself that this wasn't the Marathon. This wasn't even human territory. My shoulders went cold as the shock blanketed me: *people were dying. Was it always like this? Why didn't we know?* And then, from what sounded like every direction at once came the sound of inexorable grating and a kind of mechanical chanting. The bloody statues. Still coming. *And I could die ...*

Shock cut rational thought out and let my hindbrain do the thinking. As usual, my subconscious was a lot more intelligent than my conscious and also a hell of a lot better at self-preservation, and I had a momentary flashback to an evening on watch out here not so long ago, waiting for a vampire that had broken its territorial bounds in Leeds.

A mental map of the city pulsed behind my eyes like an expensive effect in CSI and I turned. There, in the gap where two shops didn't quite touch, was my advantage: a metal fire-escape, rising from ground level up to a platform close to the roofline. It looked rusty and frail, but I'd climbed it that evening to watch for the vamp in the crowded streets, so I knew it could take my weight. I grabbed the handrail, swinging myself up half-a-dozen steps, then sprinted towards the top.

Don't think, run. Four flights of rattling fatigued metal, each step clanking as though the whole thing would topple, but it held. By the third flight I was gasping, my thighs were complaining and my lungs were groaning as I swung around the last handrail and grabbed the safety-bar at the top. Bent double and wheezing, I appreciated the view, which was chiefly the statues gathering at the base of the staircase and rolling their heads back to try to look up at me.

As I looked down I was filled with a sudden anger. *Bloody* Otherworlders! I was a sodding council employee, for God's sake. I did *paperwork* and made tea and didn't understand the computers, like any normal person, so how had I ended up on a rooftop being held at bay by a bunch of jumped-up statuary?

There was a brief moment of huddled quiet down below before the first of them started on up the fire escape. One, then two, and when I looked down I found each of the lower steps occupied by a sculpture. Shit. Metal graunched and screamed at the weight, vibrations ran the full length of the flight and the lower part of the handrail fell away in a rain of rust, but still they climbed.

Mouth dry, I scrambled on to the upper rail surrounding the balcony, gripping the protruding guttering with both hands to keep my balance as I kicked at the few supporting struts which attached the structure to the building. With the weight down below already pulling the metal pins almost beyond their endurance it only took a few moments of fevered wrenching before the entire fire escape peeled from beneath me. As I looked down between my wildly waving legs I could see the entire rank of stone people hitting the pavement, detonating on impact into a suitcase-load of body parts and random carvings.

This would all have been far better news if I hadn't now been dangling from an only partly supported plastic gutter high above the street. For one moment of desperate weakness I considered bursting into tears. My lungs were howling at me and my arm muscles were lines of fire ending in rapidly numbing fingers. *I could let go. I could just drop and have this over.* But then reality cut in. I had to get out of here, if only so that I could make good on my promise to punch Sil really hard, and I gritted my teeth, ignored the shriek of pain from my shoulders and swung my legs. My knees caught on the edge of the building and I managed to pull myself up on to the flat roof. Noisy panting ensued. My tights were laddered and my dress was rucked to above my waist but right now I didn't care. I was alive. Gradually my breathing slowed and I sat down on the pitted surface to get my bearings.

I knew this street. Knew each and every shop, every crack

in the pavement, every gobbet of spat-out chewing gum – this was my city. *Make that knowledge work, Jess.* I wiped my sour-tasting mouth on my bare wrist and thought. *Safer up here. Travel at roof level.* I stood up carefully and made my way to the edge of the roof, where it joined the next building. I was about to step up when in front of me a shape formed, grew and flowed across the grey rooftop, sinuous and fluid. A Shadow. I barely had time to register it before it was on me.

I fell, slumping down on to my knees. Every single thing in my world was revealed in all its tawdry, pathetic hopelessness. *I* was nothing. I had no-one. The one I wanted was the one I couldn't have; I'd die painfully and alone –

Wait a minute. *Shadow*, think, Jessie, what do you know about Shadows? That they're nasty, and can kill and *they feed off desperation.* Almost against my will my muscles contracted and pushed me a step closer to the edge of the roof, shuffling along on my knees. Thirty feet or so of air was all that lay between me and the impact that would stop this horror. The Shadow pushed at my mind, felt almost excited – deriving nourishment from the depression that causes the ending of a life – *I just wanted it to stop, now.*

Only one thing to do, and I welcomed the blackness and oblivion.

When I woke up, the rooftop was deserted. My thigh ached from the tranq shot and my head was thumping – that stuff was *disgusting*. But the Shadow had left me; lost interest when my mind was no longer able to feed its habit. Life, once again, didn't seem quite so bad.

Until I heard the scream.

Ignoring the bad-hangover sensation and the dry lips, I ran. Belted all the way down the line of roofs, occasionally leaping gaps like a cheap cop-show detective, until I reached the end of the row and clambered down the fancy brickwork of Barclays Bank. The female vampire had made it all the way to Coppergate and I headed to where I could see her, a huddled bundle that I hoped was still alive.

'Are you all right?'

'Help me.' The vampire seemed to be in shock, eyes frozen wide and, despite the fact that vampires don't have much of a circulatory system, she was shivering and pumping blood on to the fancy paved walkway. 'My leg – '

'I can see.' I pulled off my shoes and tights and wadded the black mesh into a ball. 'Press this up against it.' She did as I said, which shows how far gone she was; normally a vampire will chew off their own arm rather than obey a human command. But I didn't have time to be diplomatic. 'You're Caro?' I had to get her talking, keep her mind off her injury. 'Keep pressing, it'll stop the bleeding. What happened?'

'There was this thing, came at me out of nowhere. It slashed my leg and I think it would have eaten me, except – ' she winced. 'The zombie, he came along that road there.'

'I didn't see him.'

'No,' she said, rather pointedly.

'Oh.' This wasn't a race, it was a bloodbath. 'I think we ought to keep moving. Whatever took him might still be hungry.' I tied the remnants of my tights around Caro's leg, tightly enough to stop the bleeding and, with her leaning on me and hopping, we managed to make some progress through the eerily deserted centre. 'There's something not right about this race.'

'I think, maybe. Yes.' Caro hopped carefully beside me.

'I thought it was a bit of fun!' I wailed. 'I mean, come on! Against a *Shadow*? What chance did I have?'

'You think that the race was purposely made to be dangerous?'

'Someone entered me in that draw,' I said, thinking aloud. 'I think something was supposed to happen to me in the Run.'

Caro was shaking her head. 'You must be very important then, for someone to rig the race.'

'But I'm *not*! I'm not even on the sodding *council*. I don't do deals, I don't have any power over anybody, unless you count Liam, and getting me killed would be a bit extreme; he could just not send me a Christmas card.' I shook my head. 'I'm a filing clerk.' It came out as a wail. 'Who'd want to kill a filing clerk?'

Caro shrugged, exotically. Clinging together, we hauled ourselves through the narrow exit and out into the open space behind the shopping mall. There, where Clifford's Tower should have stood, was a pair of bone gates, the matching pair of those in the Hagg Baba.

'So what will you do?'

'I don't know. Try not to get killed.'

Caro gave me a peculiar look out of her green eyes. 'Welcome to our world. Do you know how many humans want vampires killed? At the last count? The Britain for Humans party comprises fifty thousand people. Fifty *thousand*, Jessica, would happily see me dead tomorrow. Today. Five minutes ago. Trying not to get killed is a way of life for us.'

'I thought things had settled down after the Troubles.'

'For some people things will never "settle down". Those were bad times, a lot of people on both sides got hurt.' The vampire sighed. 'And a long life isn't necessarily a good thing, when it comes with memories like those.'

'I'm sorry,' I said, and meant it.

Caro gave a brief smile. Her fangs weren't visible and the smile made her look almost human. 'You do the best you can, and your liaison work makes people more tolerant, so, it's not your fault.'

'Well, thanks for that.'

The bone gates arched above us. 'All this place needs –

– 'is a Foo Fighters track playing in the background. Whoa!' And we were, as they say, back in the room.

The crowd were gathered around a huge glass sphere, which must be the watching device, but they stepped back as we reappeared and there was a very respectable round of applause. I let go of Caro and headed off to the toilets, spent a couple of minutes in there fiddling with my remaining tranq tube, and by the time I came out, she'd been declared the Dead Run winner (there was still no sign of the ghoul). She threw me an apologetic look over the heads of her congratulators, but I just shrugged and went off looking for Malfaire.

Chapter Ten

He was sitting in the crowded main restaurant, obviously not bothered enough to even watch the race. Sil was hovering in the background, talking to a waiter – he clearly *had* watched the race because my appearance didn't even cause him a raised eyebrow. When he saw me walk in, Malfaire jumped to his feet.

'Jessica!'

'Yup.' God, I even impressed myself. I'd ruined yet more tights, had sweat staining and – I did not *believe* it – I'd broken another heel, but I was positively refrigerator-cool. 'I'm fine. It was a bit bloodthirsty in there – did the ghoul get out?'

Malfaire shrugged. Over his shoulder I saw Sil shake his head slowly and I let my macho façade slip a fraction as tears welled behind my eyes. 'Come and have a drink.' Malfaire led me to a now-empty table, filled a glass from the wine bottle that stood on it and we both sat down. In the circumstances, in fact, in *any* circumstances, drinking with Malfaire was the last thing I wanted to do, but I had an ulterior motive here, and tried to stop myself from fingering the tube in my pocket. Malfaire raised his glass to me, 'You survived the Dead Run! Let's drink to that.'

'I'd rather drink to the ones that didn't make it.'

'As you like.'

Sil was looking daggers at me across the room but I ignored him. I was enjoying upsetting him; after all, he didn't know that I found Malfaire creepy.

'So.' Malfaire pushed his chair away from the table a little so that he could tip his head back and look at me.

It was the kind of 'so' that quite often precedes a night of debauchery, and I felt a tingle down the length of my spine. Magic? Possibly. 'How do you usually wrap up a night like this one? I bet it's not by drinking in a closed restaurant with a vampire onlooker and the staff tidying up around you.'

No, I thought, do you really think it's as easy as that? A bit of magic, a flick of your highlights and I'll fall into bed with you? Time to put my plan into action. Feeling a bit *Agatha Christie* I flipped a hand around my head. 'Sorry. There's a wasp, there, look. Bloody things, they get everywhere.'

Malfaire's eyes were intent on me, almost hypnotic. 'I really think I'd like to come home with you tonight.'

Well, all right, everyone seemed to think he was totally gorgeous except me, but even so there was something in his persistence which was off-putting. A bit full-on and up-front ... surely I merited some flowers, maybe chocolates, some casual charm, perhaps. 'That's very sweet and everything, but ...' hastily trying to think of an excuse, 'my place is a bit difficult. I share, you see, with my friend Rachel.' Who might, judging by the way she'd been looking at Zan when they left, be entertaining in her own right. If it were possible to 'entertain' Zan, and the jury was still out on that one.

'Anyway, didn't *I* promise to walk you home?' It was Sil. I wasn't sure if he was coming to my rescue or letting rampant jealousy get the better of him. 'We have things to talk about.' He glanced at Malfaire. 'There's a lot of catching up to do.'

But at least he was a distraction. I performed a little dextrous jiggery-pokery under the table while the two men eyeballed one another and Malfaire jumped. 'What the –! Ow! Something stabbed me in the leg!'

'I told you there was a wasp – rub some vinegar on it.' I kept my eyes on Sil. Didn't want my expression to give anything away, and looking at Sil made me think of other things, disturbing things.

'I shall complain to the management.' But the mood was broken. Malfaire no longer seemed to want to seduce me, which was good, and anyway I make it a rule never to sleep with someone until I know what species they are. Sil was already pulling me backwards out of the Hagg Baba and before I knew it I was out on the chilly pre-dawn street, stumbling over the cobbles with Sil beside me, looking severely disgruntled.

'You would have, wouldn't you?' he said, before we'd even got halfway down the road. 'You'd have bloody well shagged him! And what was all that "ooh look, a wasp" bullshit? What was he supposed to do, fight it to the death in front of you?'

'What the *hell* is the matter with you?' I stopped blundering over the uneven surface and turned to face him. Sil had completely dropped the concerned act, and was standing with one hand around a lamp-post as though he wished it was my neck. His knuckles were white, and his face was, too.

'It's you! All that fawning over the creep as though he is your ideal man, flashing your bosom and your legs and flicking your hair like a cheap streetwalker chasing a penny tumble!'

'Excuse *me*! Fawning? I did no such thing, and anyway, am I not now walking away? Did I not just turn him down? Although, may I point out, that going home and being given a good time by Malfaire pales in comparison to being shouted at and called a ho by you!'

'Did I say that? Did *I* call you anything? I don't think *so*.' Sil's eyes were hard. 'But, okay, maybe you enjoy being treated the way he was treating you, like you're nothing more than a piece of ass.'

I felt the shock hit me. Something in Sil's anger had unlocked it and the cool calmness that had held me since I'd passed back through those bone gates evaporated; a bone-numbing horror crept in in its place. I stumbled as though I'd been struck.

'Jessie?' Sil grabbed my arm, held me up.

'Oh, God! Oh, God, Sil, I could have been *killed*.' My legs gave out and my arms felt that gravity-suction again as though I still hung from the side of that building. 'Oh, God.'

'Yes. You could. But you weren't.' For a second – the briefest flash of time – his body was against me, rigid and strong. 'Listen. You're the only human ever to have run and you came back, helping a *vampire* over the line. That is pretty impressive, you know that?'

He took half a step back, but his arm stayed, still supporting my weight.

'I nearly died.' A shrill giggle. 'That is so *stupid*.'

Sil flipped me round, gazed at me with huge eyes. 'I'm taking you home. You're hysterical.'

'You're pretty funny yourself.'

'Jessica. Shut. Up.'

So, you see why I couldn't work with Sil? He marched me to my door, where he let go of my arm as though it smelled of wet fish and turned away into the night. I was left, leaning against the front door, legs trembling and with the terrible feeling that I might be sick.

I let myself in, cautiously, but I needn't have worried. The buzz-saw snoring from Rach's room told me that she was sleeping alone, although the disgust on the face of Jasper, regarding me severely from the top of the freezer, told me that she had let Zan accompany her past the front door. Jasper liked vampires about as much as I did, right now.

I couldn't sleep. The shock left me alternately freezing cold or drenched-sweaty and I spent the hours lurching up and down the temperature scale thinking of all the clever remarks I should have made to Sil.

I didn't fall asleep until an hour before I had to get up, so when I finally dragged myself into the office I probably looked more vampire than human.

'God, I heard the Run was tough, but you look *terrible*!' Liam exploded up out of his seat and, for the first time in his employment, held the door open for me.

'And where did you hear that?' Feeling about a hundred and three, I lowered myself into my chair and fired up the computer. There was a vase of flowers on my desk. Hmmm. I hoped Liam wasn't getting all mushy over me, just because I nearly died.

'Caro came over. She was just leaving, heading back to, where's she from? Halifax, Harrogate, yep, Harrogate, that's it. She brought some flowers for you, to say thanks, said that she wouldn't have won without you. Said she owes you one, and those are not words that vampires utter very often, unless it's in the context of bitey-bitey.'

'Right. That's nice.' Only a vampire would have selected a vase full of white lilies. 'Liam, you remember that blood-analysis we had done that time, can you remember which lab did it for us? Only, I've got another job for them.' From my bag I withdrew the narrow metal tube.

'That's a tranq,' Liam said, clearly thinking I'd gone completely barking.

'No, it's not.' I held it out to show him the inside of the unit.

'That looks like – is it *blood*?'

'I emptied the tranq down a toilet and used the syringe to get a blood sample from Mr Malfaire. Hopefully,' I held the narrow cylinder up to the light, 'this will tell us exactly *what* he is.'

'Hang on. This is all a bit James Bond, isn't it? Isn't it illegal to obtain genetic material surreptitiously?' Liam sounded dubious but actually looked thrilled. I suspected he'd always wanted to be 'Q', or was it 'M', some mid-alphabet letter anyway, hence all that fiddling with the computer.

'Ah, now that's interesting. There *is* a law, but it only applies to humans.' I grinned across the desk, 'Don't you *love* discrimination?'

Sil stared across the office at Zan. 'The Run was rigged?'

Zan inclined his head. 'I strongly suspect so. Jessica has repeatedly stated that she didn't enter her name. Somebody did, somebody prevented the Committee from cancelling the Run, and somebody allowed a demon, a Shadow and sufficient magic to animate statues to gain ingress. To what end we must wait to establish.'

'Not a fluke. Not a joke.'

'No.'

'Shit.'

Another graceful inclination. 'As you say.'

'But why?' Sil started to pace the floor, the bottle of O swinging between his fingers. His demon, liking the feelings of uncertainty, moved inside him. 'Why do that? She could have died, nearly did by the sounds of it.'

'Yes.' Zan's fingers clattered over his keyboard. 'If she hadn't broken all the rules by going armed, she would have done.'

'They broke the rules first.' Sil knew he sounded sulky. 'Humans do not run.' He took a huge swig from the bottle, wincing a bit at the chalky aftertaste. Tonight he was *definitely* going out to score. It had been too long. 'So. Someone wants Jessica dead. Why?'

'Because of you, maybe?' Zan didn't look up from the screen. 'Someone who knows that you ... she is your weakness, after all.'

'Oh, that is absolute damned bull!' Sil took another long drink. *Jessie, with your slow smile and your quick mouth, if someone harmed you, what would I do? Would anyone survive?* 'Bull,' he repeated and the bottle hit a fang, sending a sharp pain spearing through his skull.

'All right.' Zan leaned back in his chair, stretching out his legs. 'Then maybe it is personal. Someone she has upset.'

'In that case, no-one's beyond suspicion. Jessie upsets people like we drink blood. It's practically her hobby,' he added, thinking of her perpetual ability to scrape down his nerves like a hot wire inside a tooth.

'You have a meeting in ten minutes,' Zan said, checking his Blackberry. 'Chief Constable. Do you want me to cancel so that you can go and make sure she's all right?'

Sil put the bottle down and wiped his hand over his mouth. 'No. No. Jessie made it very clear to me that she doesn't want me, doesn't want anything to do with me. I am not about to start protecting her just because she's aggravated someone. Let her work it out for herself.'

Zan wrinkled his nose. 'You're not going to start charging about like some kind of animal, breaking things, are you?'

'No.'

'Because you did last time she rejected you.'

'Yes, I know.'

'And it was expensive.'

'Yes, Zan, I *know*. It's all right, I'm a vampire not a teenage girl. I have coped with a few rejections over the years, I think I'll manage.' He scraped his hair away from his face with both hands and sauntered out of the office.

On his way to the conference room he kicked a table and broke a large and valuable statue. *Didn't say I was perfect, Zan, did I?*

Chapter Eleven

The next day should have been my day off, as near as I could calculate with our weird shift patterns. I'd been looking forward to a lie-in and some therapeutic window-shopping, but after the events of the previous couple of days, and given the number of Otherworlders still wafting around our streets like unwanted relatives at a wedding, we'd decided it was better to keep the office staffed. But, because we were *never*, in any possible version of the universe, going to get overtime, we worked pretty much in spirit, rather than body.

At one o'clock I left Liam reading his latest *Doctor Who* magazine and headed out of the office in search of lunch. Almost immediately Malfaire was beside me. I might have suspected him of lying in wait, if I hadn't had the world's tiniest ego, and most of that had seeped out after the last few years of romantic disappointment.

'May I take you to lunch, Jessica?'

Okay, he was strange, okay, I didn't fancy him, but he was polite, he didn't seem to be dangerous and he was offering me free food. We went to a bistro in the shadow of the Minster, where we looked at each other over long glasses of ice and a drink called virgin's blood that I really hoped was nothing more than tomato juice and vodka. He was wearing sunglasses pushed high against his face so that no trace of his eyes showed and his hair was carefully dishevelled. The overall effect was that of a designer hangover.

'So,' he began when the waiter had taken our order. 'Tell me about yourself, Jessica. Are you from York?'

It was an unexpected question. I'd been expecting

something more sexually pointed and I'd been bracing myself to beat him off with the cutlery. 'I was born in Devon, but my parents moved to York when I was only a few weeks old. Apparently things were really bad in the South during the Troubles.'

'They were indeed. Whereabouts in Devon? I knew the area quite well, once upon a time.'

'Exeter.'

'Ah. Lovely city.'

I took a sip of my drink and my eyes watered. 'Back then you could only get Residency Rights in York if you were local, what with it being a Safe Area. We were lucky, my dad is from here originally and he managed to wangle it so that we could move to the city, then he and my mum got jobs teaching at local schools. My sister was at a Protected boarding school in the Midlands, and they reckoned they could visit her just as well from here as from Devon, so, here I am.'

Malfaire looked amused. 'You have a sister? What's she like?'

'Oh, Abbie? She's nothing like me for a start. She's very sensible.'

He raised his eyebrows above the rims of his sunglasses. 'Does that mean that you aren't sensible, Jessica?' His arms came forward across the table, and he leaned on them.

'No, I'm sensible, too. Very sensible. Positively prudent.' I moved myself and my glass further back.

The waiter brought our plates of seafood and buttered pasta and Malfaire watched me the whole time it was being fussily arranged on the table. I found myself finishing my drink, to give my fingers something to do. 'Now, tell me more about yourself, about growing up. What sort of a child were you? Because I have to say,' he lowered his voice a little bit, but not enough, and the waiter smirked, 'that I find you a most *fascinating* adult.'

In my back pocket my mobile vibrated. 'Hi, Liam, what's up?'

'Wow, is that relief in your voice? What are you up to … please tell me it doesn't involve the words "bail" "breaking" and "injunction"? Anyway, look, this is important … Daim's dead.'

'*What?*' I swivelled around in my chair so that I no longer faced Malfaire, but he craned forward as though trying to listen in to my call.

There was a furtive rummaging around at the other end of the phone, from which I surmised that Liam had been fiddling with the new electric pencil sharpener. 'He was killed, about an hour ago. They've got the guy who did it, but Sil wants you. He's not convinced it's quite as straightforward as it looks.'

I caught Malfaire's eye. He mouthed 'problem?' at me, around a prawn he was sucking in a most lascivious way. I shook my head. 'What about Tez? Did he get out?'

'Daim's demon? I dunno; you'll have to ask Sil. He's down there now, wants you to get over the river ASAP.'

'But I'm –'

'Sil, Jessie, not me. You know what he's like, and he sounded a bit uptight when he rang in.'

Tez had warned me about danger, and now Daim was dead? My meal no longer looked delicious; it became pellets of greasy gunk in a slimy sauce, as my appetite retreated. Daim was a kid, a stupid, mixed-up kid without much of a life, and then he'd become a vampire without any notable change of circumstance. I owed him.

'But what about Enforcement?'

Daim came from over the river to the South, which meant

that his Enforcement team should have been led by Laurie Denham, he of the shaky hands and even shakier grasp of concepts. Sil being involved in something that ought to have been an open-and-shut case for the mop-and-bucket brigade was worrying.

'Laurie's pie-eyed drunk as usual. Natalie Andrews has gone over to fill in, but Sil wants you there, too. Reckon he thinks it's got something to do with the Run business. Probably wants you to investigate.'

'Oh, great. So now the city vamp has got me down as York's answer to Miss bloody Marple, has he? That's great, I'll be lucky to get an uninterrupted lunch break before Christmas now!'

'No-one would *ever* mistake you for Miss Marple, Jessie. Poirot possibly, given the incipient moustache ... Now, do you want the address or not, only I've got to get on with this filing.'

'Suppose.' I took down the dictated address and hung up, to see Malfaire still smiling at me.

'Well, off you go and clear up your mystery. I wouldn't want to be the man responsible for keeping you when your Master has called.' This was said in a slightly derisory tone.

I stood rather awkwardly, not sure how to take my leave. Malfaire sorted it for me by standing and giving me a cool, continental double-kiss. 'We must do this again,' he said, 'only without the sudden death element.'

I looked at him across the table doing shabby rock-god for all he was worth, and wondered again at the lack of sex appeal. Given his appearance, I should have been a little puddle of liquid by now ... instead, all I could do was criticise his eyes as being a bit too golden and his hair as over-dramatic. Maybe my sex drive had driven off.

Looking over my shoulder as I left, I saw that Malfaire

was smiling broadly into his drink, almost laughing. I hadn't been *that* amusing, had I?

I hailed a taxi and managed the cross-city journey in less than half-an-hour, wondering all the while about what could have happened to Daim. 'They've got the person who did it,' Liam had said, so he'd been killed. Not, as I might have expected, managed to damage himself spectacularly by, say, trying to microwave his head or see if vampires really could fly ... Had it been an accident? I knew vampires were hard to kill unless you really, *really* meant it – it was unlikely that someone had slipped whilst holding a sharp knife or anything.

All in all, I was feeling pretty shaken when I hauled myself up the five flights of stairs to the flat in which Daim Willis had had his last brief encounter.

I was surprised to find, on entering the flat, a certain lack of the paraphernalia of a fight. The front door was intact, the fixtures and fittings were still fitted and fixed, and only the presence of a spreading pool of blood gave away the fact that something untoward had happened there.

Daim's body was crumpled on the floor in a kitchen which smelled of old chips and more recent sausages, the plain pine stake jutting from his spine as though he'd been nailed into place. He was cold and there was no sign that his demon had escaped. I felt my heart give a little twitch; he may not have been a friend, but it seemed ridiculous that he had ended in a sticky mess, disregarded.

'Tez?' I whispered, but there was no reply, no movement.

'He has gone, Jessie.'

I swivelled and found Zan standing behind me. 'What happened?'

Zan looked around the flat. It obviously fell way below his standards, but then I think Buckingham Palace lacked that certain something as far as Zan was concerned. 'I am unsure. That is why we need you.'

'I don't know what use I can be.' A boy was brought into the kitchen, escorted by Sil, who looked about as pleased to see me as the corpse did. 'Why did you ask me to come over?'

'This is the killer. Human.' Sil pushed and, being vampire, he didn't have to push too hard before the boy was physically shunted in front of me.

I glanced him over. 'Yes.' The lad looked frozen, scared, certainly not as cocky as I would have expected from someone who'd just killed himself a vampire. He wasn't wearing any of the badges which would affiliate him to an anti-vamp organisation and he didn't look hard enough to be a chancy free-agent. In fact he seemed rather baffled as to why he was there at all. 'And he's terrified of *you*.'

'So. Maybe he will talk to you.'

Natalie Andrews came in from the living room and greeted me, warmly enough when you consider that this was, technically, her patch. Although not up to her to actually *do* anything, this being an Otherworld matter and therefore under Sil's jurisdiction, it was her job as Enforcement for this bit of York to oversee proceedings.

'Why can't Nat talk to him?'

'I already have.' Natalie flicked a look at Sil. 'He doesn't know anything, or he *says* he doesn't know anything. Yet he was found in here, standing over Daim. That has to put him in the knowing something category.' She shook her long, dark-red hair back over her shoulders, for Sil's benefit.

'And I cannot read anything from him. I think magic may be involved but …' Sil shrugged. Apart from the ability to control minds, vampires have less magic than the average chat-show host.

'What's your name?' I turned to the boy, who'd acquired a certain defiance from being talked about in his presence.

'Mike.' Surly, but at least he'd answered.

'So, Mike – you're, what? A friend of Daim's from … before?'

'Yeah.' A trace of uncertainty.

There was something about the boy, something about the flicker in his eyes. They were an unusual pale-hazel colour, the most attractive thing about him, and as I stared deep, deep into them, something stared back. A whiteness passed over the pupils, as though for one second Mike had been struck blind. I turned to Sil. 'He's been glamoured. Some bastard's put him under an enchantment.'

'Are you sure?'

I turned back to Mike. That *something* was still there, inside his head. Fading now, melting like a cloud into the air. 'Yes. And whoever did it is very, very confident that this lad won't remember anything that could give them away.' I looked down at Daim, spread out on the grubby lino floor. 'Where'd you get the stake?'

Mike blinked at me. 'Wha'?'

'The stake. Where did you get it? Did you buy it, or were you given it, or –?'

'It were here.' The boy gave his head a little shake, as though to dislodge a troublesome memory. 'It were already here. I found it there, on table.'

Sil's face was momentarily occupied by an expression I couldn't read. 'You are saying that you came into a vampire's flat, and there *happened* to be a stake on the table?'

Mike nearly wet himself at being directly addressed. 'Errr, yeah. Sir.'

'Sil, it's not his fault. One of your lot has glamoured him so thoroughly that he wouldn't have known if he was in

Canterbury Cathedral knifing David Beckham. You've got to let him go.'

'One of *my lot*?'

'You know what I mean. An Otherworlder.'

Sil walked around Mike, peering into his face like someone looking through the windows of an empty house. He let his fangs show a touch and Mike whimpered. 'Someone would do this? Glamour a human to kill another vampire? But why? Why not ride in and do the job himself?'

'That's up to you to find out, isn't it? You're in charge of Otherworld Affairs in this city. But bear in mind this guy's not really a killer, he's been got at by someone ... by one of *yours*, Sil. Just like ...' I gulped at the coincidence, 'Harry and Eleanor. I'm beginning to think –' I tailed off. Enforcement were still investigating; it was none of Sil's business. 'It's a bit like blaming a gun for a shooting.'

Sil glanced at Natalie, looked away and then looked back. They made big-time eye-contact and I saw the flare of interest in his eyes. He was a sucker for a flicky-haired girl. It would all end in tears, of course; trouble was, they wouldn't be his. I curled my nails into my palms and wondered why I was so angry about the prospect.

'But who on *earth* would want Daim Willis dead?' Natalie pulled herself away from Sil's dubious, if undoubted, attractions for a second. 'Want him dead enough to go to the trouble of glamouring one of his friends into doing it, rather than waiting for him to fall off a bridge or something?'

'Jessica? You knew him, who would want him dead?'

I looked once more at the body on the floor. In death Daim was even more pathetic than in life; he resembled a bunch of old clothes with a face on. And not even a very prepossessing face, at that. I found that I was shaking. 'I think it might have been because of me.'

Sil rolled his eyes. 'Everything still has to be about you, doesn't it, Jessie?'

'No, listen. Tez warned me about some kind of danger he thought I was in, which does, incidentally, seem to be the case, should anyone actually be *interested*, so, I think, Tez had been picking up information he wasn't supposed to have.'

Zan was looking from Sil to me. 'But,' he said slowly, 'who would arrange this to stop a demon from informing a human? You humans, you're just –' He tailed off.

'Lesser meat? Oh, don't worry Zan, I'm well aware of what you think of us. Anyway I don't think it was prevention, I think it was punishment.'

Sil snorted. 'Very Mafioso,' he snapped. 'And what has suddenly made you so important?'

'I don't know,' I said, genuine terror tiptoeing up and down my spine. 'I really don't. But first Enforcement go crackers on me, then there's the Run business, and now Daim's dead ...'

Natalie was looking Sil up and down and he was pretending not to notice. I guess some women like that whole man-in-charge thing, even if the man in question is five foot ten, skinny as a heron and – well, not really a man. I hated myself for the burst of jealousy that fired off inside me so strongly that if I'd had a demon it would have been lying down and fanning itself. I mean, come on. *Sil?* Wouldn't touch him if he'd been made of chocolate. I needed a bloke, that was all. It had been too long.

'So, can we let Mike go?'

Sil stared out of the window. I think it was to give Natalie a chance to check out his back view and she certainly made the most of it. He'd obviously come from a meeting of some kind because he was wearing a beautifully tailored suit, slightly out of date, but that's what you get with vampires, they have a made-to-measure suit and they keep wearing it, century after century. It had taken me months of pointed comments to get Zan out of frock coats. 'But that will send the wrong message. It'll look as though I turned a blind eye.'

'Well, can't you, I dunno, scare him up a bit? Give him a bit of the old vamp power thing.'

Sil closed his eyes. 'What the hell do you think this is, an episode of Scooby Doo?'

I looked over to where Zan was leaning against the wall, playing with one of his interminable devices. He really was Liam's vampire twin. 'Zan? Any suggestions?'

Zan fiddled with the tiny palm top for a bit longer. 'Take his mind?'

Sil straightened. 'Obtain power over him? To what end?'

'Tell him to forget the glamour.' The two vampires locked eyes. 'It can be done,' Zan went on, 'if your mind is strong enough to supersede the hex. You will not remove it; merely force it to be ignored.'

I hadn't the faintest idea what he was talking about, but Sil had. 'So.' He walked around Mike again and Mike cringed. 'You think I can force him to remember who glamoured him?' He smiled and Natalie gave a little moan. I wondered what she'd do if she saw one of his special smiles, when he genuinely found something amusing. They were better than an erotic novelist's entire output. But don't quote me on that.

'Perhaps not.' Zan gave an alien shrug. 'But worth a try.'

'I haven't done this in a long time.' Sil shot Natalie a quick look. He was turning her on, and that was exciting his demon, which was ratcheting up the tension and locking the pair of them in a self-feeding loop. Oh, I knew how it worked all right. I bet he was loving it. 'Here we go.'

Grey eyes darkened. His pupils seemed to bleed out, the grey shrinking further and further under the darkness, and then further out, beyond the iris and into the pale whites, until the whole eye was a black, mirrorlike surface. 'Mike. Look at me.'

Mike was a mass of fear. Sil's voice added to that fear and I watched with a measure of pity as a large damp stain spread across the front of his jeans.

'Look. At. Me.'

I had to fight my own feet from turning me round, the voice was that compelling. Natalie took two steps towards Sil and I put my hand on her arm to stop her from walking right into the vampire glamour. And glamour was the right word for it. Sil looked amazing. The huge, dark pits that his eyes had become made his skin look translucently pale, and his hair look like slashes into midnight where its blackness trailed across his face. His perfect bone structure stood out like a porcelain mask and he looked taller, more alien than ever before. Something inside me squeezed painfully.

'I can't ...' Natalie moved another step closer.

'Don't look at the eyes,' I said, keeping my voice low so as not to break the hold Sil had on Mike. 'Try the groin,' I added, rather tightly. 'It seems to be distracting you already.' She gave me a sharp look which I returned with extra edges. 'You're welcome to him, believe me, just don't start choosing curtains. He's typical vamp, all about the novelty.'

After a few seconds of mental lock-down, Sil released his hold and Mike crumpled to the floor, sprawling on Daim's less-than-savoury floor covering with his face in something that looked like the remnants of a pasty. 'He'll remember killing,' Sil said, his voice sounding rather far away. 'I thought that was punishment enough, to remember killing your best friend.'

'But you couldn't tell who glamoured him first time round?'

'No. I couldn't take him back that far. There's a block in there, something that cut out whenever I got close to the memory.' Sil shook his head as though clearing a thought. 'Something that could stop me getting deep into his head. Into a *human*'s head.'

Forgetting Natalie, forgetting Zan, we stared at each other for a moment. 'Something powerful,' I whispered.

'*Really* powerful.'

'But then, you're not exactly Mister Alpha Vampire, are you? I mean, couldn't someone higher up the chain break through it?'

'Hey, you do know I run this city, right?'

'Well, yeah, but it's not like you're all thews and biceps, is it? You're more the cerebral type.'

'Was that a compliment?'

I looked him up and down. 'No.'

'It wasn't another vampire, Jessie.' Sil came in close. I was uncomfortably reminded of those last days in the office. 'It's something else.'

'What, then? I thought, apart from your lot and the weres and the zombies ... that was it for the human-based component. And I can't imagine a vampire, even one with Daim's lack of attributes, letting anything else get close enough to glamour him.'

'*Neither can I.*' We were nearly nose to nose now. I could feel the static from his hair pulling at my skin. There was a huge chasm of ache inside me, regret, loss, grief, and I nearly fell into it when he reached out a hand and touched my wrist. 'Something is very, very wrong.'

Zan's voice brought me down. 'Can I suggest that we leave Mike to come round in his own time and go and complete all the necessary paperwork back at the office? I need to charge the Blackberry.'

The spell holding me to Sil broke completely when I saw him move towards Natalie. 'Yeah, good idea. Get the bodsquad in, deal with the mortal remains, then send someone to check that the boy is okay, will you?'

Zan typed the notes.

'You softie,' I said.

'Yeah? You were the one who wanted to let him go. I'm letting him go.'

'Knowing what he did.'

'Should make sure he never does it again then, shouldn't it? Nothing like the memory of death to ...' He stopped suddenly.

'Sil?'

No response.

Natalie looked from Sil to me. 'Do you two do this all the time?' she asked.

'Pretty much.' Sil leaned closer to her. 'We have a kind of hate-hate relationship.'

'We don't have *any* kind of relationship,' I said, and marched out of the flat.

The music was loud, the lights garish and the dancers as desperate as they always were. If he weren't so fucked-up right now he'd feel sorry for them, for their oh-so-transparent ploys and desires, their pathetically human mindsets. But not tonight. Tonight even the interlude he'd enjoyed with Natalie hadn't been enough to wipe the memory of Jess's expression from his mind, even sex hadn't helped him to lose himself enough. He needed more to rid himself of the thought of those flame-coloured eyes scorching his, the weight of loathing in her voice as she'd dismissed any thought of him. Needed to forget ...

The beat thrummed. *Want. Crave. Choose carefully, choose one who knows what you're asking. Who wants what you offer. You don't want even a hint of coercion.*

Sil circled, feeling the power and the grace that the demon lent flowing through him, muscle and bone. He found it increasingly hard to remember those days of humanity before this wondrous new vitality gripped him; all that came to mind when he tried was an overbearing sadness. But one of the most incredible things about carrying this demon was that he never *had* to recollect those times. Never had to live on 'befores' or 'yesterdays' because 'now' swept all in front of it. 'Now' was all that mattered. *Carpe diem* might have been composed for vampires – the day was theirs to seize. A girl slithered past him, all silk and lace and scent of willingness, and he turned to watch her pass, watching her watch him as he did so.

He had a sudden, unwanted, image of Jessica as he'd once caught her, trying on a dress in the office. Horrible, mismatched underwear and cartoon-covered socks, yet so, *so* desirable, even when her cold fury and hot embarrassment met to floor him in the resultant snowstorm of insults. *Hell. Here I am, surrounded by eager women and I'm still thinking about Jessica. Who doesn't want me. What am I, some kind of masochist? Am I getting off on wanting a woman who must be about the only female on the planet who doesn't fall for the vampire image? What is wrong with me?*

And there she was. A tall girl, all dressed in black, one of the vampire groupies. Not ideal; he would have preferred someone a little more innocent but hey, beggars and choosers and all that.

'Not seen you in here before.' She leaned up against him at the bar. 'You new?'

Sil laughed. 'Oh no. Far, far from it, in fact. Old as they come.'

'Then you *don't* come here often.'

The laughter died. 'No. Shall we ... dance?'

And as she cruised in his arms and he sated the other hunger, he closed his eyes and wondered what Jessie would say if she could see him now, what she would say if she knew about the emptiness that still lay in that corner of his heart. Felt her presence with another tug along that invisible wire that bound them, and wished he knew what the hell to do about it.

Chapter Twelve

In comparison to CSI-type Enforcement, the hell-hound hunt and the staked body, the next week was dull, dull, dull. Hey, I wasn't complaining, I got to nag Liam into sorting out some bugs in the computer system, while I caught up with a filing backlog that had been propping the inner door open for weeks and finally read the instructions for that damned electric pencil sharpener. Dull was good. Dull was reassuring.

'Uh oh, bad news, Jessie.' Liam was checking his e-mails.

'Please tell me they aren't cancelling *Doctor Who*? Not sure I can stand you if you can't do the "plot rundown" every Monday morning. And anyway I'm still not speaking to you.' I was watching the tracker screen. Numbers of Otherworlders had returned to near normal now, which made boring viewing so I was also ordering a Tesco delivery. Extra HobNobs. 'I do *not* have a moustache.'

'It's not my fault your nose throws a shadow on your upper lip – ow! No, look, it's a mail from the blood-checking service we sent that sample to.' He swung the screen of his computer around so that I could see. 'They can't do anything.'

I read. '"Due to lack of current data … blah, blah we are unable to verify the type stroke variety of lifeform stroke creature, any further queries please contact …" What on earth is *that* all about?'

'Even *they* don't know what Mr Malfaire is.' Liam flipped the screen back around to continue checking eBay for mint-condition Cyberman suits. Wasn't sure what he wanted them for and certainly wasn't going to ask. 'We'll have to try something else.'

'How much blood is left?'

'Quite a bit. More than enough for another test. Why, do you know somewhere?'

'No, but I think Sil does. Give him a ring and ask him, would you?'

Liam looked at me levelly. 'You call him.'

'He was horrible to me the other day.'

'Sil's only horrible to people he likes. It's when he's *polite* you have to worry.'

'Okay, fine, if you're going to make a big deal of it, I'll ring him!'

'Or you could go over there.'

'Don't push your luck.'

But, as the unpushed luck would have it, two minutes after I'd agreed to call, just as I was gathering up the necessary vitriol for a conversation with Sil, he arrived in the office.

I tried to pretend to type but the alphabet had become meaningless.

'You've decorated,' he said.

'You left stains. Look, did you just come round to criticise the décor, or what? Only, we're busy.'

'So I see.' Sil looked pointedly at Liam's computer, showing the list of items that he was 'watching' on eBay. 'I came over to see whether you've found out anything about Malfaire. Any *inside information.*' He gave the last phrase a spin.

'You mean you've come to pry into my sex life, don't you? It's a bit of a menial job, isn't it, for a city vamp? Don't you have henchmen for that sort of thing, or is it that you're getting all prurient in your old age and want all the details first hand?' And … *breathe.*

Sil just looked at me. He was standing inside the doorway, as though reluctant to enter any further into my territory, looking thin and drawn. His hair was straggling down over the collar of the big velvet coat he wore and his customary dark stubble seemed almost to be drilling holes in his unusually pale skin. He looked awful.

'And anyway, it's none of your business what I might – or might *not* – get up to with Malfaire. My private life is just that, private.' I half-stood, daring him to accuse me, to make something of it.

'What Jessie *means*,' Liam threw me a querying glance, obviously unable to work out why I was being so short and snappish, 'is why didn't you phone?'

Sil swayed and his eyes half-closed. One hand reached to grab at the doorframe and missed, then his whole body crumpled inside his coat, going down on to the floor in a tangle of fabric, limbs and hair like a collapsing tent.

'*Shit.*' I shot out of my seat and over to the fallen vampire, checking for a pulse and feeling the clamminess of his skin against my fingers. 'Sil? Can you hear me?' I pulled open the neck of his shirt and slid a hand inside, groping across his smooth chest until I could feel the reassuring heartbeat and the tiny, settling movement of his demon reacting to my touch. '*Sil.*'

'He needs blood,' Liam observed. 'He looks as though he's starved.'

'Is there any in?'

'I think there's a half-bottle of synth in the cupboard in the kitchen. Hold on, I'll go and see if I can find it. It's not out of date yet, shouldn't be clotted.'

I stayed where I was, crouched down beside Sil, trying not to admire his long eyelashes fanned out across his cheekbones or the blueish, sloe-black of his hair contrasting with his bloodless skin like a monochrome photograph. He had the kind of sharp good looks that sit best on young faces. Fortunately he'd been infected nearly a hundred years ago, at the age of twenty-nine and had aged approximately half-an-hour since then. So, so beautiful. My fingers itched with the urge to touch his skin again. Except that, at the moment, he had all the sex appeal of a picnic table.

Eyelids fluttered, but when they opened his pupils shone in white irises and I couldn't tell whether he could see me. 'Jessie?'

'I'm here. What's up?'

'Is there anything to drink around here?'

'Liam's fetching something.'

'I can't –' Sil struck. Jerking himself forward as smoothly as a snake he missed my neck by a whisker, biting into the air as I moved away.

'Sil!' But he wasn't listening. Crouching to his feet he hunched under the drape of his coat, lips drawn back to protect them from impact. He was hissing too, a long, blown-out breath of anger and frustration at missing his target, and when a vampire is hissing then it's time to leave the room.

It was amazing how quickly I switched from admiring his unconscious beauty to trying to put as much furniture between us as possible. He was in front of the door otherwise I'd have run; instead I slid myself down behind my computer.

But, *Sil*? Attacking? All right he'd got that vampire attitude that made even cats look shamefaced, but this was way, *way* outside his normal behaviour. I dared a quick look between the legs of the office chair.

He was huddled, arms around his body, crawled up against himself as though resisting an invisible enemy. He was shaking his head and muttering. His eyes were closed and there was a feeling in the air as though ropes and nets were being woven from his words.

I closed my eyes and fought the ache. The urge to put my arms around him was almost a solid lump in my throat; the terrible, terrifying desire to touch, to ease his pain. I forced it away with every ounce of willpower that I had, trying to let common sense come to the fore – did I *want* to get bitten?

Oh, hell! *Did I?*

No. Stupid, stupid. *Come on Jessie, you know what a vampire's life is like. Do you really want to say goodbye to having proper, deep, real feelings? Do you want your entire existence to be ruled by the constant need for sex and thrills, all buzz and highs and never caring about anyone else?*

And the one final thought. *Just to be close to him?*

My fingers grasped a wooden object from the floor. An HB pencil, not a stake – we weren't allowed to keep any in the office – but it would do in an emergency. 'Sil.' I braced myself against the desk and came up sharply, my weapon held pointy-end first. 'If you can't explain yourself – and you've got two seconds, mate – then I'm coming for you.'

'What are you going to do, sketch him to death?' Liam appeared in the doorway, bottle of blood steaming gently in his hands.

'He went for me!' I said, aggrieved. 'I mean, *really.*'

Liam stared. He knew, we both knew – *all of us* knew – the penalties for a vampire attack on a human and it made his skin pull tight and pallid around an expression of disbelief. '*Jessie* ...'

I gave my head a tiny shake. Found that I would even have been prepared to lie and say that I'd invited the bite, it being illegal to solicit blood but not to actually drink it, in one of the Treaty's more convoluted sub-clauses. What was done between consenting, if somewhat deluded, adults, was not a matter for the law. This was one strike that would go unreported.

Sil grabbed the bottle from Liam and chugged it down in one long, long swallow, still crouched down on the floor. 'More,' was all he said, casting the empty away so that it rolled off behind the water-cooler. 'Quickly.'

'What the hell is *up* with you?'

Sil looked at me, a vampire-fast flick of a glance. 'Talk later. More blood.'

Liam and I exchanged a look. 'I'll pop across the road to the newsagents,' he said. 'They've usually got some, if you ask. Are you sure you'll be …?'

'Can you run?'

'Sure.' Liam was looking as though leaving me alone with Sil was probably even higher up his list of 'things not to do' than forgetting to record *Misfits*, but he took off anyway.

'Right, you. Talk, now. I don't give a bunny's uncle how hungry you are, you can still talk, and I warn you, bitey-boy, you'd better make it *good*.'

Sil opened his eyes and I was reassured to see that they were their usual shifting grey. 'Aren't you afraid?'

'What, of you? Nope. Was that the object of the exercise?'

'I don't – shit, Jessie, I didn't bite you, did I?' Again he huddled back into his coat, crossed his arms over his head and pulled it down on to his knees. 'I can't – I tried, God, I really *tried*, but it's like – a *craving*, a need, like, worse than sex, worse than anything.'

'The blood?'

'Yeah. Coming round there, with you bending over me … I can *smell* you, I can feel your blood, feel it beating in your veins and I was so *hungry*.'

'Sounds like me, with doughnuts.'

Sil gave a little smile. His fangs were still down, stained

with the blood he'd drunk. 'Yes, I remember you with doughnuts.' The smile died. 'But it was – I've never known it like that, yes, I've been hungry before, we all have. This was beyond that, it was all-consuming.'

Liam battered back up the stairs, arms full of bottles of lukewarm blood. 'They didn't have any in the heater, so these were the best I could do.'

'You,' Sil grasped two bottles, opened them both with his teeth, 'have probably saved all our lives.' Down went the contents of the bottles. I deliberately didn't notice the overspill that trickled across his chin and ran into his hair. His skin was already a healthier colour, even his eyes had darkened.

'Why so hungry? Haven't you been ...' I tailed off, too squeamish to voice what he – what *all* vampires – did.

'Feeding? Not for the last couple of days. Had no appetite.'

'Until just now.' I watched him drain another bottle. Liam stood close, put an arm around my shoulders.

'Did he really strike?'

'Yeah.' Laconically, Sil placed the bottle on the floor.

'Jessie!' Liam turned my head, forcing it back so that he could see my neck. 'Where did he get you? Did he seed? I'll call the blood-wash unit, tell them to have ...'

'He didn't.' Liam's hand was so warm compared to Sil's skin. 'He missed.'

'*Missed?*' Liam let me go and stepped back. 'Wow. Sil, have you got really shit in the last few months or something? Vampires don't *miss*.'

'She moved.'

'Wow, Jessie, when did you become an Olympic athlete?'

'Look, guys. This is all irrelevant right now. What matters is ... I think you were magicked, Sil. Your eyes were white when you struck, and the only time I've ever seen that before is in that young lad who'd been glamoured into killing Daim. And Harry and Eleanor, their eyes were wrong, too.'

Sil stood up. 'There is something very strange going on,' he said. 'And I have the feeling that you're right in the middle of it, Jessie.'

'Strange isn't the half of it.' Liam, Mister *How Clean is Your House*, lobbed the empty bottles into the recycling bin, and carried the untouched ones into the kitchen. 'Do you have any idea how hard it is to glamour a vampire?'

'Why, do you?' My nerves were beginning to settle now but the adrenaline wanted me to fight something and either one of these two would do. 'You got some kind of secret life, Liam?'

He came back in and perched on his desk. 'Barely got an unsecret one. But, unlike you Jessie, I actually *read* the e-mails that we get from Head Office. And there was one not so long ago about vampires being nearly immune to glamour. So, whoever did this is incredibly powerful. And wants you to know it, otherwise they would have used any old vampire from off the street, someone disposable. Someone you'd have staked in a second if you could have.' He tried not to look at either of us. 'No comebacks for killing a vamp that's gone for you, Jess. Totally legal, you know that, right? Using Sil shows ...' He hesitated because I was giving him a look so evil you could have put it in a suit and called it Satan. 'Um. It shows it's someone who knows you,' he tailed off.

The three of us stared at each other.

'You think *Zan*?' I whispered. 'No. He wouldn't.'

Sil rolled his eyes. 'What, because you desire him, you believe he wouldn't wipe you off the face of the earth? You really think he'd hesitate to eliminate you if you stood between him and something he wanted?'

'I do *not* desire him!'

'Oh, please, I saw the way you were eyeing him up over at Daim's flat! You were *this* close to dropping your drawers!'

'Well, thank you *very* much, Mr Morality! So, you and Natalie were admiring one another's clothes, were you?'

'Children!' Liam held up his hands. 'There is a time and place for discussing who wants to get off with whom, and I shall be opening an online forum shortly, but for now, can we please *concentrate*!'

Sil and I, slightly ashamed, dropped our heads. 'Sorry.'

'Right. So, Sil got himself glamoured. Yes?'

'Yes.'

'And you think it was Zan?'

I shook my head. 'He has the proximity, so he could have done but – come on, this is Zan we're talking about! The guy lives for his computer systems, he'd no more glamour Sil than he'd … I dunno, take to the streets and live off rats' blood. And anyway, why?' I turned to Sil. 'I realise that I am probably going to live to regret asking this, but, what's the last thing you remember before you lost your appetite?'

Sil dropped one shoulder. 'It was after Daim died. I … I went on to a club. Got a bit – out of things.'

'But drink and drugs don't affect vampires.'

'Drugs don't work on us at all, different metabolic system. But alcohol taken secondhand does.'

Liam cleared his throat. 'Okay. And that's the last thing you remember?'

'Pretty much. I was dancing, there was music. It got hot, I went outside and …' The shrug again. 'After that I didn't feel hungry until just now.'

'What about Malfaire?' Liam said, suddenly. 'Things have started since he turned up.'

I thought of Malfaire's tawny eyes, the boil and roll of magic that seemed to move along with him in his personal space. His unidentifiability. His *creepiness*. 'Yeah, but, like you said, he's just turned up, he hasn't got any reason to have a grudge against me.'

Sil's eyes were almost black. 'Have you slept with him?'

'What, you reckon a guy would try to kill me because I didn't get into bed with him? Bit extreme.'

'Or you were so bad he thought he'd better take you out for the good of humanity.'

'Ha! Like you'd know!'

We glowered at each other for a moment, like a tethered pair of fighting dogs.

'Still not helping.' Liam glanced from me to Sil and back again. 'Can't you two get a room or something? Sort all this out in bed and leave my sanity intact? I'm messaging your office, Sil, by the way, letting them know what happened here, so don't think for *one minute* that you're going to let this drop.' His fingers clattered over the keyboard as he sent an instant report.

'Are you insinuating,' I said slowly, not taking my eyes off the vampire, 'that I might *under any circumstances* – and I warn you to think *very carefully* about your answer, Liam, bearing in mind that you still owe petty cash fifteen quid and I know what you spent it on because your drawer doesn't close properly – that I might have *any* kind of feelings for this *thing*?'

'Oh, come on! It's far more of an insult from where *I'm* standing, I mean, please, will you look at her!' Sil held his arms out in a wide appeal for Liam's sympathy. 'Wouldn't poke her with yours.'

'I'm just saying.' Liam wagged a finger at us both. 'That's all. You used to be good together and then, wham, *you've* taken up running the city as if it's the only thing in your life and *you're* like Toad Woman every time his name is mentioned!'

Sil and I looked at each other properly now. 'We – it's not that simple,' I began.

'She didn't want me,' Sil stated, baldly. 'She didn't want me because I'm vampire. That's all there is to it, Liam.'

'You didn't give me the chance!' I glared at the metal-grey eyes and the blood-splattered hair. 'You said you wanted to talk and I thought – I thought we were chatting and next thing I know –'

There was a pause. Eventually Liam cleared his throat. 'I'm thinking that I'm going to have to steam clean the office chairs. Or my brain, whichever is easier.'

'I vote for your brain. Maybe we can get you reprogrammed without an imagination. And get a proper sense of humour put in,' I said, without taking my eyes off Sil. His pupils were huge.

'Then can you *please* tell me what really happened, because, I warn you, the pathetic amount of imagination I *was* granted is about to put in a bill for overtime.'

'Which won't be paid,' finished Sil.

'Sil.' But how could I say it? That I knew vampires and their behaviour inside out and I didn't *dare* feel for him. That feeling any kind of emotion for a vampire was asking for that knife-in-the-gut sensation when you realised that the only emotion they could feel was the kind that fed their demon. Nothing softer remained, nothing kind or loving … nothing that we could relate to. They were alien; their emotions were alien. It would be like trying to love a Dalek.

'Jessie – I – ' His face was inches from mine, centimetres. I could feel the coolness radiating from his skin, the soft flick of his hair brushing my shoulder.

'I'm averting my eyes.' Liam covered his face, dramatically. 'Try not to make too much noise.'

'I'm not scared of –' I'd begun, bracing myself for the inevitable explanation, when the telephone rang and shocked us all into jumping a few inches clear of each other.

'Oh, *bugger*!' Liam uncovered his eyes. 'Why does the phone always go during the *denouement*? I'm telling you, if this is my aunt calling to let me know that her leg is better I will *not* be responsible for my actions,' and he picked up the receiver. Sil and I carefully avoided one another's glance for fear that we might see the same scared acknowledgement in each other. 'Sil, it's for you. Zan.'

'I'll just – um, outside, if I can?' Sil took the handset and moved out of the office, carefully closing the door behind him. I wondered what they could have to say that we shouldn't hear.

'You get worse by the day,' I said to Liam, who was collecting mugs from the desks. I presumed he was off to the kitchen to wash them so that he could eavesdrop on Sil's conversation in passing. 'I bet Sarah half-expects you to start wearing a very long scarf and going to conventions ... oh, Lord, the shame of it!'

Liam turned around. His eyes were sad. 'You're screwing with him, Jessie,' he said. 'He's mad for you, and you're messing with his mind – I know things are all over the place, but do him a favour and either shag him or leave him alone.'

'*Me* leave *him* alone? Er, hello? I've spent two years trying to keep out of his way and what happens? Every time I turn around, there he is, growling at me from the sidelines like a ghoul on a bender!'

Liam shrugged, but before he could reply, Sil was back. 'Zan thinks there might be something in Jessica's fears. Something wants her dead.'

'Hallelujah! Someone's decided to listen to me, at last!'

'And if that's the case ...' Sil squared his shoulders, drew himself up. His full height wasn't intimidating, barely four inches taller than me but when he pulled the whole Otherworld thing he seemed to occupy more space, as though his presence extended through other dimensions. 'Jessica Amelia Grant. I offer you the protection of my services, my body and my time.'

'Wow,' said Liam.

'I'm not bloody marrying you; I just don't want to die.'

'It's the Official Protection Act.' Liam stared at Sil. 'Legally binding. And I never knew your middle name was Amelia.'

'Well it is. And *that* is the OPA? I always thought there'd be ... I dunno, bells and whistles, or at least some minor government official standing by with the paperwork. Is there some formal process for saying "thanks a lot, but I'm not sure I want it"?'

'Be sensible, Jessie. If someone wants you dead, and Sil is offering you protection, what's wrong with taking it? It's a big deal. He doesn't jump up and offer service to everyone who comes to him saying they're in danger.'

'No, he'd never get any biting done.'

Sil shrugged. 'But I still don't understand, why *you*?'

I pulled a face. 'Your guess is as good as mine. I'm no threat to anyone. I don't know anything. I can't even work that bloody pencil sharpener.'

Sil gave me a very 'vampire' look. Deep, dark, unreadable and slightly hungry. 'You know something you don't know you know.'

'Very erudite. I've tried to think, but, you *know* what I do! I'm like – you know that brick at the bottom of the pile? That's me.'

Sil shrugged and the coat fell around him like a cape. 'But if that brick is removed, a whole edifice may fall.'

'Wow, you've really got aphorisms today, haven't you? So, if I accept your offer of protection, who's meant to keep me safe from *you*?'

'The spell is finished. We beat it.' We'd almost managed a whole conversation without arguing. Things were looking up.

'*You* beat it. Kudos to you, you're stronger than you seem.'

Sil shook his head. 'Jessie, when I went to bite, I missed.'

'Yeah. Duh. Otherwise I'd be back at the blood-wash unit again, and I think I'm on the verge of getting my own named chair up there.'

'No. *I missed*. You've no idea; it was like red-mist time. Killing frenzy. Not that I'd know, obviously,' he added quickly, 'but that sort of thing. It was you, you *moved*. I've never seen anything like it.'

'You can't know that, red mist, remember? I saw you coming, I moved. I got lucky. End of story.'

'If you say so.'

'I do.'

I lowered my voice. 'Can I think about it – the protection thing? I don't want to sound ungrateful –' Sil made a snorting noise – 'but it would be stupid for you to have to tie yourself to keeping me out of danger when (a) I can manage perfectly well by myself and (b) nothing else might happen. Ever.' I put a hand on his arm. 'You've got a city to run. York is more important than me, Sil. The needs of the many outweigh the needs of the few and all that.'

'I cannot believe you are quoting *Star Trek* at me.'

'Would you prefer *Buffy*?'

Liam was watching this exchange with a strange

127

expression. 'Do you have to be around Jessie to protect her, Sil? I mean, tell me to shut up if you want, but you two have so much tension I'm thinking of hanging my washing up on the air between you.'

'Shut up,' I said. 'Sil, we need the address of the blood-testing service we used to use. I've still got some of Malfaire's blood and the other place has let us down.'

Sil went over to the corner where his desk used to stand. 'Did you chuck out the old ledgers?'

Liam could, of course, lay his hand directly on the books required, and Sil flipped straight to the right page with an expression of disdain for my own chaotic methods of filing.

'Right, Liam, we need a sample from you.'

Liam nearly dropped the ledger stack. 'Well, if you insist, Jessie, but – be gentle with me.'

'Not *that* kind of sample, you loon.' Even Sil was sniggering now; it was almost like old times. 'Blood.'

Sil flashed his fangs, Liam stuck out his tongue. 'Not if Mr Sucky is doing the sampling. You know how much I hate it!'

'You are so in the wrong job for someone who hates the sight of blood.'

'Can't we send some bottled stuff?' Liam was backing away, trying to keep both arms behind his back.

'It has to be real blood,' Sil grinned lazily, 'so that the lab can use it as a contrast for Malfaire's sample.'

'Oh, for heaven's sake!' I pulled back a sleeve to expose the vein running down my arm. 'Have some of mine!'

Liam sucked in a breath. 'Hardly tactful, Jessie.' He nodded at Sil, who'd become very still, staring at my skin as though he could see through it to the pulsing beneath. 'What if the spell is still working?'

'Nah. That's not a spell, that's blood-lust.' I nudged Sil. 'Hey. Manners.'

For a second his face was alien, then, with difficulty Sil pulled his eyes up to my face. His were huge and darkened with desire. 'Synth. Now.'

'In the kitchen.'

Sil ran for it and we could hear the frenzied sound of blood being gulped. 'Come on, make it quick. If he has to sit and watch, he might not be able to control himself.'

Liam found a clean syringe from a tranq kit and I stuck the needle into my own vein. Honestly, what's the use of staff when one of them passes out at the sight of blood and the other is overcome with the urge to ravage bystanders? I filled two phials and put one spare in the fridge with the rest of Malfaire's blood, just in case the testing unit decided they wanted another go. Then we parcelled up the two samples and Liam promised to courier them straight over so by the time Sil finished drinking, it was all over, nothing to see.

'I'd better go.' Sil came back in, dragging his coat closely around his body. 'Things to do, you know how it goes.'

'Yeah, me too.' I located my own coat under a pile of paperwork on the floor. 'But separately, you do understand that, Liam, don't you?'

Liam made a face, but when Sil had left he grabbed my sleeve to stop me. 'Jessie.' His voice was serious, and Liam was hardly ever serious. 'Are you afraid of him vamping you? Is that what this is all about?'

I had a momentary urge to throw myself into Liam's arms and cry on his shoulder. But it *was* only momentary. 'No. Honestly, Liam. I just think, when it comes to Sil, distance is a good thing.'

'Is it because of Cameron?'

No-one had dared mention that name to me for a good

few months now. My whole body went still at the sound. 'No,' I eventually whispered. 'No, Liam.'

'You know lightning doesn't strike twice, Jessie. You shouldn't let losing Cameron prejudice you against all men.'

'I didn't *lose* him. Look, I'm really going now. Lock up, will you?'

The mood changed like a coin-flip. 'Okay. But be sure to go straight home now. No hanky-panky!'

'Would I commit "hanky-panky"?'

Liam gave me an arch look. 'The way you're looking right now you're more likely to commit murder, and I don't think I can raise the cash to keep you out of prison, so, you know, hanky-panky would be cheaper. I've got the tea money to think of here, and if you ever want to see another Kit Kat …'

I threw my phone at his head again on my way out. This time I missed.

Chapter Thirteen

When I got home, Malfaire was waiting.

'Jessie!' Rach looked almost shifty as I walked in. 'You've got a visitor!' A heavy wink and a tactful withdrawal told me she'd got him down as a prospective partner for me. She was probably busying herself in the kitchen icing heart shapes on to a million fat-and-dairy-free fairy cakes, in case I hadn't fully got the message.

Malfaire stood up and held a hand out. 'Hello, Jessica.' He took my fingers in his and turned my hand over to examine the palm. He was wearing those dark glasses again, and his hair loose. The magic that pulled and tugged around him like the swell of an invisible sea brushed my skin and raised a nettle rash along my arms. 'I must say, you don't appear very pleased to see me.'

I breathed deeply. 'I want to know what you're playing at.'

'Playing at? Jessica, surely I have made it clear that I find you attractive. Why should I need to be playing?' Slowly he peeled the glasses away from his face to reveal his eyes clouded with what looked like disappointment, and he dropped his head so that his hair concealed his face.

I sat down on the couch, knees carefully together. 'There's a lot of things that have started happening to me just as you turned up. I've got demons talking about some kind of danger, vampires trying to bite me – all right, I never trusted him anyway but, even so, it's not the kind of thing he'd do, and Enforcement tried to shoot me in a bloody *chemist's* for God's sake, and I only got away because curlers are really, really heavy!' I realised that my voice was becoming shrill and that I might not be making a lot of sense. 'And then there was the Run, and you were there. And you are – whatever it is that you are, I don't know.'

'You can't tell?' He looked pleased, raising those pale amber eyes to mine. 'You can't read me, Jessica? Perhaps you haven't tried yet.'

'Oh, I have. So has Liam, but neither of us can get anything.'

'Then try again, now. Come.' He took my hands and drew me up again, so that we stood face-to-face in the middle of the living room. 'Look into me.'

Taking a deep breath I looked. Stepped into his eyes, where the cool tawny shades met the merest hint of green, like walking from shadows into light. Gold flecks moved through the colours, dancing and weaving a complicated pattern and hints of distant, half-remembered things swam in the darker hues at the centre.

But nothing spoke to me. Not the weird duality that you got in a vampire's eyes, where the demon and the subjugated human co-existed in the single space. Not the tight, focused feel that you got from staring at a werewolf's eyes either. Zombies I'd never needed to identify from the eyes; the fingers hanging by gristle was normally the clincher there.

'Well, Jessica?' Malfaire's voice seemed to come from a long way off. 'What are you seeing?'

'I'm not … you bastard, are you trying to glamour me?' I took a rapid two steps back until I collided with the small table. 'Wow, I nearly fell for that one!'

Malfaire looked a little perturbed. 'Glamour you? Why should I want to glamour you?'

'I don't know.' Suddenly I was riding a tiger. And I didn't know if it was safer to hang on, or get off and face it. 'Why should you want to call a hell-hound, or glamour Harry and

Ellie? Or get my name pulled out for the Dead Run? Or try to magic Sil into biting me?'

He turned to me, and the planes and angles of his face were harder. 'Because I wanted to know how strong you are.'

'Great, I feel so much better. You didn't actually want me *dead*.'

'No. Although, if you *had* died, I would have had my answer, wouldn't I?'

I didn't know whether to laugh in his face or crumple up and cry. 'Did you kill Daim Willis?'

Malfaire blank-faced me.

'All right, wrong question. Did you arrange to have Daim Willis killed?'

Malfaire turned away from me. 'He was vampire. He deserved death.'

'He was nineteen years old, Malfaire, and thick as a pig sandwich.' This was all moving way too fast for me. 'All right then. Let's deal with the elephant in the room, shall we. Why the *hell* would you want to know how strong I am? Couldn't you have – I dunno – got me to take part in a lorry-pull or something? Because, I warn you, those things were all false positives and flukes. I am absolutely Missis Pathetico in the muscleman stakes.'

'Oh, you are *so much more* than that.' Malfaire sat opposite me, leaned forward deliberately and seemed amused when I sat down and leaned back an equivalent amount so that we sat in a kind of reciprocating action. 'One day there will be war again, Jessica. The vampires will be driven from this dimension.'

'And what, exactly, does that have to do with me?' My brain was whirring – I must have sounded as though I had a clockwork head. *But if the vampires go ... the Pact will break. It's only the fact that they are the strongest of the Others, that they want peace, that keeps everything holding together. And if they go, what makes them leave?* A cold feeling rose up inside me and chilled my throat as an unknown future stretched long and dark and full of conflict.

'Because you will be at the forefront!' Malfaire's voice was almost inaudible. 'That is why I wanted to test your strengths, your audacity.'

Uh oh. 'I don't think so! I mean, what use would I be? I'm an office worker. In fact there's probably something in my contract about not fighting. I'm not even supposed to alter the height on my adjustable chair.'

The battle-light died in Malfaire's eyes, and his expression softened. 'Ah, there's so much you don't know, little Jessica.' A finger traced along the line of my cheek. 'And so much I hope you never know.'

'All right, if you've quite finished patronising me.' I stood up. 'I've known Zan and Sil aeons longer than I've known you, so why you'd think I'd take your part against them, I have no idea. And I've heard all this before; there's always some drunk raving on in the park about how we should kick the vampires out, send them back where they came from, crap like that. But, d'you know, there's a theory that says that it's having the Otherworlders to hate that's united mankind, stopped us fighting and hating each other. Made this world a better place. So, before you start spouting your tired rhetoric, perhaps you might like to think of that. Whatever you are.'

Malfaire sighed and picked his sunglasses up off the table, pulled them on tight against his eyes. He shook his head slowly, so that his hair fell over his face and caught against the cunning stubble decorating his exquisite cheekbones. 'It wasn't that,' he said, flatly. 'You must be with me.'

'Okay, why now? I'm presuming you – whatever you are – came through when the field shifted? You and your kind have been here a hundred years?'

Malfaire gave a squeezed-looking smile, as though he was trying to avoid laughing out loud, and then tipped his head in acknowledgement. 'If you must be precise, then yes.'

'So, what's been stopping you up to now? I should point out that I only want to know so that I can make sure that there's much, *much* more of it.'

Again that small smile. 'There is a rising faction, Jessica. Those who are increasingly unhappy with the terms of the Treaty; those terms that keep whole races suppressed, keep them from giving free rein to their natures. There is movement afoot to remove the vampires from their position of power and hand that power to those who have a more ... shall we say *egalitarian* view.'

'We all have to live here! We can all get along but there have to be rules!'

Malfaire moved towards the door. 'But rules in whose favour? Perhaps you should think about that, my dear, before you lay yourself at the feet of your vampire lovers.'

'You have *so* got the wrong idea about me!'

Rach bustled into the hallway, clearly distressed at the sound of my raised voice. 'Oh, are you going, Mr Malfaire? Wouldn't you like to stay for dinner, or you could take Jessie out, she never goes out these days, she's always working, work, work, work; honestly, she never stops.' Over her shoulder in the kitchen I could see Jasper, poised on the work surface, frozen in the moment of a full-blown, arched-back, hissing session in the direction of Malfaire.

Malfaire moved like I'd only ever seen a vampire move – raised a hand and sent a stream of words in the direction of the cat, who shuddered once and fell quiet. There was a nasty smell of smouldering fur, Jasper gave a sudden un-catlike yelp and leapt into Rach's arms with the end of his tail scribing a smoky trail as he came.

'And with that, you said goodbye to my *ever* being on your side!' I half-whispered, as Rach gave a strangled cry and tightened her arms around Jasper. It was a lie; he'd blown any chance of me siding with him when he'd said that Daim deserved to die. 'Now, go.'

Malfaire paused on his way through the door and smiled, an amused-as-though-I'd-been-a-clever-pet smile. 'The time will come, yes, it is not far now, when you will *beg* for me.' Then he laughed, and clicked the door shut, leaving me steaming with anger on the inside.

Bastard. I didn't waste any time, I was straight on the phone to Sil, who, ten minutes later, appeared at the front door. I let him in and then went back to comforting Rach, who was slumped on the sofa still weeping into Jasper's, by now rather irritated, fur.

'You're having a rethink?' Sil winced at the sight of the cat. Vampires actually like cats, they're very alike in a lot of ways. Particularly the killing ways.

'Bloody Malfaire,' I answered, tightly, and brought him up to speed on what had happened. Sil sat and listened, one hand absentmindedly stroking Jasper's ears. When I'd finished talking, he sat back, his fangs showing a touch, which meant he was angry. Either that or aroused, and I was betting that a crying woman, an annoyed, if head-locked, cat and me were not the sort of things that Sil got off on.

'Rachel,' he said. 'Look. At. Me.'

Rach turned, instinctively, to look at him, and gave a little whimper. 'Yes?' then went silent. Jasper jumped to the floor with a spiked-fur look of relief and began washing himself under the table. I glanced across and met a pair of eyes which shone pure black, iris and pupil bled together into one, like a hole in the soul. Sil's almost classically beautiful face was emotionless.

'You're glamouring her!'

His eyes stayed fixed on Rach's eerily expressionless face. 'Yes, Jessica, I know.'

'Why?'

Sil waved a hand. 'We need to talk. Seriously. And I remember you talking about your friend and her tendency to press snacks on people as soon as they sit down, and I'm feeling pretty hair trigger here at the moment, Jessie, I don't know if I can stand someone offering me hummus dip and carrot sticks without my turning round and doing something REALLY NASTY, okay?'

Definitely angry then.

'So.' I waited for his eyes to return to as near normal as was normal for him. 'What are we talking about?'

He dropped his head towards his chest, so that his dark fringe flopped over his face. 'Jessica,' he sounded a bit strangled, 'I don't know if you are being incredibly dense or incredibly brave here, but, knowing you I'd go for dense.' Now the head came up fast and I didn't look away quickly enough to avoid meeting his eye. 'Take the protection, in the name of all that's holy, just *take it*.' The speed with which he jumped to his feet made the cat bristle at him suddenly and dash behind the sofa. It even made *me* start and I'd been expecting it; Sil was showing all the signs of buttoned-down anger that had manifested in our previous Great Bust Up. His eyes were flickering black to silver and his jaw was tight.

I took a deep breath and sighed it out, trying to lose the frustration and general low-level annoyance that being close to Sil brought on. 'I'm not dead. Malfaire might be on my case but even with what he's pulled so far, I'm still here.

So maybe I don't need your protection, and I am managing to deduce – even though by your definition I've got the intellectual capacity of a slug – that the whole protection thing is bigger than you presenting me with an Uzi and an instruction manual. Am I right?'

'Like I'd let you loose with an Uzi! You'd probably manage to destroy all the major tourist attractions in one afternoon.'

Yelling at belt-level made me feel at a disadvantage, so I stood up too, to face him. 'Yeah, well, *I'm* not the one who got themselves glamoured into trying to kill someone, am I?' We stared huffily at one another for a few moments, then I sighed and sat down again next to the unnaturally still Rachel. 'Sil. You've got a city to run, all those meetings and civic things and being the Face of York. You couldn't do that if you were trying to keep me out of trouble, could you?'

He sat opposite me so fast that our knees nearly cracked together under the central table. 'I'm going to tell you something,' he said, lowering his voice and leaning towards me with his elbows on the table. 'It's confidential, all right? I mean, completely, not a word to anyone, Rachel or Liam or anyone.'

'You're secretly a woman.' I leaned forward, too.

'Well, obviously.' Unexpectedly he reached out, spreading long fingers on the tabletop like he wanted to touch me but was trying not to. 'Jessie. I came to work with you ...'

'... to learn more about human/Otherworld interactions, I know, I remember. To help you run the city better.'

'To report back to Zan.' The fingers curled back under his palms. 'Do you understand?'

'Well, yes, he's in charge of all the admin stuff ... oh.' I let myself meet his eyes for the first time, properly. 'You mean Zan is the one who's *really* in charge? He's running the city and you're like, what, a figurehead?'

Sil dropped his eyes as though he was ashamed. 'I'm the disposable one. Anything happens to me, things run on as normal. They just appoint someone else to do the high-visibility stuff, because all the real negotiations and political stuff is being dealt with behind the scenes by the same vamp who has been doing it for the last sixty years. Before me there was Strel, he was killed in a firefight during the Troubles, so Zan asked me to take his job. I do the face-to-face stuff but Zan briefs me on what to say and who to say it to. Except now, obviously,' he added quickly. 'This is just me.'

'That's quite clever.' I almost smiled for a minute, before I remembered that I was more than a bit aggravated with him. 'Oh, for a bunch of bloodsucking, parasitic life-forms, of course. What about if something happens to Zan?'

'Who the hell would want to take out an admin assistant? You've got to admit it, Jessie, he plays the part well, all that fussing with computers and being obsessed with the state of the technology; he's like Über Geek.'

'You mean it's like protective colouration?'

'No, he actually is a geek. But a much more powerful one than anyone thinks. So then. What do you think?'

'About Zan really being the one who runs the city? Why should I care? It's only your bit he's in charge of, after all, the Otherworlder part. I still have to work my way through ninety layers of council authority before I even get near anyone who can give permission to buy new biros.'

Sil snapped to his feet, vampire-fast. I carefully didn't jump again. 'No! Jessie ...' He let out a brief hiss and his fangs slid over his bottom lip. I found myself looking around the room for potential weaponry. 'I told you all that so that you'd trust me!'

There was a wooden candlestick with a fairly pointy end on the table. It would do as a stake if nothing else presented itself. Why, *why*, had I left the tranqs in my room? 'Oh yeah, 'cos you look *really* trustworthy right now.'

'Sorry.' He put both hands on the table again and took a deep breath. 'You are winding me up beyond all mortal understanding.'

There was a pain where my heart should have been. I wanted to stretch out an arm and touch his cheek, make him look at me, make him smile ... I shook my head fast enough to descramble my brain. *God, I have got to get out more.*

'Remember ... remember how it used to be?' His voice had softened a bit and the fangs were gone. 'You and me working together? We were a good team, Jessie; you could trust me then to watch your back. In fact, I saved your skin a few times, if memory serves.'

'I might have ...'

'*Jessica.* When trouble came, it was you and me. Oh, and Liam, but then trouble rarely comes in the form of something that can be beaten off with paperwork.'

'Unless it comes from the Town Hall.'

He nodded slowly. 'True. For beating off bureaucracy, Liam heads the team. But for other things ... without me, you wouldn't be here, in this room!'

'Being shouted at by you!'

'At least you're alive to *be* shouted at.' Now he touched me, just the tips of his fingers against the back of my hand, but I felt every single nerve-ending go into overdrive. 'I'm vampire, as you take pleasure in pointing out at every single bloody opportunity. All right, I got glamoured, but that *will not* be happening again, and I have the speed, the strength, the power to protect you. Whatever this Malfaire is, whatever he wants from you, you can't win against him.'

'But he knows I've survived so far. The hell-hound and

you attacking me and all the other stuff – I got through it.'
The feel of his skin against mine was beginning to twist my thoughts, turn them hot and uncomfortable.

'Yes.' Now Sil lowered his voice until I had to lean closer. His fingertips slid to my wrist, where my pulse was banging away ... *no, not banging, don't think about banging* ... beating fast. 'Now he knows *exactly* how strong you are. He's taken your measure, do you see? Now you've turned against him, next time he's only got to –' a sudden sweep of his elbow and he knocked the wooden candleholder to the floor, where it cracked and the end fell off in a particularly illustrative way. 'Please, Jessie, *please* take my protection.'

I stared at him. 'I don't think I've ever heard you say please before.'

'I will recite the works of William Shakespeare if it means you'll do it.'

The air was thick and heavy and smelled of singed cat fur. I looked at the immobile figure of Rach, her arms still posed as though holding Jasper. He could do that. He could glamour, he could move like a rattlesnake and he had the power of every vampire in the city at his disposal – or at least, as I now knew, Zan did, but same thing.

And, call me Missus Superficial, but *damn*, he was gorgeous.

'Oh, all right then,' I said, aware that I sounded less than bowled over. 'I'll take your protection stuff.'

'All *right*!' Sil said, more schoolboy than vampire. Trouble was, he'd been a schoolboy when *Dracula* was first published. 'Then, Jessica Amelia Grant, I extend to you my protection.'

There was a momentary silence.

'Is that it? I'm still waiting for the fireworks.'

Sil gave me a sideways grin. 'No, Jessie. The fireworks come later,' he said, in a tone I wasn't quite sure I liked.

'You look – is that expression *happy*?' Zan swivelled to watch Sil's entrance to the office.

'Better believe it.' Sil leaned against the doorframe for a second longer, enjoying the other vampire's incredulity. 'Jessica Grant has taken my protection.'

Zan whistled. 'And you, of course, made her aware of all the … ahem … implications of this? Having you watching her for all the hours of the day?'

Sil shrugged. 'I skirted round those.' Deep inside his demon was turning cartwheels in the hormonal soup that he had become. *Jessie. Why the hell do I want her so much? And why did it feel so good when I touched her hand?* 'And I had to tell her about you.'

Was it his imagination or did Zan jump a little. 'What about me?'

'About the city.'

'Oh. Should I be concerned?'

'Not sure.' Sil slithered into the seat opposite Zan and put his feet up on the desk. 'That Malfaire creature is up to something. Been mouthing off about vampires being thrown from this dimension and war coming, usual megalomaniac ramblings, but there is definitely something different about this one. You found out what he is yet?'

Zan shook his head. 'Feet. Off.'

Sil wrinkled his nose, but complied. He let his eyes unfocus, riding the ridiculous high that simply having a conversation with Jessica had brought. His fingers still tingled with the warmth of her skin, but the rest of him was a nameless ache. His demon moved and he was suddenly hungry. 'Think I might pop into Hagg Baba,' he said, trying for casual. 'Anything you want?'

Zan, debugging a file, barely looked at him. 'I've eaten.' He was nodding towards the empty bottles when his body

142

gave a sudden twitch, and the old vampire's green eyes slid to Sil's. 'Oh, no.'

Sil shrugged.

'I felt that one. You are seriously affected by something, aren't you? You've not got a problem …? Because, you know, this new synth is as near to the real thing as I have ever tasted.'

Sil felt slightly insulted. 'You cussed fool; it's easy to tell it's been a long time since you were human. It's not the blood. It's her. Jessica. She makes me feel …' He wasn't even aware that his fangs were locked down until he bit his own lip.

'Yes, I take the point, she is an unwilling doxie.' Zan looked back to his screen. 'Either bite her or let her go.'

'She doesn't want me to bite her.' Sil licked the blood off his mouth. It made his stomach rumble.

'*Oh.*' Zan kicked his chair back away from the desk and leaned towards Sil. 'Right. I see. If you truly wish her blood … Would you like me to oblige you by concealing her death? Let me see … an unplanned trip to the Americas, possibly? Or would her fellow worker find that suspicious?' He sighed. 'These damnable portable telephone devices …' Another sigh. 'Bodies were so much easier to dispose of in the old days …'

'What? *No.* You'd do that? No.' *Wow! We like the idea of that way too much. No. Jessie is different. It's not sex, it's not blood, it's something else that runs separate to those and yet entwined. And she won't give me blood, I'm pretty sure of that, and I will not take it without permission, not from her – not from anyone. The sex… yes, she might go for the sex, she looks at me sometimes as though … but sex is nothing, it's just a means to an end.* 'Truly. It will be fine.' Sil got to his feet. 'So, I'll go and get food, then.'

'To the Hagg Baba.' It wasn't a question.

'What's wrong with that?'

'To the only place in the city where you can obtain the genuine article? Apart from the clubs, which you know that I frown upon. Biting is biting and we cannot afford to sully our reputations, however willing the participants may be. Are you sure you don't have a problem?' Zan's stare was like a needle. 'Not going to run rogue on me, are you?'

'No. It's Jessica, something about her makes me ...'

The old vampire raised an exquisite eyebrow. 'And she's asked for your protection? I sincerely hope you both know what you're doing.'

Sil threw him a grin and wondered if he had time for a cold shower.

Chapter Fourteen

Next morning, things got worse.

My first indication of this was, as I went to leave the flat to walk to the office, Sil fell into step beside me. Or tried to, but the overall effect must have been that of the trial run of a push-pull device.

'Go away.'

'You want my protection.'

'Ah, but "*quod custodiet ipsos custodes?*"'

Sil gave me a pained look.

'"Who guards the guards"?'

'Yes, I know what it means, Jessica. And it's "quis". Not "quod". I may have a demon, but I also have a classical education.'

'Ah, so you'll know that saying about vampires, then.' I accelerated and managed to put a few strides between us.

'Which saying?' He caught up, effortlessly.

'That they should piss off and leave me alone.'

'Very funny.' He fell back a few steps, his big, black coat swirling around his ankles like an enthusiastic dog on its first walk of the day. 'Anyway, get used to it. You have my protection for as long as Malfaire is still around.'

'I'm surprised Zan can spare you for babysitting duties. I'd have thought he needed you closer to home in case he had any dry-cleaning to pick up.'

'Cheap shot, Jessica.' Sil shoved his hands into the pockets of the coat and walked along with his elbows jutting out and his shoulders hunched. 'And that thing about Zan? I told you in the strictest confidence. We don't want it getting out, and if it does – well, then I may have to kill you.' He flashed me a look out of eyes that were gull-grey. 'So. What's on the agenda for today?'

I was instantly irritated. 'Oh, I thought I might go out and wrestle a few werewolves into submission, then bait some Shadows.'

We'd arrived at the main door to the office building, ajar because Liam had already gone up. I went to push the door fully open, but Sil leaned across in front of me, barring my way. When he spoke, his fangs showed.

'You are not taking any of this seriously, are you, Jessie? Getting my protection is no laughing matter. It ties us together for the foreseeable future or at least until Malfaire is dealt with. Now, neither your office nor mine have even got close to finding out what this guy is, or what he can do, so I suggest that you keep your head down and do your job, and *let me do mine*.'

'Okay, Lord Machismo,' I pushed his arm until I could get past, 'you've made your position clear. But I only signed up for your protection, not for you following me around like we're the result of some new surgical procedure. So, if you'll excuse me, I have work to do.'

I stomped up the stairs, aware of him following me, not noisily because he was wearing suede boots which made no sound, but his presence filled the narrow passageway as he whirled along at my heels.

'Morning, Liam!' I flung myself down into my seat and fired up my computer. 'Anything to know?'

'Er, we appear to have a vampire stuck to our spare chair? Honestly, Sil, isn't a protector supposed to be looming around all mysteriously, rather than forming part of the workforce?'

'You're thinking of Batman. Where's my coffee?'

'Here. It's a bit cool; you're late.'

'Yeah well, I had to do the "Me and My Shadow" dance all the way here.'

Liam and Sil raised their eyebrows at each other. 'You don't think, maybe, you're over-reacting a bit?' Liam asked. 'After all, you know Malfaire has been trying to kill you, or at least mangle your carcass into something unrecognisable; surely it can't hurt to have a bit of protection?'

'*That* is not protection, that is an impediment! No, don't make him *drinks*.'

'Bottle of O, if you're going to the kitchen, my dear friend.' Sil waved a lazy hand. 'Anyway, how come you know that Jessie finally saw sense and agreed to accept my protection?'

Liam blushed. 'She Facebooked me.'

Sil looked at me steadily until I had to pretend a very sturdy interest in a file. 'It was a private message,' I muttered. 'It's not like I plastered it all over the 'net. Anyway,' I rallied, 'if you're going to be hanging around, you can at least make yourself useful.' I shoved a pile of envelopes at him. 'Here's this morning's mail, get reading.'

Sil stood up and I thought for a moment he was going to walk out, but he just took his coat off and hung it on the back of the chair, then sat down again, legs crossed at the ankle, looking elegant and in it for the long haul. 'What do you do with them these days?'

'They'll mostly be complaints; we've got a tray for those. Where's the complaints tray, Liam?'

'Box marked recycling.' Liam's voice drifted back from the kitchen.

'There you go. Anything else, well, I'm sure it will all come back to you quickly enough.'

I turned to my screen and called up the Tracker sheet, but after a few moments I realised that Sil was looking at me and swivelled my chair to face him. 'What?'

'Nothing.' He had his head tilted to one side and was looking at me, one hand combing the hair away from his face. 'Just wondering.'

Liam came back with a bottle of blood for Sil and a new, improved coffee for me. 'So, you two do anything nice last night?' he asked, brightly.

'Facebook. Bit of telly and then off to bed with a new Katie Fforde,' I said.

'Right. How about you, Sil? Let's hope you had a salacious night of bouncing off the walls, because Madame Dull here is *not* doing much for the gossip quotient lately!'

'Well, you know how it is. The clubs, the sex, the sex-clubs.' Thankfully at that point the telephone rang and I lost the end of the run-down on a vampire's night-time exploits as I answered it.

'This is OBSU. You sent us a sample yesterday? Only, you haven't sent us a human contrast.'

Oh *damn*! All I wanted was one simple blood test. It really shouldn't be *this* hard. 'I'm sure we did.'

'There must have been a mix-up then.'

'Must have been.'

'Only it's going to cost more than the estimate, you know that, don't you? We had to provide the contrast blood ourselves, using a neutral donor.'

'That's fine. Give me a rundown.' I listened to Richard at OBSU. Then I thanked him politely, put the phone down, shut off my computer and stood up. 'I have to go out.'

'I've just made you a coffee!'

'Yeah, sorry Liam, but I have to.'

Sil looked up from Liam's screen and something in my face made him flinch. 'I'm coming, too.'

'No. You stay here. This is private.'

Sil was already standing, pulling his coat from the back

of the chair. 'You can still get killed on private business. I'm coming.'

Our eyes met with an almost audible clash. Liam ducked. 'You two are scary,' he said. 'Next time, I'm working with ghouls – they might be horrible but at least they're predictable.' His gaze ran over me. 'Jessie? Take Sil. You look like you're going to need backup, wherever it is that you're going.'

'You can't come,' I said to Sil, who was staring me down.

He'd wrapped both his arms around over his coat like he was hugging himself. 'Not negotiable. You get killed, it's all right for you but then we have the whole Malfaire thing flying around, and maybe the reason that you're not dead yet is that he wants you alive for something.' Sil's pupils were huge but his eyes were cold. 'And until we know ... I won't interfere. I'll be there, in case.' He was getting wound up now, his demon was flickering around in the background, feeding off the emotion, casting shadows over his face. 'Jessica, you asked. You asked for my protection. So I must give it.'

'And it gives you the right to order me about.'

Sil shrugged. 'I'm trying to do what I think is best.'

I opened my mouth to argue that how could he possibly know what was best for me? Right now I hardly even knew. But the effort was beyond me. 'Oh, come on then, I haven't got time to play games.' Or the inclination. Things were getting very, very bad and I couldn't, *daren't*, confide in anyone.

I drove out of town and north towards the moors. 'Where are we going?' Sil eventually asked, after staring out of the window for twenty miles.

'Up on the moors,' I answered shortly.

'Yeah, I can see that. Anywhere specific, or do you just fancy a drive around?'

'Don't.'

Sil glanced at me. 'What is it, Jessica? What happened back at the office? And don't tell me it was nothing, because you're acting even more fucked-up than usual right now.'

I shook my head. Tears weren't far away and I didn't trust myself to speak. Instead, I turned the car down a narrow lane between two high hedges acned with hawthorn berries and sloes, bumping over the grassy line that grew down the middle of the road. The track eventually led down the hill, over a cattle grid and between two paddocks filled with grazing Jacob sheep. I pulled up in front of the low, two-storied house, with the tiny windows and off-centre front door.

'Nice,' Sil said, getting out. 'Very homely.'

I pushed on the front door, which was never locked. It opened on to the stone-flagged hall, where coats decorated the walls and Wellingtons covered the floor. An old Labrador padded up to greet us with a wet nose in the groin before following us down to the big kitchen at the back, heated as usual by the Aga, which bubbled like a spell. The air was full of baking and drying cotton.

'Jessica!' My mother, coming out of the pantry, held a hand to her heart. 'My dear girl, you nearly gave me a stroke! Why didn't you say you were coming? And who,' her eyes widened at the sight of the vampire, 'is *this* rather lovely specimen?' She couldn't help it, I knew, but I saw her eyes flicker to my left hand. She'd have a long wait to see an engagement ring on it. 'Was there something you wanted to tell me?'

'Yes.' My voice sounded strangled. 'You'd better sit down. Where's Dad?'

'Oh, he's up at the top paddock, fixing some fences. I keep telling him we ought to get a man in, but you know how he is.' Her eyes were worried.

'Sil.' He was looking around, seeing those things that I never noticed anymore, the hairy dog-beds in front of the Aga, the big, scrubbed table in the middle of the room, scattered with baking in various stages, the three generations of cats squeezed on to a sofa, the dresser scattered with family photographs. I felt sick, wanted to smash things. 'Will you go up to the top field and fetch my father?'

His head came up. 'But –'

'I'm safe enough here. Please. Go.' I needed him gone, I needed my father here.

'Jessie – '

Without thinking I touched his arm. 'Please, Sil.' And our eyes met. His held an expression that I didn't want to analyse, not right now. 'Just go.'

With an inclination of his head towards us both, Sil took himself off back down the hallway and through the front door, the old dog getting up to follow in the hope of a walk, but waddling stiffly back to his bed by the Aga when Sil outdistanced him.

My mother pulled two chairs out from the pine table, and sat down carefully on one. 'So this isn't a social visit then?' she asked, resting elbows on the table and rubbing at the back of her neck. 'Not work, I hope?'

I sat down, but jumped back up again. My mouth was dry. I ran a fingernail down a crack in the wood grain, an action so familiar from childhood that it was like an echo. 'Mum – ' My eyes roamed the walls, up to the ceiling, where they carefully enumerated all the items of clothing drying on the rack suspended above the Aga.

'Is it something to do with that young man? I must say, he's very nice looking. Could do with a square meal though. I do hope it's not frustrated mothering instinct with you, dear.'

'He's a vampire.'

'Ah.' And a world of anxious pain was contained within that single syllable.

'But he's not the problem.'

'Oh?' And how could the fact that her daughter was involved with a vampire *not* be a problem, I could see her thinking. 'So then, what *is* the problem?'

I dug my nails into my hands. 'You are.'

'Ah.' And my mother, my usually unflustered mother, began tugging at her sleeves, trying to pull them down over her hands, fussing with the cuffs of her wrap-around jumper. 'And what makes you say that?'

'Mum, I *know*. Look, before Dad gets here, you'd better tell me – how did you meet him?'

'Your father? I'm sure I've told you, we were at teacher-training together.'

'No! Not Dad! My *real* father! Malfaire!'

My mother's face closed down. Fell into itself, as though fifty years of ageing had caught up with her all at once. 'How did you – ?' she whispered.

'Blood tests. We sent a sample of his blood, and one of mine as the human contrast.' I gave a snuffly giggle of irony. 'They assumed there had been a mistake because the two samples were so similar. One was a blood sample from something they called a ghyst, the other was only partly human. When they did the full range of testing they found that it only made sense if the ghyst was the paternal relative of the other. So, what happened? Does Dad know?'

'Oh, my God.' My mother covered her eyes with her hands.

'Who am I, Mum? More to the point, *what* am I? What on earth is a ghyst? What does it do? What has it done to *me*?'

She stood up and went over to the Aga, fussing with the

kettle. She shook it to check for water, put it down, picked it up, filled it and put it down again. 'You weren't supposed to find out,' she said, and her voice was different, strange. Like I'd never known her.

'Well, obviously. Thirty-one years is a long time to keep a secret, especially one like this. Did he seduce you? I could see how you might –'

My mother turned around, her back to the Aga now. She looked furious. 'How could you ever think such a thing! That I would ever do *that* with a monster like him!' Her hands were fists on the Aga rail. She stood in such contrast to the cosy farmhouse kitchen that I began to wonder if this was really the woman I'd known all my life, or some impostor.

'Um … Mum, I *do* know the facts of life, you know.' I held up one hand. 'Malfaire. Father.' I held up the other. 'Mother. You.' I linked the fingers together. 'Me.' She stared at me. Just stared, her hair coming loose from its pony-tail, wisping down over her face. 'Oh.' I said, realisation trying to break through but being pushed down by hope and horror. 'Oh. No.'

She nodded. 'Yes.'

'You're not my mother.'

'I'm sorry.'

'Shit.'

'Mother or no, I will *not* have swearing in this house!' And it was so familiar, so dear, that I couldn't help smiling.

'Sorry.'

A confusion of dog at the back door, and my father entered breathless from what must have been a down-hill sprint, the two farm collies circling his feet in their attempts to get into the kitchen, and Sil, looking as though mud was a foreign language, stepping over them to come inside.

'Oh, thank heavens!'

'What on earth is the matter? This young man wouldn't tell me anything. I thought I was being abducted for a moment.'

'She knows, Brian.'

'Knows? Knows what?' He hung his full-length waterproof on the inside of the back door and turned to warm himself at the Aga, standing next to my mother and illustrating, once again, how unlike them I was.

'She knows about Malfaire.'

Sil twitched but he didn't react any more than that. Instead he scooped a ginger cat off the sofa and held it to his shoulder, where it sat, stunned.

'Oh. How much does she know?' The kettle squealed and, without thinking, my father began making tea for all of us.

'I wanted you here before I told her.'

'It isn't my decision, Jen. It's up to you to say.'

'Please, someone.' My voice sounded very little, very far away. Sil's grey glance settled on me with physical weight. 'You can go now.'

'I will not leave you.'

I was tired, too loaded with weariness to fight him. 'Please. Just … go and look round the farm or something.'

My parents exchanged a glance.

'Sil …'

He plopped the cat gently back on to the cushions and came over to me. 'Jessica. The Protection Act. It isn't just words you know. Not just something we *say*. It's …' A clenched fist crossed his chest in an almost ceremonial gesture. 'It's here. *I* am here. And I will not leave you.'

My stomach felt as though someone was twisting a knife in it and I looked up at these two people I no longer understood. Betrayal turned the knife again. They were so familiar, they'd been so predictable, and all the time … *this*.

I met Sil's eyes again. His gaze was steady and his hand cupped my shoulder briefly in a touch of support. *He might be vampire, his moral high-ground might be at sub-sea level, but he'd never lied to me about who I was.*

'All right.'

And while we all sat around the pale pine table, handling mugs of tea strong enough to have run the farm on their own, my erstwhile parents told me the story of my life.

Chapter Fifteen

'When we lived in Exeter, it was a war zone.' My mother – *Jen* – sipped at her tea. 'And there was such misery, such suffering ...' She put out a hand and touched my arm, as though to reassure herself that I was still there, still alive. 'You have to remember, Jessica, that this was at the height of the Troubles, the prejudice and the discrimination were terrible things to see, and the hatred.'

She looked across at my father. He would never be anything other than Dad, this man who'd taught me to read and helped with my homework. Malfaire was never going to qualify for the title for anything other than DNA input. My father looked back, reached out a hand and covered her fingers with his. 'Go on, Jen,' he whispered. 'It's time. You know it.'

A deep breath and she went on. 'I worked as a volunteer when I wasn't teaching. In a women's shelter. It was a frightening time, Jessica, more than you can ever imagine, back then, even admitting to *knowing* someone who wasn't human was to invite a petrol bomb through your window. Whole areas had zero-tolerance policies, there were zombies and ghouls walking the night, you'll never know.'

'I read my history, I've seen the films. What has it all to do with anything?'

'There were women ... little more than children some of them, starving, out on the streets. Parents dead, often killed by the mon–' a flick of a look in Sil's direction – 'by Otherworlders. The welfare system was hard to negotiate if you had no home ... these people were *desperate*, Jessica, alone, terrified, hungry, some of them had children of their own to feed, they would do whatever it took to keep themselves alive. Even ... Well. You said you've read your history. You know what people had to do.' She dropped her eyes, fingers plucking at my sleeve as though she could pick a conclusion into my mind through the wool. 'And there was a girl ...'

'My mother.'

A nod over the cooling tea. 'She came to us so shocked that she barely knew her own name. She'd been in ... well, one could hardly call it a relationship ... she'd been the plaything, I think is the best way to put it, of a demon. Who had grown tired of her and thrown her back on to the streets with only the clothes she stood up in, and they weren't good for much by then, either. And then she'd found out she was pregnant.'

The cold finger that ran down my spine was so distinct that I half-turned to check that Sil was still sitting at the table corner. My fingers were blue around my mug and I couldn't think of anything to say. Sil was concentrating on the floor, looking a bit embarrassed. Let him, he'd been the one who insisted on coming; if my family's dirty laundry was going to get aired in front of him it served him right.

'She ... her name was Rune, by the way. Rune Atrasia. Rune was so, *so* scared. She said that everyone knew about her and the demon, that everyone would know that the baby was his and ... There were mobs out, killing children – *children*, mind you, for being Otherworlders. And I think ...' There was a bit of a pause. My parents' eyes met over the tabletop clutter that had once been so comforting and was now so alien. 'I think that she was afraid the child would be born ... not quite right.'

'We tried to persuade her to move somewhere.' My father ... *Brian* ... went to refill the kettle. 'We had friends, someone who would take her in, help her make a new life. But she ... ah, never mind. Dead set on staying put.'

My entire body was cold now. 'She didn't want me.' I had to take my hands from the table and sit on them to stop the shaking.

'You mustn't think that.' My mother moved her chair a scraped inch closer to me. 'She was afraid.'

'Of *me*? Of her own *baby*?' The tendons in my neck were so tight that my mouth was pulled open.

'Things have changed so much. You see, Jessie,' her eyes rose to mine, a half-smile of fondness curved her mouth, 'you must understand, it wasn't like it is now. Nowadays you can –' her glance rode over Sil like a ferry over a queasy sea – 'you can date Otherworlders, even,' she swallowed hard, 'even *sleep* with them and nothing is said. It's fashionable, I think, isn't it?'

I refused to admit to anything. Sil kept on staring at the floor. From the carefully cultivated blankness of his expression I had to assume that there was something really *fascinating* about those flagstones.

'She was very young and very scared and things were very different. You can't ... you *mustn't* judge her, Jess.'

'Don't you *dare* tell me how to feel!' I'd jumped to my feet; the kitchen was suddenly full of scattered cats in states of alarm and a silence you could have bent nails around.

'Sit down.' Sil's words dropped into the silence, heavy as bricks.

'This is none of your business.'

'*Sit. Down.*' Power flared, Sil was pulling Otherworld on me. I could feel the movement of his demon inside him. 'You need to know this, Jessica. Losing your temper won't achieve anything.'

'Except make me feel better,' I muttered.

'No, it won't.'

I sat, reluctantly. Waited for more words until the gap made me look at my mother again. There were tears on her cheek and an old pain in her eyes. 'We'd just ... your father and I ... there was a baby ... but I was too old and ...' My father dropped a hand on to her shoulder and squeezed it lightly. He didn't need to speak. She straightened her back, gave her head a slight shake and went on. 'So we offered to adopt Rune's baby. She didn't want her child to carry the stigma of being Otherworld, so we came up with a plan; and I know this sounds very odd, but everything was so confused and impermanent back then, and I'd only just lost ... we didn't tell people that it wasn't my baby. Rune came and hid with us, I wore lots of loose clothes, Abbie only came on a home visit once during those months.'

'Not safe to travel, you see.' A tin of biscuits materialised with the refreshed tea pot. 'Abigail was at a Protected boarding school and they weren't keen on letting the children move about the country much. She came home for that Christmas, I think, wasn't it, Jen?'

'Probably. We told her she was going to have a baby brother or sister, but she wasn't much bothered. I think she'd got a crush on some teacher or other and that was all she could think about back then.'

'Mr Collins.'

'Are you sure, Brian? I thought it was that Matthew chap, the one that taught French, you remember, with all that limp hair, looked like he needed a good scrub.'

'No, it was Collins. Had a saxophone.'

'*Please.*' Everyone looked at me. 'Just tell me.'

'Always so impatient, Jess!'

'Yes, well, I've got work to do.' *And I want to get out of this place that isn't my home any more.*

My mother raised her eyebrows. 'All right, dear, we understand.'

'No. You really don't.'

Sil rolled his eyes.

'I delivered you, in fact, such a little scrap you were, all eyes and these *strange* expressions.'

'No change there,' Sil muttered.

'We thought everything was all right. Even so, we moved up here, to be safe, to be sure.'

There was a long, concrete-filled silence. 'So,' I said slowly, 'can I meet her? My mother? You must know where she is.' My other mother glanced quickly at my father, and in that second I knew. 'She's dead, isn't she?'

How *could* I feel sad about the death of a woman whose existence I had only just discovered? But I did. Believe it.

'We don't know what happened and we only found out quite recently. We'd been in touch, on and off, over the years … just photographs sometimes, just so she could see the kind of woman you'd become, and then … one day a phone call from Exeter police, they'd found our address in among her things.'

'How did she die?'

'I said, we don't know.'

Questions were flashing into my mind, a whole series of them at light speed, barely chance to register each new one before the next came screaming through. *Does Malfaire know, what does this make me, who am I really, what really happened to my mother, how many people know, can anyone tell I'm not fully human by looking* … and over and above it all *WHAT AM I?*

'Jess.' My father's voice was gentle, calm. 'Whatever Rune did or didn't do, she loved you. She couldn't keep you, but she loved you. And we wanted you so much … We all did what we did for you. To keep you safe.'

'Safe? Is that what I am?' I stood up abruptly again and the cats all repeated the flat-eared run for the worktops. 'I have to go now.'

My mother stood up too. 'Come to supper tomorrow,' she suggested. 'We'll have Abbie over as well. Maybe your father could bring out some of his sloe gin.'

'I don't know. I'm not sure how I feel about playing happy families at the moment.' It was cruel, I knew it as I said it. But hadn't they lied to me for the last thirty-one years? It was unfair of them to even *ask* me to pretend.

I climbed into the car, knowing that they were watching me drive away, as ever, hand-in-hand in the doorway to the cosy little house, which had once been my home, my retreat, and was now a place I knew I would never feel safe again.

'Do you want me to drive?'

'Shut up, Sil.' My hands were shaking on the wheel but driving would keep my mind busy, stop me thinking about the implications of the story I'd been told. 'I'm fine.'

'You, Jessie, you're anything but fine.'

I turned to him so suddenly that the car twitched in the lane and scarlet hawthorn tips ran a squealing line down the paintwork. 'How did your life change when you were vamped?'

'God, I don't know.' He raked his fingers through his hair. 'I don't remember. It was a long time ago!'

'Over ninety years. You've been a vampire for over ninety years. You've lived with it, every day, knowing that you used to be human.'

'But you're not vampire.'

'No.'

'Jessie.' There was a curious note in Sil's voice, an

undercurrent. He hid his expression by turning his head to look out of the window. 'You are still *you*. Nothing's changed. You haven't had to spend six months wondering what you're going to turn into when the demon inside you hatches, you *know* what you are. You'll never have to face all your friends, all your family growing old and dying while you stay young, watching your children –'

'You had *children?*' *How long had I known him? And he'd never mentioned ...*

'Two.'

'Sil.'

'They're dead now.'

Oh God, I *really* didn't need this. 'But at least you started out human. I look human, I walk and talk human, but –' my flesh was creeping on my bones. 'What the hell *am* I?'

'At least we know you're half-ghyst. Gives us something to go on, and now we know what Malfaire is we can work on a way to defeat him.'

Oh yeah, that would *really* help. Here I am finding out that I'm half-demon and I'm supposed to get all enthused by the fact that it might give us a hint as to how to get rid of my biological father? I stared out of the windscreen as though I'd never seen this world before. 'Did it hurt? Becoming a vampire?'

Beside me Sil took a deep breath. 'Jessie, you're aren't vampire. You aren't going to change, you are going to go on being the same irritating minx that you started out. All right?' His voice softened. 'Let's get back and get our respective geeks on to the problem of finding out what being half-demon is going to mean for you.' A sly smile. 'You might be able to do tricks.'

'Bastard.'

Chapter Sixteen

'You were gone a long time.' There was a question there, carefully hidden.

'Yeah, sorry. Anything happening?'

Liam looked from me to Sil and back again. 'Nah. Just paperwork. Oh, there was a call out to Enforcement about an hour ago but no-one came back to ask us to attend, so it was probably some local getting a bit daylight-happy.' He swivelled his chair around so that his back was to us. 'So, you two have a nice time?'

'No. Liam, can you run through a search for me? I need to know all there is to know about the ghyst.'

'Are you sure – ?' Sil began.

'Yes. I have to know.'

'Wouldn't you like to take a little time over this?'

'And what part of "I have to know" didn't you get?'

'Hello? Still here.' Liam swivelled back to wave his hand in front of my face. 'If you two are going to have private conversations, then can you at least have them in private?'

I ignored him and turned on Sil. 'Can you get Zan on to it?'

He stood and looked at me out of those infuriatingly unreadable eyes. 'I think you should take a moment.'

'Liam, could you call Zan's office and see if you can get hold of him?'

Liam gave me a tired, pitying look and pointed at Sil. 'Jessie, an enormous percentage of Zan's office is standing next to you. Looking, if I am not mistaken, severely pissed-off.'

Sil sighed. 'Wouldn't you be?' I made my eyes pleading-shaped, and glared at the vampire, who held both his hands up defensively. 'Yes, it's all right, Jessie, I know. Not in front of anyone else.'

'Oh, whoa, what is this, death-match time? Any bodies turn up floating down the river and you know I go straight to Head Office and tell tales.'

'Liam, you really are the most disloyal person I know, and given that I know a *lot* of vampires, that's a pretty shocking statistic.' I absentmindedly picked up my several-hours-old coffee and drank the dregs. 'I'm going home.'

'What about the search?'

'Mail me the results. I've got to go and spend a clichéd few hours looking through some old photo albums. No, not you.' This to Sil, who had risen to his feet from the edge of Liam's desk. 'You stay here.'

'What, suddenly you're not at risk any more? I don't think so, Jessie.'

'I want to be on my own for a bit. Surely you can understand, after what happened today?'

'Look at yourself. You're vulnerable, even more so than usual and you're normally as vulnerable as a day-old chick in the open, so you're going to need protection. Besides, I'm not sure you *should* be alone.'

'You're doing it again, having those coded conversations. If there's something going on, then why can't *I* know, at least? Or, a clue, a clue would do – ' Liam's voice faded as I started down the stairs, hearing him plaintively calling after us – 'or a mime? How many syllables?'

It was dusk on the pavement outside the office, a warm and muggy night was settling over the city, with a fog rising from the river through which people were moving like footless ghosts. Sil and I walked against the tide towards the flat.

'What are you going to do?' Sil asked, shaking beads

of moisture from his hair. 'After you've finished with the wallowing in self-pity, obviously.'

'I am *not* wallowing!' I snapped back. 'I'm trying to come to terms with things here!'

'You'd better come to terms fast then. Everything's changed for you, Jessie, and this isn't the time for weeping and wailing. There will be time for that later, if you feel you must.'

'Why? You were the one telling me that I am still who I've always been! So what's changed that is so desperate that I deal with it?'

Sil looked at me from under lashes pearlised in fog. 'Because you're one of us now,' he said softly. 'You're an Otherworlder. I don't know if we've ever had a half-breed before. Vamps don't breed true, werewolves can't cross-breed, and none of the other races ever interact sexually with humans, so you are quite the curiosity.'

I stopped walking so suddenly that he was a few steps ahead before he realised. '*Nothing* has changed! I'm still who I've always been, still *what* I've always been! I do not have anything to do with the Otherworld.'

'I think the law might disagree.'

'I am *not* one of you. I've been human for thirty-one years, and I shall carry on being human.'

'You're half-demon, Jessie. You can't fight it.'

'What were *your* parents like?' I asked, nastily. 'Or can't you remember that far back?'

'Victorian. Hardly ever met them. I had nannies.'

Touché. 'Look, I'm home now. Why don't you go back to your office? No-one is going to do anything to me tonight; there's no Run, I'm expecting no visitors and,' I checked up and down the street, 'no sign of Enforcement coming over all peculiar. I'll catch up with you tomorrow when I've had a chance to think about all this.'

Sil shook his head and a fine mist of water from his hair hit me in the face. 'No.'

'I'll be safe enough in the flat.' I went through the main door and started to climb the stairs. 'No-one's going to break in; we've got locks and everything.'

'Even so.' Sil followed me.

'You can't guard me all day and all night! What about sleep?'

'Jessie, I'm a bloody *vampire*! You know, the whole "children of the night" thing! I don't need sleep and I'm not going to be taking up the spare room, if that is what you're worried about.'

'We haven't *got* a spare room.' I stopped on the landing and turned around to face him. 'And *that's* what I'm worried about.'

'You've made your position very clear, Jessica.' Sil's voice was cool. 'You don't want me, fine. Believe me, there's plenty that do, and I'm not putting myself up for humiliation at *your* hands again.'

'Ooh, listen to you!' I put the key in the lock. 'We all know you're boombastic, you don't have to keep on about it!'

'Jealous, Jessie?' Sil's voice had a little laugh in it. 'I notice *you* don't seem to be getting any action these days?'

'Yes, well, my last boyfriend-experience ended in him getting blasted to kingdom-come, so it's not something I'm in a hurry to repeat!' I leaned against the partially opened door, feeling the slight prick behind my eyes which meant I might cry if he kept prodding me.

Sil seemed to know it too. 'Yes, I'm sorry. That was a cheap shot. A mere repetition of vile tattle.'

'No, you pretentious nineteenth-century prat, it was a bloody wicked thing to say. How come you're all "yeah, okay" and then you suddenly get an attack of the Oscar Wilde's?'

He shrugged. 'One can adapt, but upbringing is still uppermost. Do you miss him?'

'Cameron? Sometimes.'

'But I shouldn't think you miss having to chain him up every full moon. Sorry! Sorry!'

'You are *such* a bastard.'

I pushed the door fully open and walked through, into the arms of Malfaire, who was standing inside.

'Ah, Jessica, there you are. I was beginning to worry.'

I jumped and recoiled at the same time. 'How did you get in?' A tiny part of me was looking him over thinking *this is your father. You carry his genes. You are alike in ways you don't know.* A slightly larger part was screaming *what the hell is he?*

'Your charming flatmate. She let me in. I have … er … *persuaded* her to go out for the evening.' He leaned against the wall and crossed his arms, louchely. 'Lovely girl.'

'But … she … you …' No way. No way would Rach have let Malfaire into the flat willingly. Especially after he'd flamed her cat. Not even to force-feed him her healthy snacks until he died of mouth-boredom. And *going out?* After *dark?* Rachel considered the night to be nature's way of telling us to watch *EastEnders*. 'She wouldn't.'

Sil was standing at my shoulder. 'Did you glamour her?'

Malfaire straightened. 'Maybe. A little.' He moved to walk around us both. 'Hmm. I wonder, Jessica, is *this* the love-interest in the tale that is your life?' Malfaire eyed Sil up and down like a second-hand horse. 'A little too skinny for my tastes, although the bone structure is good. Nice long legs, to pull you deep. Or does that part of you belong to the other one, the old vampire, with those *gorgeous* green eyes?'

Sil hissed at him, fangs out.

'Now, now. Jessica, can't you control your pet?'

Focus on being angry. On the here and now. 'Pet? He's no pet of mine!'

'Really?' Malfaire sounded superciliously uninterested.

'I repeat, why are you here?'

Malfaire walked through and lounged down on one of the sofas, for all the world as though this was *his* home, not mine. 'When we last parted ... I'm not sure you fully understood the implications.'

Tonight he looked as though he had been dipped in caramel, from the top of his softly blond head to the tips of his brown leather shoes, he was one-tone, creamy-toffee coloured, wrapped in a super-soft mohair jacket, which reached halfway to his knees and probably cost more than this flat.

Beside me, Sil was vibrating with anger. His fangs were so far out that he'd bitten his tongue and a tiny drizzle of blood was running down the dark stubble peppering his chin. 'You have no business here with Jessica.'

Malfaire leaned forward on the sofa, resting his elbows on his knees. I was still standing, but found myself leaning forward too, meeting him halfway. His eyes scanned me. 'You know what you are,' he said, quietly. 'I can see in your face.'

Inside me, a battle was being fought. On one side, I wanted *so badly* to know things: What I truly was – demon, human? What was my mother like? What did she look like, sound like, smell like? Did I get my hair from her, or my eyes, or my triumphant bosom? *What did you do to her that made her so terrified of her own child that she didn't want to keep me?*

And on the other side stood Jessica Grant, human by adoption and upbringing, by habit and convention. Not wanting to reveal herself hurt by today's shaking news, not wishing to put herself in humiliation's way by opening up to Malfaire and giving him the chance to get the upper hand.

'It has taken me a long time to find you, my daughter.'

'And that's why you want me to go along with your anti-vampire league stuff? Because I happen to have fifty per cent of your genes, you think I ought to be unable to make up my own mind about good and evil? Okay, the vampires haven't always been the good guys, but now we've got a Peace Treaty that works in everyone's favour, we've developed synthetic blood which means humans don't die for lack of compatible transfusions any more, and vampires living longer than us means there's continuity in organisations where that's a good thing. We all bumble along nicely enough. Now you come along trying to raise hate and intolerance and ... what, I'm supposed to join in because you're my good old, long lost dad?' There were tears in my eyes and my voice had dropped into the hoarseness of swallowed misery. 'Just ... just piss off, Malfaire.'

He sighed, a deep, seemingly heartfelt sigh. 'But I am all you have, in this world.' The unmistakable threat rolled and rippled beneath his words. 'You and I, we could rule!'

Sil put his hand on my arm. I glanced up at him and saw the pulsating, gleaming form of his demon breaking its way to the surface, fighting its way from glands and nerves to coalesce along the front of his suit. I grimaced, not at its appearance, but at the thought of the dry-cleaning bill, as the dual creature that the vampire truly was stood before me, strong and imperious. 'Why do you want, Jessica?' It spoke with Sil's voice but no inflection, as though the words meant nothing, were just something that seeped out.

I'd never seen Sil's demon before. It had an elegance, a kind of pared-down simplicity of form that wasn't ugly or stomach-churning as some could be; it was more like a very thin humanoid that occupied the same body space as him. More of a symbiote than a parasite, I found myself thinking, then wondering why on earth I wasn't more traumatised by this demon in my home. 'Yes, it's rather the twenty-four million-dollar question, isn't it, Malfaire? What the hell do you want with me? I've made it clear that I'm never going to be on your side in whatever mythical "battles" you've dreamed up, so why don't you just leave me alone and go and shout your rhetoric from a box down in the park, like the other nutters?'

Malfaire sighed again. 'I had wished to protect my bloodline,' he said, still sitting relaxed on the sofa, 'but it appears that you have to die.' A wave of his hand and Sil and I were encased in a hex, a greenish-yellow staining in the air around us. 'I do hope you realise that this is nothing personal.' Malfaire's voice drifted in, strained through the magic so the words sounded hollow. 'Purely self-protection.'

Sil leapt. In cat-like silence he flew for Malfaire's throat, head back and fangs to the fore, but was unable to break through the spell, despite his demon tearing at the walls of magic with claws and teeth. I tried to move to help, but the air was thick and I didn't have the vampire's strength to fight it. I began to sag at the knees, pressed slowly, slowly to the floor by the increasing pressure inside the circle, feeling the blood rising as my head started to pound.

'Keep still.' Sil's words were hissed and low. 'You cannot battle this demon; he is one of our kind. To fight will mean the end comes sooner for you.'

'But ...'

When he spoke again it was more 'Sil' and less demon. 'Protection Act, Jess, for the sake of all the heavens, leave me to do this!'

My headache was increasing now, my eyes felt full and

overripe. A drip fell on my hand and when I looked at it I found that my nose was bleeding. The greasy smell made me feel sick, the sheer energy of the magic was pushing me low to the ground, driving my head towards the carpet, and even Sil was hunched under the weight of it. But his demon was fighting back, still rending at the swirling bilious mist of the spell, punching holes that seemed to hang in the air before the green mist came eddying in to fill the space. With each gap he made, the pressure lessened for a moment; I could feel it in my whole body, before it built again and the walls were renewed. 'Sil?'

'I ...' Sil bent close to me. Outside the circle I could see Malfaire examining his nails as though none of this was his doing. Only the smile spreading across his face told me that he knew exactly how much we were suffering. 'I can break this. My demon can separate and move through the walls to Malfaire. It may be able to kill him before it dies of the magic ...'

'No.' I dabbed again at my bleeding nose. 'If your demon separates from your body, you'll die.'

We were hunched together now on the floor. Malfaire's smile had grown broader.

'If I don't, we will *both* die.' Sil touched my hand. 'I'm not afraid, Jess. A hundred years. It's enough. And you are worth the ending.'

Tears joined the blood dripping on to my hand. 'No. I'm really not. Please, don't. Someone will come, something will happen ... you can't ... *don't*, Sil.'

The pressure eased. I looked towards the outside of the circle with hope bursting through me, only to see Malfaire looking in.

'Oh, do go on,' he said. 'I am *such* a sucker for romance at times like these.'

I found that Sil had both arms wrapped round me. His demon had slithered around so that I could no longer see it, leaving only the human form pressed against my body, his face close to mine. 'Jess,' he said, my name a breath against my cheek. 'Jess.' And then I saw it, his demon pulling away, drawing itself from him, appearing on the ground at his side like a cat reluctantly leaving the lap of a warm owner.

'I won't let you die for me,' I breathed back. 'It's just stupid. Romantic, but stupid.'

'I may be stupid but you are important, Jessica.' Sil's voice was already faint, his body slumping slowly as the life force began to drain away. 'This is the best way …'

Anger rose. *How dare Malfaire! How dare he hurt me, how dare he try to kill my … Sil! How dare he be my father!* Propelled by sheer resentment, I managed to crawl within a foot of the pus-coloured magical field.

Malfaire was still watching us. 'The vampire desires you, my little Jessica. He wants your body, your blood, his whole being pulses with his longing for you.'

'You've been reading too many romantic novels,' I said. 'Nobody's "being pulses with longing", least of all his.' Out of the corner of my eye I could see the lanky form of Sil's demon slowly pulling its limbs free, and Sil's body curling forwards, closer and closer to death. I managed to stand against the pressure, forcing my body upright. 'You're getting off on this, aren't you?' For some reason the pressure eased and I was able to breathe properly. 'You pervert.'

Malfaire still stood smiling slightly, but his expression was increasingly one of astonishment. 'You fight the spell?'

'Don't I just.' I took a careful step forward. My legs felt spongey, but held. I had no idea how I was doing any of this, but if it took the wind out of Malfaire's sails then I was going to carry on. 'Let us go.'

'Or?'

Damn, forward planning, not really my thing. 'Or, I'll walk through this magic circle of yours and pull your brains out through your nose.' I walked forward. One step, then another. It was like walking over custard, but I did it. Another step. The circle stank, the air around it prickled like an infestation and his power hung heavy; it was like trying to walk through wet lead sheets. And another step. I was right at the edge now, feeling the spell strobing against my mind like a migraine, scattering thought processes, short-circuiting my body. My legs wouldn't go on, my arms wrapped around my waist in an attempt to pull me back.

'Not as easy as you thought?'

That bastard was *laughing* at me! *Nobody* laughs at me! Well, except Liam, but he's earned that privilege – Malfaire was doing it simply because he *could*.

And then I saw Sil. Crouched to the ground, his life leaving him with the demon as it prepared to separate completely. *For me. He was willing to die, for me.* And the thought of life without him gave me the spur I needed. Sheer force of will. That's all it was. Foot before foot, legs groaning with the effort and the desire to turn round, but I did it. I walked through the scalding walls of enchantment.

As I walked out of the circle, Malfaire's power broke. Sil's demon shot back into his body like a rubber band had snapped, leaving him still crouched but shaking his head blearily. Malfaire stared at me. He looked slightly scared.

'What's the matter? Didn't you think I could do it?'

His face told me, very clearly, that he hadn't. And that he wasn't quite sure what I might do now. 'Stay away.' His voice was harsh, hoarse.

'And if I don't?' One step forward and I was almost within touching distance. To my huge surprise, Malfaire took a step back. Then another. Almost as though *he* was afraid of *me*.

'You have no power!' His voice was a bit desperate. Rising up the scale. 'You have no *power*!' he repeated.

'I have the bloody power to slap you senseless if you don't get out of here.' I didn't have the faintest idea how I was doing this, but I seemed to be terrifying Malfaire. I must have a *really* scary expression.

He drew himself up, carefully beyond my reach. Assumed a little more of his previous air of dignity. 'This ends,' he said, and was gone. Leaving behind a smell of scorched sofa, the collapsed remains of a circle of power staining the carpet, and a vampire staring very sharp daggers at me.

Rachel was *so* going to triple my rent.

Chapter Seventeen

I would have loved to have spent the rest of the evening under my duvet, alternately crying and swearing, eating Mars Bars and reading *The Bell Jar*. But by the time I'd endured half-an-hour of Sil yelling at me for not letting him die – yep, I didn't really understand that either, but vampires and gratitude? Not so much – I'd rather lost the urge. Now I wanted ... I wanted to be out, where real people were enjoying themselves. I wanted to reinforce my humanity with vodka and coke, cheesy chips and drum and bass. I wanted to shake my hips to music I wouldn't even have on in the car, to drink overpriced alcohol in a dark club and dance with men I'd never have to see again. I e-mailed the office while Sil took some deep breaths and a delivery from his staff, brought personally by possibly the flunkiest flunky I had ever seen. It looked suspiciously like a suitcase of clothes, but Sil's sartorial arrangements came underneath cleaning the oven on my list of topics to worry about right now. Liam's answering mail came back before I was even changed. He'd spoken to Zan in Vampire High Command but found out nothing about ghysts.

His rapid reply meant that he was sitting at his computer with not enough to do, always a disastrous combination, so I decided to go in and spoil his fun. There were a couple of hours to kill before the clubs got warmed up and the men got drunk enough to dance; I might as well spend the time annoying Liam. It was that or sit in Costa eating chocolate brownies and, given the dress I'd chosen, any extra calories might be a bit of a disaster. Actually, from the look on Sil's face when he saw my sartorial choice, the dress might be a disaster anyway. He'd wrinkled his lip and walked three steps behind me all the way to the office, and whenever I'd caught a glimpse of him out of the corner of my eye, he'd been trying to avert his gaze, as though he was ashamed to be seen in the same space-time continuum as me.

When I got there, Liam was waiting for me with a hold-all slung over his arm.

'You off somewhere?' I asked.

'It's the gear. There's a ghoul, gone to ground in a kids' play area. What on *earth* are you wearing?'

'I thought I might go out tonight.' I took the bag from him. 'Give me that. You know Head Office doesn't like you going outside.'

'You weren't here.'

'I am now. You go and ... scrub the software or whatever it is you do. I'll tranq the ghoul and hit the clubs afterwards.'

Liam gave me a dark look. 'Oh, yes? And why? Something I'm still not allowed to know anything about?'

'Ask The Incredible Mouth over there. He can't seem to shut up about my business.' I nodded towards Sil, who was standing by my desk, looking over a clipboard with a list of names and addresses on it. 'No, it's all right, Liam. I just want to – ah, have an evening out. Don't think I'm really in the mood for an evening of *Made in Chelsea* with Rach.' She'd wandered in just before I left, with unfocused eyes, a headache, and no memory of letting Malfaire in to the flat, and started making one of her meat-, fat- and dairy-free meals. Vodka and cheesy chips had increased their appeal at that point. 'I want to get on the outside of a few drinks, have a bit of a dance.' *Get off my face. Forget any of the stuff that happened today.* 'Nothing big, personal stuff. Anyway, what's wrong with what I'm wearing?'

Liam gave me a look up and down. 'It's a bit sexy. You're ghoul-bagging, not walking the ring-road touting for business.'

'Thank you, mother. And what about Sil, he's wearing less per square inch than I am; how come you're not telling him off?'

'He's a vampire, he'd be sexy in a Tesco bag and slippers. You look like you're off to see the wizard. What the hell are you going to do with the ghoul – cover yourself in sequins and try to gay him into submission?'

I was wearing a body-hugging, strappy and largely backless dress in dark red with shoes to match. 'I wasn't anticipating a tranquing. I only popped in here to make sure you weren't wasting tax-payers money, or at least the pitiful amount of tax-payers money that we get. Then I thought I'd go straight out.'

'Yes.' Liam gave me a look more pointed than a tranq dart. 'That's pretty much how it looks. I just thought I'd familiarise myself with your outfit because I have a *very strong* feeling – I dunno, call me psychic if you like – that you'll be wearing exactly the same clothes tomorrow morning when you turn up for work.'

'You think I'm going to seduce some innocent clubber?' Behind my desk Sil made a sarcastic blowing noise. 'That's rubbish! Anyway, I'm an adult woman; I can make my own decisions.'

Sil snorted now. 'Looking like that, the only decision you'll have to make is which position doesn't make you look fat.'

'Oh right, from a man in leather trousers and a shirt you could use to catch cod!'

'Yes, what's with the fishnet and leather look, Sil? You on a promise, tonight?'

Sil didn't look up from the clipboard. 'If she's going clubbing then I'm rather obliged to go along as well, and I'm steering her towards the club down by the river.'

'I thought you were supposed to be guarding me, not enjoying yourself!'

'Oh, I can enjoy myself at the same time.' He looked up at me. 'You'll fit right in there. They have pole dancing on Fridays.'

Liam sucked in a breath. 'For a straight guy, Sil, you can be a real *bitch*, you know that?'

'I wouldn't be so sure about the straight.' I checked the contents of the bag and prepared to move out. 'Not dressed like that.' Pulled my big coat down off the rack and used it to cover the offending dress. 'Mind you, Liam, sometimes I have my doubts about *you*.'

'I'm in touch with my feminine side,' Liam came back. 'You should be grateful!'

'Yeah, if this tranquing goes pear-shaped, at least we can sit around afterwards and talk about *Hollyoaks*. Is all the gear in?'

'You're ready to go. Good luck.'

'Cheers,' and Sil and I were off, running down the stairs with a hold-all swinging against my thigh – just like the old days, except in the old days Sil wasn't dressed like a rent boy and I wasn't wearing heels.

The ghoul had been caught by the dawn and had hidden all day underneath a ramp in a skate-park cum playground right on the edge of our jurisdiction, but out of area for the ghoul and, therefore, fair game for us.

'It's under there.' I pointed with the handle of the tranq gun. 'You can see it, faintly.'

Sil held the bag open for me to find the tranq darts. 'I always wondered how you did it, you know. How you managed to be so quick, so good at finding the mark. I guess it was obvious, really.'

I screwed the special darts into the barrel of the gun. 'It's my job, I *have* to see, *have* to be quick, or I'd be getting even worse headlines in the local press than I do now.'

'And you never thought there might be more to it than that?'

'Oh yes, every day I'd wake up and think, "gosh, I wonder if my parents were both human?" It's not the sort of thing that springs to mind, you know?'

Leaving Sil with the gear, I advanced on the area of darkness behind the skate ramp. Ghouls aren't actual killers, not intentionally anyway. In their own dimension, apparently, they're quite solitary and live off wild creatures. In this one they're a bloody nuisance, but at least they're not Shadows.

'Jessica Grant?' The scratchy voice came from the shadowy angle hard against the ground, where the windblown cigarette butts collected half-a-dozen deep. *'They send you?'*

'Yeah, James Bond was busy.' I couldn't get a shot in if I couldn't see. 'Who are you?'

'Carrerwear. I am ghoul.'

'Uh-huh. I sort of guessed.'

'I ask this, that you hear me.'

'I'm listening.'

'The demon who wants you. He wishes you to know, he no longer acts alone in his desire for war.'

'Who? No, don't tell me, Malfaire.' Deep inside me, anger fought with reason. 'Am I *really* meant to be intimidated by that?'

The ghoul snapped out at me, caught me on the wrist, sent the gun spinning from my hand across the grass. *'Yes,'* it said, simply, and flowed forward out of its hiding place.

The gun was too far away, over the other side of the

concrete skate ramp. If I threw myself across the half-tube then the ghoul would be on me before I touched the ground and I didn't trust myself to be able to fight it off. Damn! Ghouls usually had all the tactical ability of a pub darts team, but this one was intelligent, careful.

'So then, what do you get out of this? You lot hunt me down, then what happens? Some kind of reward thing?'

'We become allied to the demon Malfaire. There will be advantages, in the war to come.' The ghoul was standing over the gun. Bastard.

'Everyone's talking war all of a sudden. I thought the pact was working well.'

'He will lead us and there will be power. No more hiding.'

Okay, so I couldn't get the gun, couldn't run away, couldn't fight. What *could* I do? I could think.

Dropped to the ground like a felled bullock. I hurt my shoulder on impact, but that didn't matter. The ghoul hesitated, then began to come towards me, moving off the gun and into the space between us. It seemed uncertain; flowed almost reluctantly, keeping its edges against the side of the ramp. I jerked myself to my feet, one smooth quick movement, and I was behind the ghoul, picking up the gun before it could react. Levelled the gun, braced my wrist and pulled the trigger, all in one, and hit it square in the mid-section where it solidified as the chemicals took effect.

'You were a fat lot of good.'

'What did you want me to do?' Sil curled a lip at me. 'Only one gun; what was I supposed to do, bore it to sleep?'

'You could have distracted it.'

'You were having a nice, cosy chat.'

The gun was still in my hand. I ran my fingers over the familiarity of the handle, felt the way it balanced against my palm. 'Your eyes look different.'

Under the new moonlight his eyes were dark. Sil's eyes never looked *that* dark.

'I'm hungry, all right?'

Uh-oh. 'This club that you want us to go to? Would it happen to be the kind of club where consenting adults get together for a bit of bitey-action?'

Sil slid over the grass space between us almost without moving and was in front of me in a fraction of a second. 'What's your *problem*, Jessie? I'm vampire, a fucking *vampire* – blood, sex and high emotional drama are rather the point!' He was shouting at me now, his eyes shone black as polished coal, while his skin was whiter than white. 'And after that ... *thing* with Malfaire I need blood, warm blood, gushing into my mouth with the pound of a pulse! Okay, yeah, I can get by on the artificial, but sometimes I just want to be what I am, let all the dark come out. Feed my demon properly.'

Behind me the ghoul gave a muffled whimper. I reached my gun-hand out and fired another tranq straight into the rolled shape, without looking. 'It's illegal, Sil.' I dropped my eyes so I didn't have to look at him. It was like lemon juice in a mouth ulcer, hearing his careful enunciation of exactly what it was that made him so alien, so unavailable to me.

'Not if they offer blood. What's done behind closed doors is no-one's business but the people's concerned. And no-one ever complains, Jessie, no-one ever runs to the police. They're there because they want it; we're there because we do it. Cause and effect, supply and demand.'

'You tart.'

'*I'm* not the one running out to pull in a tight dress and high heels, because I've had some family drama, am I? You be careful throwing stones, Jessie, because some of them might bounce right back.'

He turned and began walking away, leaving the bag of paraphernalia on the ground. 'You'd better phone in to Enforcement to take this guy.'

'Are you going?'

'Like I said, I'm hungry.'

'But you're supposed to be protecting me. What if Malfaire turns up?'

Sil glanced over his shoulder and gave my outfit a once up-and-down look. 'I'm sure you'll manage to – talk your way out of things.' His shoulders were set absolutely rigid under the lacy shirt as he turned away again.

The animosity hurt. 'What's pissing you off so much, Sil?'

Maybe it was the serious way I asked, not shouting, only raising my voice enough to cross the air to him. He stopped walking. 'On this occasion, or generally? You, Jessie. Always, you. Judging me for what I am, what I have to do. I didn't *choose* to be what I am. I got unlucky one night down a dark alley with a woman who wasn't what she seemed to be.'

'I didn't know.'

'Ninety years ago things weren't like they are now. There were stories … sightings, but Otherworlders were hiding, creeping in the night, not knowing what reaction they might get in this new world. Most people didn't even know what a vampire could do, or *would* do. My wife refused to see me and took the children away. I think she told them I was dead.'

'Sil.'

'When you've lost something, Jessie, something that really *mattered*, you lose a little part of yourself as well. The part that *feels*. I know you all think we have no emotions; that we can't experience anything that doesn't feed our demon, but it's not true, Jess. Vampires can feel as much as any human. More, in fact, given the number of years we have to feel *in*.' He stopped talking and raised his face to the newly dark sky. 'You have no idea,' he added softly. 'No idea what I feel.'

'But I thought … everyone says …' *He could feel. So why didn't he?*

'Yes. Everyone who isn't vampire says. Us, now, we say nothing. And do you know why we say nothing?'

I shook my head. He was still staring upwards, his eyes searching between the stars.

'No. You don't know, how can you?' A sigh that sounded as though it contained a century of held breath. 'Now we're something new, a bit dangerous, the perfect partner for those with the jaded sexual palate, but what it is, you see,' and again he'd crossed the space between us without me seeing him move, 'I bite and I drink and I fuck, and I've learned not to let any of it touch me. But I was prepared to *die* for you today.' He'd lowered his voice so much that I had to get right up close to hear him. 'To give it all up, all this …' His hands went wide to indicate the chilly park. 'The blood, the sex, all of it. I'd give it up *for you*, Jessica Grant. And that seems to mean nothing to you.'

His eyes were completely black now. Empty holes. There was a frisson shuddering in the air, a tangible wall of things unsaid.

'Come on then.'

'What?'

'Let's go. To this club.'

Sil shook his head, slowly. His hair swung free from the collar of the fishnet shirt and blew back to drag over his face. 'Thought you didn't agree with the bitey-action. Why the change of heart?'

I didn't know how to begin to say what was in my head,

in my heart. That his death would have killed something deep inside me; that his speech about loss could just as well have applied to me. But I couldn't. He was vampire. As he said, how could I know what that felt like? 'You're set on going there, I'm under your protection, so,' I shrugged, 'I guess I have to come. Besides, they do have music, don't they? And dancing?'

There was a slow nod and the moon came out again to highlight his cheekbones. 'Yes.'

'Right then.' And then I looked up and met the jet-black stare. 'Are you all right?'

Behind us, the ghoul rolled and fell gloopily into the mud.

'Nothing wrong with me.'

'Are you sure? All that about your wife and children – '

He was standing closer than was comfortable. 'My business, Jessie, my pain.'

My heart had come loose in my chest. *Vampires can feel. They simply choose not to, for alien reasons of their own. He can feel pain.* The memories hurt him – I could see that much in those nuclear eyes. '*Sil.*'

'Right, come on then, let's get to the club. But you can buy your own drinks.'

'I'd insist on it.' My voice held a pretended strength, a pretended carelessness.

'And no getting uptight if things get a bit rough.'

'Check.'

'Okay,' and he smiled, but because his fangs were down and his eyes were a couple of featureless pits, it wasn't pleasant, 'call Enforcement and let's go.'

Sil strode along. She was following, he could sense her heat and uncertainty bobbing along behind him. *What possessed me? Why in the seven hells did I bring up the children?* He swallowed and focused on keeping his steps even and slow enough for Jessie to keep up with.

He could see her now, if he looked sideways. Looking good in that dress, however much he might deride her for her choice; it hugged her curves and revealed enough of her long legs to make a lesser man dream of heaven; she walked tall and strangely sure of herself for someone whose life had just been destroyed and rebuilt on new foundations. *I would have done it, Jess. I'd have taken the lives of my demon and myself to keep you safe from that bastard Malfaire. And for you I lowered the barriers enough to talk about my children ...*

Through his open-weave shirt the night air was cool against his skin, soothing his demon into temporary peace, even as it drove through his brain with the need for the blood. And what on earth did he think was going to happen at the club? She'd freak, almost certainly. Freak, then maybe get a little angry, a bit sick perhaps. *But she has to know. What I am, what lies at the heart of me. What I have to do to stay sane.*

He didn't need the turned heads to know he looked good. Women, some men, breaking stride as he swept along the pavement. *Are you seeing, Jessie? They want me, every one of them. All I have to do is stop, smile, speak and I can have any one I choose: blood and sex. But it won't stop the hunger. Only you can do that, Jessica Grant. I think you're the only one who can make the pain go away. But you don't want to. I offered you my life and you still dismiss me. I am a monster in your eyes, and after tonight it's going to get worse ...* He tried to force himself not to care.

The club was incredibly hot, the amount of energy being generated by the bodies inside pressed close together could have powered the National Grid. A blue cloud of smoke hung over the heads of the occupants, the air smelled of perfume, BO, machine-smoke and regurgitated alcohol and amid all this, people were dancing. Groin-to-groin couples swayed in time, more or less, to the beat of a relentless dance track.

Sil was, by now, one of the dancers. Almost as soon as we'd walked in he'd found himself a companion: a small, blonde girl with very long hair and a white lace dress which made me look positively nunnery-bound in my body-hugging red number. She was all over him now, out on the dance floor, wrapping her lean limbs up and down his body as they simulated something multiple-orgasmic to the electric rhythm. He danced well, fluidly. As if he was trying not to think.

'Hey!' I looked at the person who'd arrived next to me. He was tall, skinny and dark with hair caught up in a pony-tail at the back. Werewolf. 'D'you want to dance?'

'I'm –' I was going to make an excuse, maybe cite the greasy cocktail I was drinking, but one look at Sil's ecstatic face as his partner danced in closer, and I changed my mind. 'Yeah, why not?'

I let myself be whirled into the press of bodies on the dance floor. To my surprise, the werewolf was a pretty good dancer, and we bounced along in harmony for a while. Then he leaned in close. 'Didn't you use to go out with Cameron? Thought I recognised your face. Who'd you come with tonight?'

I jerked a thumb at Sil, dancing with his eyes closed now as his new friend gyrated herself against him.

'Him.'

'Oh, yeah, right. Are you two, y'know, like an item, then?'

'No. Absolutely not. In fact, about as far away from an item as you can get. Decidedly single.'

'Cool.'

The rhythm changed to something slower, silkier; the lights became blue. The smell changed too, the chemical scent from the smoke machine replaced by something heavier, deeper, more like incense, woody and intense. A wailing vocal harmonic started up over the top of the music and the werewolf moved in closer, put his arms around me. 'What's your name?'

'Tobe.'

Pressed together like this, it was a lot easier to talk. 'And you knew me when I was with Cameron?'

'Yeah. It was terrible, what they did to him.'

'The court said it was a misunderstanding. Tragic but not anyone's fault.' I trotted out the party line; inside I was clenched.

'Yeah, I heard you gave evidence. Cameron would never have hurt anyone.' Tobe leaned into me. He smelled of Aramis and dope, and it was vaguely comforting. '*Never.*'

'No.'

'And it wouldn't have happened if he'd been human.'

I felt a sudden jolt to my stomach. Humans and Otherworlders. Which side did I belong on? Did I have to choose? And what would happen if I did?

We were dancing very, *very* close now. I could feel the particular werewolf energy against my skin, dancing along with us. This Tobe was well in control of his nature but there were other parts of him he couldn't control and I could tell that he thought his luck was definitely in tonight. 'You're a great dancer, Jessica.'

'Thanks.' I was watching Sil but because Tobe was taller than me I had to look sideways around his chest. When we next circled, Sil had his face tight into the neck of his partner. A thin trickle of blood was running down her shoulder into the white lace of her dress, but her head was thrown back, her mouth curved into a slack line of acquiescent bliss. 'God!'

'What?'

'He's feeding off her!'

Tobe shrugged. 'That's why she's here. Tell you what,' he dropped his mouth against my ear, 'they've got rooms, why don't we go on back there? I could, y'know, *change* for you.' His tongue flickered out along my neck. 'Did Cameron ever change while you were doing it? It'll drive you *wild*, know what I'm saying?'

Sil was a vampire. Well, I'd hardly thought he was some guy with odd dentistry and an especially effective skin-care regime, had I? Vampire. Yes. Blood-sucker. Hormone-junkie. *Otherworlder.* Not my problem.

Tobe was running his fingers up and down my spine, lingering a little longer each time around the lower levels. I moved a step back. 'Look, I'm sorry, you're very sweet, but –'

'It's the vamp, huh? You two've been watching each other all night. What is it, you into threesomes? I can do that, yeah.'

'No, it's – what do you mean, watching each other?'

'You can't take your eyes off him and he's been looking over here every time that blonde bitch took her hands off his cock long enough for him to focus.' Tobe looked curiously into my face. 'You *sure* you're not together?'

The music was still playing, a curious throbbing tone like a metal pulse. Hypnotic. 'Positive.'

'Then maybe you should be.' And Tobe released me, walking off into the crowd circling the dance floor. Bodies coupled, parted, writhed. Down on the floor a demon of some kind was indulging itself, feeding on the aura of a young man who squirmed and gasped in the kind of rapture

I would normally expect to be on-screen and faked. I seemed to be the only single-unit in the room.

A touch on my shoulder and I whirled, ready to punch. But it was Sil, flushed and panting as though he'd run the circuit, pupils dilated to almost cover the silver of his eyes. 'Hey.'

'You didn't tell me it would be like *this*.' I waved a hand at the conjoined bodies, the occasional spray of blood, the sounds of moaning overlaying the regular thump of the beat.

He shrugged and wiped the back of his hand over his mouth. 'It varies. Sometimes it's crazy, other times it's more laid back. Like this.'

'How often do you *do* this?' I asked, thinking – this is *laid back*?

'Not often. It's just …' And he shrugged again. 'Do you want to go?' His eyes were unfocused, sliding from my face to the action and back again, and for all the healthy glow of his skin, he was shivering slightly.

'Are you okay?'

'I – yes, I – ' I saw the blonde he'd bitten, sitting on the floor at the other side of the room with her head on her arms. 'I think we should go.'

'She's not going to change, is she? You haven't vamped her?'

'What?' Sil dragged his eyes back to me, reluctantly. 'Oh, her. No. I let go before the demon seeded into her.' Again his eyes went back to the bloodstained floor.

'You old romantic, you.'

A smile and a flash of fangs. 'Yeah, well. That *would* be illegal.'

We walked unnoticed back to the entrance of the club, where I collected my tranq bag from a human cloakroom attendant. I saw Tobe deep in discussion with a pretty dark girl, her braided hair piled on top of her head. As we walked past he looked up and winked.

'He try to pick you up?'

'A bit.'

'Yet you're leaving with me.' Sil lurched and put a hand against a bridge parapet to steady himself. 'Wow. She'd had a skinful, that young lady. Second-hand vodka always gets me this way. Why didn't you go with him? Bit scruffy but that's the wolves for you; when the Dimensional attributes were being handed out, the vamps definitely got all the style.'

'You think? You're creaking.'

'That's the boots. Seriously, Jessie, why *didn't* you go? Even as a recreational shag? I mean, it's not as if you've not done werewolves before, meant to be pretty good as a species, so I hear. Lots of howling action.' He wiggled his hips suggestively, lurched again and hiccupped. 'Bugger.'

'You're pissed.'

'Mmmmm.' Light, gymnastic, he leapt up on to the bridge parapet, began walking along with his arms outstretched. 'At least I'm not singing. So, go on then. Why didn't you go make jiggy-jiggy with the beasty-boy there?' He turned a graceful, if wobbly, cartwheel along the handrail, landing back on the pavement next to me.

'Do you really think I'm the kind of girl to go off with some bloke she's just met in a club? What about the danger?'

'Oh come on, you're not *that* dangerous.'

'Ha, ha. Do you really think I'm that much of a tart?'

Sil leaned back against the edge of the bridge. 'It's been a long time since Cameron. I wouldn't blame you for wanting a bit of action. Werewolves are supposed to be addictive, you know. One's never enough.'

'I wouldn't know. I never slept with Cameron.'

The instant the words were out I wanted to shoot myself.

I covered my mouth with my hand and bit my lip. Sil's eyes widened.

'But ... but it looked as if you and he were practically living together! What were you waiting for, a ring?'

'I didn't say – look, I've been drinking, too. Let's forget it, okay?'

Sil put his hands on my shoulders and pulled me around. 'No. What really happened with you and him, Jessie?'

'I can't tell you!' I could smell vodka coming from him, but it wasn't on his breath, it was more like it came from inside him, making his skin and hair smell of it. 'I *can't*, Sil, it's not safe!'

'He's been dead, what, a year?'

I nodded. 'Ten months.'

'So, where's the harm?'

I took a shaky breath. Ever since that showdown, when Enforcement had turned up mob-handed and Eleanor had ended up ripping Cameron to pieces with silver bullets, I'd sworn that everything Cam had told me would die with him. It had been terrible, tragic, a mistake. 'He –'

'Didn't you love him? Is that it, Jessie?'

'I did, but not like that. Sil, Cameron was gay. I was his cover.'

Sil let go of my shoulders and leaned his head so far back over the edge of the bridge I was afraid he'd fall. He was laughing. 'A gay *werewolf*? I didn't even know that was possible! Oh, that's terrific!'

'You don't understand! Werewolves are all about dominance, about power. Imagine what it's like to be so in love with your dominant male that you have trouble staying the same shape when he's about! How long do you think you can last, if you won't fight him, won't mate with the ones he's chosen for you, can't think straight when he's around? So Cameron asked me to pretend. It took some of the pressure off; people stopped asking awkward questions.'

'And the day he was killed?'

'Cameron had formed a focus for gay shifters. They were going to come out *en masse*, form their own group. Not a pack, because there were wolves and cats and all sorts, but a group. Word got out, someone overheard and misunderstood the nature of his rally. It got round that he was going to stage a challenge for the leadership of his pack, that he didn't care who got hurt and – '

'Enforcement, silver bullets, the end.'

I blotted my cheeks with my fingers. 'It wasn't fair. He would never have hurt anybody. It shouldn't have happened.'

'I'm sorry.'

This time I shrugged.

'God, I am *sooooo* pissed.' Sil hiccupped again. 'Jessie – '

'What now? More intrusive questions about my love life? You must *swear*, Sil, not to say anything about what I told you. Because Cameron died the other gay shifters never did come out; there's a lot of people could get hurt if it became general knowledge.'

'You are lovely, you know that?'

'Sil, don't.'

'Don't?'

'Don't come on to me when you've got a stomach full of some girl's blood.'

'My side of the fence now. Remember? When it comes to it, Jessie, when it comes right down to it, you aren't human any more. You don't have the luxury of being all censorious and upright about it, not when half your genetics is something worse than vampire. You don't know yet, you've not been put in the position, but one day – you'll be faced with some situation and *something* will out. It may be demon.' He shouldered himself away from the stonework and took a staggering few steps forward. 'And when that happens, we'll go back to the club. See what you think of it then, when you're one of the ones down on the floor with someone's life hanging there, right in front of you, for the taking.' His fangs slid into place, locked down, and for a moment I thought he was going to lunge at me, he looked so tense and excited.

'You certainly know how to sweet-talk a girl. No wonder you're never short of them.' The bitter edge to my voice seemed to bring him down a bit.

'Yeah. And doesn't that just screw you up.'

'What are you insinuating?'

'You know.'

'You reckon that I'm desperate for you?'

'Oh, you're fooling no-one. You're avoiding it.'

I smacked him in the face, said, 'Avoid that, you bastard,' and stalked off.

Sil followed her home without being spotted, and leaned against a convenient garden wall, waiting until her bedroom light went out. He listened to the distant sounds of taps running and tried to ignore the soft sound of crying that came two minutes after the darkness. *My side of the line now, Jessica.* He rubbed his head. Drawing out his demon had hurt more than he'd expected, and he certainly hadn't expected to be around for the aftermath – his demon writhed at the memory of its near-death experience. *You broke Malfaire's magic. Are you thinking about that, up in your room, with the chocolate wrappers and the old school photographs? Are you wondering how you did it, what it means? What you might become?*

The crying broke into hiccups and he felt something drag inside him. His demon, still reeling from the double

193

effect of fresh blood and second-hand alcohol, was reacting sluggishly to her misery. Or rather, to his reaction to her misery. *Never done that before. But maybe I've never felt like this before, have I?*

A flashback, and suddenly his demon sobered up. *Watching from a distance, the doctor arriving. His white face, shaking head, at the door, my wife ... God, my wife, breaking down, and I couldn't touch her, couldn't reach her to tell her ... The funeral, one among many in that vicious influenza-ridden time, two small wreaths and the bunch of hastily picked daisies that I barely had time to lay before the other mourners arrived. The white coffins ...*

He wiped his hand across his face, amazed to find it wet. *Sadness? Where did that come from?* His teeth gritted, fangs nicking his lip, as he felt his demon squirm for a second under the sensation. *If only Jess knew, just for one second, what it was to be vampire. What it felt like to have to live without emotion, to know it was there and be forced to ride the instinct and the reaction without allowing any of the repercussions to cut through and let you see what you had become.*

The hiccups had stopped now; the only sound coming from Jessie's room was a kind of sleep-sob as she settled into troubled dreaming. Sil stared at her window for a moment longer, his demon whirling smugly, then bunched a fist. *I look great. I'm strong. I'll live another two hundred years at least. I can glamour humans into doing anything I want them to. Fuck you, Jessica. Fuck you, fuck the Protection Act, fuck it all.* A stride that broke into a jog and then into a run and he was out into the main street, heading back towards the club by the river.

Chapter Eighteen

Liam looked me over as I arrived at the office in my pointedly very different outfit of jeans and T-shirt. 'Sil not with you?'

I looked around exaggeratedly. 'Ooh, no. I wonder what could have happened to him? Maybe I sleep-kill. Anyway, thought today was your turn for the annual day off?'

'Yes, Mister Scrooge, it was. But ... I decided to come in.' Liam pushed a still-tepid mug of coffee my way. 'Sarah's taken Charlotte to visit her mother. That's Sarah's mother, what with her being Charlotte's mother herself and everything. Didn't fancy sitting in the house on my own, might be expected to perform some archaic "man task" like hanging a door or something. Besides, yesterday –'

'Yesterday was mad, I'm sorry.' I had a sudden, horrible mental jigsaw-image of some of yesterday's events, a bit like a 'previously, in my life' pre-credits sequence. 'Wow. Yes. Really mad.'

'Something to do with the bloods?'

I'd forgotten Liam's ability to put two-and-two together and make ... well, yes, in this case four, but sometimes he'd get two-and-two to make bread pudding. 'It ... there are *implications*, Liam. Things might be difficult.'

'Tell me.'

And I did. So, shoot me, Liam's been my friend a long time, and I know how to do edited highlights. It took me two coffees and a large bar of Galaxy to cover everything I was willing to cover, and I was sniffing again by the time I got to the end.

'Oh, Jessie.' Liam had tears in his own eyes and I saw his

gaze keep turning to the framed photo of his baby daughter which he kept on his desk. 'Your poor parents.'

'What about poor me?' I sniffed again and wiped my nose on my sleeve. 'I don't even know what species I am.'

He shrugged. 'You cry like a woman. You shovel chocolate down your neck like a woman, you're a miserable cow once a month, you think your bum is fat, you go all gooey over baby pictures and you dribble over Zan and Sil. Tell me how you could be any *more* human and I'll go and buy you a bottle of it.'

'Well, thank you, Mr Supportive. I take back everything I said about you being gay.'

Liam grinned. 'Thanks. Now. You need to find out all you can about the ghyst-demons, I suppose. And you need to do it before Malfaire recovers from his ass-whupping and comes after you, yes?'

I froze, hand halfway to a Kit Kat. 'God, I never thought … he's not going to take it well, is he?'

'Uh, no, Jessie, probably not. So, what I was thinking – ' He typed rapidly for a moment and a large flashing icon descended on the middle of his screen. 'I've forwarded it to you, too.'

I groaned. 'Please tell me that's not what I think it is.'

'Copies of all the info-mails the council have sent us for the last five years. All the accumulated wisdom of the ages.' He bent down and fetched up from under his desk the papers that I stood on to reach the so-called hidden chocolate, split the pile in two and slammed half down on my desk, with an accompanying puff of dust and smell of old budgie cages. 'And these are the ones from before we all went digital. There's bound to be something in here somewhere.'

I poked the papers. 'Is there an index?'

'No. I started to make one a couple of years ago but,'

a shrug, 'you know, life intervened and everything. So I guess we just have to truck through all of them.' He leaned forward. 'Are you okay? I mean, wouldn't you be better leaving this to me and taking some time off? You still look pretty shitty.'

'Pay cut, that man.' But I was flattered that he'd noticed, when all Sil had done was nag me about not being human. There was a tiny prickle down my spine, like a woodlouse had crawled up my shirt. *Not human* ...

'What are we doing?' Sil's lanky figure slunk into view. 'Making up filthy headlines again?'

Now he *was* wearing last night's clothes, unless his wardrobe held more than one pair of leather trousers and lace-effect shirt. He looked slightly spaced-out and he'd tied his hair back to show off his cheekbones. 'Second-hand alcohol,' he said, throwing himself into the spare chair like he belonged there and drinking the now stone-cold coffee that I'd left in my mug down in one. 'What a night.'

His demon was almost asleep inside him; I could feel its drowsy relish. 'Well, as long as one of us had a good time.' I felt shrewish and snappy and not sure why. 'Try to stay awake long enough to help go through these. We're looking for mentions of ghyst.'

Sil picked up some of the papers and winked at me in an annoying way. 'Okay, boss.'

'Liam and I can split the e-versions; I'll do the last three years, Liam you do the two years before, Sil, you can do the old paper copies. Oh, and make more coffee.'

We sat and skimmed through the council hand-outs until our eyes bulged.

'Otherworld office has all this kind of thing on e-files.' Sil had put his feet up on Liam's desk and was flipping pages at twice the speed that we could have read at, being mere ... humans.

'I know. I hacked in. Couldn't open your file. I think Zan might be reading them your end. Or trying to stop us getting in.' Liam said without looking up.

'He will have run a word-search function.'

'All right, don't rub it in, we all know how much better you are than us,' I said irritably. The dust from the paper copies was in my eyes now and they itched, although not as much as my hands from wanting to punch Sil firmly in his self-satisfied face. 'We don't want to have to rely on Zan beating us to it. Even if he's quite clearly going to.'

'Just saying,' he turned over a page, infuriatingly calmly, 'that's all. Gotcha!' Sil laid down his leaflet like a winning poker hand. 'Here. Ghyst-demon.' He pushed the paper towards me, but the council's relentless money-saving investment in tiny print meant that we all ended up huddled together trying to read.

'Oh, no.' I might not have a vampire's skills, but I could speed read when I wanted to. 'No.' Shoved my chair back so hard that it cannoned off the far wall and nearly dropped me on the floor.

The boys exchanged a look. 'It might not be that bad, Jessie.'

'Right.' I tapped the offending page and quoted. '"Ghyst-demon. Rare and semi-mythical, blah blah ... rumoured to be unable to be killed, except by its own flesh and blood." Look, they've spelled immortal with only one "m".'

Sil patted my arm. 'Well, at least we know now why Malfaire wants you. If you're on his side he's invincible. If not – '

' – then I'm better off dead,' I finished. 'Oh, shit.'

'If you die, do I get your computer?' Liam asked, shakily trying to lighten the mood. 'And your special mug?'

I sat with my head in my hands. If Malfaire killed me, there would be nothing on earth to stop him from forming an army of ghouls, Shadows, any vampire that felt restricted by the current rules and regulations, any Otherworlder, in fact, that wanted to stage a take-over bid. If he left me alive, then he'd want me to fight alongside him.

'Jessie.' Sil's patting had turned into more of a rub. 'You're still under my protection.'

'Oh yeah, and that worked really well last time, didn't it? I seem to remember that you ... It wouldn't have ended well.' I didn't even look up. 'What do I do? Liam?'

'He won't kill you.' Liam sounded desperate. 'He won't. You're his daughter. I couldn't harm Charlotte for all the money in the world, and he must have some kind of feelings for you, otherwise why search you out? Why not let it lie? You'd never have found out that you were anything to do with him otherwise.'

'Perhaps he wants to be sure of winning.' Sil stood and leaned against the desk, legs crossed and hands in pockets. 'If he's certain that there's no danger to him, he can attack with impunity.' He seemed to come to a decision. 'Jessie, I think you ought to move in with Zan and me.'

I blinked. 'What, the pair of you live in one house? It must be like an episode of *Big Bang Theory* round your place. Anyway, I've got a flat, and I don't anticipate moving out any time soon.'

Now Sil crouched down to look me straight in the eye. 'Remember danger, Jessie? Remember the big bad demon who wants you dead? If you're in Vampire Central then we can both keep an eye on you, and anywhere has to be more secure than your place.'

'Vegan Central,' added Liam.

'You really call your place Vampire Central?' Sil lived

in an impressive three-storey Georgian house near York Minster. You could see Betty's Tea Room from one of the upstairs bathrooms, if you stood on the vanity unit; just don't ask me how I know. 'Rachel needs me to pay the rent.'

'Yes, but I glamoured Rachel once. That means she's under my ... ah, I was going to say power, but suddenly realise that makes me sound like a stage hypnotist. I've formed a mental link with her. I can make her forget that you ever lived there. Just like this.' And Sil clicked his fingers. 'So we can do this the easy way – the "I'm moving out for a few days" way – or we can do it the hard way.' He clicked his fingers again. 'Leaving you nowhere to go back to, when all this is over.'

'Bastard,' I managed, but my heart wasn't really in it.

'Sensible bastard, though,' Liam said. 'At least it would mean you had back-up 24/7.'

'Or two more people to have to worry about.' I sighed. It was a foregone conclusion already, obviously. I couldn't think of a good reason not to do as Sil said, and a hundred reasons to go along with it, number one being 'I don't want to die alone'. 'And what about Rach? What if Malfaire decides to ... I dunno, find out where I've gone? He might ... torture her.'

'Force her to eat a cream scone?' Liam gave me a direct look. 'Malfaire hasn't exactly had to struggle to find you so far, has he? You're going to the vamps for protection, not to hide. I think he'll know where you are if he wants you.'

'Well, that's reassuring,' I said. 'Remind me to send you on that empathy course next time it comes round.'

'That would be dangerously close to Professional Development, and you know what you always say about that ...' Liam gave me a grin, but it was thin.

We were whistling in the wind, and we all knew it.

Chapter Nineteen

We put in possibly the least effective working day ever, mostly consisting of picturesque brooding on Sil's part, half-heartedly monitoring the tracker programme on mine and fiddling with the pencil sharpener on Liam's, but six o'clock eventually rolled around. 'Better go home.' I shut down the computer and eased my back. 'No callouts, Liam, so we can all leave.'

'Great! I'll get a takeaway and sit around the house in my pants. What? Sarah's at her mother's, there have *got* to be *some* perks ...'

'I'll buzz Zan to expect us.' Sil took out his mobile.

'Uh-huh. I need to go back to the flat tonight. Just tonight. It's all right, I've given in to your macho demands that I come to your place. But, you know, I need to pack.'

'Oh God, not all of it,' Sil groaned. 'Not the cuddly toys as well.'

'Only for tonight, while I ... how do you know about the cuddly toys?'

Sil sighed. 'I have been in your flat, remember.'

'Only when Malfaire ...'

'And I had to change my clothes.'

'You changed in *my bedroom*?' Indignation made me shrill.

'I'm not sure. It was either your bedroom or a small offshoot of Hamleys' toyshop, with an option on Cadbury's best-selling chocolates and photographs of girls in school uniform ... I really don't think that this is important right now.'

Liam sighed. 'Just one more night, Sil.' He put on his

coat. 'And I shall see you both back here tomorrow morning, bright and shiny and probably wearing each other's jumpers.'

'Shut up, Liam.' If I'd had my mobile to hand I would have thrown it at him, but it was in the pocket of my coat, which was hung up by the door. 'Do you really have to come everywhere with me, Sil? What about last night; you let me go home alone then.'

Sil looked as if he was about to say something, then changed his mind. 'Yep, everywhere.' He pulled his soft black coat around himself like a cloak. 'It might prevent Malfaire from harming you, if he's got an audience.'

'Oh yeah, 'cos that always stops the bad guys,' I said sarcastically, dragging my coat down from the door and over my shoulders. Liam made a face.

'You two should *so* get it on.'

This time both of us spoke in unison. 'Shut up, Liam,' and Sil held the door open for me, taking my arm as we marched out in pretended umbrage. At least, my umbrage was pretend, I couldn't speak for Sil's, but he was walking fast and unevenly, which was usually a sign that the vampire was pissed off.

'Slow down!'

'Why? You're in danger, or haven't you heard?'

'Because at this rate, Malfaire won't need to attack, he can wait for me to catch fire from the air friction. I'm not vampire, Sil. If you want to keep belting around like that then you're going to have to let go of me first.'

Slowly he released me. 'Sorry.'

'Wow, you're apologising again? Call the *Guinness Book of Records*. Anyway, why don't we take a taxi?'

'Because I can't guarantee that a taxi-driver hasn't been glamoured to drive straight into the river with you.' He then muttered something which sounded like 'merciful relief for us all' but I charitably ignored it.

We headed down the main tourist area, now empty of all but the most determined sightseer, and towards the river. As we reached the walkway which led down the side of the bridge, I touched his arm. 'Sil, I'm sorry, too.'

'What?' He swung round towards me.

'About – you know. Everything. I never meant us to be enemies.'

'Enemies. Is that what we are?' His hair was escaping, one wisp at a time, from the ponytail behind his head, the locks joining to form a flopping straggle that made his cheeks look thinner and paler than usual.

'I'm scared,' I finally confessed. 'I don't know what to do. I don't need any more people with grudges against me. Can't we go back to how we used to be when you first came to work for me?'

His eyes softened, running to that almost blue-grey that they turned when he was being nice. 'Oh, yes?' He took a step towards me. 'And how was that again?'

I couldn't help myself. I wanted to but I felt so shaky, so confused, and Sil was standing there all nicely rumpled and, well, *there*. I stepped in, and his arms came around me and pulled me close until I could feel the solidity of his body against mine. As he tilted his head forward, I lifted my chin and moved towards his mouth as though he'd become magnetic.

There must have been mere millimetres of air between our lips, when I was hit a massive blow from the side and sent tumbling on to the cobbles with a wight on top of me, its white-sheeted, skeletal form pinning me to the ground. Sil made it two steps before another wight grabbed him around the neck and pulled him backwards down on to the flagstones beside the river.

The wights fought like Schwarzenegger on crack. I saw Sil's head slam into the pavement just before I was dragged under the bridge by the wight which had me. It used my hair as a handle to hold me down whilst its bones were everywhere, striking out at me. Every blow connected, every blow hurt and with each impact my hair was pulled a little tighter. I kicked out at the legs but there was no flesh to impact on, no muscles to bruise, only a hawser-like strength.

The lipless face came in close, grinning obscenely with the mouth open for a bite which would remove half my cheek. I summoned all my hatred in one solid, leaden ball, twisted around, ignoring the pain from my head, then flung myself down on to the ground with the unbalanced wight underneath me.

There was a satisfying snapping sound as part of the ribcage gave way, shards of bone stabbing into the palms of my hands, with the wight making a noise like a hurricane trapped in a lift shaft and struggling to bring its legs underneath it. I sat on its damaged chest, one of its arms pinned under my knee, and tried to peer out of the gloom to see what was happening to Sil, but the wight took the opportunity to bring its free arm up and elbow me in the side of the head. My vision swung so that the lights across the river dipped and appeared to fall into the water for a few seconds. Without thinking I struck out sideways, catching the arm on the downswing and giving it such momentum that it bounced off the flagstones with a sound like a whip-crack. 'You *bastard*!'

I didn't think, I reacted. Leaned forward further into the shattered ribs and grabbed at the skull with both hands, which freed the wight's arms. It closed them around my body, grabbing my waist and squeezing until it felt as though my kidneys were being forced into my windpipe, but I didn't let go; I pulled at the skull and twisted. Kept on pulling, twisting until with one final crack the skull came free of the spinal column and the body collapsed back.

I slowly became aware of the splinters of bone piercing my legs and my face dripping blood; my hands were peppered with tiny slices from the broken ribs. But I was *alive*.

There was no noise from the walkway beyond the black cavern. Nothing but the distant cries of revellers heading home, a muted traffic whoosh from the bridge above. I disentangled myself from the remains of the wight and dragged myself on shaky legs to the corner of the steps, where I could grab on to the stonework for support and move hand-over-hand until I was in the open air. 'Sil?'

He was braced against the brick wall, hands on thighs, bent nearly double and was gasping for breath, but, like me, alive. Head raised at my voice. 'Jessie?'

His eyes were swollen and there was a bite out of his neck. 'You okay?' I couldn't move to get any closer; it was taking all my energy to hang on to the step in front of me.

'Yes.'

'Where is it?'

He flicked his head at the water. 'Threw it in the river.' Coughed deeply and retched. 'Yours?'

'Pulled its head off.'

We hung in our random positions for a few moments, then caught each other's eye and started laughing, the breathless, hysterical laughter of people who hadn't expected to survive. Hiccupping, ridiculous laughing, until tears made my face sting, and Sil had a coughing fit which brought him to his knees on the cobbles.

'I think I peed myself.' I held my arms around me to ease

the ache in my stomach, blood from the bone-cuts smeared across my T-shirt. 'Ow, that hurts.'

Sil had to climb up the side of the building to get upright, ending up facing the brickwork with his forehead resting against it. 'We need to get out of here.'

'Let's get back to the flat. Although I warn you, Rach might ask some very pointed questions about your presence. Either that or flirt with you, but I think her blood might be ninety per cent soya.'

'Not sure I can walk, Jessie.' Sil flicked a hand towards his leg. 'Got a bit … bitten …' The giggles threatened again briefly, but he managed to contain them.

'You'll have to lean on me.' Cautiously, because I wasn't completely sure of my own roadworthiness, I slid my way over to him and got an arm around his waist. Sil put his arm across my shoulders and we began a strange, limping process along the river walk. I tried to ignore how our bodies moved in rhythm and how he felt so cool and hard against me.

'Bloody hell man, don't you ever *eat*?'

'Jessie, I'm trying *very, very hard* not to notice the fact that you are bleeding from at least three places. This is no time to bring up the subject of food!'

'All right, forget I mentioned – '

And we stopped. Five strides ahead of us stood Malfaire, a Shadow at either side. He was watching us come, a quizzical eyebrow kinked and a half-smile on his impeccable lips. I wondered how long he'd been working on that expression.

'Good evening,' he said. 'And how are the love-birds flitting tonight, hmm?'

'Piss off.' Not exactly a quip to be proud of I know, but not bad for someone as beaten-up as I was.

'Just heading home, are we? Are you finally intending to indulge our young vampire in his darkest desires, Jessica?'

Sil hissed. I could feel his demon rising, but it couldn't help him. His body was too weak to sustain another attack.

Malfaire was looking us up and down so insolently, so *knowingly*, that I felt myself blush. 'What do you want?'

'Want? Well, I want you, Jessica, did I not say?'

'And the wights?'

He made a dismissive gesture with both hands. 'A courtesy detail. Flowers seemed inappropriate. And less lethal.' He took a step closer and the Shadows came with him. 'You're my daughter, a chip off the old block, as I think you proved. Despatching a pair of wights was very impressive.' Still coming. 'I am giving you a final chance to listen to reason and come and fight alongside me, because the alternative will not be pleasant. But,' he shrugged, 'there you go, some people need a lot of persuasion.'

I stepped back and stumbled over a metal hook, the kind of thing the rivermen used to pull the boats to shore. It banged my already bruised ankle and tears came into my eyes. 'You want me dead.'

'Baldly put, but – yes, if you refuse to fight *with* me, then you must be *against* me.' Another dismissive wave. 'Although I think simply killing you would rather spoil the fun, don't you?' His gaze flickered over Sil. 'I can do that at any time. But there are so many that you care for, I think I might enjoy reducing their number a little first. While you watch, and appreciate their pain.'

The Shadows moved a step closer and I bent down and snatched up the rusty metal hook. 'Get those things away from us, you arrogant git.'

Malfaire stared at me for a second, then grinned. 'My dear, I don't think for one second that you mean me harm. After all, you're a council employee, so you keep telling everyone, as though by denying your heritage you can make it cease to exist.'

By now there was only a couple of feet between us, and I could feel the chill air coming from the Shadows. If I'd leaned forward I could have kissed him. 'You're willing to gamble?'

Sil hissed again. 'Your vampire knows more about killing than you do, Jessie.' Malfaire's voice was silky. 'Why don't you let him threaten me? It would be far more convincing.'

'He's *not* "my vampire".' The metal was chilly, rough under my fingers. 'And he couldn't kill you; it has to be me. Your own flesh and blood, Malfaire. That's what it would take to kill you. And that's me.'

There was more space between us now. Without my noticing, Malfaire had pulled back, although the Shadows were still way, *way* too close for comfort. 'You – ' was all Malfaire had time to say, before I raised my arm and waved the metal hook and Malfaire was standing close enough that the razor-sharp tip caught in his impeccable clothing, tangled in his beautiful coat and ripped through it like tissue paper. Malfaire looked down in shock. I, equally shocked, tried to pull free but somehow he took an inadvertent step towards me and the coiled iron dug deep. As I flailed, feeling the resistance of his body, the hook snatched upward.

His hands fluttered. Bright blood fanned from the wound as he staggered under the impact and the stain began creeping from behind his clothes. I just stood and stared. Firstly at Malfaire, who was grappling with both hands in the air, as though he was trying to force breaths in, and then at the stained metal in my hand.

'For fuck's sake let's get out of here.' Sil half-turned, but I couldn't move, watching Malfaire pumping blood over the pavement and his impeccable suit. He leaned forward, struggling for air and I took half a step towards him, wanting ... *needing* to help.

Sil tugged at me. 'Jessie! There's no *time*,' and I simultaneously felt the brush of a Shadow at my back and Sil's bodyweight hitting me sideways on. I grabbed at him but he kept moving and we both fell, hitting the river tangled together in a slowly rotating heap of coat and limbs.

Chapter Twenty

The water clanged closed over our heads like a bell. Sil was a whirling presence beside me; the frantic rippling and gasping seemed to indicate that vampires had all the natural buoyancy of a house-brick. The sinking went on as we were swept downstream. The hull of a moored barge threatened to crush us, I grabbed at Sil, at passing flotsam, but the current carried us too fast to fight. We surfaced and sank, sank and surfaced, finally crashing into a small rowing boat which had jammed against a bridge support, and managing to surface together.

'Police.' I gasped. 'I ought ...' My lungs ached. I tried to hang on to the side of the boat but my fingers were numb and had no grip and we were swept another hundred yards before an underwater obstruction provided us with another breathing space. 'It was an accident, Sil! I never meant ...'

'Forget police.' Sil shook his head. 'We have to get out of here. Going to freeze to death.'

The spring had brought the usual flood of meltwater down from the high moors, and although the air temperature was pleasantly mild, the water was bitterly cold. I'd lost the feeling in my legs. I wouldn't be able to make the scramble up the nearby bank without falling back into the water. 'Can't.'

Sil closed his eyes. 'Me, neither.' Under the water his hand fumbled for mine and squeezed. I felt the cuts along my palm.

'Your demon can.'

Now his eyes opened. 'What?'

'You don't need to separate, just let it have control. Call it.'

'It isn't like having a dog, Jessie. My demon ...' He let go

210

of my hand and crossed the released arm over his chest. 'It will try to preserve itself, do you understand?'

I held up my released hand. The cold water had washed clean the cuts, but they gaped like open mouths. 'Use blood.'

'I – ' He tried to turn his head away, but his eyes wouldn't move from the bright beads of blood appearing along the edge of my hand. 'Don't do this.'

'Have you got a better plan?' My teeth chattered.

'No, but – you can't.' His face was paling. 'You *don't* understand. When … when Malfaire had us … we were going to die. My demon is all about self-preservation. If I let it have control it will save me, if it can but … it will be the demon in charge, not me.'

I looked him in the eye and whispered, 'I trust you. You won't let it seed.'

There was a moment's silence. Then he said, 'Jessie,' and let loose.

It only took a second – his demon must have been hovering under the surface. It burst its way free, half in and half out of his body; a snatch and it had grabbed my hand, licking the arc of blood from my grey-white skin with a tongue which felt like fire against the chill. I closed my eyes so as not to see. 'We need to get out of the water,' I said, trying to sound calm. I didn't want to panic the demon into doing something unnecessarily brutal – of course, being a demon, it wouldn't see anything unnecessary in brutality – but I was becoming increasingly aware that outlying parts of my body were no longer receiving brain signals. 'Can you get us out?'

And now I met the demon's eyes, black-red, like domesticated hell. 'Out?' it said, pulling its mouth free of my hand.

'Out of the water.' Then, because it seemed to want to go straight back to licking my palm. 'There's more blood, if we get out of the water.'

'More?' It moved Sil's body like a puppeteer, moving as part of him and yet distinct. I'd never asked a vampire what it felt like to let the demon have control and I didn't think I wanted to know. 'More!'

The grip on my hand intensified and the demon propelled us through the water, then leapt for the bank. He hit it, dragging me along by the wrist, which smacked me into the concrete embankment, then crawled up the near-vertical wall and on to the cobbled rise.

Then he struck. I didn't have time to brace myself or prepare at all; he hit me in the vein in the side of my neck, but maybe because I was so cold it didn't really hurt. All I could feel was the heat of his mouth against my skin and a kind of aching, heavy sensation which ran down the muscles of my arm.

There was something very sexual about it, the closeness of our bodies and the firmness of the demon's grip. Dreamily I felt his skin heating up as I lay in his arms, a warmth that made me tingle where our flesh touched, along with a pleasant drowsiness. My eyes flickered, lids too heavy to stay open.

Suddenly I thought back to the girl in the club. Her half-drugged look after Sil had fed. How much blood could a demon take? How much blood could a human afford to lose, and how fast, before the body went into shock? And, given my previous experiences, I had about another thirty seconds before it seeded into me ... 'Sil!' It came out as a squeak. The demon ignored me, although its eyes flicked open for a second; I saw them shine out hell-bright from under the fall of hair. 'Sil. Remember, I trust you.'

'He cannot hear you, human woman. I have his body and mind.'

'But he can send you back down, can't he? That's how it works – you are the *éminence grise* of the relationship, but he runs you.' Another rush of weakness. 'Sil. Please.'

The demon jolted. Another mouthful of me and it jerked again, then hurled itself upright and away. When I managed to move my poor, battered body into a sitting position, Sil's demon had slithered back to wherever it lived inside him and he was back in control, head down, on all fours.

'Hey.'

He looked up as I spoke. The fire-glow died away from his eyes but there was still blood spread along his cheek and on his mouth. '*God!*' Dazed, unfocused. He brought a hand up to his face and stared at it, as though he'd been expecting more fingers. 'What a power!'

'Oh, don't worry about it; I'm fine, hardly bleeding to death at all.'

Sil sat back, inhaling and flexing his fingers with his eyes shut. 'Oh,' he kept saying. 'Oh, let the devil take me now …'

'We need to get under cover.' I couldn't just sit here, I was freezing again. 'Sil?'

'Can't move. Need to ride this out.'

'You don't usually have any trouble in getting away from the scene of the crime. In fact, you're usually all energetic.'

'This is … your blood is …' He put a hand to his chest as though to either quieten his demon or make sure it was still there. 'It's *sensational*,' he slurred.

'Oh, great. Well, we'll both sit here then, shall we, while you enjoy the party in your head and I die of *gangrene*!'

'I can taste you.' He ran his tongue over his lips, over the tips of still-protruding fangs. 'It's sweet.' He shook his head in slow motion. '*God!*'

I tried to stand. 'Oh, damn.' A wave of dizziness broke over my head and the lamp-lit night disintegrated into thousands of tiny grey pieces. I clutched at the air and stumbled a couple of steps forward. My knees finally gave way and I plummeted on top of the vampire, who, at least, managed to catch me, although whether he knew he was doing it was debatable. 'Right. So *I* can't walk, either. Great. Hypothermia, here we come.'

I hadn't known it was possible to feel this cold. At least when we'd been submerged I'd been numb; now I could feel how much everything hurt. I tried to move from my position half-wrapped around Sil, his clammy coat dripping diesel-flavoured water on my face, and touched his skin.

'God! You're so *warm*!' His body was a temperature that I didn't think mine would ever reach again, outside the crematorium. 'How is that possible?'

'The blood,' he said, eyes still closed. 'It's burning through me like a furnace. I can feel you in my heart, in my veins, you're glowing like a sun in my head.'

'Why? It doesn't always do this, does it?'

A ponderous headshake. 'You –' he enunciated carefully – 'are pure Class A.' Sil stretched a hand free of his clinging coat and ripped the front of his shirt open, smiling as more of his pale skin was exposed to the night air.

'You're *high*.'

'I am. But I am also *warm*.' And Sil opened his eyes and smiled. His pupils were all over the place.

'We need to get under cover.' I looked around. A few yards further down, where the murky brown river's edge lapped against the cement of the river frontage, there was an indentation; storm drain, sewage outlet, right now I didn't care. 'If I can get out of the night air, I'll be okay. Just ... get my breath back and we can go home.'

Cautiously I tried to stand up but the filmy curtains of unconsciousness threatened to draw closed again, and I ended up crawling the ten yards to the mouth of the drain. Sil crawled alongside me, still smiling. The ground inside the tunnel was dry and sandy and thankfully free from rats. It was also out of the wind.

Sil collapsed and lay immobile, which was reassuring. The heat of his body was tremendous. I could see steam beginning to rise from beneath his coat, his black leather jeans looked as though they were drying already. Very, *very* carefully I moved one hand and laid it on his chest, where the skin was almost improbably smooth, only a brief line of hair running down the centre. The heat *hurt*.

Sil lay there. I half-raised my head to look down on him and felt my heart move. I mean, who wouldn't? Physically he was perfect. Slender and pale, stubbled enough to show off his faultless cheekbones and with eyes that changed colour more often than traffic lights. I couldn't help it. Although, God knows, I'd tried. Feeling anything for a vampire other than pure, hot-blooded lust, was asking to get your heart ripped out and handed back to you, dripping. And probably not in a metaphorical way, either.

Sil spoke without opening his eyes, it made me jump. 'You need to get warm all over.'

'I thought you'd passed out.'

Eyes switched open. 'Metabolising.' A thoughtful look at where the neck of my T-shirt gaped, revealing the double bite mark. 'I would really enjoy another hit though, if you're offering.'

'I'm not.'

'Shame.' He was still looking thoughtful, and his eyes were the pure grey of chinchilla fur. 'Why won't you let me warm you up? You're freezing to death, you've probably got exposure, and I'm burning up. What is the *matter* with you, Jessie?'

'Nothing.' I scooted a bit closer. The heat was radiating off him like a car bonnet in the sun, making my skin ache. Very carefully he reached out and began pulling the sodden T-shirt off my shoulders 'What are you doing?'

'Take it off and you'll warm up faster.'

I was clumsy, uncoordinated. My fingers hadn't recovered enough to grip the hem and pull it up over my head and I wasn't sure that what I was doing was sensible. Undressing in front of Sil, even an off-his-face Sil, had to have repercussions. 'I can't.'

'Yes.' Warm hands drew the T-shirt up my body.

'You're enjoying this.'

Huge, nearly white, his eyes dominated his face. 'You have no idea.'

'That's it! I'm not taking anything else off. I don't care if I freeze to death. I am *not* sitting around in a tunnel with you, in my knickers.'

'You're enjoying this too, aren't you?'

'What?'

'Stripping for me.' He looked down at my chest, which was quite nicely adorned with a pink-and-black stripey number, although I usually liked my nipples considerably less perky than they were at present. I folded my arms.

'I'm cold, all right?'

'Did I say anything?'

'You looked.'

Sil, somewhat wobbly, got to his knees and faced me. 'Jessie.' He reached out and ran his hands down my arms, the heat was almost unbearable. 'How long is it since you last had sex?'

'What's that got to do with anything?'

'You've got this whole attitude thing going on, and yet something in you wants me. My demon can feel it. What in the seven hells is going on with you? You push me away all the time, but – '

'God, you fancy yourself a bit, don't you?' I shut my eyes. It wasn't so bad if I couldn't see him. 'Four years.'

'You're *joking*! Four years since you last had sex? No wonder you're leaving a trail of pheromones that every vampire for miles can pick up. Why? Why so long?'

I shrugged. This was the bit that *really* hurt. It had been four years since I'd met Sil for the first time. Four years since I'd fallen completely for his sharp-tongued comebacks, his sniping, argumentative ways and that loose-limbed body. Four years. I was mad for him, but I didn't dare express it. And no-one else measured up. 'Work, I suppose.'

Yes, I wanted him. But I didn't want *this*. He had a demon riding his endocrine system, making him fight and crave and live on the edge so that it could taste the hormones and surf the highs. And, while I could just about bear to watch Sil behaving like all the others, I could only do it because no part of him, however small, had ever been mine. And it was moments like this, when he got close, which hurt the most.

'I always thought, maybe you and Liam – '

'Liam?' I was so appalled I almost forgot to shiver. 'You think I was shagging *Liam*?'

A shrug. 'He is a kind man.'

'You shag him then. Anyway, he's got Sarah and the baby.'

'Oh, so you *have* thought about it. But honestly, Jessie, four *years* – ' He sat back and dropped his hands. 'Go on. You're sitting there, horny as hell for me, well, here I am.' Now he held his arms out wide. 'Come on. Do it. Touch me.'

I shrugged again and tried to look away. 'Some of us can go more than twenty minutes without sex, you know.'

'Jessie.' Sil was leaning in. 'Your lips have gone blue.' He leaned in further and kissed me firmly on the mouth and, for a second, the shivering stopped, as though he fed me warmth. He moved back and dropped his voice to a murmur. 'You say you trust me. So prove it.'

Hands closed around my shoulders and he pulled me in, tight, against him, drawing my head up so that his lips could close over mine. I could feel his fangs sliding down half-inside my own mouth, one point grazed against my lip and I made a tiny sound of protest, but the warmth was too overpowering, felt so good against my skin that I was never in any danger of drawing away. As long as he was kissing me, *just* kissing me, it was all right. I could handle it.

So, what happened? One minute he was pouring heat into my mouth and I was kneeling there feeling the smooth, dry warmth from his skin, tasting the metallic tang of my blood on his lips, and the next I was kissing him back, running my tongue along the inside of his lip and feeling the hardness of the fangs as they locked into place. There must be a scientific explanation for the fact that I didn't fight his hands as they travelled across my body, a chemical reason for my reaction to his touch. My whole body felt his skin like electricity, the tiny hairs on the back of my neck stood on end as his fingers traced around the clothes I still wore.

'Jessica – ' His mouth left mine to whisper along my jawline, down my neck, across my shoulder.

'Yes.' Single syllable, he could take it to mean what he wanted. Was he asking permission? Questioning the reasoning behind this? I didn't *care*.

He unsnapped the pink-and-black striped bra and I felt the pure heat of his body against my bare skin. His eyes flickered to mine; once, twice, and they were the bruise-grey of storm driven clouds, backlit with sunrise as I pulled his clothes away from his body and ran fingers down newly

218

uncovered flesh. He kissed the score-lines down my face, stroked gentle fingers over the greenish bruising across my ribs, whispered words I couldn't understand into my hair. How long had I dreamed of this? How long had I waited, wanting?

I unwrapped him as one might a longed-for Christmas present. Slowly, prolonging the moment of the reveal, loving the way his breath caught in his throat each time I dragged fingertips over his skin.

The leather jeans had shrunk skin-tight during our river swim, fitting so tightly the fabric was stretched and thick across the fly so Sil had to help, unbuttoning with one hand while the other stroked my skin, raising goose pimples that had nothing to do with the temperature.

He was impressively ready for action, his skin damp and so hot that when I reached my fingers in to touch him it made me jump. 'You're *really* hot.'

'And you are dying of the cold. You just killed a demon, Jessica. I think, now, you are allowed a little fun ...' He smiled against me, as though he understood that I had been dying of a heart forced to remain cool, which was now thawing into mush under the heat of his longed-for attention. His hands wound into my hair, my hands slithered around the silky hardness of him until I was aching, gasping, wanting him so badly that I could hear his name breathed out with every sighing exhalation. And then, with one movement, he was inside me, breathing my name in time, in rhythm, as his own name was in my mouth. *So warm.*

We moved as though dancing, a tempo we'd never attained during even our most frenzied arguments; moved and turned and touched, and I felt every inch of him not only with my body but with my mind. I wanted to experience it all; to photograph it with my memory so that not one second of this pulsing beat would go to waste; that ever afterwards I would be able to call to mind the smell of his skin, the shadow moving behind his eyes, the drifting brush of his hair across parts of me rendered so sensitive that it was all I could do not to shout out.

I don't know what I'd expected sex with Sil to be like. I think that I'd expected more violence – there was something in the way he walked, something that hinted at things restrained. But I'd never expected tenderness. Never expected him to cry my name as he came, never expected his wanting to make me scream for him, too – and *God*, he was good at that. Years and years of experience behind that mouth, those fingers, all combined in teasing and leading me on until I lay, pinned beneath his weight, shaking with unspoken words sobbing in my throat.

And I hadn't expected him to hold me. Although I was glowing with warmth, he put his arms around me and closed me against him. I could feel his breathing slowing, the fluttering of the demon locked inside as it fed off the energy and the desire. 'Christ, Jessie.'

Had he guessed? I refused to let him see my face. 'What?'

'That was – I haven't had sex like that since – before.'

'Before what?' My voice sounded thick because I was trying not to cry. Trying not to think that now it would all be different, that I'd never again be able to watch him drag another girl into some back room, and heckle him when he reappeared ten minutes later all dishevelled and unfocused.

'Before the demon.' His voice sounded as heavy with regret as mine did with tears. 'I'd forgotten how good it felt to come without wanting the blood at the same time.'

'And usually you do?'

'Oh, *yes*.' He moved beside me as though even the thought of it made him hard. 'I want it, all the time, watching her throat, watching the blood rise, and knowing it's there, for the taking.'

It made me uneasy, the cool lust in his voice. Made me wonder how many times he took the blood, whether it was offered or not. 'But you didn't want mine?'

A half-laugh. 'I wanted more than your blood.'

'So what was it like with me?'

He went very quiet then. Lay almost totally still. 'It was like it was with my wife,' he said at last. 'Human.'

The lump in my throat was almost insurmountable. 'What was her name?' I asked.

'Christie. Christina Margaret.' He said the name slowly, as though he'd had it in his mind for a very long time but had forgotten how to say it. 'Christie,' he said again, faintly.

'And what was your name?'

'Does it matter?' Sil sat up. It made me feel awkward and I found I was scrunching myself up, trying to cover myself with bits of my clothes.

'I'd like to know.'

'What, first fuck in four years, you want my name and address?' Sil gave a ghostly smile. 'Jonathan. I was Jonathan Charles Wilberforce.'

Jonathan. Jonathan and his wife, Christina.

'What about your children?'

'Stop it, Jessica.'

It hurt. God, how it hurt. Every word, every name, every detail, let me know how different it was now. That our friendship was gone, blown to dust by one momentary dream-realisation.

'I thought you might like to talk about them. You never do, and it must be hard to pretend that they never existed, particularly when, well, when you've done something like this.'

For a long, long time Sil sat with his forehead resting on his knees. 'Joseph,' he said at last. 'Joseph and Constance.' And then he cried and I wrapped my arms around him.

Sil had to wait until Jessie fell asleep before he could even start to examine what had happened. His body felt better than it had for years – no sign of any adverse reaction to the immense high that he'd ridden, nothing but a slight heaviness, a slowness of thought and that, he concluded, was probably a result of the sex rather than the blood. Or it could be the feelings he was finally allowing. He glanced across at her, head pillowed on what was left of his shirt, skin still glowing from the heat he'd transferred to her, and there was a sudden contraction in his chest as his demon jolted. *All these years. All these years I have managed simply by never acknowledging what I lost, Christie, Constance, Joseph.* And the slow realisation of what he had become crept through his mind. *I have never sat down and looked back at the things that made me human because, now I know that is how we must live, we vampires. We are only able to exist by never admitting that once we loved, once we, too, laughed and cried … because to accept the things we lost means that we must admit our loss of humanity. We deal with the guilt for the killings and the using of the humans by pretending that we were never one of them.*

How many years now has it been? The flu pandemic was in 1918. Nearly a hundred years ago, and I'd been a vampire for four years by then …

His breath caught and broke into staccato gasps as he fought the tears again. *First Constance, then Joseph. Seven and eight years old, too fragile to fight the virus that took so many; might have taken me, if I'd still been human enough to be subject to infections. Left Christie alone. Weeping and*

222

grieving and I'd been unable to comfort her; that's when I lost what was left of my humanity, not when I was infected, not when the demon hatched, but then, that night when the children died and I could do nothing, not even help my wife through the pain.

He wept again then, this time without Jessie's arms around him.

Chapter Twenty-One

'God, Jessie!' Rachel met me at the front door. 'Have you been out all night?'

I pushed past her to get into my room. 'There was … a party.'

'You could have invited me. I've still got that blue dress I borrowed from Laura for the Run thing. Anyway, why is your hair all straggly?' Rach followed and perched herself on the end of my bed, wide blue eyes innocently regarding me from under her poodle-curly fringe. I stood for a second, trying to think of an explanation. Then, quite unreasonably, I burst into tears.

Rach began to fuss around. She pulled my duvet from the bed to draw over my shoulders, then hustled me out of the bedroom, settling me on the sofa. 'Can you tell me what happened?' She put her head on one side. 'Or is it some kind of Official Secrets thing?'

I laughed through the tears. 'I work for the council, not MI5.'

The duvet must have slipped, taken my collar down with it, because Rach's eyes were suddenly on my neck, pupils wide and her face paling. 'Oh *no*, Jess, no.' Her hand flew to cover her mouth, fingertips between her teeth. 'No, please.' Now there were tears in her eyes, too. 'You're my only real friend and I've always thought your job was just silly stuff and you've always been so good at it, and the Treaty and everything is working and this hardly ever happens any more!'

Her reaction stopped my own shock dead. 'What?'

Rach pointed at my neck. 'The bite. You're … you're

going to be a *vampire* ...' Heavy sobs broke her words into single, almost inaudible fragments. 'I ... can't ... my ... family ... noooooo ...'

I raised a finger and touched the mark. It was healing fast, as vampire bites did, but was still visible; precise and raw. 'Rach, listen. Yes, I got bitten. It was ... look, it's all a bit complicated to explain but the important thing is that *he didn't seed.*'

'You're sure?'

A sudden flashback to Sil, fighting his own demon for control, those glowing coals of eyes dying back to the clouded grey. 'Honestly.'

Rach stood up and slowly made her way to the kitchen. I heard sounds of the kettle being filled and Rach trying to compose herself with the aid of kitchen roll and much nose blowing. As my own eyes continued to leak tears and my body shuddered, I wished my own emotional state could be so easily calmed.

'It's not Liam, is it?' Two brimming cups of PG Tips arrived on the low table, accompanied, to my amazement, by half a packet of chocolate digestives.

'Why is everyone fixated on Liam?' I wiped my eyes and nose on a corner of the duvet. 'He's not a vampire; thought you'd be able to tell, what with his total lack of style and his *Doctor Who* obsession. And where did these biscuits come from? I thought you regarded all processed foods as Produce of the Devil?'

'Jessie, even *I* get pre-menstrual.' Rach sipped at the scalding tea. It reminded me of the heat from Sil's skin. But right now, even the cuckoo-clock which hung tastelessly from the shelf reminded me of Sil. I could still see his eyes, feel his fingers, taste him on the roof of my mouth ... 'You're crying again.'

'I think I may have done something really, *really* stupid,'

I sniffed. 'I've – well, look, I've – oh, sod it, I slept with someone last night.'

'Yes? And?' Rachel took a biscuit and ate it without even looking at it first, which told me all I needed to know about her alleged suspicion of wheat-based comestibles. 'I've slept with hundreds of men and I hardly ever come home in tears.'

'Really? *Hundreds?*'

'All right, maybe not hundreds. But some. So why has this one made you cry?' Then she added with sudden wide-eyed comprehension, 'is he married?'

'No. Quite the opposite.' The tea was helping calm me.

'So he's single ...'

No, Rach, I thought. *The opposite of married is vampire. No attachments, no faithfulness. No happy-ever-after. How can I possibly expect her to understand?* 'Look, forget it. It'll be fine. I'll have a quick shower and go to work. That'll take my mind off everything.' And besides, Liam *would* understand. I suddenly wanted to pour my heart out to my co-worker, rather than my best friend, and I knew that was terribly wrong. 'I'll drink my tea first.'

Rach was looking at me oddly. 'What's happened to you, Jessie?' she finally asked. 'You used to be so ... normal. You'd come home from work and we'd watch *Desperate Housewives*, me eating something nutritious and you shovelling down crap. Then we'd talk about men and ... well, mostly men. Now this weird shutter thing has come down.'

'It was a tough party.'

'Not just this morning. For a few days now.' She tilted her head and looked at me out of the corner of her eye.

'I'm sorry, Rach. Things have been a bit strange lately.'

She shrugged. 'And you're obviously not going to tell me any more. Well, good luck with that.' Rach leaned in and removed the chocolate digestive that I was about to dunk.

'Perhaps you ought to go to the office. Then you can eat your own biscuits.'

'Grief, Jessie!' Liam coming up the stairs to the office surprised me. I was sitting in front of my computer, staring at its empty screen. 'It's a bit early for you.' He began fussing around, putting down his bags behind his desk, fetching out the coffee jar and searching out clean mugs. 'Why so crack of dawn? And where's Sil?'

'Couldn't sleep.'

'But you went home, oh, right, I get it.' Liam tapped the side of his nose. 'Right. Say no more. No questions asked.' He picked up both our mugs in one hand and headed out on to the landing towards the kitchen, but then reappeared, head only, poking through the doorway. 'Well, just the one. Who, what species, did you stay at his and how was it? Oh. That's four questions. Never mind, give.'

I turned my eyes on him. Eyes that had watched a vampire cry while I held him. There was so much to say, so much on my mind, that I didn't know how to even start to let it out.

'Ohhh ... kaaay, sorry I asked.' Liam's head disappeared.

Not fair, I know. It wasn't Liam's fault that I'd fallen for Sil all those years ago, or that I'd ended up having wild sex in a storm drain. And I only had myself to blame for the aftermath, when the vampire had finally broken down, wrapping his arms around me and weeping for his lost family. But not blaming Liam didn't help *me*; didn't take away this feeling that I'd blown possibly the most precious relationship I'd ever have into a thousand smoking smithereens; so, right now, Liam was on the blunt end of something that had the other end impaled inside my heart.

'Where's that *bloody* coffee?' was all I could think of to say, so far.

'Coming right up, boss-man.' Liam carried a tray through, which was unusual. Normally he balanced the cups in his fist and then complained about scalded knuckles all morning. 'I've put two sugars in because you look like you're in shock. And I've brought the biscuits, because I've got a feeling that you're going to say something that's going to put *me* in shock.'

'I think I killed Malfaire last night.'

'Whoa, there it was; shortbread I think, for that one.'

'And two wights attacked Sil and me; we only just got away.'

'And a chocolate HobNob –'

'And then we ended up in the river and spent most of the night trying to avoid hypothermia.'

'Sod it, I'll open the custard creams. Anything else? Because I think there's some emergency Kit Kats in the cupboard, if you haven't found them already.'

I tried really hard to keep my mouth shut. To regulate the flow of words so that I could be cool, emotionless, tell Liam what had happened with a joke and a shrug. Bit the inside of my cheek and everything, but it was useless. 'Sil – ' and then the tears came again.

I was dimly aware of Liam's, 'Oh shit,' and then frantic rummaging in a desk drawer before I was presented with a large box of tissues and a hug. 'Jesus, Jessie, couldn't you have spread this out over a week or so?' He smelled nice, I registered, of clean shirt and aftershave, with a hint of baby sick. It was great to be able to lean in to someone who'd understand the full implications of last night. 'You've set a new world record for workplace stress, by the way. In fact, announcements like that probably contravene Health and Safety guidelines.'

'It's just shock.' I hiccupped, trying to breathe.

'Jesus, what did he do to you!'

I gave a snotty laugh. 'How graphic would you like me to be?'

A hand stroked my hair. 'If you wouldn't see it on *Doctor Who*, then I don't need to know, all right?' There was a long silence, during which Liam uncomplainingly hugged me. Then he let out a sigh. 'Okay. Can we go back to "you *think* you killed Malfaire"? I mean, what happened, did you plank him or what?'

The cold feeling came creeping back. 'No – he – ' and another lump of tissue was brought into play – 'there was blood, he couldn't breathe.'

'I'm going to run the channels,' Liam said firmly. 'If there's any news on him, we'll know. Or someone will.' His hand lingered on my shoulder. 'How are you doing now? You up to this?'

I nodded and sniffed. Shock did funny things to the system. I would never have cried in front of Liam in the normal course of events. It made him come over all *Master and Commander* and hyper-butch.

'You're not up the duff are you?' Liam's sudden question came over the top of the monitor. 'Sarah cried for seven months when she was expecting.'

'That was because she knew you were the father,' I replied.

'Ah, the return of the Jessica Grant we all know and love.' Liam sighed. 'Before we go any further, Jessie, are you going to tell me what happened with you and Sil? The thing that made you cry – and don't try giving me that "shock" crap. I've *seen* you in shock and it makes you want to rip heads off, not sit around with a lifetime's supply of tissues – oh. Oh, whoa.'

'What?'

Liam stared at his computer for a few more seconds, then

swung the monitor to face me and turned up the volume on his speakers. Malfaire's image filled the screen, his face a bleached-bone white but his marmalade eyes full of a kind of triumph. His clothes were messy, torn-about looking, but there was no sign of any wound. I glanced at Liam. 'What is it?'

'News clip. From this morning, some minor station that deals in Otherworlder affairs. Picked it up in a general sweep.'

'Can you re-run? From the start?'

Liam blinked. 'Hold on a sec,' and he fiddled with his keyboard for a moment. The image on screen pixellated and broke, then the position of Malfaire's head changed and we were back at the beginning.

'While I admit that I was grievously injured, my healing abilities were only slightly compromised, and I appear before you today to show the demon world that I am, indeed, immortal. Our victory against the humankind is assured.'

Liam switched the screen off so quickly that the monitor rocked.

'Not dead.' I was alarmed by the sweep of relief. I wasn't a murderer.

'No.'

My mobile rang. I snatched it out of my pocket and threw it to Liam. 'See who it is, will you?'

'Why? Who aren't you speaking to?'

'*Liam –* '

'All right, all right.' He flipped down the screen. 'It's Zan. Are we open for business, or shall I tell him that you're having a breakdown?' Great. Like I wanted *Zan* to know.

'Is he webcamming?'

'Probably. The number's his internet phone.'

'Right, flip him up. I want to shout at him.'

230

'I know you're in shock, Jessie, but – is that wise?'

'D'you know, I don't think I care?'

On screen Zan was looking paler and taller than usual, as though he'd spent the last few weeks in a dark cupboard. 'Jessica. I have seen the latest broadcasts. They have not yet reached the human channels, and hopefully he will be dismissed as another scaremonger, but ...' A frown creased his otherwise perfect forehead. 'I fear danger may walk abroad.'

'*That* bad? So he's more than just a nutter?'

Zan gave a muted shrug. 'He seems truly invincible. If *you* could not kill him, then ... who can?'

I had a sudden thought, a memory of my mother ... of *Jen*, sitting at the farm table, head in her hands, mourning. 'My family – Zan ... are they in danger? He threatened ...'

The low-level shrug was repeated. 'His invincibility may save them. If he feels himself supreme, then why should he concern himself with a petty collection of humans? I fear that they are beneath his notice now.' He glanced down at something on his desk. 'You, however, have taken a stand against him and he will have you punished as an example to others.'

A movement behind Zan. 'Hey.'

'Hello, Sil.' My heart shot up into my throat at the sight of him and I had to do some special breathing exercises to get over the feeling that I was going to fall off my chair. While I was wearing the first clothes that I'd stepped on, he looked sassy and slick. Black shirt over black T over black jeans. It made his hair almost purple-dark and his skin very pale. No trace of the tears or the anguish, or of the ecstasy either, come to that. 'How are you this morning?'

His face appeared in front of Zan. 'Yeah, I'm good.'

My heart sank down into my stomach. His tone was brisk,

upbeat, nicely impersonal; no softness in the way he spoke or looked at me. Everything that had happened between us, *everything*, was nothing to him. 'Well, that's nice.' God, I was proud of myself. *Jonathan*, whispered a tiny voice deep in my mind, *his name is Jonathan*. And another piece of me folded in half and curled around itself. I focused on the webcam.

Zan was standing up now, readjusting the camera, so all I could see was a close-up of his stomach. A wide leather belt rode around his narrow hips, a shirt which looked very much as though it was made of silk was tucked into it. Even as things were falling apart, Zan dressed for the catwalk. His face had thinned. Become feral. His fangs were down and his pupils red. 'Stay there,' he said and abruptly ended the call. He seemed to have dropped the pretence of being in charge of nothing more dangerous than a particularly savage stapler and I wondered where that left Sil.

I was shaking. Liam came and perched on the desk in front of me. 'So, then,' he said carefully. 'You reckoned you were a murderer, now you know you're not, but you still look like you're minus one Happy Hour and Sil is being way too laid back for it to be natural. What exactly has been going on, Jessie?'

'Sil – ' I tried to start again but words wouldn't come past the lump in my throat.

Liam raised his eyebrows. 'So *he's* the vamp responsible for the bite on your neck then, is he? Thought it must be something like that ... Oh come on, Jessie, did you think I wouldn't notice? You can pull your collar up all you like, but how long have I worked in this office?'

My hands flew to the incriminating marks. 'It wasn't – it's not like it looks.'

'Yeah? Well, you tell me what it looks like to *you*, and

I'll tell you that to me it looks like you and the city vamp have been getting down and dirty, and if you don't tell me *everything* then you could be watching your coffee for laxatives for the next three weeks.'

And then I started crying again.

Liam watched me impassively for a moment, then disappeared into the kitchen. There were clanking sounds and the noise of the emergency bucket being displaced, before he reappeared carrying a bottle of whisky. 'When biscuits are no longer enough – ' he explained, pouring two mugfuls – 'time for the heavy stuff.'

I sobbed down a mouthful. Liam was still watching me. 'This is horrible.'

'Yeah. I use it to clean the spoons.' He moved suddenly, to crouch in front of me. 'So. It was Sil. It's all come to this.' Gently he hooked a sticky strand of hair behind my ear. 'Just tell me, Jessie.'

So I told him. All of it. Even the bits that made me blush to admit. Liam listened and drained his mug, poured me another even though I could hardly bear to sip at it. 'You and Sil. You were always hot for each other.'

'It's worse than that.' Tears flowed faster. 'Oh God, Liam, what am I going to do? I think I'm in love with him.'

I bent forward, crying so hard that whisky slopped up my arm. Liam put the mug down and took my hand. '*Fuck*, Jessie. After all we've been told, with all that you know? Talk about a slow boat to nowhere.'

'I *know*. There's nothing you can tell me about vampires. They don't form relationships, they make stoats look sexually circumspect and they have all the emotional warmth of a slug. I *know* all this! Hell, I probably wrote the pamphlet. But – ' I shrugged.

He rubbed a thumb across my cheek, smearing the tears.

'Oh, Jessie. What do you want me to do? I can kill him, if you like.'

That made me laugh. I looked up into Liam's oh-so-human eyes, a gentle brown without all the clouding and shifting that marks out a vampire. 'No. You're all right. I'll have to deal with it as best I can.'

'But can you? Can you really deal with him, feeling like this? What if – hell I hate to say it, Jessie, but you must have thought it – what if he goes rogue? Could you stake him?'

'Look.' I took a huge breath, regained some self-control. 'I don't know, okay? Last night he … he was almost *human*. He cried, Liam. He told me about his kids, his wife, and he cried. So, maybe there is hope for him. But for now, I can only take things a little bit at a time. And Malfaire is still out there, he still wants me dead, and now we have no idea what to do about it, that's the most pressing problem. Being in love with a vampire – well, I'll have to dig out that T-shirt you brought me back from London and keep wearing it until the message sinks in.'

'The "What Would Buffy Do?" one? Jessie, you do know that *Buffy* wasn't a documentary don't you?'

I shrugged tiredly. 'I'm not sure what I know any more.'

Chapter Twenty-Two

Zan looked as though he had changed especially to come over. The silk shirt had been exchanged for a linen one, topped with a thigh-length black wool coat lined in red satin. The trousers were velvet, and fine calf-leather black boots finished it all off.

'You look like you've dressed for the blind,' I said. 'Very tactile.'

'You don't want to know what it says in Braille.' Sil slumped down on to my desk. Liam began fiddling with his computer.

'Honestly, Zan, I've got Malfaire on my tail, threatening me with God knows what and you're dressed like the poster-boy for the new undead revolution. Boy, do you have a problem with priorities!'

Green eyes laced with gold met mine and locked on. 'Who gave you the mark, Jessica?' Zan's voice was deceptively gentle. 'Did some demon feed from you?' One long finger flicked the collar of my crumpled shirt away from the bite, still bruised and tender. 'Was it with your permission?'

'And *you* are changing the subject!'

'It was mine.' Sil shuffled paperwork, looking as though he was trying to keep his hands occupied. 'It demanded payment in blood for getting us out of the river.'

'Interesting,' Zan hadn't let the collar go yet, kept his finger between the cotton and my skin. 'And how did it taste?'

Sil's eyes were cool as they met mine, but there was a shivering remembrance of the rush behind them. 'It was *amazing*, Zan. I've never tasted anything so powerful. It nearly knocked me out for a while. Back when I was human one of my friends ... well, there was opium involved, and it was a bit like that, only more.'

'Hmmm.' Zan looked at the wound. 'That may be her blood combination. Human and ghyst, something in the mixture of the two. Interesting.'

I didn't like the thoughtful way I was being looked at. 'Oy, excuse me guys. Things are bad enough without you two looking at me like I'm some kind of living happy-pill! Could you try to control yourselves for a few minutes? At least until you tell me why you came over here. I'm sure it wasn't to give me the pleasure of watching you walk in velvet trousers.'

Liam went and fetched the bottles of synth for the vampires and two more coffees for him and me, then sat down on the edge of my desk, watching Sil.

'We came to collect you, Jessie.' Sil raised his head so that the light drew attention to his perfect bone structure. 'Malfaire will need to make an example of you now you've actually tried to kill him, so we're taking you back to where we may protect you.'

'But surely, if Jessie can't kill Malfaire, he'll leave her alone.' Liam kept his eyes on Sil, as though he expected him to leap up and defile me at any moment.

Zan was on his feet now. 'Jessica,' he said, and his words were heavy as stones, 'you are in danger. You are also our only weapon against Malfaire, however you may be used. And Sil has invoked the Protection Act.'

'But I didn't kill him ...'

'No. And yet.'

I felt my pupils distend with shock. 'This is big, isn't it?' My voice crouched low in my throat and came out as a whisper. 'He's going to try to fight?'

Zan nodded slowly. 'Everything we have worked for may be in danger. Malfaire is rallying all those who have been held in check only by their fear of a war that they would never win. This may be the end of peace, Jessica.'

'Jessie.' Sil managed to get past Liam. 'Zan is right; you know it.' He touched me then, just the lightest of brushes against my arm with his hand but I jumped like he'd burned me. 'Please – '

And I wanted to tell him my peace had ended as soon as I'd felt his body against mine. But this was about so, so much more than me and him. And yet … yet … Even though I knew we were in danger I wanted to make him forget his long-gone family, his Christie and the horror of the loss of his children, I wanted to say 'I love you' into those sea-grey troubled eyes, to feel his body eager against me again, that soaring hugeness inside my heart. But instead I whispered '*Jonathan*'. Watched him go still.

'Oh, Jessie,' he said.

'I know.'

'It's – maybe – I need – I don't know. But it – '

'I know.' And I did know. I'd always known I couldn't have him. That was all there was to it. He was vampire, and that would always win out.

'Wow, you two are erudite this morning.' Liam broke the silence. I became aware that all three men were standing very, very close to me. I could have walked into either one's arms with only half a step.

'Can you lot back up a bit?' I said, clearing my throat, 'only it's kind of hard to breathe with all this testosterone in the air, and I'd quite like to be able to turn around without facing a sexual harassment charge.' I could do this. 'Okay, I get it. We bed down at Vamp Central and try to work out what to do next. But please can we take the office stuff with us?'

'You are dedicated to your job, Jessica.' Zan moved obediently a few steps away.

'Not really. End of the world or not, you know what they're like if the tracker programme isn't backed up every twenty-four hours.'

Sil was looking at me, unblinking. I had no idea what he was thinking, and that worried me.

Chapter Twenty-Three

I left Sil and Liam manhandling office furniture into Zan's chilly living room – well, Sil was handling and Liam was saying 'up your end' rather a worrying number of times – so that we could keep our office running whilst remaining under the eye of the vampires, or "safe" as Zan kept insisting on calling it. I had the feeling we would have been just as safe if we'd stayed in our own office, i.e., about as safe as we would have been inside a damp paper bag, but I'd lost the will to argue. I followed the old vampire up the huge oak staircase. We trekked along miles of portrait-hung corridor, past acres of ornate furniture and through swamps of deep-pile carpets, until Zan stopped outside a carved, gothic door. 'This will be your room.'

'What? I have to *sleep* here?'

Zan reached behind him and opened the door. 'Sleep, play charades, whatever pleases you, Jessica.' He stood aside and I walked past him into the room. It was the size of a small African country with a vast four-posted double bed in the middle, and windows looking out over an exquisitely landscaped garden. There was an en-suite bathroom with gaudily patterned gold taps, and a bowl of fruit on a small writing table just inside the door. Instead of paper, the walls were ornamented with embroidered hangings alternated with mahogany panelling; it was like a cross between a bridal suite and a porn set.

'You do have electricity, don't you? And the toilet flushes?'

Zan had followed me into the room. 'Of course.' He walked across to the window, pausing on his way to run a possessive hand over an enormously ugly chest-of-drawers and the spiral-carved bed supports. 'Among the things that this century has to recommend it, the lavatorial facilities come fairly high up the list.' He stood at the waist-level sill, gazing down over the gardens with his back to me.

'It's a bit *Brideshead Revisited*.'

Without turning around Zan said, 'If you tell me that what this place needs is a woman's touch, I am afraid I may have to tear your throat out.'

Whoa. I was going to treat that as a joke. 'So. How long am I going to have to stay? I mean, is it worth bringing more of my clothes over or what?'

Now Zan turned. He said absolutely nothing, he didn't need to. The look in his jade eyes was enough.

'*What*? Oh, no, that's stupid, Zan. We have to do something.'

'And you suggest …?'

'We can't just wait for Malfaire to decide the next move! There are people's lives at stake here … remember the Troubles?' Intimations of mortality were beginning to creep into my head. I didn't want to die, not like this, cowering in a vampire's glorified flat-share. Actually, I didn't want to die at all, apart from possibly in my own bed aged a hundred and three.

'I agree. We must seize the initiative.' Zan's voice was low, business-like. And also he was speaking to me as an equal, as though I carried as much weight in this as he did, and that scared me almost more than anything. 'And yes, Jessica. I remember the Troubles only too well. And I also remember that many of the deaths during that time were caused by actions without consideration. We must take time here to consider what may best be done.'

Just when I thought I'd sunk as low as my spirits could possibly go, there was a slow knock at the half-open door.

Sil stood on the threshold, propping himself by one arm against the door frame. 'Jessie – '

Zan gave me a grin. The very tips of his fangs showed. 'You will need to talk.' His expression was amused but the teeth gave the lie to the smile. 'I shall leave you. But Sil, when you are ready, one of us needs to go to Jessica's flat and fetch what remains of her possessions.'

'Hold on.' The thought of Sil rummaging through my underwear and trying to find wearable clothes in my jumble-sale of a wardrobe did not fill me with pleasure. And Zan would only do it if he was allowed to wear those creepy latex gloves. 'Can't I go myself?'

'Of course.' Zan inclined his head towards me. 'If you feel that having coordinating shoes and bags is worth dying for.' Another supercilious smile and he wafted from the room, passing Sil with barely a nod of acknowledgement. I sat on the bed and stared.

'Does he know? About us, about what we did?'

Sil waved a non-committal hand. 'Zan knows pretty much everything,' he said. 'Now, you going to let me in there, or have you got some hunky young stud naked in that bathroom already, now that you've broken your four-year celibacy rule?'

'Where would I get a hunky young stud from? There's at least one person too many in this house already.' I didn't exactly let him in; I just walked over towards the window, and he followed. He kicked the door shut behind him and the slam echoed down the landing like a cough. 'Very butch. You don't have to prove you're a man to me, Sil, remember?'

I had my back to him, trying to fix my attention on the garden and not on Sil's reflection in the window.

'Jessie. What happened last night ... I don't think you

understand what it meant … what it *means* to me. But you know it's not like I can *stop* being vampire.'

'A demon is for several lifetimes, not just for Christmas?'

He smiled. 'You're special, Jessie. And I don't want to hurt you.'

'Fine by me.' I turned around to face him. 'So, you can see yourself out then.'

'There's something in you, something that *pulls* me, something that I want more of. I can feel you, when you think of me there's this …' He made a fist and punched it towards his ribcage. 'I don't understand it.'

'You're going to get to the sex in a minute, aren't you?'

'The sex? Oh yeah, well, goes without saying, doesn't it? I mean, it was incredible. It was – '

'All right, so I'm a world-class shag.' I had to be cruel, had to be hard. Otherwise I was going to go down underneath the longing that hid inside me.

'There were *layers*, it was feeling and thinking and being, all wrapped up in you. Jesus, Jessie, you made me remember the past like I never do, like I never *want* to do. You bring it all back, the sadness and the pain.'

'I'm sorry,' I whispered.

'No! No, don't be sorry. It's *good*. You don't understand, do you, Jessica? You think you know us so well; you read the pamphlets and the officially sanctioned books and you think that genuinely gives you an insight into our natures?'

'Oh, I know you, all right. You're a bunch of arrogant, emotionless, neutered killers.'

He dipped his head and took a small step closer to me. 'And you truly believe that is all we are?' A cool hand touched my cheek. 'Truly? In your heart?'

'Jonathan,' I said, very softly. Almost under my breath. Rolled with the feeling, let the whole thing take me under until I felt it in my lungs, drowned in it. 'Not Sil. Not with me.'

'But I have to experience, to feel, the blood and the white-heat of the lust and the danger, do you see?'

I took a deep breath. If this was all going to end in war and death – and I was *not* accepting that as a foregone conclusion, but you never knew – I was not leaving unfinished business. 'And that's the problem. How on earth can I let myself love you when I'd never know where you were, or who you were with? Vampires are like Jeremy Kyle's secret weapon in the viewing figures war; you said it yourself, Sil. You feed and fuck and it doesn't touch you. *Nothing* touches you.'

The vampire moved closer and I didn't know who I was seeing, Sil with his white-eyed disdain, or Jonathan, shaking with pain he was trying to forget. 'Love?'

'Four years, Sil. And every time I see you with someone else it's like broken glass behind my eyes.'

A slow shake of the head. 'I never knew.'

'No, of course you didn't! Too busy shaking everybody else up. Why did you think I slapped you when you tried to kiss me?'

Sil sat on the edge of the bed. 'I thought you were scared of me. I –' He broke off and ran his hands through his hair. 'I can't believe I'm hearing this. So, last night was – what?'

'An aberration. I slipped, all right? You were there and ...' the tears began to leak out, 'and I'm frightened, and I was cold and you ... you.'

The vampire closed his eyes and threw himself back on the bed, lying sprawled. 'So you refused to allow your feelings for me even when I kissed you? You really are the most utterly exasperating person I have ever known, and I have known quite a few lawyers, so that is really saying something.'

'That's not fair, Sil. I can't control the way I feel, but I *can* control what happens to me, and I refuse to trail along behind you with my tongue hanging out, just waiting for that moment when you decide to turn around and notice me. When your bed is cold and you fancy a quick fuck to warm it up ready for the next victim – I won't be that woman, Sil. I might love you but that doesn't mean I'm going to lie down and let you walk all over me.' I sniffed hard and tried to drag the tears back up my cheeks by the power of suction.

His eyes opened; a dark, slate colour now. 'You still have no real understanding, do you? Of my kind, of how we have to live?' He moved from prone to standing beside me in one slick, vampire-move. 'Try. Just for one second step outside your oh-so-human mindset and imagine what it is to be one of us.'

I was crying properly now. 'What do you mean? Jonathan?' I looked into his face, felt his demon relishing the moment.

His hands went up, reached around to cup the back of my head, hold me steady. 'As you keep reminding me, I have been vampire for nearly a hundred years.'

'What do you want, a party?' I dropped my eyes from his, stared at the garish pattern on the carpet, where swirls and broken colour blocks made it look as though someone had been violently ill several centuries ago and no-one had cleared up.

'Jessica. You judge me, you judge all vampires, by your human standards. You humans, you believe we can't feel, that we are the ultimate in emotional detachment.' His hand was insistent on my neck, not letting me turn my head away; all I could do was keep my eyes on that horrible carpet.

'Well, you can't, can you? You shag around and you party like it's the end of the world and you don't love or care for anyone except yourselves. I've seen you, Sil, don't forget. I was at that club when you danced as though you and she were wearing the same knickers and then you ...' I swallowed. 'Then you drank her blood.' My gaze travelled back up, almost against my will. 'Now tell me that's the behaviour of a caring, compassionate member of society.'

There was a sudden draught at the back of my neck as his hands fell away. 'All right,' he said, and his voice was very quiet now. 'All right. We party. We need the thrills and the highs ... our *demons* need those. But tell me this, Jessica –' His voice became so quiet that I had to lean in close to hear his words. Felt them breathed against my cheek. 'If we have no feelings, if we care so little, *why does the memory of my wife and children make me weep?*'

He was only voicing something that I'd wondered myself, but I'd pushed the thought away, squirrelled it somewhere under my ribs, behind my heart. *If he felt ... if he could feel ... could he feel for me? And, if he could, then what on earth was all the vampire cold-bloodedness about?* 'I don't ...'

'Jessica. The reason vampires don't feel? The reason we dare not?' And there he was again, right in front of me, head slightly tilted and his eyes holding me, preventing me from looking away. 'It is because we are cowards. If we allow ourselves to feel, then we have to live with our guilt.' He turned, swift and lithe, and began pacing the carpet of the ornate room, like a wolf moving through Versailles. 'A century, Jess. A hundred years, and most of those spent living on the edge. Killing, feeding, turning those we desired.' His voice was matter-of-fact, but I could see the way his hands twisted around one another, fingers interlocking and releasing, as though he was trying to squeeze the pain from his words to keep his tone level. 'I've done ... we've *all* done things ... And after a few years, we learn to stop feeling. To lock away every trace of emotion, because otherwise ...'

245

He stopped. Put his hands on the window ledge and leaned to stare out over the gardens. 'Because otherwise the guilt would kill us.'

'Sil …'

'The only way to live is to forget. But I carry that guilt. And uppermost is the guilt of the night they died. Joseph and Constance. I wasn't there, Jess. I wasn't there to hold them or protect them or …' A sudden biting-off of the words and his head dropped. His shoulders moved, jerked twice and when he spoke again his voice was thin. 'Christie was right to send me away. Because I would have turned them. If I'd been there, I would have turned my own children. Her, too. I might have condemned them to lives that needed lethal amounts of adrenaline to function, and back then there wasn't the synth; we had to bite to live.' I felt his demon give a shiver, felt it rise within him, called by whatever feelings he was working so hard to suppress, and watched him straighten as though it drove steel through his spine. 'And *that* is why vampires are emotionless. Not because we *cannot* feel but because we *dare* not.'

He faced me again, eyes pale grey once more. There was no trace of the suffering on his face now.

'So you don't *want* to feel, because you don't like feeling guilty? Damn it, Sil, that's like cutting off your head because you don't like your hairstyle! What about all the good stuff – do you deny yourselves that just so that you don't have to suffer a few sleepless nights? Because that's pretty crazy.'

A shake of his head. 'You still do not understand, Jessica. Half-demon, and yet you still think like a human.' He sighed and closed his eyes. 'Imagine the worst thing you have ever done.' A flicker of a smile moved across his lips, almost invisibly fast, 'and no, breaking the tracker programme was *not* the worst thing. Worse than that.'

I frowned. 'I've never …' and then a huge flashback to the sight of Malfaire, hands raking at the air and blood seeping through his immaculate jacket. The terrible feeling that had settled over me before we hit the river; I'd taken a life, and nothing would ever be the same again. 'Oh.'

His eyes opened, dark now. Brewing-storm dark. 'I have done terrible things, Jessica. Terrible, evil, wicked things. I have killed, men, women, children, just to satisfy my hunger. I took …' Cool fingers touched my neck and I became aware of my pulse, leaping in my veins as if my corpuscles were taking part in a skipping contest; when I looked up at Sil's face his fangs were down, touching his lower lip and making his mouth flex. 'I could take you. Now, here, tear your throat out and walk away without even a moment's remorse. Because that is what it truly means to be vampire. *That* is what sets us apart from the humans, not our desire for blood, but our ability to know that guilt exists, and to deny it.'

'To save you from pain.'

'Because we are spineless and weak.'

I looked up into a face that should have seemed cruel, predatory. But all I saw was the man behind the predator – the man who'd been willing to die for me, the man who had sat with me as I found out the truth about my parentage. The man who had held me and cried when he'd finally let himself feel. 'No. You aren't weak, Jonathan. You acknowledge what you've done, and a weak man could never do that.'

'Thank you.' Now his hands moved to tilt my chin, to cup my cheek as his mouth moved closer. 'Thank you.'

This time his lips were cool on my mouth, but there was nothing different in the way our bodies reacted to one another. Mine liquefied and his leapt. The mystery was gone but was replaced by a sureness, a deftness. I knew now how much he liked my fingers touching, stroking, rewarded by a hardness that reflected the fact that he was, still, really only twenty-nine. He knew how to make me squirm against the pressure of his hand until I gasped his name, his *real* name, and dug my nails into the skin of his back while he held my weight and looked into my eyes. And then, on the complex woven covering to the intricately carved bed, we rode one another hard. The confusion and the repressed emotion we both carried drove us on to extremes, to wordless sounds and our names, whispered over and over, as our bodies hummed with a passion that was almost flamethrower-strong.

Whoever said that it was better to have loved and lost had clearly never spent any time in bed with a vampire.

And, of course, I woke up an hour or so later, alone.

'Stupid, stupid,' I berated myself, once I'd blearily opened my eyes and stopped patting the evidently smooth sheet on the other side of the bed. 'What did you *expect*?' And I climbed out of the bed, although, given the height, it was more like climbing off, and headed for the shower, still chastising myself for having even considered the possibility that Sil would have held me until I woke; would have *stayed*.

My mobile rang as I stood in the shower, my head lathered as I sang 'Gonna wash that man right out of my hair' under my breath. I shot out from under the water to pick it up, my still-active inner teenager hoping that it might be Sil, whilst my over-thirty outer self knew that he would have just knocked on the door.

At first there was no voice on the other end, and I feared that I'd suffered shampoo-eye for a sales call, until I heard the whispered words, sibilant through the tiny speaker. 'I have your family.' Malfaire.

Hysteria didn't even come close. I ran from the shower, covering myself with my mobile phone and the hand towel, with my hair dripping soap down my back. I dialled the farm, got the 'unavailable' tone and dialled again, one-handed, as I mopped water from my eyes. Unavailable. Again. And again, until I'd covered the bedroom floor in wet footprints and stood at the door, screaming. Zan arrived first, actually managing to look reasonably human as he pounded up the stairs still clutching a glass of freshly poured blood. Sil was close behind and Liam puffed along last, carrying an unexplained screwdriver.

'If this is a spider,' Sil began, but I flung myself at Zan with blatant disregard for the tiny towel.

'This is your fault, you said they were safe! You said he wouldn't touch them and – oh God, I never thought – he might have Abbie as well; he said he was going to try to hurt me through other people and now he's at the farm, the phones are dead, and they could be *dying*; I never *thought*, I should have *thought* … it's my fault. Why didn't I warn them? My family … *I* need to get up there.' I slapped at Zan's rock-hard chest, wanting, *needing* him to feel my anguish, to hurry, to *do something*.

Zan's hand was so cold on my water-warmed flesh that I nearly dropped the towel. 'Go and dress, Jessica.' Over my head, he and Sil exchanged a look. 'Sil, find transport. Take her.'

'On it now.' Ignoring me, Sil swung away back down the stairs. Liam dropped the screwdriver and I realised that my boobs were totally uncovered.

'Go and dress,' Zan repeated, seemingly unmoved by my chestal anatomy. 'And finish washing your hair.'

I managed a world-record shower and hair-rinse and found my discarded jeans and knickers at the foot of the bed. My bra and top were nowhere to be seen, so I pulled Sil's black shirt from where it had fallen and been forgotten, and put that on. When I opened the bedroom door again,

Zan was still standing there. He looked me up and down with what might have been a sigh.

'We need to go *now*!'

Without speaking Zan turned and headed down the stairs. I followed fast and nearly cannoned into Liam who was waiting at the bottom.

'It'll be all right, Jessie. Don't worry.'

'Now say that again, to my face this time, Liam.'

He dragged his eyes upwards with an unashamed grin. 'Sorry.'

The two vampires were muttering to one another in the hallway. Sil was juggling a set of car keys. 'It's outside. We can be gone in two minutes.'

'And I shall hold things here.'

'Yes. But be careful, this is probably …'

'Can we just *go*!'

The vampires exchanged another look. 'We cannot take the risk he is lying,' Sil said. 'We may have been wrong to assume that he would direct his anger at Jessica alone. He really may have her family. He *did* threaten to kill those close to her. First.'

'Are you armed?'

'What do you think this is, the *High Chaparral*? Let's leave, now! Sil!'

Sil and Zan gave one another a curt nod, which looked oddly formal and then Sil grabbed my elbow, dragged me out of the door, and I shut up totally. He was tugging me towards the most beautiful car I had ever seen in my life.

'Is this yours?'

He shrugged and slid into the driving seat. 'Among others,' he said, as though owning a Bugatti Veyron Pur Sang was meaningless. 'Get in.'

I hardly dared touch the immaculate chrome of the door;

this was less of a car and more of a machine for taking your fingerprints. Behind the wheel, Sil looked so coolly at home that my throat hurt; something about his slender sexiness was perfectly matched to the vehicle. 'But this car …'

'Built by vampires, for vampires.' Sil barely waited for me to belt myself into place before we were squealing our way out of the centre of York. It was like being strapped inside a bullet.

I stared out of the dark-tinted window, willing the countryside past faster. 'He'll have those Shadows with him again, and maybe more wights. Can't this thing go any quicker?'

'Have you got a plan?'

I shook my head. 'No. No plan. But it struck me earlier, Sil. *Nothing* is unkillable. If he was, I mean really, *truly* immortal, then why would he need to be able to breed? And anything that *can* produce offspring *must* die. Fundamental rule of the Universe.'

'Earlier. You mean when we were …?'

He looked so affronted that, despite everything, I laughed. 'No! Good grief, I hardly had time to draw breath, let alone think deep thoughts.'

'Well. Good.'

'Can't this thing go any faster?'

'You're repeating yourself. No, it can't.'

Capable hands spun the wheel and I imagined my mother facing down Malfaire in the cluttered kitchen, with only the old Labrador as defence. '*Please* make it go faster.'

Sil nudged a bit more speed out of the engine. 'So, we are hurrying now, are we? Have you spoken to your parents since you found out about Malfaire? Or are we dashing to the rescue of some people you're going to pretend are nothing to do with you when this is over?'

I stared at him. 'Don't you dare moralise to me.'

'Someone has to, Jessie. Think of what they've been through. First they lost a child, then they took on the offspring of a demon without knowing who or what you may turn out to be. Your own natural mother was afraid of what you might be and yet they lied and dissembled in order to bring you up, to keep you safe; they even moved here, away from what they knew, so that your identity would be kept secret. You are their daughter and a simple fact of genetics doesn't change that. Haven't you ever thought of that? And that they must have worried themselves sick about what you might be – but they loved you all the same, brought you up with human values despite it all?' He shook his head. 'You need to start thinking about that, Jessie, not just yourself.'

'Turn here.'

'You're avoiding the subject.'

'We need to turn left here to get to the farm,' I repeated. 'And we're doing nearly two hundred miles an hour.' I kept my tone level and even. The car started to slow, and made the turn with the rear spoiler brake fully extended while he concentrated on the ridiculously complicated gear-change mechanism and the Sat Nav device which was currently telling us we were in the middle of Hampshire.

I made him park in the small paddock out of sight of the house. 'If Malfaire is still there, if he's holding them there, he'll be waiting for us.'

'Then what do you suggest?'

'I spent my teenage years going to parties despite being grounded. I know at least seventeen ways of getting in and out of the house without being seen.'

Sil raised his eyebrows at me. 'Show me.'

His tight trousers weren't the best things for skulking

along the ditch line in, but he never mentioned the mud or the brambles or anything. We hustled along the sunken trench, crept through the old dairy-house door and in the back of the walk-in larder, arriving in the kitchen in time to cause my mother to drop an entire tray of scones.

'Oh, my dear Lord!' The Labrador, sensing a unique opportunity, began gobbling down the oven-hot scones as my mother ... Jenny ... collapsed on to a chair. 'Where did you come from?'

'Over the fields. Where is he?'

'Over in the barn, I think. Jessica, I'm so glad you came ...'

'Has he got Dad? Or Abbie?'

She stared harder. 'Has *who* got your father? I told you that he's in the barn, doing something to that dratted tractor. Abbie will still be at work.'

Sil and I looked at one another. The horrified conclusions that I was drawing were also beginning to drop into place across his features. 'Oh *shit*,' I whispered.

'Distraction.' Sil sounded resigned. 'He's tampered with the phones to get you to come here. He'll be at the house.'

'You *knew*?'

'Suspected. But we couldn't take the chance.'

My mother was staring at us. 'Jessica, what have you got yourself involved in now?' I noticed her trying not to look at Sil. 'Is something wrong?'

'Look, Mum.' I touched her hand and her eyes brightened. I hadn't realised how faded she'd looked, how stooped and old, until she straightened and smiled at me. 'I'll explain everything some time soon. But please, just for now, don't ask me anything. Get Dad in here and lock the door, don't let anyone in except Abbie when she comes over.'

'Is it Malfaire?' Her voice was thin, papery. 'Is it all going wrong, what we did?'

'No.' I patted her arm, felt Sil look at me. 'No. It's fine. Just a precaution. But we have to go now, Mum, I'm sorry.'

'Just …' and now she wasn't looking at me but at Sil, 'keep her safe. Please.'

He nodded once, solemnly. 'I will,' and then we were off again, racing down to the paddock, spinning the Veyron off the slick grass and out on to the road.

Jessica went quiet, chewing her fingernails and staring out of the window as though willpower could make the car go faster. Sil pushed his foot to the floor. One way or another this wasn't going to end well and dying in a flaming sports car at least had a photogenic quality to it, rather than dying under torture at the hand of a jumped-up, semi-immortal poser like Malfaire.

Jessie gave a little whimper and he eased up. He'd promised her mother he'd keep her safe, *and what the hell was that all about? When did I start kowtowing to their bloody mothers? I'm a vampire, silent killer, sexual predator, not a henpecked husband.* But he let the car slow to a safer speed, despite riding the leading edge of a hormone surge that was trying to push him into mindless acceleration. Malfaire was in York, probably in his house right now; all right, Zan had a few tricks which might manage to fool him long enough to keep them out of trouble but … Jessie really cared about Liam. If anything had happened to him, then maybe she'd lose her last link with the humanity she so wanted to claim. *Maybe she'll go demon on Malfaire's ass. Would that be so bad? She might not be able to kill him, but she might have some kind of demon power to take him down, weaken him, so that the vampires could banish him or something?* The thought made his demon quicken and writhe and a flash of blood-longing made him close his eyes for a second. *Jessie.*

You know me now, all of me. You've seen the emptiness where my heart once was, and made me feel whole again. He looked at her now, taking his eyes off the road for long enough to see her shiver. *Is it enough? Would it ever be enough? You excite me in ways I never dreamed of. But is it enough? You say you love me. A human emotion, one of those I cut myself free from a long, long time ago, in that bleak graveyard, between two tiny humps of earth, and now I don't even remember what they felt like. Because, however you try to justify it, Jess, we vampires are craven excuses for beings. The truth is that we are not supreme, we just wish to feel that way, and we do that by pretending ...*

'Will Zan be all right?' she surprised him by asking. 'I suppose he's got Liam but ... God, Liam ...'

'Hey.' Sil touched her, the car swinging alarmingly as he took his hand off the wheel. 'They'll be fine. Malfaire might just be winding you up, he might be nowhere near York by now. Might even have decided to let you be, since you can't seem to do him any damage.'

He saw the hope flash momentarily through her tawny eyes and then fade. 'He wants me dead,' she said, and the awful finality of the words made him shudder. *I'll keep her safe. I promised.*

Chapter Twenty-Four

I tried to ring Liam from the car, but his mobile went to voicemail every time. Then I tried Rachel, home and mobile, and my sister on *her* mobile, with the same results. I tried again, but my hands were shaking too hard for accurate dialling. 'Do you think they're at the house? Has Malfaire ...?'

Without looking, Sil reached out a hand and stilled my trembling fingers. 'Almost certainly,' he said, eyes on the road. 'But he won't have killed them, Jess. Not if you aren't there to see it happen. He's taken them to force you to do something, and bodies are no use for blackmail.'

I took a deep breath. 'Then he's going to try to kill you, too.'

The car wobbled a bit as he allowed his eyes to meet mine for a brief moment. 'Yes. And I really do not want to sound self-interested here, but *that* is why we need a plan.'

We spent the rest of the journey trying to come up with one, but we weren't natural co-operators. Sil's plans always consisted of smashing our way in and trying to cause Malfaire as much damage as possible, while mine consisted of trying to talk our way out of things. When we eventually pulled up in the York square next to the house, we were still arguing.

'If he can't be killed, there's no point going in guns blazing.'

'Talking will do nothing. He won't listen to anything you have to say.'

I stopped, halfway out of the Bugatti. 'He might,' I said slowly. 'If it's something he wants to hear.' The very beginnings of a kind of plan were starting to form. I had no idea how far I could take it, and still no idea how we were going to actually defeat Malfaire, but I thought I could at least hold him for a while. 'Sil.' I put a hand on the vampire's arm. 'Whatever is going on with us, whatever we decide to do afterwards, split up or go back to the way we were before … you will help me now, won't you?'

He stood rigid. 'Jessie. Do you really think this is the time and place for a big "Where Is This Going?" relationship talk?'

'Er, no, I suppose not really. But that wasn't where I was heading. Listen.' I whispered my sketchy idea, all the while aware of the feel of him under my hand, the flexing of his muscles as his fist bunched and the occasional slip and glide as his demon freewheeled on the tension.

'It will never work, Jessica. It depends on your friend being here.'

'Look, Rach isn't answering her phone. I cannot get it over to you strongly enough, what with you being a bloody nineteenth-century Dorian-Grey-alike, that, short of some of the more extreme forms of death, *nothing* stops Rachel from answering her phone. She lives in constant hope that Damian Lewis is going to come for her, and, besides, she's got the vet on speed-dial. If she's not answering, something is very, very wrong, and Malfaire is kind of the definition of very, very wrong.'

'But …'

'Got a better idea, plotmeister?'

A pause. 'I suppose it is the best we have. But you … he could harm you.'

'Sil, the entire *world* could be at stake here. If the Treaty goes tits-up, we've all had it anyway, pretty much. It'll be back to the guerrilla warfare and hiding in burned-out cars and baiting traps with designer footwear.' Sil gave me a sideways look. 'I know, I know, my view of the Troubles all comes from films and some of them were comedies, but you know what I mean. If I stand any chance of stopping him, then I have to take it.' We stared at the front of the house for a moment. 'So, we ought to go in then.'

Sil pulled a face. 'Yes.'

'No point standing around out here.'

'No.'

'Are you scared?'

He rolled his eyes. 'Let's just bloody do it, shall we? Rubbish plan or no, we can't stand out here all day debating.' His long, thin fingertips closed around the handle of the huge front door.

'Wait! What happened to the element of surprise?'

'I live here and Malfaire knows it. I rather think the element of surprise burned itself out at that point, Jessica.' Sil gathered himself to full height and stalked in through his own doorway. I tiptoed along behind, cautiously staying in his shadow. The hallways and landings were chilly, hushed places at the best of times and, right now, with my skin dread-clammy, they felt positively mausoleumic.

'It shouldn't be this quiet,' I whispered as we slid like an ill-matched pair of Charlie's Angels around corners. 'At least if people were screaming I'd know they were still alive.'

Right on cue a sudden scream filled the corridor. It was a female scream of fear and horror.

'That was Rach!'

Without thinking, I headed towards the sound. Took the stairs two at a time, spun around the top landing and stopped outside a bedroom door. 'They're in here.'

The vampire and I stood and contemplated the bedroom door for a couple of seconds. Finally I muttered, 'Oh, what the hell,' and opened it. Inside, the room stank of magic. It was thick with spells, enough to cast mutant silhouettes across the floor and furniture. There, on the bed, sprawled Rach, rubbing at a sore-looking forearm, with Abbie huddled against her. Liam was attempting to keep himself in front of both women which, considering Liam could have stunt-doubled for a pipe-cleaner, was an heroic effort. In the middle of the green, greasy smoke of the magic lay Zan, Harry and Eleanor, trussed with invisible ropes. Only their eyes moved.

Malfaire stood in the centre of the room. The magic rolled and boiled around him and completely ruined the toning effect of his autumnal ensemble.

'Let them go.'

He jumped. If that was to be my only triumph this evening, it was worth it. 'Ah. Hello, Jessica. I had hoped that you would be joining us. And now the fun may truly begin.'

'For a given value of "fun".' I stared into Malfaire's face. 'Let them go. This has nothing to do with them; what you really want is me, so, here I am.'

The magic billowed as he turned to face me fully. 'Actually, Jessica, what I really want is you to watch them die.'

I looked at Liam. 'What did he do?'

'I called Enforcement as soon as you'd gone. Thought we might need back up, but I was too late.' Liam sounded breathless, desperate to impart information. 'He turned up just after, with your sister and your friend in tow and when Harry and Ellie got here, he ... We tried to call you but ...' His voice broke. 'I'm sorry, Jessie. We wanted to fight ...'

Malfaire inclined his head in agreement. 'This one put up quite the struggle.' He nudged Zan with one, immaculately booted foot. 'But ultimately I am the better man. As you will discover.' His eyes flicked uninterestedly over Sil and then away. He was so certain of himself, so smug, he made vampires look positively self-deprecating.

'What will it take for you to let them go?' Rach and Abbie were boggling at me as though they'd never seen me before. Eleanor had her eyes fixed on me as though she was memorising my every move for the court case, and Harry had his eyes shut. There were occasional twitches around his mouth, and I wondered if he was praying.

'You have already declined my offer, Jessica. More than once. It should hardly be necessary to repeat it.'

'You still want me to fight at your side?' God, what was it with everyone? Apart from work I'd gone thirty-one years without being involved in so much as a scuffle outside a nightclub, and suddenly everyone and his dog wants me armed.

'You are prepared to reconsider?'

'If it means saving these people, then yes, I'll reconsider.'

Sil moved a little closer to me. 'Here we go,' he whispered on an almost inaudible outbreath.

Malfaire gave a triumphant grin. 'Ah, my daughter. I knew you would come around to my way of thinking, in the end.'

'Hard not to, when you've got everyone hostage. Let them go, and we'll talk.'

The magic threw little golden sparks off the edges of the furniture. Pretty. Lethal, but pretty. 'Now, I would be a fool indeed to release everyone, wouldn't I? Do you consider me a fool, Jessica?'

I folded my arms. 'Let them go or I won't say another word.'

'Promises, promises,' Liam cut in.

'I'm *so* glad you're on my side, I'd hate to think of you bitching for the opposition,' I said without looking at him.

Malfaire pounced. Took me by one hand and moved me to a corner of the room. I rolled my eyes at Sil, hoping he'd take this as 'try to get everyone out of here', but he just frowned. We really needed to work on our subliminal signalling.

'Be with me, daughter, and everyone will be safe.' Magic whispered across my skin like a fresh breeze. 'Together we may protect whomever we wish. And *destroy* whatever stands before us.'

I breathed as calmly as I could. 'You're immortal,' I said.

He looked absurdly proud. 'Yes, it does seem that way, doesn't it?' he agreed. 'No hard feelings about the whole – ' A hand wafted along his torso. 'You had to try, after all. I would admire you less if I'd thought you were unable to kill.' His hand gently squeezed mine. 'But what's made you reconsider your position? I thought that you and this –' a hand waved towards Sil – 'were playing happy families.'

Eleanor's eyes narrowed even further and I might not have telepathy but I'd be willing to hazard a guess at what she was thinking right then.

'Since I found out about the whole demon thing, I'm not so sure where I fit in any more. Now I've had time to think ... my whole *life* turns out to have been a lie, I'm in –' Whoops. Managed to catch myself in time there – 'in deep with a vampire who can't stop himself from screwing around and living on the edge, so there's no happy-ever-after for me there either. If I'm enough of a demon to have something to offer you – well, that's starting to look like a better bet, from where I'm standing.'

I could see Eleanor was taking mental notes. I was probably *never* going to be out of the frame for any crime now, as far as she was concerned; if I so much as dropped a crisp packet in the street I'd probably be looking at ten years to life. Abbie and Rach were holding hands. Harry was still praying silently.

I let myself look at Sil. Our plan was little more than rudimentary and there were many fine details that we hadn't had time to work out but it was all we had, and now was the time to put it into action.

Sil hurled himself across the floor, meeting Malfaire's magical shielding with the noise of a thousand tin cans falling. His fangs were down and he was halfway to demon by the look in his eyes. They stood grimacing, face to face, as the magic streamed over and past them; Malfaire's cheeks were rattling with the force of it and Sil's dark mane of hair was flapping like a flag. Sil punched out, slashed at the pale-green shielding and Malfaire stepped back, his face tight, nose wrinkled against the metallic stink of impact. When the blow failed to penetrate, Malfaire's mouth started to curve in a little smile which broadened with each attempt Sil made. 'Vampire,' he said contemptuously, as though the word was synonymous with rubbish. 'Don't you know that I can't die?'

If you can't die, I thought, with a sudden, rising hope, *then why bother shielding? Even you aren't quite sure, are you?* Zan seemed to be conscious in the middle of all that magical rope-stuff. 'Are you okay?' I mouthed around the edge of the glam-rock combat.

He twitched an eyebrow.

'Is that yes or no?' I mouthed back.

He rolled his eyes, and I concluded that if he was capable of silent sarcasm he was probably all right. It made me feel a bit better.

'Aren't you going to do something?' It was Abigail. Ghostly pale, she'd used Malfaire's inattention to take the chance to stand up and face me. 'This all seems to be something to do with you, Jessica. Don't you think you ought to make these monsters stop?'

'Monsters' was a bit rich coming from someone who'd had Zan's picture tacked up on her bedroom wall throughout her formative years. 'It will be over soon,' I said. The magic was blazing around them now; Sil was outlined in a livid green while Malfaire stood, seemingly unmoved, in a yellowish glow. But Sil was weakening; the green was tightening, closing in around the vampire and, as I watched, it formed a noose-shape in the air, drew down around the flailing form and snared him, binding his arms to his sides.

Sil rolled, or rather, the magic rolled him, until he lined up next to Zan and the Enforcement pair, eyes flaring. He'd probably never been this helpless in his entire, long, life.

Abbie sat down again. She and Rach resumed their pallid, silent staring while Liam merely sat, hands in his lap. He looked defeated and hopeless, as though he was waiting to die.

'All right,' I said to Malfaire. 'You're more powerful than the vampires, I get that.'

It was Sil's turn to be poked with the toe. 'Now, where were we?' Poke, poke. 'Ah, yes. You were telling me that you felt more demon than human, I think.'

'I'll be on your side,' I said quickly, before I could change my mind. Knew I sounded like we were picking school-yard football teams, but couldn't think of any other way to phrase it. Malfaire gave me a long, slow look. It was hot and hungry. 'If you're so powerful, then what's the point in me sticking with the vampires? If I can protect the people I love then I'd rather be on the winning side.'

Malfaire's look intensified; you could have fried eggs on the air between us. Eleanor and Zan were giving me joint evils. I quite liked them trussed up and silent.

'Mmmm,' Malfaire said slowly. 'But I'm not sure I trust this sudden turnaround, daughter.'

'What do you want me to do to prove it?' I tried not to let my eyes stray over to Sil. This was such a big gamble that it made the whole of Las Vegas look like a 'just for pennies' pontoon evening at the local Senior Citizens club. 'I could kill one of them – would that do?'

Malfaire's eyes were syrup-gold. 'Hmm. It may.' He lifted his gaze from mine and stared at his captives. 'But which?'

I forced down the leap of panic. 'A hard choice.'

'One of the humans. The vampires are mine to deal with.'

I had to let him think that the choice was his, but without that actually being the case. 'I have history with the Enforcement team. I'm due some revenge …'

Eleanor's pupils distended. I tried to beam her good vibes but … couldn't quite bring myself to do it. A little suffering would be good for her. The bitch.

Malfaire shook his head. 'No. That would be too easy. Cold blood is so much more *satisfying*.'

Good. 'That leaves my adopted sister, my colleague or my best friend.'

Abbie gave a squeal and Liam started. They all fixed their eyes on my face.

'Hmm. I don't believe your workmate is sufficiently close to you.'

Malfaire clearly didn't know about just how much time Liam and I spent in one another's company or how personal our conversations could get when we were. 'Fine.'

'And your sister is not truly your sister, is she? You will be undergoing some distancing from your family.'

'So. Rachel then.' I tried to look as though I didn't care one way or the other.

The women both started yelling at once; Rach jumped

to her feet and Abbie pushed herself in front of her. 'Now, listen here, you're not going to ...'

'Jessie?' Liam's eyes met mine. 'Can you?'

'I have to.' I tried to will him to understand, whilst widening my eyes at Sil. The vampire's expression never faltered, but then he'd had more practice than me at this sort of thing. 'I have to, Liam.'

Liam looked me up and down, then nodded. 'Yeah.'

'Go to your friend, Rachel.' Malfaire gave Rach a little shove and she tottered out from Abigail's shielding bulk. 'Say goodbye, everyone.'

Another shove and Rach wobbled into my arms. A coil of magic came with her, keeping her from flailing at me, as she so clearly wanted to do. Her face was shocked blank. 'Jessie, you won't,' she said, as though trying to convince herself. 'You won't.'

I raised my hands to either side of her head. Couldn't look her in the eye. 'I am so sorry, Rach.'

She squeaked and tried to move her head away, but Malfaire had her trussed. Every ounce of blood had drained from her skin, she was blueish pale and her eyes looked drugged. 'Jessie ...'

I flicked a glance at the bound vampires. Sil was still not blinking. Okay. We could do this. Carefully positioned my hands, palms cupping her above the ears. Twisted.

Rachel gave a little sigh and dropped at my feet. Revulsion crawled down my spine like a bug and I must have gone pale myself, because Liam came over and grabbed my arm. 'It's over, Jessie,' he whispered. 'You did it, it's over.'

Abbie, her face shocked immobile, whispered, 'You are no sister of mine.'

Malfaire, on the other hand, looked jubilant. 'My daughter.' He sounded almost fond. 'I knew you could do it.'

I huddled into Liam, not wanting to see the results of my actions. Chanced one quick look at Sil. He'd closed his eyes. Good.

'Now you'll let them go?'

Malfaire wrinkled his nose at me. 'Oh, all right. They were no fun anyway.' And then an alien stare. 'And, of course, I know where your parents live, should you need additional persuasion.'

I clenched both hands into Liam's shirt. 'Liam. He stays with me.'

A perfect eyebrow rose. 'Really? This one, too? Jessica, you greedy girl. Yes, he can stay. After all, once we call the full force of the Dark to us it's hardly going to matter who we left alive at this juncture. None of them will live through the battle.'

'Can I ...?' I let go of Liam, faced Malfaire. Had to do this right or he'd never go for it. 'Malfaire ...' That smile curled his lips again. 'Could I beg a favour?'

A sigh, as though he over-indulged me all the time. 'Go on.'

'Could I have a few minutes alone, to say goodbye to them before you let them leave? I may never see them again and it would mean a lot to me.'

A shrewd look. Had I pushed it too far? 'You cannot escape, Jessica. And now that you have killed, in full view of your pathetic Enforcement, well, you would be hunted even should you try to leave.'

'I know.' Yes, go on Malfaire, remind everyone that I come under the Otherworld heading now, that Enforcement are my nemeses instead of ... well, Eleanor and I hadn't exactly been doing one another's hair, but at least we'd been in it together. Now I'd very definitely stepped over the species line. 'Believe me, Malfaire, running away is the last thing on my mind.'

'Well then. All right. Oh, but I'll keep this one until you rejoin me, in case you decide to change your mind.' Malfaire hooked one arm around Liam's shoulders in a kind of prison-buddy hug.

'But …'

'Your choice.' His arm tightened painfully. I could see Liam's skinny shoulders being forced inwards under the pressure.

'Yes. As long as I can say goodbye.'

Malfaire gave a short nod. 'Very well. You have ten minutes. If any of them are still here after that time,' he gave Liam a matey squeeze that nearly drove him to his knees, 'I'm sure you wouldn't like the effects,' he finished, and he and Liam, moving in step like a hellish three-legged race entrant, left the room.

Slowly the magic around the vampires and Enforcement dissolved and they sat up. 'Well. I suppose that's bought us a few minutes.' Eleanor's voice was bitter.

'A few minutes might be enough.' Harry sounded harsh.

'Is this what the Treaty has come to? You opposing us? *War*?' Zan stood, straight-backed and imposing and, for a second, I felt a tiny shiver of warning down my spine.

'God, you all have a high opinion of me, don't you? You think I'd really ally myself with Malfaire? I'm beginning to hate myself by association.' I put my hands on my hips and stood over Rach's fallen body. 'Sil? Do your hocus-pocus.'

Getting stiffly to his feet Sil joined me. 'You took one hell of a risk, Jessica.'

'Better than the alternative.'

He inclined his head, bent down beside Rach and whispered something in her ear.

'This carpet smells funny,' were her first, unLazaruslike words. 'What happened?'

'Sil still has a mind-tie with you. He kind of put you under, so Malfaire would think you were dead.'

My sister stared accusingly at me from the bed. 'You bitch,' she said, between sobs. 'I always knew. You're evil, Jessica.' It felt like she'd pushed her hand between my ribs and was clawing at my heart.

Rachel stared at me. 'You killed me,' she said, rubbing her neck.

'But you aren't dead. Evidently.'

'But you chose me. You killed me. Not Liam, not Abigail. Not even *Eleanor*. I thought you were my *friend*.'

'It had to be you, Rach. You're the only one Sil has ever glamoured, or, at least, the only one he's admitting to. The only one he has an influence over. I'm glad he was paying attention.' I looked at the vampire and got a dark-glass gaze in response.

'Okay, so now what?' Harry was rubbing his arms. I noted that Eleanor had grasped at his jacket cuff and was holding on for dear life; this touch of vulnerability almost made me stand down from Hatred Defcon One, until I remembered the silver bullets, and I forced myself to look away. Now was not the time to weaken on the loathing front.

Zan looked at me. 'Jessica?'

'What? I think I've done you lot enough favours for one day.'

Sil was giving me the stare. 'I think it might be time for Plan B,' he said.

'Plan B? What on earth is that? We never came up with a Plan B. We barely had a Plan A.'

Zan leaned in close, his mouth against my ear. Little tickles of breath made my hair stand on end along my neck. 'Jessica,' he whispered. 'There are several panicked humans in here. I suggest you think of a Plan B with some alacrity.'

268

Sil gave me a small smile. 'She's never been the world's greatest planner.'

'I know. I've seen her office.'

The two vamps flanked me like a couple of bookends as I stared at the humans, now huddled around one another on the bed. Rach kept rubbing her neck and Abbie was avoiding looking directly at me.

'Okay. Plan B it is.' They had to get out of here. Malfaire wouldn't hesitate to kill everyone if his mood dictated it. 'Zan, can you get them to Harrogate?'

The vampires stared at me. 'Harrogate?' Zan repeated.

'What for, a bit of pre-apocalyptic shopping?' Sil's eyes were munitions grey again.

'Caro. The vampire I helped at the Dead Run, she owes me. Take them to her and ask her to … I dunno, look after them until they get the all-clear. Malfaire won't know where they've gone so he won't be able to come after them if everything goes wrong this end. Get my parents there as well.'

Zan turned to Sil. 'Take them, as she says.'

'I'm not leaving Jessie. You go.' Sil grabbed my hand.

'Nor I.' Zan took my other hand. I felt as though they'd tethered me, but their rigidity, useless as I knew it to be, was somehow comforting.

'It's all right, we'll take the van.' Eleanor stood up, obviously trying for control. 'I think we have to radio through a report in any case.' She glanced to Harry for confirmation, but he wouldn't meet her eye, just kept his gaze firmly fixed on the carpet.

'Phone Mum and Dad,' I said to Abbie. 'Tell them to meet you there. If Malfaire is still doing his phone-block thing, ring the neighbours and give them the message that way.'

Abbie barely glanced at me. 'I don't know what's going on here, Jessica,' she said. 'You were my baby sister, now you're not even human and you're some kind of killer planning on fighting demons and letting war break out again.' She shook her head. 'I used to change your nappy! *But you're not even human ...*'

'Talk to Mum and Dad, Abbs. It's their story really, not mine. I didn't ask for any of this and now I'm just doing the best I can. Oh, and I'm trying to avert war, not let it happen.' I took a breath. 'And you *never* changed my nappy. If you don't count that time you were looking for that necklace thing that I swallowed.'

The vampires exchanged a look, and then a shrug.

Abbie walked over to Zan with Rach clinging to her like a toddler. 'Where do we find this Caro?'

Zan wrote the address on a bit of card. Abbie blushed as she took it from him; that was one serious crush she had going. Then Zan took them all to the back stairs, returning to Sil and me with a weary expression. 'I instructed them to leave quickly and quietly. It was a clever thought, Jessica, to send them to Caro.'

'What about you two? Malfaire will kill you if he finds you're still here.'

Zan and Sil exchanged a quick glance, then Sil laid a hand gently on my cheek. 'We're not leaving you, Jessie. He's a monster and, let's face it, if *we* think that ...'

'You want us to go, and yet, a human remains,' Zan said. 'Why?'

'Liam and I have been team-mates for a long time and I trust him to do exactly as I ask, not fanny about asking daft questions, present company very much included there, guys. And, I don't think Malfaire will see him as any kind of threat, so he'll be safer than you would be. Is that enough?'

'But …' Sil began. Zan silenced him with a raised hand.

'I fear any questions will merely justify point one.'

'Thank you.'

Sil looked into my eyes. As I've said, I'm immune to the whole vamp mind control thing so he can only have done it to let me see the shifting of the darkness inside him. 'Zan and I will stay in the house.'

'But he's beaten you so many times already, what makes you think …?'

Sil pulled me closer towards him. 'Jessie, if anything happens to you, Zan and I will go out fighting, know that.'

Gosh.

The two vampires melted away into the darkness, of which there was quite a lot in this house. Slowly, stomach churning, I went down the main staircase, keeping one hand on the oak banister for support.

'Ginger Rogers had more style.' Liam was standing in the hallway.

'She didn't work for York City Council.' I reached the bottom and lowered my voice. 'Are you okay?'

The 'I'm so cool I can make jokes' act fell away. 'I am fucking *terrified*, Jessie.' His skin was taut with fear and a silken gloss of sweat lay sheer on his skin. 'What now?'

'Thanks for not asking why I didn't get Malfaire to let you go with the others.'

'Hey!' A return of the sense of humour. 'You're my boss. Let you stay here alone and I kiss goodbye to the Christmas bonus.' But his fingers dug into the skin of my arm. 'Sarah and Charlotte,' he breathed. 'Does he *know* about them?'

'They'll be fine at Sarah's mother's; even if he does know, he won't know where to look for them.'

He closed his eyes for a second and a little of the tension left him. 'Okay then. What's the plan? As Malfaire can't even be killed by his own flesh and blood – what do we try next?'

'Oh. My. God.' It must have been the terror and the dread that did it. Like the tumblers of a lock suddenly freeing up to allow access to a safe, my brain clicked into gear. 'Is it really as simple as that?'

'Er, Jessie? Human, no telepathy.'

'I've just, ohhh, it could be, but how can, ohhh …'

'And again, in English?'

Where was Malfaire? How long had we got before he turned up? I lowered my voice and started to talk really fast. 'When you brought the office stuff here, did you bring everything? Everything we had in the fridge?'

'Yep. Pretty much.'

'No, it's important. *All* the stuff from the fridge?'

'Er, yes. There wasn't much in there. And we brought the paperwork. We left the dead files, but I picked up everything that's open at the moment. Why?'

'Because I have a plan.'

At almost cartoon-speed I outlined my idea to Liam, who flinched. 'You think that's it? That'll work?'

'It's the only hope we've got right now. You wait for …' I tailed off as Malfaire came sauntering around the corner accompanied by his pair of Shadows.

'Jessica.' He clicked his fingers and the Shadows flowed off into hidden corners. I was clearly supposed to be aware they were still present. 'We find ourselves alone at last.'

'Hello.' Liam gave a little wave. 'Still here, still listening, still paying the fan club subscription fees. I might not be armed but I can bite bloody hard if you're after a fight.'

Malfaire hardly gave him a glance. 'Humans do clutter the place up, don't they?' he said to me. 'Perhaps we should …'

'Malfaire.' I had to stop him thinking about Liam, although it already helped that he considered my front-line weapon to be beneath contempt. 'I think we should let Liam carry on staffing the office. If people notice the tracker programme is down, we could have chaos breaking out on the streets.' The demon's expression went thoughtful, so I pressed home my advantage, 'I mean, yes, we want chaos, ultimately, but we want chaos we can be in charge of. Not chaotic chaos,' I finished lamely. 'Keep things running until we can step in and take over. We don't want the humans implementing some kind of "scorched earth" policy, do we?'

Liam's eyes flashed wide for a second. The reality of the danger we might be in if I couldn't do something fairly drastic was clearly sinking in. And I knew that there were plans in high government for terminal action should the vampires try to rise. I'd once slept with a blabbermouth journalist – something Liam *didn't* know about. At least, I hoped he didn't.

Malfaire waved a hand. Didn't even seem bothered enough to waste words on a mere human. I leaned towards Liam, steadied myself against his shoulder, and gave him a quick peck on the cheek. 'See you later,' I said, and then under cover of wiping away non-existent lipstick (I worked for the *council*, lipstick in my job would have been like clothes on dogs) I whispered in his ear, 'Sil and Zan are in the house.'

Malfaire pulled me away rather more roughly than I thought the situation warranted. I barely had time to grimace at Liam in a way that I *really* hoped he understood, before I found myself in a high-ceilinged reception room, with the double doors firmly closed behind us.

Malfaire glanced around at the furnishings. 'How odd,' he said. 'Usually vampires have more of a sense of style.' He turned to face me. 'That's all they are, of course, a triumph of style over substance. You seemed surprised that I could so easily subdue both your pet and the old one, but, as you will find out, vampires are pathetic creatures, really.' He removed his jacket and hung it carefully over the back of a Louis XIV chair, stroking the folds so that it wouldn't crease. 'Yes,' he went on. 'With vampires it's all blood and thrills, which is not a basis for a system of government. This world will be so much better when demons run it properly.' He gave me a long-lashed look. 'And by demons, of course, I mean you and me.'

This was good. This was the bad guy wanting to talk. And the longer he talked, the more chance there was of Liam being able to do what I'd asked. If I could keep him talking a while longer ...

'So.' I perched on the edge of a ridiculously over-gilded chair. There seemed to be a lot of gilt around this house. I wondered if Zan was being metaphorical through the medium of furniture. 'Where do we go from here?'

Malfaire leaned against the wall and stared down his nose at me. 'You are very like your mother, Jessica,' he said suddenly. 'In appearance, I mean. She was an easily broken thing, ultimately, and I do hope that you have not inherited that tendency.'

I held my breath. Tried to keep my expression neutral. 'I see.'

The demon fussed with the creases in his trousers, lining them perfectly down the front. 'You should never have been born, of course,' he continued. 'Ghyst do not willingly breed unless threatened with extinction; we are not prone to giving birth to our own downfall. Although that now seems to have been little more than unsubstantiated rumour.'

'Well, you wouldn't, I suppose. It would be like giving birth to a life-sentence.' I swallowed hard. 'My mother – what was she like?'

Malfaire gave a little smile. 'Ah. There was a lot more to your mother than met the eye, my dear. Very much more.' The smile thinned at the corners. 'But, if it is all the same to you, I don't think it a good idea to give you *too* much information. Added incentive to keep me alive and well, do you see? If anything happens to me, all knowledge of your parentage will die with me.' He studied his nails. 'And, of course, when we rule her picture will hang –' a glance at the walls – 'just *there*, I think.'

He has pictures of her. He knows all about her, my mother, Rune Atrasia. The information I most want in the world. But ...

'Would you like some wine?' I blurted out, trying to cover the tumult of emotion that was rioting through me. If I'd had a vampire demon it would have been a very, very happy bunny right now. 'Zan keeps ... *kept* a pretty swanky cellar; there's some expensive stuff down there.'

Malfaire shrugged. 'You need alcohol?'

'Oh yes,' I said, with very heavy emphasis. 'Right now, I think I do.'

'Then we shall share a bottle of the vampire's finest. Order your human to fetch us some.'

'I'll go and find him.' Leaving the demon lounging in an antique chair, I fled down the corridor to the living room, where Liam had all the office equipment. He was crouched in front of the fridge. 'Jessie, this had better work,' he said, straightening up as I came in. 'I am really not up for spending the rest of my life as that man's domestic servant.' He handed me a bottle. 'Well, not unless it comes with a really smart uniform,' he added.

'This is it?'

'Yeah. Zan helped out. He's ace at mixing cocktails, it seems. Particularly this sort, which makes you wonder. Jessie, are you …?'

'Don't. Please. Where are the vamps now?'

Liam nodded at the wall. 'Secret passageways run all over the house. Perfect for that mob-and-blazing-torch moment.'

'They think of everything. Right. You know what you're doing?'

'Yep. The boys are waiting for the cue. They'll let me know when you're ready.'

'You mean they'll be watching? What if this,' I shook the bottle, 'doesn't work?'

Liam gave a little grin. 'Then I think we all die horribly in some kind of cinematic slo-mo.' Then he reached out and unexpectedly touched my cheek. 'Are you all right?'

I felt the tears heavy behind my eyelids. 'I have to be. Otherwise …' I choked off and shook my head. 'I don't think we'd like the alternative.'

'Well, look at it this way. There can't be many people who've had to get drunk on very expensive wine to save the world.'

'Thanks.' We stood a moment longer, then I waved the bottle and left. Couldn't speak for the lump in my throat. If I messed this up then I'd never see Liam again. Not alive, anyway.

Sil waited in the passage behind the panelling for Zan to catch up. 'She's good, you've got to admit.'

The old vampire nodded. 'Clever. Devious. Almost like one of us.'

Sil half-laughed. 'I think that is what frightens her most.' He pressed his eye to the crack, which gave a fish-eye view of the room beyond. 'She has left the room.' His stomach lurched in a way he recognised from when he'd been human. He was actually *scared*. It had been a long time since anything had had the power to frighten him, but the thought of Jessie alone with that demon was sending adrenaline spurts through his system and making his own demon writhe inside him. He closed his eyes for a second, feeling the thrashing monster that lay within him as though for the first time. The trade off. The thing that gave him long life and the strength to hunt, the thing that fed off the blood and the power and the thrills. The thing that made him what he was. His mind choked on the thought. *Jonathan died in the alley with a vampire's bite in his throat and a vampire's seed in his blood. Sil walked away. And now I co-exist with a creature that has the power to kill me simply by leaving, a creature I sustain by allowing it to feed on any emotion which connects me to humanity.*

He drew his fingers down the rough plaster inside the wall, digging his nails through the surface, trying to reach a sensation that would bring his mind back to where it should be. But all he could think of was her expression when she'd known she had to fight Malfaire alone. Her golden eyes holding all that fear and all that terrible knowledge as she'd tried to send him away. His demon pinched at his lungs. *I can't let her face it alone. It's going to hurt her, it's going to make her feel a little less human. She shouldn't be alone.*

Malfaire had moved into one of the State receiving rooms. An enormous desk, which must have been built *in situ*, took up the centre of the room. The remainder of the furniture, a green velvet *chaise-longue*, some over-polished mahogany woodwork and some truly horrible paintings, were all racked along the walls, leaving the desk looking like an island in an over-fished sea.

'Ah. There you are. Thought I was going to have to come looking.' Malfaire was reclining on the velvet day-bed effort, like Byron on his day off.

'Liam found us this.' I waved the bottle, and the two glasses. 'So we can drink to our success in style.'

Malfaire took the bottle and scrutinised the label. 'Not bad. Chateau Latour Pauillac. 1990, too. I almost revise my opinion of vampires.'

'He's opened it for us, but I'm not sure it's had time to breathe.' I put the glasses on a side table, hoping he wasn't going to come over all posh wine critic and insist on giving it time to reach optimal drinking temperature. I wasn't sure I could keep polite conversation going for much longer. 'Shall I pour some?'

The demon yawned. 'Why not? It may relax you sufficiently to begin discussions of our future together. I am considering giving you the North to rule.'

'Lovely!' I said brightly, wondering why Malfaire merited London and the ports, while I got the chilly half and the pigeon racing. Still, at least the M25 would be his problem. I wondered if that would hold up his plans for world-domination. I poured two glasses of the black-red wine. It was thick, almost gloopy, and smelled of blackberries with a metallic edge.

He raised his glass to me. 'Let this be the first of many.'

I clinked my glass against his and took a small swallow. It tasted foul, but then I've never had much of a palate for wine. Give me a bottle of lager and a packet of cheese-and-onion crisps and I'm happy; the expensive stuff always reminds me of paint-thinner.

Malfaire, however, seemed to appreciate it. He sniffed his glass, took a sip and followed this with a larger gulp. 'Hmm. A little tinny. Odd sort of aftertaste … seems to me that this has been massively over-rated.' He did the whole slooshing about in the mouth thing beloved of professional wine-tasters. 'But drinkable. Very drinkable.' At last he swallowed. 'Now. What do you think of my proposal?'

I refilled his glass. 'Have some more.'

'Jessica, are you trying to get me drunk? I'm a demon. It won't work.'

'Then there's no problem. Drink up.' I pressed the glass into his hand. 'Can we negotiate for Birmingham, or do we have to draw lots or something?'

Malfaire gulped the whole glass down in one, clearly pleased that I was going along with his plan. 'I will take the Midlands. Sheffield, however, is all yours.'

'That's ... very nice. Trams. Meadowhall. All the ... shopping I can take. Wow, you must be thirsty. Another?' Without waiting for an answer I refilled.

'There will be no need for shopping.' Malfaire drained the glass in another single swig; he'd clearly stopped worrying about the bouquet and the after-taste. The wine, and its addition, must be cutting in already. 'That is why we have the humans. They may be a nuisance, but we need to retain some to feed the vampires that we choose to keep alive.' He smiled. 'I am thinking we may spend the weekends hunting them for sport.'

'Well, I've never liked football much.'

'I thought of starting with your pet. He looks as though he could run quite quickly, doesn't he? Particularly with ... what, Shadows after him? Or wights? Which would you prefer to see tear him apart, Jessica?'

'No!' I wasn't fast enough to keep my mouth shut and a sudden flare of magic sparked between us, sending a flash of pain all the way up to my shoulder. 'Ow!'

'I apologise. Automatic response.' Malfaire smiled that

cat-like smile again. 'Purely defensive, you understand, nothing personal.'

So he doesn't really trust me, I thought. *He's not completely stupid.* I tried to move smoothly, unthreateningly and not say anything inflammatory. 'No, I should apologise. I'm still getting my head around ...' I waved an arm. 'It's taking some getting used to.' My heart raced as he slumped back against the velvet of the *chaise*. His expression had changed to surprise, tinged with a vacant kind of bliss and I felt a momentary relaxation of the muscles between my shoulder blades. *This just might work. But it means ...*

Malfaire breathed heavily. 'What *is* this? It's like my whole skin is alive ... dancing.' Another deep breath. 'I've never felt anything like it.'

'You obviously don't go to the right parties.'

I waited until his eyes rolled closed, then moved towards the door. 'Where are you going?' Malfaire's voice was slurred as though his tongue was numb. 'Jessica?'

Keep him calm. Don't risk him firing off more spells; someone could get hurt. 'Yeah, I'm here. Just getting myself another glass of wine.'

I tiptoed over the carpet to the door. I'd been expecting Liam, but it was Sil crouched behind it holding my gun.

'What are you ...?' I began, but he raised a finger to his lips.

'Hush.' He pushed the tranq gun into my hand. 'I don't want you to be alone, Jessie.'

'Do you mean now, or generally?' I whispered.

'Still not the right time for this conversation,' he hissed back.

'Jessica? Jessica, where are you?' Malfaire's voice floated from the *chaise*. 'I feel *fantastic*.'

'I'm here.' I motioned to Sil to follow me but he stayed

where he was, eyes fixed on my braless chest and I had to poke him quite vigorously before he'd shift.

Malfaire's eyes were black. No trace of the gold now; just two huge pupils trying to focus. 'I'm flying.'

'Damn straight.' I approached his slumped form and hefted the tranq gun. Felt its familiar weight against my palm and looked down on the demon. He'd begun to laugh, bonelessly sprawled across the velvet, unsuspecting. This wasn't right. I didn't have the power to take a life, not when he was so out of things, so unable to defend himself or even to know what was happening. I lowered the gun again. 'I can't do this.'

Malfaire was suddenly focusing. On me. On the gun. I heard Sil shout, 'Jessie, look out!' and then there was a confusion of movement and a sting of energy flipped the gun from my hand to slither underneath the *chaise*; suddenly I couldn't breathe, couldn't move, wrapped in those coils of magic and held rigid.

'I'm impressed, I really am.' Malfaire's voice was dreamy, the blood that we'd mixed into the wine was still pounding through his system; the lack of coordination it produced was probably the only reason that I wasn't already dead. 'But you do realise, don't you –' my body rotated until my head pointed downwards and I started to feel sick – 'that getting you on my side for the war was purely out of the goodness of my heart. I was always going to end you, Jessica, whether you were with me or not.' A vomit-inducing movement wafted me into the air above him and he raised his head to smile an unfocused smile into my face. 'And the killing part is always so much *fun*. It's a shame you can't ask your mother about it.'

Sil shouted, some wordless sound, and charged, getting halfway across the room before the magic caught him in its coils and flung him through the doorway. I heard the crack as he hit the door frame on his way, a rising shriek which ended suddenly in a loud bump, and then the regular thumping and scuffing sound of a body sliding along the tiled hallway, hitting panelling and furniture all the way to the front door.

'Sil!' I moved and the magic surrounding me turned to jelly then to air and I was down on the floor beside the *chaise*, hand closed around the gun. I felt shakily cold and my fingers were numb but the tranq gun sat easily in my hand, slightly warm.

I brought it up suddenly, slid it over the edge of the *chaise*, along Malfaire's side to rest against the bottom of his rib cage. 'Sil,' was all I could say. Then I bit my lip, hard, and pulled the trigger.

There was a moment of confusion. Malfaire gave a gasp. I stood up to make sure my shot had hit home and he grabbed me, pressed me against his chest. He was smiling. Then I saw his eyes clear, the effects of my blood falling from him. 'What's happening?'

'It's called dying.' I wrenched myself from his grasp and knelt beside him. 'And I'm sorry. Really I am. But you shouldn't have killed my mother and hurt Sil.'

'I am *immortal*!' It was a choked shout, one with more hope than expectation behind it. 'This cannot ...'

A sudden backwash of loathing scalded through my veins. 'Yes, it can.' I held up the gun. 'You can only be killed by your own flesh and blood. Remember?' Thanks to Liam, thanks to his organisation, his compulsion to keep, to file, we'd kept the rest of my blood sample that I'd taken for the testing unit and Zan had mixed it in with the wine. The tissue sample from Malfaire, the sample I'd stolen in the Hagg Baba for testing, Liam had loaded into an empty tranq cartridge. And I'd fired it. Without the needle, it had scythed through his flesh into his body and passed right through whatever organ he had that stood in place of a heart. 'Your own flesh and blood, armed with your own flesh and blood. That's what it takes,' I leaned down and hissed into his ear, 'for future reference.'

Then my knees gave way and I collapsed backwards, off the *chaise* and on to the carpet, as Malfaire writhed once more and lay still. The room became silent; an odd, cold silence that crept under my skin and into my veins with the chill.

'I killed him. I killed him.' The words were sobbed out with my breath. 'I killed him.'

Sudden arms around my shoulders. I shrugged them off but they came back. 'Jessica.'

'I killed him.' I looked up. Zan was standing, staring at the body with an expression of hunger. Liam was beside me, drawing me into his chest. 'I killed him.'

Liam looked into my face. It clearly took some effort and I wished I'd had time to find my bra. 'Oh, Jessie. You did it.'

'Sil. We must go to Sil. Malfaire threw him …' I couldn't even finish the sentence.

'We saw.' Liam stood up, pulling me from the blood-soaked carpet with him despite the weakness in my legs.

'Is he all right?' I was shivering now, uncontrollably, leaning against him simply to stop myself going down again. '*Is he?*'

'He'll be fine. He's lying there groaning, but he looks *way* too good to be dying, if you ask me.'

I tore from the room, my feet leaving bloody prints and sticking slightly to the carpet as I went. 'Sil!' Down the hallway, half-noticing the broken newel-post, the shards of wood, the random splinters of plastic and the shine of electrical components from the smashed telephone. 'Oh God, Sil.'

He lay against the front door, his body coiled around itself and his eyes a complicated colour. 'Hey, Jessie.' He managed a grin. 'You got him then.'

'Don't you dare die, you bastard.'

'I don't intend to.' A wince and a grimace. 'But I've damaged a leg, I think.'

'I thought he'd killed you. I couldn't have pulled the trigger otherwise.'

Sil smiled. 'So my plan worked?'

'That was not a plan! That was the opposite of a plan, the antithesis of planning. That was dashing in and ruining what would have been a perfectly good plan if you hadn't spoiled it all by trying to be a hero!'

'So, you did have a plan, did you?'

The adrenaline was beginning to slide out of my body, leaving me cold. I watched his demon take the last draught of my elation and panic, moving behind his eyes like an unwanted thought. 'No. No plan. Just terror.'

Sil stretched out a hand, palm up and I stared at it for a moment. I couldn't tell if he meant it as a gesture of surrender or to ward me off until he spoke. 'Help me up, will you? I'm healing but I'm not that fast.' I reached out and pulled and he slid easily against me. 'I promised your mother I'd keep you safe,' he said quietly. 'Didn't do much of a job, did I?'

I gave a half-sob but muffled it. 'I'm fine. Well, feeling a bit sordid, but it could have been worse.'

Oh-so-gently he touched my face. 'You aren't a monster, Jessie. You did what you had to do for all of us.' Those grey-green eyes looked down through mine, into my heart. 'He would have mustered an army of the Dark against the Treaty, killed everyone who stood against him. Hell, you've probably saved the world.'

'Well, I suppose that's something.' I wiped the back of my hand across my eyes. 'So why do I feel like I've lost everything, *Jonathan*?' I whispered.

Sil flicked his eyes along the corridor. Zan and Liam were hanging around trying not to look as if they were listening. 'Give us a second, guys.'

'Jessie?' Liam half-called. 'Are you sure?'

'Yes.' I couldn't tear my eyes away from Sil. 'We need to put an insurance claim in to the council, you could write it up. Do a spreadsheet; you know it always calms you down, writing a spreadsheet.'

He laughed. 'Okay. As long as you're all right with Mister Bitey.'

I felt Sil's demon move, reacting to my proximity. 'Yeah, I'll be fine.' My voice shook a bit but sounded strong. I was proud of myself. As Sil said, I'd probably saved the world and that was pretty good going for someone who wasn't sure what HTML was.

Sil's demon was still moving. I could sense its presence behind his eyes; they changed as I watched, blue-green to grey and then on to an iron-grey like a night sky. 'Oh,' he said and touched his chest as though it hurt. 'Oh. God.'

'What? Are you all right? Have you broken a rib or something? Do vampires *have* ribs? Oh, duh, Jessie, of course they do, otherwise their insides would be their outsides.' I knew I was rambling but I was afraid. There was something terribly intense about Sil's expression.

'No. Just … a touch too much for even *my* demon to manage.'

'Too much what?'

His hands laced behind me. 'Too much emotion. For a second there … I almost felt human again'

'And that's a bad thing?' The old-chocolate-box smell

of him was almost neutralising the smell of blood, the cool stillness of his body steadying my own shaking one.

'No. Yes. I don't … It makes me feel things, Jessica. The pain, the guilt, the remorse … I don't think I can live with those, not even to feel the … to feel anything else.'

'You won't love me because it means facing up to what you are?' Anger made me bite my lip and I watched as his flickering eyes beamed in on the sudden bloom of blood. 'I'm sorry, Sil, you were right before. You *are* a coward.'

'I lost my family, Jessica.' His voice wavered a touch. 'I had to hide at my own children's funeral because of what I am. I watched my wife remarry. A man she loved until the day she died – a man who made her forget me …' I felt his ribs move as he buried a sob beneath an attempt at a cool tone. 'I have a *right* not to want to feel.'

'I've lost my family too, now.' I felt a brief hotness on my cheek, which turned out to be a tear. 'And loving you is all I've got left.' I gave in for just one, quick, Germaine-Greer-bothering second and rested my face against his chest, felt his demon squirm. 'And you *do* feel, you told me so yourself. You just deny it. Feed it to your demon. Like … like Rachel sometimes buys bacon and then feeds it to Jasper. Sometimes she actually makes herself a sandwich and she thinks I don't know, and if you tell her that then I'll stake you myself, but …'

'So you think you could be my bacon sandwich?' There was another tremble in his voice now, but it sounded different. 'My one weakness?'

I took half-a-step backwards but kept my arms around him. 'Everyone should let themselves have one thing that makes all the rest of the denial worthwhile. I loved you for four years, wouldn't even so much as *date* anyone; Cameron was as much my cover as I was his, because I wanted you so much that no-one else was ever going to come close. Believe me, I know about denial.' I lowered my voice, aware that Liam might well be hovering. '*But it was worthwhile, for that night in the drain. If there's never any more than that, it was worthwhile.*'

'And you can love me, knowing what I've done?' There was a note of wonder in his voice. 'Knowing how I have been? *What* I have been?'

'Hey, no-one's perfect. I broke the tracker programme. We've all got our nasty little secrets – my parentage is probably going to turn out to be the least of mine – but, yes. I love you whatever. Because that's what love is, Jonathan, it's knowing and *still* caring.'

His demon moved. 'And it's learning to live with the guilt.' He stroked my hair, long fingers twisting through, pulling my head up so I had to meet his eyes, still shifting colour. 'There will still be the blood. And the clubs. But I can dance and drink synth, it doesn't have to be, well, what it was. I think I can do this, Jessica. If you feel that you can take that chance.' With the inevitability of winter, he touched my lips with his. 'You give me peace. And in return you'll get my love. If you want it.' A momentary uncertainty. 'Do you?'

His demon felt my surge of pure joy and beat ecstatically in time to his pulse. 'Well, I've got around a hundred years to come to terms with it,' I said, reaching up to pull his mouth down to mine again.

The love for her was unleashed inside him, sending his demon into the kind of frenzied bliss that would have taken several blood-donors and a night of hyperactive sex before. *Jessie. Who would have thought it? All it needed was for me to find what I'd lost, and here it was all the time. Right in front of me. I didn't know it for what it was, even when I was willing* to die for her, even when I told her mother I would keep her safe ... this slender girl with the quite incredibly untidy hair was all I needed to make me feel human again. Joseph and Constance ... it won't go away, the pain of losing you, but the more I remember you, the less it hurts. And now I have Jessica I can think of you as you were; I can remember the times before. Remember throwing you in the air and hearing you laugh as I caught you, and building endless castles in the shrubbery for you to hide in. And Christie ... you'd have liked Jessica, Christie. You and she are very alike. I can imagine you both now, sitting around the parlour table, sipping tea and listing my more peculiar habits, laughing together over my failings. And the guilt ... the guilt for all those times before the Treaty, all those things I did not to survive, but for pleasure? That can remain, to remind me of how it was. Of what *I* was. Like those photographs of a past life, a warning ...

For now the love is all. And it will save me.

About the Author

fresh-photographic.co.uk
(the fabulous Phil, who managed to make me look
half-way human!)

Jane was born in Devon and now lives in Yorkshire.
She has five children, four cats and two dogs. She works in
a local school and also teaches creative writing. Jane is a
member of the Romantic Novelists' Association and has a
first-class honours degree in creative writing.

Jane writes comedies which are often described as 'quirky'.
This is Jane's third Choc Lit novel. Her UK debut, *Please
don't stop the music*, won the 2012 Romantic Novel of the
Year and the Romantic Comedy Novel of the Year Awards
from the Romantic Novelists' Association.

For more information on Jane visit
www.janelovering.co.uk
www.twitter.com/janelovering

More Choc Lit

From Jane Lovering

Please don't stop the music

Winner of the 2012 Best Romantic Comedy Novel of the year

Winner of the 2012 Romantic Novel of the year

How much can you hide?

Jemima Hutton is determined to build a successful new life and keep her past a dark secret. Trouble is, her jewellery business looks set to fail – until enigmatic Ben Davies offers to stock her handmade belt buckles in his guitar shop and things start looking up, on all fronts.

But Ben has secrets too. When Jemima finds out he used to be the front man of hugely successful Indie rock band Willow Down, she wants to know more. Why did he desert the band on their US tour? Why is he now a semi-recluse?

And the curiosity is mutual – which means that her own secret is no longer safe …

Visit www.choc-lit.com for more details including the first two chapters and reviews, or simply scan barcode using your mobile phone QR reader.

Star Struck

Our memories define us – don't they?

And Skye Threppel lost most of hers in a car crash that stole the lives of her best friend and fiancé. It's left scars, inside and out, which have destroyed her career and her confidence.

Skye hopes a trip to the wide dusty landscapes of Nevada – and a TV convention offering the chance to meet the actor she idolises – will help her heal. But she bumps into mysterious sci-fi writer Jack Whitaker first. He's a handsome contradiction – cool and intense, with a wild past.

Jack has enough problems already. He isn't looking for a woman with self-esteem issues and a crush on one of his leading actors. Yet he's drawn to Skye.

An instant rapport soon becomes intense attraction, but Jack fears they can't have a future if Skye ever finds out about his past …

Will their memories tear them apart, or can they build new ones together?

Why not try something else from the Choc Lit selection?
Here's a sample:

Love & Freedom
Sue Moorcroft

Winner of the Festival of Romance Best Romantic Read Award 2011

New start, new love.

That's what Honor Sontag needs after her life falls apart, leaving her reputation in tatters and her head all over the place. So she flees her native America and heads for Brighton, England.

Honor's hoping for a much-deserved break and the chance to find the mother who abandoned her as a baby. What she gets is an entanglement with a mysterious male whose family seems to have a finger in every pot in town.

Martyn Mayfair has sworn off women with strings attached, but is irresistibly drawn to Honor, the American who keeps popping up in his life. All he wants is an uncomplicated relationship built on honesty, but Honor's past threatens to undermine everything. Then secrets about her mother start to spill out …

Honor has to make an agonising choice. Will she live up to her dutiful name and please others? Or will she choose freedom?

Visit www.choc-lit.com for more details including the first two chapters and reviews, or simply scan barcode using your mobile phone QR reader.

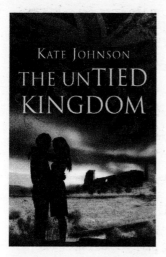

The UnTied Kingdom

Kate Johnson

Shortlisted for the 2012 RoNA Contemporary Romantic Novel Category Award

The portal to an alternate world was the start of all her troubles – or was it?

When Eve Carpenter lands with a splash in the Thames, it's not the London or England she's used to. No one has a telephone or knows what a computer is. England's a third-world country and Princess Di is still alive. But worst of all, everyone thinks Eve's a spy.

Including Major Harker who has his own problems. His sworn enemy is looking for a promotion. The General wants him to undertake some ridiculous mission to capture a computer, which Harker vaguely envisions running wild somewhere in Yorkshire. Turns out the best person to help him is Eve.

She claims to be a popstar. Harker doesn't know what a popstar is, although he suspects it's a fancy foreign word for 'spy'. Eve knows all about computers, and electricity. Eve is dangerous. There's every possibility she's mad.

And Harker is falling in love with her.

Visit www.choc-lit.com for more details including the first two chapters and reviews, or simply scan barcode using your mobile phone QR reader.

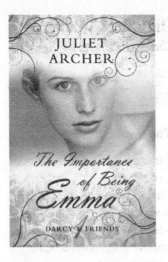

The Importance of Being Emma

Juliet Archer

Winner of The Big Red Reads Fiction Award 2011

A modern retelling of Jane Austen's *Emma*.

Mark Knightley – handsome, clever, rich – is used to women falling at his feet. Except Emma Woodhouse, who's like part of the family – and the furniture. When their relationship changes dramatically, is it an ending or a new beginning?

Emma's grown into a stunningly attractive young woman, full of ideas for modernising her family business. Then Mark gets involved and the sparks begin to fly. It's just like the old days, except that now he's seeing her through totally new eyes.

While Mark struggles to keep his feelings in check, Emma remains immune to the Knightley charm. She's never forgotten that embarrassing moment when he discovered her teenage crush on him. He's still pouring scorn on all her projects, especially her beautifully orchestrated campaign to find Mr Right for her ditzy PA. And finally, when the mysterious Flynn Churchill – the man of her dreams – turns up, how could she have eyes for anyone else? …

Visit www.choc-lit.com for more details including the first two chapters and reviews, or simply scan barcode using your mobile phone QR reader.

Highland Storms
Christina Courtenay

 Winner of the 2012 Best Historical Romantic Novel of the year

Who can you trust?

Betrayed by his brother and his childhood love, Brice Kinross needs a fresh start. So he welcomes the opportunity to leave Sweden for the Scottish Highlands to take over the family estate.

But there's trouble afoot at Rosyth in 1754 and Brice finds himself unwelcome. The estate's in ruin and money is disappearing. He discovers an ally in Marsaili Buchanan, the beautiful redheaded housekeeper, but can he trust her?

Marsaili is determined to build a good life. She works hard at being a housekeeper and harder still at avoiding men who want to take advantage of her. But she's irresistibly drawn to the new clan chief, even though he's made it plain he doesn't want to be shackled to anyone.

And the young laird has more than romance on his mind. His investigations are stirring up an enemy. Someone who will stop at nothing to get what he wants – including Marsaili – even if that means destroying Brice's life forever …

Sequel to Trade Winds

Visit www.choc-lit.com for more details including the first two chapters and reviews, or simply scan barcode using your mobile phone QR reader.

Introducing Choc Lit

We're an independent publisher creating
a delicious selection of fiction.
Where heroes are like chocolate – irresistible!
Quality stories with a romance at the heart.

Choc Lit novels are selected by genuine readers like yourself.
We only publish stories our Choc Lit Tasting Panel want to
see in print. Our reviews and awards speak for themselves.

Come and support our authors and join them in our
Author's Corner, read their interviews and see their latest
events, reviews and gossip.

Visit: www.choc-lit.com for more details.

Available in paperback and as ebooks from most stores.

We'd also love to hear how you enjoyed *Vampire State of
Mind*. Just visit www.choc-lit.com and give your feedback.
Describe Sil in terms of chocolate and you could win a
Choc Lit novel in our Flavour of the Month competition.

 Follow us on twitter: www.twitter.com/
ChocLituk, or simply scan barcode using
your mobile phone QR reader.